A NEW ERA

The Reaper Tomes Book 1

MARILU MOSER

First paperback edition September 2022

Copyediting and Formatting done by: Miss Eloquent Edits
Cover Design done by: Moonpress Designs

ISBN 978-8-9864261-0-5
Published by Tome Dragon Publishing LLC

For my husband, who kept me on track with my deadlines and occupied our spirited children so they wouldn't derail my plans every time I sat down to write. I couldn't have done this without you.

Thank you, and I adore you.

If you know me in real life and read this . . . no you don't and no you didn't. Let's not make it awkward.

Before You Read

Your mental health, emotional health, boundaries, and limits are important to me. Before you continue reading, please note there are some darker themes and subject matter in this book. This is an adult urban fantasy novel, with mature content. Recommended age is 18 years and over. This book does discuss death and subjects pertaining to death. There is also a scene in a later chapter in the book that has child death, while not discussed how the child dies, it is in a hospital setting along with another hospitalization scene.

Other elements contain, explicit sexual content, self harm, Demons (Infernal's), elements of gore and murder, blood, occult, profanity, alcohol, gore, kidnapping, murder, and mild praise (good girl).

For a complete, detailed, and up-to-date list, please scan this QR code or visit marilumoser.com

Happy Reading

Shadows danced across the walls in a private performance for her. Every twirl flawlessly executed helped to still her ragged breath. Her sweat tinted the sheets with a perfect silhouette of her body. It was the fourth time that week the nightmare had invited itself. The images assaulted her mind.

Darkness surrounded her, comforting her in its embrace. Creaking metal groaned, and a loud pitch rang through her ears. She clutched them to muffle the sound, but it was useless. The frequency had penetrated her brain, and her eyes burned. A metallic taste lingered on her tongue. With no warning, the cold metal blade ripped through her chest.

She scrubbed her face with one hand to rid her mind of the intrusive replay. The other hand laid on her chest, ensuring she was safe. It had all felt so real, so familiar. Esme laid back down, the contrast of warm sheets and cold sweat against her back induced chills down her spine. She huffed as she sat back up.

The rising sun expelled those unwelcomed pictures, and the onyx walls drank in the warm rays. The world around her woke with each passing minute. Footsteps thumped as others entered their apartment; the night shift had ended.

That was the only time when her large apartment didn't feel so lonely. Hollow and alone was her new normal since Jensen had moved out six months earlier.

"Time to start my day," she muttered to herself, running her hands down her face. While she never required a lot of sleep, the three interrupted hours she had would surely affect that day. "Please let today go smoothly." She sent her plea to the powers that be.

Even if no one was there to listen to her rambling, she always had the best conversations with herself. Esme walked to the small bathroom and took a long hot shower, staring at the tiled wall. She pulled her clothes from the closet without giving them much thought. Dark wash jeans with a loosely fitted white V-neck shirt was her go-to outfit for work. She completed it with a light brown button-down jacket and worn brown boots. Wiping the remainder of sleep from her eyes, she dragged herself to the kitchen and prepared a cup of coffee. What she craved was the bursting flavor of coffee from her favorite corner café, the one with the green exterior and red door on the other side of town. After a quick look in the mirror, phone in pocket, and coffee in hand, she was ready for the day.

She arrived at the monthly conference barely on time. Why Jensen had asked her to this meeting was beyond her. She normally worked the night shift in an entirely different department, and they hadn't spoken since he'd moved out.

When Esme walked into the local reaper bar, The Twisted Sickle, all eyes were on her.

Her appearance wasn't like other reapers. Her hair was ink-black, curling wildly, brushing the top of her shoulders. Her ironically warm, steel-gray eyes contrasted her glowing, rich, olive skin beautifully. The average reaper was over six feet tall, while Esme stood proudly at five feet four inches. Between her appearance and short stature, every reaper and other beings with whom she had encountered would theorize where she had come from.

The truth was, no one outside the Grim Reaper and other counsel members knew how reapers were created. Neither Heaven nor Hell would claim them. It was best that way, since they had to be a neutral soul-collecting party. Esme was the real conundrum. Why was she so different? Was it a mistake or on purpose? Some had speculated she was a new breed of reaper. Others considered the possibility of her being an Infernal disguised as a reaper. All anyone could agree on was that she was unique.

"Long night of partying?" Jensen jeered when he saw Esme.

"Oh, yeah, real rager," Esme replied, before drawing out a sip of coffee. "I could say the same about you." Awkward tension hung between them. Other reapers avoided the pair like the plague.

Jensen was a tall, lean man with dirty blonde hair long enough to tuck behind his ears. It framed his alabaster face perfectly. His vivacious hazel eyes were Esme's favorite thing. While all the reapers, minus herself, shared the same eye color, his were special. She could lose herself in his eyes for hours.

Stubble dotted his razor-sharp jaw. He didn't look like himself lately. His eyes looked sunken and dull, and his hair was tousled. Jensen tapped his fingers on the tablet he carried in one hand and put his other hand in his pocket. Only Esme could recognize his telling habit when he was anxious or uncomfortable. She chuckled.

Jensen cleared his throat to get the other reapers' attention and to make it easier to avoid eye contact with Esme. "So, this past month has room for improvement. Some souls managed to escape their reapers. I won't name names. I expect better of you, considering who you are." He shot a few sharp glances around the room. "With that said, appreciate the time and effort put into locating and retrieving said souls."

Rolling her eyes, she threw a few guesses around about who they could be.

Jensen continued. "A new group of reapers arrived this morning, and some of you more experienced specialists will be assigned as mentors to these Apprentices. Your lists are lighter but not empty."

A grumbled protest settled in the atmosphere.

"Listen, I know that mentoring isn't the most pleasant experience. We all take turns, so we can all share the load of teaching. Even I'm in this round of mentorship."

The grumbling settled, while discontentment lingered in the room.

"I have sent your lists for the month. You will receive them shortly. So, if there aren't questions, get it done, and get it done right." Dings, rings, and whistles echoed.

Things have modernized since the bringer of death first gained notoriety in 14th century Europe. Back then, it was only the Grim Reaper and his scythe. Since then, the world's populations have increased tenfold. The Grim Reaper had implemented the new system.

"Did you get your list?" Jensen approached Esme casually, coffee cup in hand, as the other reapers had either left to get their list started or lingered around comparing lists.

"I sure did." Esme hated small talk. It made her uncomfortable, especially when there was an obvious answer to a question. "Did you not get yours?" she asked sarcastically.

"Ah, there's that trademark witty banter. I always look forward to it first thing in the morning."

He waited and looked at her, trying to grab her attention, but he lost her. Her phone had bewitched her.

Feeling his searing gaze, she set her eyes on him. Esme had a way of looking through people. Her stare could make anyone feel seen or feel small.

Clearing his throat, he thrusted his hand forward. "I got you a coffee from that café you like." Jensen cleared his throat and continued. "I have a new reaper to check in on later today. Cora, I believe. Are you in this round of mentoring?"

"Sounds painful for her." She looked back at her dinging phone. "You know I don't mentor; I have other job descriptions. I'm sure she'll do just fine under your watchful eye. Try not to be hard on her. It is her first day, after all."

There was a hidden touch of sincerity in her tone. She glanced at the paper cup of coffee; the delightful aroma drifted into her nose. "Thank you for the coffee. I already have some." She then refocused on the earlier conversation. "Your first day was centuries ago, so you probably don't remember too well. It's a lot to take on, especially with the new rules." She slipped her phone back into her pocket. "Did you make her list yet?" Esme's phone dinged again. She closed her eyes and groaned before becoming ensnared by technology once more.

Jensen inwardly cursed the phone; it had caused him to lose her yet again. "No, not yet. The bosses haven't passed down the excess souls list to make one yet. They're usually early about it, but they're running behind." Jensen spoke nonchalantly. He thought of something that had troubled his mind. He asked her, "I get to see any list created, never yours. Why is that?" The annoyance he felt was palpable. "Who is the lucky mortal you get to visit today?"

"Trust me, they aren't lucky." She shoved her phone in her back pocket and let out a sigh. "You know, as the Strategos, I'm not allowed to discuss it with any other reaper. He sends it to me directly, not through our database. In confidence, might I add." Esme's eyes reflected her internal exhaustion, then morphed into frustration. "Why did you ask me to be here? We're different departments. These are the reapers who fall under you; they don't work for me, and I certainly don't work for you. There isn't anything for us to discuss."

Jensen added his statement quickly, since he had her attention for the first time in a long while. "Listen, Esme, I just—I don't know. I feel like there is something important being left out. Maybe something unsaid."

Esme looked away and clenched her jaw before shooting a glance at him. If her eyes could look through him, her gaze would make him invisible.

Jensen opened his mouth, but she interrupted. "As I said, there is nothing for us to discuss. It wasn't necessary for me to be here. Right now—because I actually thought you needed me for something—I'm late. I have to help Camryn train the new reapers."

Any civilized society had a hierarchy of power; the Reaper world was no different. Esme was the only reaper to work directly next to the Grim Reaper. Wherever he went, she dutifully followed. In their hierarchy, everyone had earned titles. First were the originals, a group of three who came first, second, and third. The first and at the top of the pyramid was the Grim Reaper. After him were the second and third created, Thalia and Ansel. They were known as Directors, each in charge of global collection departments. After the Directors came the Strategos. There was only one Strategos: Esme. She answered only to the Grim Reaper and could act on his behalf. Under her directly was no one. Indirectly, she fielded all the paperwork and concerns from the Administrators of the red departments. Death was busy and difficult to get a hold of. She eased that burden for him. When she was in a city, every Administrator was subordinate to her.

Each department had their own group of Administrators for an entire coast. These reapers were usually over two hundred years old. Jensen was one of the Administrators, and Camryn was another. Philadelphia lacked a third Administrator. Esme was taking on that role, along with her normal job. They oversaw all reapers on the coast they resided in, making sure to finalize schedules, ensuring enough reapers were where they needed to be, and that soul collection happened exactly when it was supposed to happen. Under the Administrators were Specialists. Specialists were the reapers who had just finished training. They also carried the brunt of harvesting souls.

Specialists worked the longest hours, collecting statewide, with little time to recharge. Esme always made it a point to speak with as many Specialists as she could when she was in various cities. Finally, at the bottom of the hierarchy were the Apprentices. These were the brand-new reapers. Where and how they were created was kept secret to everyone except the Grim Reaper. All Esme knew was, he would enter a meeting with representatives from both Celestial and Infernal factions, and a few months later, a new batch of reapers was ready. Every year, a new group would emerge and become the newest group of Apprentices. This is where they would stay for a one year minimum, shadowing their mentor, finding which department they would work efficiently in. The older a reaper became, the more energy they'd emanate. It was an innate ability to let others know who to respect.

She went where she wanted and helped where she could. There was no place for a reaper who didn't fit in their world. It was a side effect luxury other senior reapers weren't afforded.

"Good ol' trusty Camryn. I'm sure he has a lot of wisdom to pass down." Bitterness coated Jensen's comment.

"Careful there, Jensen, green was never your color." Esme took a step forward, then lingered to glance up at him.

His scent of cedar, leather, and oranges called to her. The urge to nestle her face into his chest while he wrapped his arms around her surfaced. She lost herself in his gaze. The morning sun reflected in his eyes, reminding her of pools of honey. She shook her head, snapping out of the daze. Distance is what she needed. As she placed her hands on his chest, a warm glow emitted. The ripple of strong, calming warmth entered Jensen's chest, entwining with his own energy. He closed his eyes, feeling her warmth fill the hole that no one else could fill.

She whispered, "You shouldn't blame others for your mistakes." Her fingers skimmed down his chest as she pushed away from him. "Especially when they had nothing to do with it."

Brushing past him, Esme opened the door, letting a peek of sunlight into The Twisted Sickle.

"Esme." Jensen tried to call her back, but she had already walked away. It was an all too painful and familiar sight. A handful of reapers stood around the bar, looking at him and the remnants of their uncomfortable encounter. "Why are you still here? Don't you have some reaping to get to?" Jensen said loudly and sternly. The lingering reapers looked at each other, muttering and slowly exiting the bar.

Esme walked into the city, passing graffiti-covered walls and more coffee shops and dwindling corner cafés than she could count.

A reaper's only purpose was to take a soul to the veil, so the soul was free to move on to an afterlife. After roaming the globe for so long, mortals became faceless beings. Every city mimicked another. Transients and vagabonds tucking themselves away in whatever safety a cardboard box could provide them.

As her eyes wandered the streets and brick buildings, she spotted Infernals, attempting to make a few deals before the sun fully rose.

"Fucking demons," she said, with clear disdain in her voice. Personally, she'd never had any issues with any Infernal being, especially since reapers were strongly discouraged from socializing outside themselves. What irked her was how those damned Infernal creatures always preyed upon the vulnerable.

It was amazing how that race had managed to conceal themselves for this long. Knowledge about Infernals was widely known in every culture because they were far too reckless in their actions. They played fast and loose, greedy for more power. Then there were the Celestials, more commonly known as angels.

If there was a race Esme disliked, it would be the Celestials. Sitting high in their city somewhere above the clouds, rarely interacting with mortals, letting the Infernals roam unchecked. What was the most bothersome was how grandiose mortals portrayed angels, since they hardly did a thing.

An Infernal who had finished a deal drew his gaze from his prey and locked eyes with Esme. His red eyes flashed as he gave a sinister grin. "You poor soul. You have no idea what is going to happen to you." Her voice was heavy, carrying the burden for the one who had just made a deal for their soul. She snapped her eyes up toward the clouds before continuing her morning commute.

Sure, she could have apparated from The Twisted Sickle to headquarters, but walking provided her with a few insights. It offered her more understanding of mortals' lives she had escorted once their days were through. With lists stretching hundreds of names, thoughts were never spared on the daily rituals of mortals.

Not Esme.

Walking the streets gave her glimpses into the mortal world, and she secretly pretended to be one of them. She loved the feel of the morning hustle, the sounds of cars rushing by. Sitting on a random bench to hear the fleeting stories and gossip of mortal lives were often better and more entertaining than reading a book. What she looked forward to was watching other reapers work. Just by observing, she could tell who needed retraining or maybe a change in scenery. It wasn't often other reapers would change cities, states, or countries. Esme believed it did them well and made them more productive if they got to experience something other than the mundane.

It had been four years since she hung her hat as the roaming reaper and moved to the city of Philadelphia. The last Administrator had been transferred to another country. Esme had offered to fill the role until they would find a replacement. There was something charming about Philadelphia, all the old history and architecture. The countless museums were among her favorite places to visit. She could spend days on end visiting every single one that clustered near each other, just soaking in the history of mortals. The food, a bonus and guilty pleasure.

Her feet carried her out of Rittenhouse Square, where The Twisted Sickle sat, nestled away. The crosswalk turned red and rung an obnoxious, loud beep.

She stood still in the herd of humankind. Here she was, a reaper in plain sight, and the surrounding people were none the wiser. Esme laughed to herself. She savored a deep breath of the fresh coffee and smog-laced, warm morning air.

Esme could sense someone watching her, but who? Before she could spot who, the crosswalk light counted down— not that it meant much in this city—and the crowd started shifting. A young woman with long purple hair, shouting into her phone, brushed against Esme in an eager attempt to cross. The woman shuddered and looked back with a look of discomfort in her eyes. It was the way humans unknowingly encounter death. A sudden icy chill usually means a reaper is nearby.

Esme didn't move. She knew what was coming. She let out a sigh and could taste it. The bitterness of the end, the tang of darkness. This time was different. There was a new tartness in the air. The flavor of that nightmarish metal flooded her senses. Screeching tires, screams, and a thud broke her train of thought.

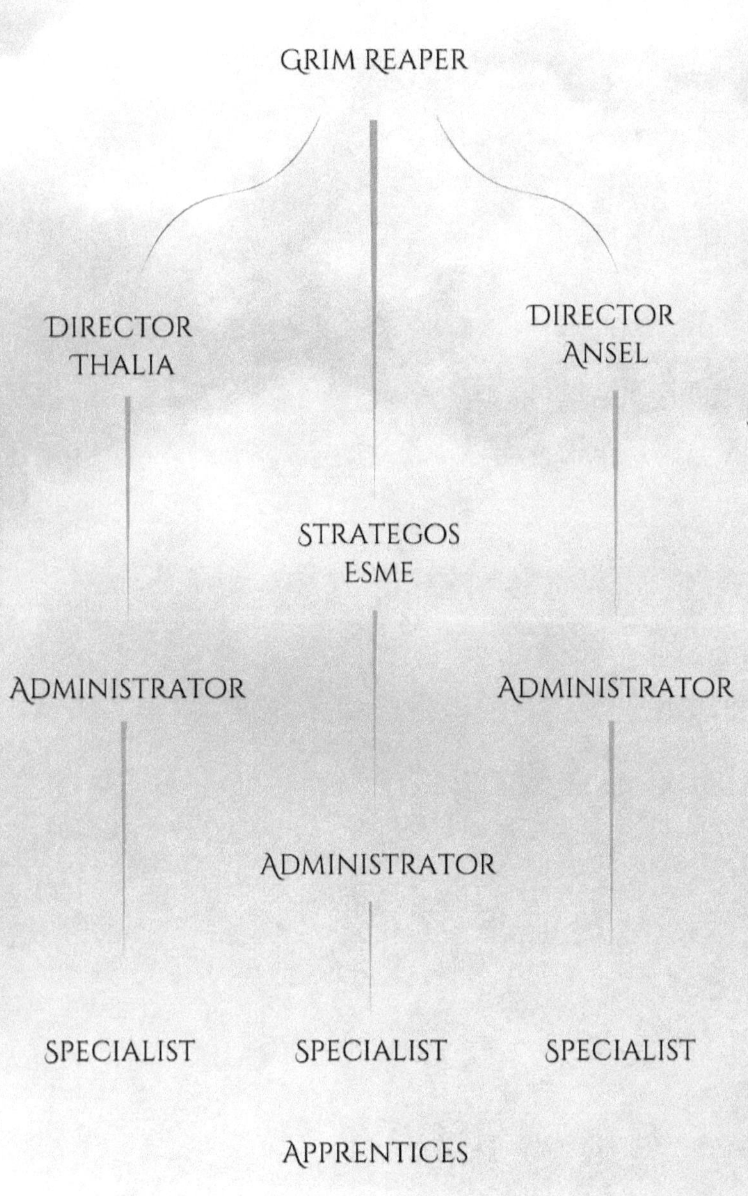

GRIM REAPER
DIRECTOR THALIA
DIRECTOR ANSEL
STRATEGOS ESME
ADMINISTRATOR
ADMINISTRATOR
ADMINISTRATOR
SPECIALIST
SPECIALIST
SPECIALIST
APPRENTICES

2

Another reaper apparated next to her. Tyler arrived as she heard the thud.

"Hey, Tyler."

"Hey, Esme. I didn't know you were working in this area today." Tyler was efficient at his job and quick with a joke.

"Oh, no, I'm not. I'm headed into the office to help train the new batch. Is she yours?" Esme asked Tyler, nodding over to the crowd.

Tyler shook his head. "Not mine. I've got the driver."

Esme nodded with curiosity. "You mean he hasn't departed yet?"

"I still have a few more minutes," he stated, checking the time on his phone.

"Then, who has the purple hair lady?" Esme asked. "I don't see or sense any other reapers here."

"It would be hard to see anything from down there." Tyler heckled.

"Ah-ha-ha. I will hurt you." Esme said this with a vacant expression.

They looked at each other for a few seconds and started laughing. They knew reapers did not possess the ability to hurt each other. High, shrill screaming cut their laughter short.

"Someone should get her," they said unanimously.

"Jinx!" Tyler called out.

"But what do I do after you call out jinx?"

"You know, all these years here on earth, and I still don't know," he replied.

They stood there on the corner, which had become a swarm of chaos. Frantic screaming interrupted their banter.

"Uh-oh, she's freaking out, and her reaper isn't here. You should probably go grab her, too, since you still have time." Esme nudged Tyler in the woman's direction.

"Seriously? I already have him, and it's going to be so awkward since, you know, he ran her over." The mere thought caused him to dramatize his objection. "Plus, I can't take her to her door in the veil; she's not mine. You know that. Which is a stupid new rule, by the way."

Esme massaged her browbone and let out a sigh. Her phone rang. "Well, I can't take her, either, and I'm already running late to training. I'll tell you what"—she scratched her head, frizzing the curls around her fingers—"take the guy and the girl, make a stop at The Twisted Sickle, and leave her with Jensen. He can figure it out. He has a light list today." She pulled her bottom lip with her teeth as she checked the time while rejecting a call.

"Yeah, that's going to go over well." His statement had a mixture of concern and sarcasm.

"Tyler, it's fine. Everything is going to be just fine. You tell Jensen to call me if he has an issue with doing his job. Now go before I pull my seniority card on you." She patted Tyler's shoulder and winked.

As she resumed her journey through the city, she caught a quick glimpse of Tyler trying to usher this sad woman's soul from her body. The only thought going through Esme's mind was how glad she was that she didn't have to deal with this mess first thing in the morning.

As Esme continued walking, she kept thinking about the woman with no reaper. A reaper's sole purpose was to escort the departed to help make their transition easier. Her mind shifted to whoever that unfortunate reaper was who left their charge for someone else to collect. They would have to answer to Jensen, who was a stickler for rules and organization. He had no issues making it known he strongly disliked it when things didn't go according to plan. One thing they could always agree on were the reprimands he would issue.

When a reaper failed to follow the rules set out for them or failed to collect a soul properly, penalties were put in place. These punishments were usually left up to the Administrator to decide and report to the Strategos or Director if available. Many times, the reaper in question would get either a heavier workload, or they would be transferred to a remote part of the world. The latter was the worst: if there was nothing for them to do, it would take away their purpose and identity. Going remote was the equivalent of a prison sentence.

The sheer thought of Jensen being inconvenienced in the morning put a smile on her face. A part of her had always enjoyed giving him a hard time. Even though it bothered him, Jensen always found a way to laugh off her nonsense. Esme knew he secretly enjoyed the way she messed with him.

The blaring horns and construction brought her back to reality. Her phone buzzed in her back pocket. Esme pulled it out to find a text message from Tyler:

> *This was a terrible idea! I want you to know I am mad at you now. You owe me a large drink!*

Esme let out an amused chuckle, shook her head, and wrote back:

> *I'm sure that two large drinks will make things better.*

She slid her phone back into the back pocket of her jeans. After five blocks, Esme arrived at the Reaper headquarters of that city. This wasn't a building that stood out or would be memorable. Wards placed around the building made it blend seamlessly of the always bustling Center City. The building was tall enough, with seven stories and wrapped in mirrored windows. No name adorned the building. The entirety of the building was a hub for reapers.

Esme pushed through the revolving door, giving friendly nods to a group who was heading out. She pushed the up button on the elevator, rocking on the balls of her feet. Her phone buzzed again. By this point, she wanted to throw her entire phone away. Never had her phone buzzed so much in one morning. She pulled the phone out of its home to see a text message from Camryn.

> *Where are you? I have to start the training without you.*

Esme rolled her eyes and replied:

In the lobby, headed up now.

Clutching the phone, she thought she might have cracked the screen. She looked it over, seeing it was unharmed, and nestled it back into its tiny home again. Esme admired the wooden reception desk that was always empty and the shine on the tile floor beneath her feet. The air in the lobby was brisk and smelled sterile, reminding her of the local hospital.

Seeing as the elevator was taking longer than any other day, she reluctantly opted to use the stairs. As she pulled open the stairwell door, the elevator chimed in the distance. She rolled her eyes, grumbling at the elevator, committed to taking the stairs. "Cardio it is."

After walking up four flights of stairs, the training department's spectacle welcomed her. All the new reapers were meeting with assigned mentors and getting phones issued to them. Groups were gathering to find out which apartment would be theirs. Across from that group, a few others mingled, exchanging numbers.

Esme could sense all eyes on her as she walked. She stopped and surveyed the eyes lingering on her. No one in this batch was like her, either. She lifted her arms out to her side, twirling in place. "You like my outfit? I dressed myself this morning."

The mentors who knew Esme let out a chuckle, while others shook their heads. They would expect nothing less from her. She placed her arms down at her sides once she sensed the new reapers' unease. Tugging at the bottom of her jacket, she made her way to the training room.

3

Camryn stood tall and confident, staring down into the eyes that gazed back at him. His light brown hair was cut and styled in a 1930s fashion. Broad shoulders complimented his brawny frame and extreme height. When Camryn stood in front of a crowd, he commanded attention and respect. He wore a denim jacket over his black T-shirt, paired with olive-green pants and canvas shoes.

"Welcome to your first day of reaping." Camryn's deep voice echoed in the still room. "I'm here to help you become the best reaper you can be."

As he opened his mouth to continue his speech, the sound of a heavy metal door closing snatched everyone's attention. Despite her stealthy attempt at entering the room, a tight-lipped Esme had effectively drawn attention to herself and flicked a small wave.

He tracked her movements until she was standing in the back of the room, tucking herself away in the shadows. He gave her a stern nod to let her know he saw her.

"There is a lot more to reaping than just escorting souls." A rhythmic, incessant chime interrupted his well-rehearsed speech. Esme grabbed at her pocket, trying to hush her phone. She could feel everyone's searing gaze. Anxiety surged in her as the chime continued. The only thing she could do was mouth a "sorry" as she found the volume button through her jeans.

"As I was saying"—Camryn hastened his head side to side, causing it to crack—"there is more to reaping than you think. We don't just walk up to any mortal and keep moving. There is a certain art to it, a certain finesse." His large hands stroked the air in front of him when a hand rose from the crowd.

Esme looked at the hand and back at Camryn. She knew he hated being interrupted.

He addressed the rising hand. "If you could just hold that question, I can almost guarantee the answer is to follow."

The slender hand sunk back into the crowd.

He extended his hand toward Esme, who was attempting to melt back into the corner. "Allow me to introduce you to Esme. She's been doing this for an exceptionally long time and has graciously agreed to help me give you a quick history lesson and training tips. Esme?"

"Exceptionally long?" She playfully pursed her lips. "Yes, I am older than you. But I don't know if I'm that old, Camryn."

A small laugh rolled across the room.

"Well, you are—" Camryn had a devilish look in his eye.

She laughed, pointing at him. "Don't you dare guess how old I am. Especially since I can neither confirm nor deny."

A snickering comment came from a row of chairs Esme passed. "Should answer that question."

Esme stopped in her tracks, turning her head slowly toward the female voice she had just heard. She allowed a fragment of energy to ripple off her as she glared at the only three females in that row. A sudden heaviness fell upon her. The room spun under her feet. Esme rubbed her brow. Distantly, Camryn called out to her.

"Es?" His voice carried a worried undertone to it. She blinked several times, adjusting her jacket, and joined Camryn at the front of the room. "Are you okay?" He held her hand delicately, rubbing his thumb over her knuckles.

Looking down at their hands, she nodded and smiled. "I'm fine." Her smile was small and forced. "It's just been a long morning. Shall we continue?" She slipped her hand out of his and stepped to the side. The feeling in the room went from lighthearted to heavy and uncomfortable.

Camryn exaggeratedly clapped both hands in front of himself and stepped closer to her. "Like I mentioned, this is Esme." He stood behind her, placing his hands on her shoulders, accentuating their size difference. His warrior-like Viking stature caused her to appear small, fragile, and doll-like. He continued. "She has graciously agreed to help me give you all a quick history lesson and some key pointers."

A voice from the other side of the room floated through the silence. "If she's a reaper, why does she look . . ." The voice paused in confusion. "Well, why does she look like that?"

Every group that had entered this room always asked this question. It never failed. Even though it was commonly asked, it was always bothersome. Her kind only saw her at face value first as different and weird.

"Wow, we are starting out strong, I see. First, raise your hand if you have questions. Second, don't speak unless called on. Third, I have no answer. When I do, I'm sure everyone will know." A wave of her energy filled the room, causing the Apprentices to shift in their seats. It was something she had never enjoyed doing but had to. Letting her energy surface let others know who she was and that she was not to be questioned.

Esme stepped forward, which made Camryn's hands slide down her arms.

She took one deep breath, slowly exhaling as she told the Grim Reaper's history. "If you haven't guessed by now, our boss is the Grim Reaper. He collects the names of those who need to be collected during his meetings with Infernal and Celestial representatives. I believe, every once in a while, Fate sits in as well. Those names are then dispersed accordingly between him and the others. It wasn't always this way, though. The Grim Reaper didn't make his existence known until the 14th century of humanity. This happens to coincide with humanity's run-in with the plague. Until that point, being escorted by the Grim Reaper was more of a VIP privilege. The ancient Greeks called him Thanatos."

As she slipped her hands in her jacket pocket, the same hand that interrupted Camryn shot up from the crowd once again. "There are variations of him depicted throughout history. But it is important to note, since the 14th century, no new portrayals have surfaced. It's because of an agreement between all factions of beings to remain hidden in the mortal world." Images of smoke, dirt, and blood flashed in her mind. A shiver ran down her spine as she rubbed her eyes to refocus. "As the population of humans increased at an alarming rate, it became quite the challenge for a single reaper to achieve this task alone." Esme scanned the faces. Boredom was taking over the room's sentiment. Sarcasm and annoyance poured out of her mouth. "I know this is all overly exciting for you to hear. This may seem pointless, but I promise there is a reason to learn our history."

A few new reapers readjusted themselves to sit up straighter. Esme began her lesson again. "Souls were not going where they needed to be or wandering off altogether. This, as you can guess, is a big problem. We serve as the 'go-between.' Every soul has a destination, and that destination needs to be reached. Too many unclaimed souls roaming the Earth affect the mortal realm. Unfortunately, we cannot tell them what happens to them in their afterlife. It is not for us to know. It may impede them from crossing over." Esme stopped and shifted her weight beneath her feet. Her head spun again. She squeezed her eyes shut and let out a sigh before continuing. "Since the Grim Reaper needed help, two more reapers appeared to help with the collection and delivery of souls, our Directors. Together, they are the three originals—or the big three, whichever you prefer." She looked over her shoulder, seeing if Camryn had anything else he wanted to add. Instead, he nodded and gave her a thumbs-up.

"It was quickly determined each reaper was better suited and had a greater chance of collecting a soul their energy matched with. This created the reaping departments we have today." Intrigue overtook the room. That same familiar hand rose again, more eager than before. Esme could feel her eye twitch but ignored the hand again. "You will be assigned to a department based on the recommendation of your mentor. You will be with your mentor for one full year." The hand fell back down again. She rocked back on her heel and turned her head toward Camryn, who was leaning against the wall. "Camryn, would you like to explain the departments, or do you want me to do this training by myself?"

Camryn walked forward with his arms open and rolled his eyes. "Well, when you put it that way." As he moved forward, the reapers laughed.

Esme walked back to the spot Camryn had just left. His calloused hand grabbed her wrist. "Are you sure you're okay?" He had a genuine look of concern on his face.

"I'm fine," she said. "Really, I'm fine, Cam."

Camryn cleared his throat. "I'm going to make this simple and quick." An audible sigh of relief filled the room. "As Esme mentioned, we now have departments. This is where you will earn the title of Specialist." He listed them off on his fingers. "We have expected departures, innocence, and violent acts."

A familiar sight flitted across Camryn's eyes: that eagerly raised hand.

Esme looked at the hand and back at Camryn. He turned, eyes widening and twitching, staring at Esme. His frustration level was visibly rising as he did all he could to keep calm. Esme crossed her arms, placing her hand over her mouth. She simply shook her head in response. He pinched his eyes together while grabbing the front of his denim jacket. He inhaled and exhaled. Esme couldn't help let a laugh escape. Camryn furrowed his brow, disapproving of her amusement.

He continued to speak, completely ignoring the rising hand yet again. "Throughout the upcoming months, you will have souls from each category to collect. Your mentor will be there with you to help you and assess the situation. As you remember, your mentor will have a large say in what your specialty will be."

A throat cleared. "Excuse me? I have a question. Several, actually." A tall, willowy figure stood.

Esme's eyes broadened and darted between the willowy figure and Camryn.

Camryn took another step forward. "I don't believe I acknowledged you." The words were stern and cold.

Esme could tell he was fed up with that hand. She squinted, examining the still-standing figure. She noticed it was one of the female reapers in the row from where the earlier snarky remark had emanated. A few seconds passed, and that figure still stood, reluctant to sit.

"This is when you sit back down." Camryn's eyes were uncompromising as he stared at this new reaper.

Slowly, she took her seat and released some tension in the room.

He was irritated but restarted the training that had been running over. "Your lists are curated for you and you alone. It means no other reaper can take the soul for you, mentors included. Other reapers can travel with you to the veil. I stress again: they cannot take the soul for you. This is a relatively new rule the boss has instilled." Puzzled expressions riddled most faces in the room. "Apparently, there were too many reapers passing off their lists to others, and it became an issue. Since you are new, whoever I assigned to show you the ropes will be there, helping you on what to do and say if need be. The actual collection falls on you."

Once again, the new reaper stood. In a frustrated tone, she said, "But you still haven't answered how we actually collect or when we get these lists. Do we just know? What happens if a soul doesn't want to go? How do we know——"

Camryn pursed his lips and spoke through his teeth. "If you just sit and quiet down, we would have had." He balled his fists as his shoulders tensed. "You know what, I-I can't. I can't do this." He threw his arms up. He turned around and gazed down at the floor.

Esme laughed, which made him look up at her. "I'm sorry, it's just"—Esme tried her best to stifle a laugh from her lips—"you look like you're trying to burn a hole in the floor." She watched as he raised his fist to his mouth and bit down on his knuckles. Esme stepped forward and placed a gentle hand on Camryn's back. She looked up at him and said, "I'll handle it, okay?" She watched as he relaxed his hands and placed them on his waist.

He nodded and walked back to look out of a window.

Esme turned to the young reapers, who all looked uncomfortable. She addressed the room. "If this is too much for you to manage, you're going to struggle out there." She shook her head and faced the source of the commotion. Esme pointed and asked, "What's your name?"

The once bold figure took time to stand again. She replied, "Cora?"

Esme looked at her with a hardened expression. "Was that a question, or is that your name? You had no issues with making yourself known before. Please don't stop now."

Cora swallowed hard and sunk into her seat.

Esme smirked and shook her head. "What you need to understand is, we run on strict schedules. We only have so much time to give you basic knowledge before sending you out there. I would have answered all the questions for all of you. You can thank Cora we no longer have time." Grumbles rolled across each row as Cora sank into her seat. "Now, if you have questions, you'll have to bombard your mentor with them. I'm sure they will absolutely love it." She looked up at the clock and sighed. "I can answer only two of your questions, 'How do you get your lists?' Well, the Grim Reaper has a collection of names. I mentioned that before." She scratched the bridge of her nose. "Those names are handed down to the respective departments. Once there, it is distributed to the Administrators, such as Camryn and the Strategos, which is me." She noticed Cora's eyes widen after hearing Esme and Camryn held such high ranks.

Esme continued. "Once we get those names, we put them out to the reaper, who is on that appropriate shift. You'll get that list on a phone provided to you. Your mentor will help you collect all the tools you need after this meeting. I promise you there isn't much." Camryn stepped forward again. "To answer what happens if they don't want to go, simply put: you are responsible for the soul assigned to you. If they run, you track them down and bring them to the veil. Your chances of them running decrease when they experience our touch. To a living mortal, we feel frigid. To a soul, we feel warm and calming. When your hand is on them, you can share your energy; a light forms in your hand and enters them. It's called ardor fragmenting."

Another hand rose from the crowd. Esme glanced at the clock and back at the new hand. "What's your question?"

A male apprentice stood, and his voice quivered. "Can you show us what the ardor fragments looks like or feels like on one of us?"

Remembering her earlier interaction with Jensen, she jerked a sad smile on her full lips. She hadn't meant to let the ardor fragment come through. It just happened so naturally. "Sorry, I can't do that. It's an intimate experience shared with those we have chosen to love forever. The feeling is different between reapers."

Camryn gently hip-checked Esme, his arms crossed. "So, Camryn, do you want to wrap this up since we're now officially out of time?" The relieved tone in her voice made him smile.

He stretched his neck and grabbed his phone from his jacket pocket. "Your mentors should be outside or getting here within the next few minutes. As I mentioned before, they will go with you and check in throughout the day. Please listen for your name, and once you have your mentors' names, please get out of here and find them on this floor."

As Camryn rattled off names, Esme's phone whirred in her pocket. Pulling it out, she glanced at Jensen's name scrolling across the screen. She hesitated to decline the call but did it, anyway. She sent a message.

Call you back later. I'm finishing up with training.

Before she could tuck her phone away, a rapid buzz caught her attention. She smiled at Jensen's rapid reply.

That was scheduled to be over 10 minutes ago.

She raised a brow as she typed back.

Yeah well, you can thank your new trainee for that one. She's quite the inquisitive one.

Esme stared at the blinking ellipses on her screen, waiting for Jensen to reply.

Oh. No. Please tell me you're joking. Please. Esme?

Esme chuckled. Something about not replying to him gave her a sense of satisfaction. She pushed her phone back into her pocket. As she looked back up, she noticed the last few reapers leaving the room.

Camryn grabbed two chairs and slid one across the floor to Esme. His brawny frame collapsed onto the chair beneath him with a frustrated sigh. "Well—that didn't go the way it normally does." The sound of defeat was a new tone for him. He sat, observing Esme standing surrounded by empty chairs under the humming, cold fluorescent lights. It was then he realized the lonely and stressed look on her face. He stretched his arms up and rested his hands behind his head, crossing an ankle over his knee, before asking, "So, Es, are you going to tell me what's bothering you this fine morning?"

A small sigh escaped her lips as her hands ran up and down her thighs. "Oh, Cam. I don't know. Nothing and everything. This morning was just off, I guess." She grabbed the chair Camryn slid to her and positioned it in front of him. She adjusted herself in the seat as he leaned forward.

He tied the laces on his canvas shoes. "I'm going to go on a crazy assumption and say Jensen?"

Esme pointed and smiled. "Bingo."

Camryn rested his forearms on his thighs, leaning forward in his chair. "What's going on with you two now? Aren't you both moving past the whole heartbreak, awkward meetings, and avoiding each other now?" He moved his hand in a circular motion in front of her face.

Esme swatted his hand away. "Yes. No? Honestly, I don't know. It's complicated, and I hate complicated. We're not together anymore, but he still believes something is unresolved. It's almost like . . ." She shook away her thought. "We accepted each other, Cam. You know that doesn't happen often with our kind. It's rare finding an eternal paramour. Some days, I just—I don't know."

Camryn tilted his head to the side and stood. "It's okay, Es, I get it. Plus, the way it went down between you two, it's going to take some time." He offered his hand to Esme to help her up.

She placed her hand in his while she stood. The room swirled again. She sat quickly, waiting for her dizziness to pass.

A genuinely concerned look filled Camryn's caramel eyes. "There's something off with you today, and it's more than love troubles." He kneeled in front of her, still holding her hand. "What's going on?"

Esme blinked a few times and pulled her hand out of Camryn's. "It's strange. This morning, there was a soul without a reaper to escort."

Camryn furrowed his brow. "It is odd but can't be everything. Go on."

Esme hesitated. Should she be saying this? "I've been getting dizzy, getting real headaches. Having a strange reoccurring dream—nightmare, really." As the words tumbled from her mouth, she looked back at Camryn with regret.

Camryn stood and took a few steps across the tile floor. "Are you sure? Es, reapers don't dream or experience any of that. We only rest to recharge our energy."

She slumped her shoulders. "I know. Why do you think I've been off? I just don't know what to make of it."

He could tell she was uncomfortable. He busied himself, folding chairs and turning away to give her space. "We don't need to talk about any more of this if you don't want to. If you want help, I'm here."

She stood, walked toward the other side of the room, and folded chairs. "I know you are, and I appreciate it. I promise, if I need help, I'll ask you."

Her mind was restless, unease creeping into every fiber of her essence. She needed a distraction. "How did pickup go this morning?" The new group of Apprentices had emerged where every group before them emerged for that side of the country, Hector Falls in the Allegheny National Forest.

"Smooth as ever. Except, this time, they were at the bottom of the falls instead of on top. We were all confused." He scratched his earlobe.

"Thanks for taking my turn for the pickup, Cam. I had a few last-minute additions to my list and then that meeting this morning," Esme said, starting a new short stack of chairs.

Camryn watched as she moved down each row. "Don't worry about it, Es. You have enough to worry about with working two roles. I really don't mind helping you."

"Don't know what I'd do without you." She smiled.

He matched her smile. "Live in a constant state of high stress with a touch of doom and gloom. Or be perfectly content. But, seeing as you're stuck with me forever, we'll never know."

They left their conversation to settle while they folded and stacked chairs in companionable peace.

4

After dismissing the loitering reapers, Jensen walked toward his private office. It was tucked away down a long, dimly lit hall. As he reached the office door, he hesitated for a moment, recalling Esme walking away from him. A heavy sigh escaped him as he placed his hand on the silver doorknob. His head dropped as the phone rang. His hands were full of haphazard random folders that were dropped off during the meeting by specialists reapers and his tablet. The rejected paper cup of coffee balanced on top of it all.

Jensen reached for his phone. It slipped from his fingertips and landed screen-side down. The impact echoed off the old wood floors and against the dingy ruby-red walls. "Ah, damn it, not again." He swore to himself as he picked up the now silent phone. Jensen winced in anticipation of the damage. He turned it over and saw a small crack running across the top. "Oh, thank the powers that be." A wave of relief washed over him.

The phone rang again. He tucked the tablet and folders under his arm. The coffee tumbled during the shift, and he stood there, blinking at the warm pool that splashed on his boots. "Slow, deep breaths, Jensen. Slow deep breaths." This time, he opted to hold the newly cracked phone with two hands. "What can I do for you, Tyler?"

With a momentary hesitation, Tyler replied, "Hey, Jensen. So, there's a tiny problem, and I mean tiny, minute, minuscule. A blip of a problem, really."

Jensen narrowed his eyes as he looked down at the spot where his phone was. "Didn't you just start your shift? It only started ten minutes ago, and you're telling me you already have a problem? What kind of minute problem? Also, you're not my department. Why aren't you telling Strategos Esme about your problem?"

He fell silent, contemplating the right words to not agitate Jensen. The only sound seeping through the phone was street noise and two faint voices arguing. Jensen leaned against the door of his office, growing incensed. "Tyler, what is the problem? I don't have the luxury of time or patience today."

Tyler spoke quickly. "Well, I ran into Esme at my first stop of the day."

Jensen interrupted, "Is she okay?"

Tyler paused in confusion. "What? Yeah, she's fine. Why wouldn't she be? And she's also fine, if you know what I mean." Tyler snickered at his statement.

Jensen grumbled.

Realizing his words were not as funny as he thought, he prattled on. "Anywho. I was there to pick up my guy's soul when there was another soul. An unclaimed soul."

In the background, a faint female voice said, "I'm not some kind of lost or unclaimed luggage, you know."

Tyler covered his phone with one hand. A muffled response was still audible. "Shh, not now. I'm trying to explain this."

Jensen stood away from the door and turned the doorknob. As he made his way into his office, he raised his usually calm voice. "Tyler, I need you to focus!"

His attention snapped back to the phone. "Never mind, I'm almost at the bar. I'll just show you. Okay, bye."

Jensen had just sat in his sleek, black leather chair when he heard Tyler call for him. "Hey, Jensen! Jensen, you didn't run away, did you?"

Looking between the papers, computer screen, and the door, he called Tyler back.

While he waited for Tyler to walk in with whatever problem he was talking about, he rifled through some papers from the folders. He sorted and placed them in his color-coded filing system. A loud and quick knock on the open door caught his attention. "Yeah, come in."

Tyler stepped in and guided two souls into the room. Jensen, who had busied himself with a mountain of paperwork, glanced up. He laid a long drawn-out gaze on the three beings before him, then at the clocks on his wall. Jensen leaned back, undoing the buttons on his cuffs. He slowly rolled each sleeve up to his elbow before he broke his silence. "What the hell is this? Please tell me there is a good reason why there are two souls in my office at a reaper bar instead of at the veil. You know, where they belong."

Tyler rubbed the back of his neck and looked around the room. Jensen's office was modern and well-kept compared to the rest of the bar. The walls were off white, and a sleek metal geometric chandelier hung over a large, dark wooden desk with metal legs. Behind the desk chair was a gallery wall with black-and-white photos of the world's most iconic landmarks.

Tyler chuckled and pointed while squinting. "Remember that blip I mentioned?" He rapidly recounted the story. His gestures were overly dramatic during his storytelling. "So, then, Esme told me to tell you to manage this since she's busy. Also, I can't watch her all day."

Jensen put his hand up with a suspicious look on his face. "Those were her exact words?"

He shrugged and cringed. "I may have rephrased here and there. Call it creative freedom." As he walked around the office, fidgeting with the few trinkets he could find, Jensen typed furiously on his phone.

Tyler turned his attention back to Jensen. "Are you trying to make your screen crack?" The only reply from Jensen was the scratching from rubbing his stubble-laced jaw. "Who are you texting, anyway?" The tone from Tyler was a mix of curiosity and jeering.

Finally, Jensen broke his gaze from the illuminated screen. "And now she's ignoring me. I swear Esme's mission is to drive me insane." He slammed his fist on the desk, filling the room with a loud thud. He started rocking in the chair, causing the leather to groan with each determined swing. Noticing the pens had shifted, he fixed them, regaining control over his emotions. He pulled his eyes to Tyler and remembered the two lingering souls.

Tyler walked toward the door and grabbed the man he was meant to collect. He pointed at all the clocks on the wall. "Wow, will you look at the time? I need to take this guy to the veil and keep checking off that list. Don't want to be tardy, right? Schedules to keep and all that."

Before Jensen could protest, Tyler pushed the man out the door. Jensen was stuck trying to figure out what happened to this woman's missing reaper. He squinted over at the woman, who pressed the back of her head against the wall. The brazen look she was giving him caused him to fidget with the folders. He leaned forward, resting his arms on the desk. "For a human who just died, you look pretty unphased." As the words left him, he intently gazed at this woman. Jensen took in her curvy frame and deep purple hair. His eyes lingered on her face. The woman opened her mouth and took a paused breath.

A wolfish grin spread across her lips. "At first, it totally pissed me off, knowing I died. But now"—she bit her bottom lip—"now I can spend eternity haunting an attractive guy like yourself."

Jensen's eyes quickly darted back to his phone. He fumbled with it as he attempted to call Esme yet again. He drummed his thumb on the edge of the desk as the phone rang. With the call rejected, disappointment crept across his face. The woman stepped away from the wall and sauntered over to him. She invited herself to sit on the edge of his desk and stared with flirtatious eyes.

He glared up at her. "First, don't sit on my desk; second, stop looking at me like that."

The woman shrugged and slowly slid off. With a heavy sigh, she replied, "A girl can dream, right?"

"Only the living dream." Jensen furrowed his brows at her. "Okay, let's get down to business so I can get you to where you belong."

The woman frowned and replied, "I really am dead, aren't I? This isn't just some trippy dream?"

Jensen shifted in his seat to face the computer screen, his eyes softening for a fraction of a second. "I'm afraid so. Now, what's your name, date of birth, and place of departure?"

Even as confusion was spreading across her face, she opened her mouth to reply. Before she could answer, Jensen raised a finger to quiet her. His phone chimed repeatedly.

The woman stood silent, uncertain of what to do or say. She clasped her hands in front of her hips and pursed her lips.

Jensen busied himself again for a few minutes, typing message after message. Finally, he tossed the phone on the desk and pinched the bridge of his nose, squeezing his eyes shut.

The woman spoke up. "Lady troubles?"

Jensen opened one eye toward her and closed it again. He ran his hand down his face. "Why are these the women in my existence?" It wasn't clear if this was a question directed toward the woman in the office or simply a thought left unfiltered. He stretched his arms, adjusting the rolled sleeves. "Anyway, you were going to tell me your name."

The woman offered a flat gaze, unconvinced it was safe for her to talk again. "Right, my name is Alicia Jones. My birthday is on July 7th. I'm a Cancer."

Jensen rolled his eyes and typed her information into a database. He stopped typing, waiting for Alicia to finish giving more information. "I need the year and place of departure."

Alicia softened the corner of her eyes. "Two thousand, and do you mean where that jerk ran me over?"

Jensen quirked the corner of his mouth. "If it's where you died, then yes."

Alicia crossed her arms and shifted her weight. "Corner of Spruce and South Broad. I was heading over to the hospital for my volunteer shift."

Jensen typed some more, letting the furious taps and clicks from the keyboard fill the conversational void. A frustrated groan released from his lips with the final click. The sound matched the confused expression on his face. The two exchanged glances.

"Well?" Alicia said. "Who forgot to fly me to heaven?"

Jensen pushed back his chair and stood. He adjusted the waistband on his pants. "We don't know if you're going to heaven; also, we reapers don't fly." The next words rushed out of his mouth as he unrolled his sleeves. "No one was assigned to escort you to the veil because you're not supposed to be dead yet."

Alicia dropped her arms at the same time as her jaw. "Excuse me?"

Shoving his hands in his pockets, he inspected the bewildered look on Alicia's face. He meandered his way to the door.

Just as he reached for the doorknob, she threw herself against it. "If I'm not supposed to be dead, then why am I? You better put me back in my body right now!"

Jensen gently grabbed hold of her shoulders and slid her away from the exit she was guarding. "Sorry, I can't do that. I believe you're looking for a necromancer. They are incredibly difficult to find and extremely frowned upon. Not to mention, their practices were outlawed quite some time ago. The disorder they create is unbelievable." He slipped through the door but heard Alicia close in on him from behind.

Alicia's eyes focused on her shoes. "Then, what now? What—what am I going to do? Where do I go?" Jensen grabbed his leather jacket off the coat rack by the front door of the bar.

He turned to look at her. "For now, you stay here. No leaving the safety The Twisted Sickle will provide you. Unless you want to be lost for all eternity with almost a zero chance of an afterlife."

Panic filled Alicia's voice. "And where do you think you're going?"

Jensen methodically adjusted the jacket. "I have to go pick up a new reaper and collect some souls myself. I'll make you two promises. One, I'll be back later today to sort all this out. Two, I won't forget about you. I will figure this out." Glassed uncertainty coated Alicia's eyes. He placed his hand on her shoulder, letting a small amount of the ardor fragment to release. "But for now, just, uh, make yourself at home here. And again, please don't go anywhere. Oh, and try not to tell anyone in here about your situation. I don't want to raise unnecessary alarms." Jensen ran a hand through his hair and made his way to headquarters to meet Cora and hopefully speak to Esme.

The door closed, and Alicia mumbled, "You have got to be kidding me." She stood in an empty bar, surveying what had been referred to as safety. Did safety always feel like prison? She hung her head at the thought. "It's fine. This is fine. I'll just be forever alone."

The door opened as a group of reapers entered. They stopped mid-stride upon seeing a soul in the place, which provided an escape from work. Seeing the crestfallen faces reflecting her own emotions, a hopeful idea sparked to life. "Hi, I'm Alicia. I'll be working here for the foreseeable future. What can I get you to drink?"

5

Jensen leaned against the elevator's wall, probing the bridge of his nose. A familiar song came over the elevator speakers. Even while lost in thought, Jensen hummed along instinctively. He glanced at the round numbered buttons, each dinging and turning orange as they met with their destination. The doors opened, revealing the training floor as Jensen begrudgingly pushed himself away from the cool elevator wall before walking out onto the floor.

In the swarm of new reapers, he nodded to a few familiar faces who were speaking with their apprentices. As he scanned the room, a new reaper, entranced by his phone, unintentionally shoulder-checked Jensen.

After the morning he had been experiencing, Jensen snapped. "Hey, watch where you're going!" The other reaper, fascinated by his new gadget, kept walking. Jensen attempted to calm himself by opening and closing his fists while exhaling sharply. "This place is like a zoo. There's no order to any of this." He voiced his disdain for the scene before him, which Camryn had overheard standing nearby.

"Can you feel it?" Camryn strolled over to Jensen with an acknowledging nod.

Jensen scanned Camryn and narrowed his eyes. "What are you talking about?"

Camryn let out a dry laugh. "The first-day jitters always charge the air differently. Wouldn't you agree?"

Jensen shook his head and crossed his arms. "You've been on duty for far too long. You enjoy this? I thought this was supposed to be a punishment for you."

Camryn squared off his shoulders while thinking of his reply. "Good one. I can't help it if I broke a rule I didn't know existed. I was just helping a friend out."

Jensen ran his hand through his hair as an unfiltered thought escaped him. "Hm, interesting. That's not what I heard. Speaking of helping a friend, did Esme make it to training on time? I don't know if I held her up too long this morning." He gave a sidelong glance to Camryn as he began walking again.

Camryn lightly jogged up to Jensen and said, "She was just in time. I'm lucky she was there to keep the train wreck of training from completely derailing. Thanks to your new trainee, Cora."

His jaw clenched, as hurt flickered in his heart at the mention of Esme. "Yeah, lucky you." He cleared his throat and shook out his shoulders. "Speaking of which, is she still here?"

Noticing the expression on Jensen's face, Camryn couldn't help let a wry smile creep in. "Of course, she's still here. She's been waiting for you since training finished."

Jensen's eyes softened for the first time in hours while scanning the crowded room. "Oh? That's—good. Yeah, that's good. I've been trying to talk to her all morning, and she hasn't exactly been answering me."

Camryn leaned against a pillar in the middle of the room and smirked. "How would she be able to answer you? Cora hasn't been issued her phone yet." Jensen whipped his head in Camryn's direction with anger rising in his eyes. "Oh, you mean Es? No, sorry, man. She slipped out as soon as training ended."

He leaned away from the pillar and grabbed Jensen's shoulders while turning him in the opposite direction. "Since you're here and your apprentice is here, let me introduce you to each other."

Just as they both stepped toward a cluster of new reapers who had gathered together, Jensen caught sight of Esme, who was hurriedly making her way through the masses. She was bogged down by a few specialists handing her reports and requests. Giving tight nods, she gathered the papers quickly and continued down a hallway. He pulled himself free of Camryn's guiding grip. Camryn followed the trail Jensen was tracing and caught sight of Esme, who headed to a spare office. Camryn tried to refocus Jensen by calling his name, but he was already on the move.

She found solitude in her corner office, quickly shutting the door behind her. She rested her head against the door for a minute, rubbing her eyes. The commotion from the crowd was now muffled. She rubbed her temples as the room spiraled around her. The succulents she had hanging on the wall became swirls and paint strokes of different greens. Walking to the window at the back of the office space, she snatched her phone. As the phone rang, she watched the flow of humankind rushing in and out of buildings. Cars became blurred objects, and the rest of the world unfocused around her. Her hand itched and tingled.

She was leaving a message as the door swung open aggressively. "Please call me back. I desperately need to speak with you again. Please." She turned to the blurry figure standing in the doorway. Esme stuffed her phone back in her pocket and closed her eyes. "You know, when the door is closed, the common courtesy is to knock first."

"I think the common courtesy is to call before pawning off a soul to another reaper." Jensen's body filled the door frame as he leaned into it.

Esme stared at the gray carpet, trying to hide her unfocused eyes. "Well, I figured it was a situation you could handle appropriately this time."

Jensen shook his head. "Wow, going there already?"

"No. Only voicing my thoughts. Also, watch your tone with me." Her reply was quick and lined with resentment. She found herself needing to sit and catch her breath. She made her way to the broken-in leather office chair. As she slouched down, stretching her legs as far as they would reach, Jensen stopped himself from walking over to her. Instead, he pressed himself harder against the doorframe.

He stood there, watching as Esme concentrated on a bare spot on the wheat-colored wall, clearly lost in her thoughts. "We need to talk, Esme." The tone in his voice was soft but urgent.

Just as she spun the chair in his direction, a larger body encompassed the rest of the doorframe. A feeling of relief washed over her. "Cam, is everything going all right out there?" Esme knew she didn't have the energy to debate whatever was on Jensen's mind.

Camryn pushed his way past Jensen to stand in between them. The air between Jensen and Esme crackled with tension. "I was about to ask you the same about in here." His eyes darting between the other two reapers.

Jensen stood tall but didn't move from the doorway. "Camryn, this doesn't concern you. Why don't you see if you can make yourself useful somewhere else?"

Camryn turned his body to put more of himself in front of Esme. "Seeing as she's my best friend and looks extremely uncomfortable right now, I'd say this is my business."

Esme swiftly stood, annoyance coursing through her. "Standing right here. Cam, thanks for checking in. I'm good. You should worry about keeping today on track. We wasted enough time in training. Jensen, I don't have time to talk about your problems right now. I have my own to figure out." Jensen opened his mouth to speak, but she put a finger up, silencing any words he had. "You have an apprentice that needs your attention. Trust me, she's going to need your undivided attention. So, if you two are finished comparing the size of your scythe, we all have jobs to get back to." Before either Camryn or Jensen could get a word in, she brushed past the two of them and pulled her phone out, ensnaring herself once again on the illuminated screen. "One more thing: I'm getting ready to redistribute my department. If there is anyone in mind that either of you think would benefit from this, please send me a relocation request. I'm missing the schedules you said you needed my help with Camryn. You have until the end of today to send it to me. If I don't receive them by then, you're on your own. I have a few countries to visit, so I'll be popping in and out of the office today." She apparated mid-step into the lobby.

Both Camryn and Jensen stood there, eyeing each other, refusing to be the first one to walk out of the room. Camryn tilted his head to the left and squinted his eyes. "Are you going to stand there all day, or do you want to meet Cora? You know, the reaper you should be worrying about right now."

Jensen let out a low grumble and turned slowly out into the hallway. "Shouldn't you be sending those schedules to Esme?" He made his way through the dwindling crowd of reapers. A face stood out, who he had never seen before. He called out, "Cora?"

The tall, willowy woman turned her head and searched the voice calling her name. Unable to determine who called her, she raised her hand. "Here."

Jensen came up to her and took her in from head to toe, committing who she was to memory. "I'm Jensen, your mentor." Wearing a stern expression, he offered his hand. Heat rose to her cheeks as she laid eyes on Jensen while shaking his hand.

He noticed the rising flush on her neck and face. "You okay?"

Cora sheepishly tucked a strand of her long golden hair behind her hair. "Oh, uh—yes! I'm just excited to start." She forced a smile, trying to hide the brightening blush on her cheeks.

Jensen arched an eyebrow. "Riiiight. I already heard about training this morning; word of mouth is still a first impression, and I'm not impressed."

Cora quickly spoke up. "I'm new, and I have questions. I don't understand—"

"I don't care if you're new or not. The way you behaved in there was and is unacceptable. Sometimes, the best way to learn is to be silent and observe."

Cora clasped her hands together and nodded in response.

Jensen turned to walk toward a desk, looking over his shoulder. "We have a schedule to stick to. I'm going to need you to keep up."

Seeing he was already halfway across the room, she hurried her pace to match his stride. He guided her to a desk to gather her official work belongings. She looked down at her hand where she had a new sleek black phone and a small brass key on a simple keyring. She glanced back up at Jensen. "Is this it? This is everything?"

Jensen scratched the stubble on his chin. "Almost everything." He ushered her into another room, where shelves were lined with books on one side and tablets on the other. "We used to issue books, now you get this." He handed her a tablet.

She took it and examined the front and back of it. "What is this for?"

"I say it's for educational purposes. You might find yourself wanting to know about the human world. You can access any book ever created and more. But more often than not, most reapers use it for fun now." Jensen shrugged.

Cora looked at the tablet again. "For fun?"

Sighing, he replied, "Yes. I'm sure you'll explore it more. We have some more things to get done first." He led her down a flight of stairs, reaching a new floor. This floor was an open room filled with necessities. It was well-lit thanks to the sun coming in from the windows. Beads of soft light bounced off the white walls and onto the clothing racks.

"Pick a few things out. I doubt you'll want to wear the same things every day."

Cora's eyes widened, looking at all the possibilities. Her eyes went to Jensen, who had busied himself by typing on his phone.

The thought of redistributing a few of the specialists bounced around in his head. He glanced at her. "We don't have all day. Go pick something out, and I'll be right back."

Cora darted her eyes around the room. "Where are you going?"

Walking out of the room, he replied, "To do my job."

Cora lost herself in the clothing racks, picking a few basic pieces of clothing and shoes. Most of her items were black except for the sneakers she picked out. They were a bright white with a platform sole. She rocked on her heels, unsure of what to get or where to go next. Time ticked slowly as she stood there, watching the sunlight dance around the room before a voice brought her out of her thoughts.

"This is for you."

Jensen's voice startled her. Cora jumped, and a small sound escaped the back of her throat. She walked over to Jensen to see what he had in his hands. There was a wallet with cash in it. "Where does this come from?"

"It used to come from those we escorted to the veil."

The casual tone in Jensen's voice caught Cora off guard. Her eyes widened. "I'm sorry what? How is that allowed?"

He let out a light, husky laugh. "Didn't I tell you you learn more from listening? I said we 'used to,' meaning we don't anymore. The higher-up reapers brokered a few deals over the years, and now, we have unrestricted access to banks around the world. Everything is in cash. Don't get greedy. Only use what you need when you need."

Since deals had been brokered, it was highly discouraged to take from those who had passed, no matter how small the item was.

Cora pursed her lips, swallowing a question and replied with a simple "mmhmm."

They exited the room with her hands full of items. Jensen took her to a desk where a few reapers busied themselves sliding boxes onto shelves. He stepped behind the desk and slid a box in her direction. "Put your stuff in here except for the phone and key, and it'll be delivered to your apartment tonight."

As she put her clothing items in the box, Jensen put a label on the outside of the box with her name and apartment number.

After the box was handed off to be placed on the shelf with all the others, Cora's phone vibrated along the desk. Picking it up, she saw a message had come in from Jensen.

He walked around to the other side and stood next to Cora. "That would be your list."

Cora swiped, looking at the names and locations. She noticed colored markers on different names. "What are the colors for?"

Jensen placed his elbows on the desk and nodded to her phone. "You're new at this, so we're trying out different souls to find your fit. Each color belongs to a department. Green is for expected, blue is for innocent, and red is for violent."

"Which department are you in?" The question slipped as she eagerly scrolled through the list.

"I'm the Administrator for the expected departures or green department." He steepled his fingers, resting his chin on his thumbs. "You met the other Administrator, Camryn. He oversees the innocents or blue department. I'm sure you remember Esme; she's the Strategos and is currently overseeing violent or red."

Cora bit the inside of her cheek, thinking about the colors on her list. "There's a lot of green on here, almost all green."

Jensen observed her face and tone. "You sound disappointed."

Cora shrugged. "A little. I was hoping for maybe something more exciting or challenging."

Jensen nodded, his eyes still on her while a smirk cracked the corner of his lips. "A wise friend suggested I start you off easy, and like always, is probably right. You have a lot to learn."

She creased her brows in protest. "Who the hell said that? Haven't they ever heard of baptism by fire?"

Jensen winced at her words. "Esme suggested it, and hearing you now makes me believe she's right. You sound like someone I used to know, and they weren't exactly the best being. That worries me." He raised his hand and waved for her to follow him to the elevator.

Cora walked behind him. "So, you three know each other? Are you all friends?"

The elevator doors opened, and Jensen stepped inside. "Something like that. Now, let's go. You have some reaping to do."

Cora stepped into the elevator just before the doors closed. She took a deep breath to ready herself for whatever came her way.

6

The afternoon sun greeted Jensen and Cora as they walked out of the mirrored building. The air was warmer and heavier than earlier in the day. Streets and sidewalks bustled with people rushing to go everywhere and nowhere at the same time. Having been a reaper in the city for so long, Jensen fell in perfect unison to the city's hustle. "Take a look at the list I just sent you." He looked to his right, expecting Cora to be there, only to notice she was missing. He looked back to see an overwhelmed young new reaper. He could tell by her stance the sights and the vast energy that electrified the city air stunned her. Cora's eyes darted around the sidewalk as people passed her.

Jensen interrupted her thoughts as he put a gentle hand on her elbow. "It's a lot to take in, isn't it? You can feel the life energy of all the humans around. Some stronger than others." Jensen eyed the city-goers and focused his attention back on Cora. She managed to nod in agreement. Jensen pulled up his jacket sleeve to check the time on his watch.

Cora followed his eyes and raised an eyebrow at him. "That looks super old. Don't we have phones for that now?"

He pulled his sleeve taut over the watch and waved for her to follow him into the alley. "It is old, but it works. It's a hell of a lot better than the candle I gave her." Jensen spoke, admiring a memory with a rueful smile.

Cora held her forearm. "Are you still friends with her?" Her voice was somewhere between hopeful and uncertain.

Jensen cleared his throat while shaking away the memory. "It's complicated right now, but that's not why I had you follow me here. You're getting overwhelmed by the energy out there. That will only make reaping a hell of a lot harder than it needs to be." He paced the alleyway before looking at Cora again. "You'll never be able to reap the souls on your list if you can't focus on their energy." A stern look grew in his eyes.

She placed her hands on her hips, attempting to ignore him.

He set his jaw, causing his sharp jawline to become more pronounced. "Patience is something I lack on a daily basis. Save the 'I know everything' act. I'm here to teach you, and you need to learn."

Cora jutted her jaw and sharply inhaled. "Fine. What do you want me to learn?"

He walked over to a brick wall covered in murals, leaning back, and placed his heel on the wall behind him. "Close your eyes and focus on your own energy. It has a distinct signature."

Cora closed her eyes tight and peeked through one open eye to see if Jensen was watching. He was still leaning against the wall, the look of disapproval was growing on his face. She shut her eye again to concentrate. A warm hum filled her ears. The world around her became quiet. Even through closed eyes, she could sense another energy. This was different from hers. This new energy was stronger and commanded more presence. Instead of a low hum like hers, this energy pulsated hypnotically. Cora cocked her head to the side while squeezing her eyes tighter. "What is that?"

"Not what but who." His voice interrupted her concentration. Slowly, she opened her eyes to find Jensen standing in front of her. "The who would be me. You'll be able to pick up different energies as you work and spend more time with other reapers." He paused to scratch his stubbled cheek. "We all have energy signatures that feel different. After a while, you'll be able to tell the difference without looking."

A series of buzzes interrupted Jensen. They reached for their phones at the same time. Jensen saw nothing on his screen and glanced over at Cora. She was busy swiping away a notification from her screen.

She looked up to meet Jensen's gaze. "I set an alarm for my first reaping to give me a ten-minute warning."

Jensen smirked and nodded in approval. "There might be hope for you yet. Open your list and see where the first stop will take us."

A flutter swept across her stomach at his smile. She pulled at the hem of her shirt. "What if I need to calm them down? How do I do that energy thing Esme mentioned?"

"You mean ardor fragments?" He rubbed his chest where he could still feel the fragments left behind from earlier. Jensen smiled at the thought. "You have to want to share it. Or at least a part of you has to want to share."

No flutter surfaced in her stomach from the glint in his smile this time. A ball formed instead, knowing his smile wasn't for her. Cora unlocked her phone and pulled a list of names. "It says Gilbert Johnson, 865 Maple Ave. Oh, and it has a green color code."

Jensen crossed his arms, then held out an inquisitive hand. "So, what does all that tell you?"

Cora narrowed her eyes, trying to recall the color code information she learned earlier that day. "Well, I'm going to go out on a limb here and guess we aren't staying in the downtown area. The green means it's expected. I still don't understand what it means."

Jensen checked the time and responded. "It means this will be easy. Now, let's go before we're late."

She rolled her eyes. "You haven't told me how yet."

He placed a hand on her shoulder and stepped next to her in the narrow alleyway. "Focus your energy on that name and address." Cora nodded before a question arose in her mind. Jensen raised his hand, stopping her before she could ask. "Get there first, then I'll tell you what's next."

She closed her eyes, and the world muted around her except for the familiar warm hum that filled her. Cora focused all her attention on that one name and address until it became a chant in her mind. A jolt in the pit of her stomach broke her chant, forcing her to open her eyes. Charming brick homes replaced the city streets and the gleaming skyscrapers. Old tall trees proudly adorned the sidewalks, shading the parked cars.

"Are we here?" Cora looked around, fascinated by the change of scenery.

Jensen released her shoulder and looked around while releasing a heavy sigh. "Does it look like there is a soul here to take?"

She let out a disappointed breath and winced, looking up into the afternoon sun. "No. No, it does not."

Jensen started walking toward the other end of the street. "You weren't too far off. You let the pull distract you. It's this way."

Cora hurried her steps to catch up. "What's the pull?"

Still focused on the street in front of him, he replied, "The pull is the feeling of you closing in on the soul. It can feel like a sharp jolt, other times like a punch. You have to focus until that feeling is over."

Satisfied with this answer, they both walked the rest of the street in comfortable silence. After passing a few homes with children playing outside and barking dogs, they reached a smaller home with a bright yellow door. Cora inhaled a nervous, ragged breath and looked over to her mentor. "What now? Do I just knock?"

Without blinking, he let out a hearty laugh and rubbed his forehead. "All my years mentoring, never have I been asked that." He took a moment to collect himself. "What would you say after you knocked? Remember, we're reapers. We don't want the mortals to see us unless we want them to."

Cora shifted her weight to one foot and huffed, trying to hide the embarrassed flush that rose in her cheeks.

Jensen checked the time once again, then muttered a curse word before becoming stern again. "We're going to start running behind. Remember what I taught you about feeling the energy? Feel for Gilbert's energy."

Cora closed her eyes once more, feeling the cool wind on her face. Sensing her concentration begin to waver out, she opened her eyes, as a feeling of frustration and inadequacy filled her. "There are a lot of energies swirling around in there. I can't find his."

It was barely noon, and Jensen had entirely run out of patience. Cora's lack of full commitment did nothing to better his mood. "His energy is the one that feels fleeting. Focus on it and pull it to you."

She closed her eyes again and focused on the dwindling energy in the house. Cora opened her eyes after a sharp shock lurched in her chest and vanished. An older man stood in front of her. He was slightly hunched over, with thin white hair. She jumped back, feeling amazed and proud of herself. "Holy crap. It worked!"

Jensen, who stood behind her, ran both palms down his face. "Unbelievable. Yes, you did your job. Now try to be professional about it."

Cora rested her eyes on the old man and stuck one hand out eagerly. "Good afternoon, sir. I'm Cora, and I'm here to escort you to the veil."

Jensen rubbed the back of his neck. "That was overly professional. You can take it down a notch or two."

The old man looked at the pair, and a jovial smile spread across his face. "Well, I thought it was nice. Made me feel like I was getting the star treatment." Gilbert and Cora shared an amused laugh.

Jensen shook his head and checked the time. He stiffened up and looked at Cora. "Time to take him to the veil."

She turned to Jensen, looking confident for a few moments, until she realized she had no idea how to escort Gilbert to the veil. She opened her mouth to ask, but Jensen anticipated her question. "To get to the veil, you need to make sure you have physical contact with the soul you're escorting. Then you think of nothing. Empty your mind completely. His soul unlocks the veil for you."

They both turned their attention to Gilbert, who shuffled over to them. His voice was raspy and deep, with mischief hidden in his tone. "Well, are we going to get this show on the road? No point in dilly-dallying here."

Cora was visibly taken aback by his eagerness. "Don't you have questions about where we're going? Where you're going? Or want to see your family one last time? I'm sure we can spare a few minutes for that."

Gilbert smiled warmly and wrapped both his hands around Cora's dainty hand. His eyes were warm and gleamed at her. "When you get to be my age, you grow old and tired. I've been ready for some time now. Anyway, I think I am quite ready for my next adventure, whether it's living in peace in the sky or atoning for my devilish youth below." He straightened a little taller as he saw his family through the living room window. He could feel his lip quiver, and before a tear dared to escape him, he cleared his throat. "Right, then. I'm ready."

Cora looked worriedly over to Jensen, hoping her mentor had something more to say or offer. He only nodded his head and placed his hand on her shoulder.

Gilbert tightened his calloused hand around hers. "Okay, then, let's get to the veil." She closed her eyes and took a few minutes to clear her mind completely. The air shifted around her, growing stale. All sounds around her vanished.

Jensen squeezed her shoulder. "We're here."

She hesitantly peeled her eyes open and glanced over to Gilbert, who tightened his grip. The world around them looked different. While the quaint street remained, the colors were muted. The once tall mighty trees appeared warped and two-dimensional. Sunshine and cool breezes were nowhere to be found. The veil felt cold and lonesome.

Gilbert paused, trying to find the right words. "This isn't what I expected, if I'm being entirely honest."

Jensen looked at Gilbert and Cora. Her expression was full of worry and confusion. "Don't worry. This is what the veil is supposed to look like. It's a world between the Earthly plane and the afterlife." He spoke reassuringly to the young reaper and old soul.

Cora's voice was soft. "Why does it look similar to the street we were just on?"

Jensen crossed his arms. "The veil looks like whatever place holds the most significance to the individual's soul."

Gilbert shuffled up the street. "I grew up in this neighborhood, met my wife on this block when we were kids. We built our life here." He let out a slight gasp when we saw his house. Even though the brick home was off on the exterior color, the bright yellow door was just as vibrant as it was on the Earthly plane. "What do I do now?"

Cora cocked her head to the side, and somehow, even though she had never been to the veil, she knew exactly what he had to do. "I believe your next adventure is behind that door, Gilbert." She looked at him, giving him a reassuring smile and a gentle squeeze of his hand.

Gilbert looked into Cora's eyes, and for a fleeting moment, the eyes of a child were all she could see. In a quiet and hesitant voice, he asked her an important question. "Can you come with me? I find my courage in short supply at the moment."

She looked over to Jensen, who sadly shook his head. "I'm sorry we aren't allowed to walk through your door. Whatever waits for you, it's not meant for us to see or experience."

Gilbert sighed. "Oh, okay, then."

Cora injected an idea quickly. "Surely, I can walk up those steps and leave you at the door. I'm sure I wouldn't be breaking any rule. Right, Jensen?"

Jensen tilted his head, thinking for a second, and a small smile crept up on the corner of his lips. "There is no rule I can think of that says you can't. Make it quick, though. You have more collections."

Hand in hand, they walked up the familiar steps to that little brick house. As Gilbert approached the door, a warmth radiated from the wood. A calming presence whisked between them.

He gave one last look toward Cora. His eyes were young and full of life. "You know, I may not know much of anything about your world." He paused, collecting the right words before finishing his thought. "But I feel incredibly lucky to have you accompany me here. Thank you."

Cora bowed her head in Gilbert's direction with a steady voice. "The pleasure was all mine, sir."

He released Cora's hand, squared his shoulders, and gently turned the silver doorknob. As Gilbert walked into the house, a warm, relaxing breeze filled the veil. Cora walked back to the sidewalk, where Jensen had been waiting for her. His face rested expressionless. She let out a heavy sigh and looked to Jensen. He glanced at her from the corner of his eye, evaluating her first reaping. "You did good."

Pride began to swell in her chest. "I did, didn't I?"

Once again, he rested a hand on her shoulder. "Don't get cocky. It was rocky and could use more work. Overall, though, you did well. Now we need to get out of here. Reapers are not intended to stay here for long. Just focus on the city and get us back home."

"I think I can do that." Cora smiled to herself and took a deep breath in, focusing on the city that was now her home. When she opened her eyes, the city skyline filled her view. Busy streets sang the city music.

Jensen checked his phone and typed before turning his attention to Cora. "No time to waste. You have more names to finish collecting."

"You're not coming with me?" she asked, uncertain if she was supposed to collect without her mentor.

He placed his phone back in his pocket. "You know how to do this now. Besides, your next few names are all green-coded. I have my list to take care of, plus some management issues to sort." Jensen walked away but stopped and looked over his shoulder back at Cora. "Don't let me down now." Before she could say or ask anything else, he vanished.

She looked around the city and checked the list on her phone. "Okay, Mary Stewart, you're next." Cora closed her eyes, remembering everything Jensen had taught her and focused her energy on the new name.

J ensen moved through his list for the next few hours. He walked out of the city hospital after escorting a soul to the veil when his phone chimed. He pulled out his phone, seeing a message from Cora.

> *Finished the first half of my list. Only a few hiccups but got them sorted. My next reaping is in 3 hours and coded red.*

As he was about to reply, he remembered his promise to Alicia. She was still waiting at The Twisted Sickle. Jensen had to track down someone who would know why Alicia was in the situation she was in. He gritted his teeth as he dialed the one reaper he knew wanted nothing to do with him, Esme. He drummed his fingers on the side of his phone as it began to ring.

The phone rang and rang. After the sixth ring, Esme picked up, and he could hear a gentle sigh.

He cleared his throat. "I need a favor from you." Silence filled the phone. "Esme?" Jensen started walking back to the bar, sliding his free hand into his pocket, waiting for a response.

"Skipping the pleasantries, are we? How unlike you, Jensen. Are you going to tell me what this favor is before I agree to anything?" Esme's voice grew increasingly flustered.

Already anticipating her answer, he tried a tactic that always worked on her in the past. "Just say yes, Esme."

There was a string of curses and mumbles on Esme's end. Her voice sounded weary. Another tone underlay there he couldn't quite place. "Jensen, that doesn't work anymore. You have ten seconds to tell me the favor, or I'm hanging up."

He turned a corner before answering. "I need you to observe Cora for her next reaping."

Without any hesitation, Esme replied, "No."

Jensen stopped walking in the middle of the sidewalk. Irritation battled the swelling anger in his chest. "Seriously? I'm going back to the bar to try and figure out the mess you left for me to clean up this morning. I'm only asking you to help me with this one thing, Esme. Is it that difficult for you to put aside our history and do me this solid?"

Esme gave a hollow laugh before she answered. "Believe it or not, Jensen, I'm actually in the middle of my own mess right now. This has nothing to do with anything that has ever happened in the history of us. Give me some credit. I'm not that petty. Why even ask me when there are other reapers in this city?"

Jensen's grip tightened on his phone as he began walking again. "I need your experience. Her next reaping is a violent case, and I know that's what you specialize in." He could hear Esme shuffling things around, walking, and having a quiet discussion with herself. "Esme, what are you doing? Are you still listening to me?"

He was standing across the street from The Twisted Sickle, watching Alicia deep in conversation with a group of reapers. Esme's voice interrupted the silence. "Yes, I'm still listening. I'm at the office looking for—it doesn't matter. Why can't you ask Tyler? He's a Violent Deaths Specialist, too."

Jensen leaned against a light post. "You know he still isn't qualified to mentor or observe anyone. Also, I trust and value you and your opinion. Please, Esme, just this once." His voice pleaded in a deep whisper.

"Hey, Jensen. Out of pure curiosity, where did you leave that soul from this morning?" She stopped shuffling papers to clearly hear his answer.

Jensen's response was muffled. "I left her at the bar. Also, her name is Alicia."

A dissatisfied huff left Esme involuntarily. "You can't be serious. You left an unclaimed soul. Sorry, Alicia in a bar full of reapers without any explanation as to why she's there. Do you know who was assigned to her?"

Scuffing the sole of his shoe on the pavement, he kept his voice light. "Well, that's the hard part. She was never assigned a reaper because she wasn't supposed to die yet. I'm working on it, at least trying to."

Realizing she did leave a mess for him to sort, guilt crept into her mind. After a protested groan, she said, "What time does this soul need to be collected? I have a list to finish tonight as well."

Before she had the chance to change her mind, Jensen quickly responded as he crossed the street. "It's in about three hours. I'll send you the address. Thank you, Esme." Jensen ended the call, jogging across the street. He pulled the door open and walked into the rowdy atmosphere.

Back across the city, Esme continued to rifle through an ornate office in the reaper headquarters. This office took up the entirety of the top floor and could only be accessed with a special key. The office had lavish, built-in bookshelves that contained knowledge and secrets of years beyond herself. The walls were moss green with a dark intricately carved chair railing trailing around the room. A giant wooden desk and high back brown leather chair sat nestled in the corner. The desk had printed schedules, calendars, and journals scattered over it.

Just behind the desk was a glass case that securely kept a scythe. This wasn't any scythe; it was the scythe. The only one ever created and used. Its crackling energy floated around the large space. It sat in the beveled glass case with light engulfing it from the bottom. The long, slender juniper handle was etched with centuries of use. A large, delicate, curved silver blade thinner than a scalpel gleamed in the soft glow with a careful polish.

She sat on the polished floor surrounded by old, weathered books and notes she hastily wrote on random pieces of paper. Esme looked over to the phone she tossed on a coffee table after the conversation with Jensen. She brought her fingers to her head and rubbed her temples. Staring off at a piece of modern art on the wall, she muttered to herself, "Ugh, Jensen, how did you get me to agree to this? I need to get someone qualified to take my place here."

The hours passed as she found herself lost in book after book. A solemn expression growing on her face as she put each book back and gathered her notes. "None of this helps me. I need more answers." Esme stood and walked over to her phone to check the address Jensen pushed upon her. Looking around the Grim Reaper's office, she made sure everything had been put back in its rightful place before flicking the light switch off.

Esme looked up at the sky. The sun was setting, giving the street an amber glow. She checked the time once more and double-checked the address to make sure she was in the right place. As she scanned her surroundings, a pinch flickered in her chest and a metallic taste filled her mouth. A breath caught in her throat as she felt someone lurking near her. Esme whipped her head in the direction of the feeling, only finding parked cars and overfilled garbage cans.

"Why are you here?" Cora was standing right behind Esme, looking around for Jensen.

Esme looked over her shoulder and rolled her eyes. "Your tone? Fix it. Jensen couldn't make it. I'm doing him a favor. I'll be observing you tonight."

Cora's shoulders sagged a little. "Oh, okay. Then, let's get this over with."

She walked toward the house until Esme held her arm out and stopped her in her tracks.

Cora looked down at Esme's arm. "What are you doing?"

Esme narrowed her eyes and lowered her voice. "I know you've only been doing this for less than one full day, but do you feel that? Something is off here."

Cora closed her eyes, trying to feel what Esme was feeling. "You're right. This doesn't feel like the other souls I collected today. Is it because this is a violent death?"

Esme dropped her arm. "No, they all have a similar feeling. The only changes are the approach and handling of each situation. Let's go see what we're dealing with." She placed her hand on Cora's arm, and they both apparated into a tiny apartment.

The apartment was clean, tidy, and quiet until a deep cry came from an adjacent room. Esme and Cora shared a curious glance as they cautiously walked toward the scream. They found themselves in a small bedroom, lit only by a small lamp on a bedside table. Next to the bed was a man slumped on the carpet with a bottle of vodka and a kitchen knife. Cora's eyes opened in horror at the bloody sight before her. Esme knitted her brows, examining the man in front of her, never flinching.

"I know I'm new at this, but"—confusion and fear filled Cora's voice and eyes—"isn't he supposed to be dead by now?"

Esme stood there with crossed arms, staring at the scene before as if it were a puzzle. She inhaled and checked the time on a clock that hung on the wall. "He should have departed two minutes ago."

Cora stuck her hand out in his direction. "So, why isn't he?"

Esme scratched her chin in thought. "That is a valid question. Unfortunately, I don't have an answer for it yet. Let me see your phone." She held her hand out.

"Why?" Cora clutched her phone like a child unwilling to share a new toy.

Esme rolled her eyes. "Because the list can change. It's rare, but it does happen. I'm sure Jensen mentioned that." She pushed her hand out farther with a stern look.

Cora reluctantly placed the phone in Esme's hand, mumbling, "Actually, he didn't."

Esme slid her finger across the screen. Growing more puzzled than before, she handed the phone back.

Cora stuffed the phone back into her jacket with more attitude than intended. "I take it there were no changes. I know how to read my list, you know. Do you think I'm an idiot?"

Esme took a few steps toward the man but quickly replied. "I don't know how you want me to answer. You are new, so." She shrugged.

Cora hurriedly stepped next to Esme as the insult nicked a wound within her.

As she opened her mouth, Esme stopped and grabbed her by the arm and spoke first. "I don't have time to care about your feelings. I'm here with you, as a favor. Right now, you're still learning. Push your pride aside and learn. There is a problem here, and I need to figure it out. Do me a favor? Shut the hell up."

Realizing the tight grip she had formed on Cora's arm, she released it and continued to crouch in front of the man. Her eyes traveled from his pale lips down to his bleeding forearms. The carpet began taking on a cranberry hue.

Cora stood behind her, cautiously taking in the sight before her.

"Derek?" Esme's voice sounded entirely different. There was no cold, harsh sass; it was soft and warm. The man groaned at the sound of her voice.

Cora stepped back nervously. "Oh, my goodness, he really isn't dead yet. He should be dead, Esme. Was the time on the list wrong?"

Esme kept her eyes fixed on Derek. "No. The lists are never wrong. They can change due to some deals but never wrong." She nudged Derek's chest softly and spoke louder. "Derek?"

He opened his eyes for the first time. As he gasped for more breath, a question slipped from his lips. "Are you angels or demons?"

Esme stood and placed her hands on her hips. "Don't insult us. We're reapers. We actually work."

Cora leaned down and whispered into Esme's ear. "He can see us. How can he see us?"

Esme spared a look at Cora. "We're seen when we are meant to be seen and when we want to be seen. He can see and hear us, not because we want him to. He was supposed to."

Curiosity washed over Cora as she lowered herself next to Derek. "But he's not dead. I don't understand."

Esme pinched the bridge of her nose and inhaled. "You're still stuck on the 'not dead' part, huh?"

Derek's eyes lingered on Esme, searching her face for answers. A small, rueful smile spread on her lips. "No, he isn't dead, despite his best efforts. He was meant to be, hence why he sees us."

Derek smiled faintly and attempted a laugh. "I can't even kill myself the right way."

Cora rose again, looking at Derek with pity. As she lingered her sight on Derek, she sidestepped to Esme. "Okay, first, you can totally tell Jensen this is without a doubt, not my niche. Second, what do I do with him now? I can't exactly take a living soul to the veil."

Esme pointed to the bedside table where a wallet, keys, and phone were stacked neatly over an envelope. "Grab his phone and call for an ambulance. Just give the address, nothing else." Cora nodded and headed in the direction of the bedside table.

Esme squatted next to Derek and leaned in. "You know, you were meant to die here this evening. You weren't meant to live, hence why we're here."

By then, the carpet glistened from the newly formed crimson pool. "Why won't I die? I just want this to be over and done with." Desperation hung on his every word. "Just about everything in my life has gone wrong. The woman I was ready to ask to marry me left me for my best friend. I lost my job." He blinked hard in an attempt to focus on the world around him before continuing. "I'm completely broke, and as my father enjoys reminding me, I have amounted to absolutely nothing."

Instinctively, Esme rested a gentle hand on Derek's shoulder, letting warmth flow freely, and brought her face closer to his. "I don't know why you didn't die, Derek, but"—she paused as she stood, looking at Cora, who was speaking on the phone—"consider this a second lease on life. You have a new story completely in your hands to write. You get to decide where you go from here. Few humans get to say that without a hefty price tag." She walked away.

Esme grabbed the phone from Cora and tossed it at Derek's side. A muted voice could be heard from the other line, asking for more information. She ushered Cora to the other side of the room. Esme looked back one more time. "I do have some advice for your new life, Derek. I've lived a long time and seen more than you could ever imagine. Don't squander this chance; make it mean something to you. Screw the expectations of others. Live up to your own." An impish smile graced Esme's face before she added one last thought. "Also, outliving your enemies is the best revenge."

Derek smirked and nodded as he watched Esme grab hold of Cora and disappear.

The sound of sirens filled the late evening air. From across the street, Cora and Esme watched as the ambulance and police cars filled the narrow street. Cora rested against a lamp post as she observed the people enter the apartment they had just left. "I'm guessing this doesn't happen often?" Cora nodded to the commotion in front of them.

Esme was busy typing on her phone, the question stealing her attention. "Got it in one."

The light from the screen put a soft glow on Esme's face. Cora couldn't help wonder who she was entranced on messaging. She leaned over Esme's shoulder, attempting to steal a glance. She couldn't catch sight of the name, only a quick message:

> *We need a serious conversation. Your office. Tonight.*

Noticing a shadow on her screen, Esme quickly turned the screen off and took a step back. "People don't escape death like this. Not without some Celestial or Infernal intervention. Like I said before, some things change, lists get updated if they do. Which it was not here."

They stood in silence for a few more minutes and watched as the paramedics wheeled Derek out of the apartment on a stretcher. Derek turned his head and caught a quick glimpse of both reapers. A small smile grew on his face, followed by a tear. He closed his eyes as he was lifted into the ambulance.

Cora stretched her arm and rested it on Esme's shoulder. "Man, this was weird. It will definitely be the best story tonight!"

Esme pushed Cora's arm off and turned. Her eyes were cold and determined. Any warmth she showed in the apartment had since faded. Her voice was low and certain. "This will be told to no one. As far as you're concerned, your list has been completed, and all souls were taken to the veil. Understood?"

Cora looked down at Esme, defiance gleaming in her eyes.

Before she could protest, Esme's phone buzzed. "Do not test me, Cora." Without another look or word, Esme started walking down the street. Cora lagged behind, unsure if she was willing to accept the instruction given to her. Esme called out behind her, "I'm going now. Are you coming or not?"

Cora huffed and crossed her arms. "I guess so."

They continued walking as the sun finished setting in silence. The hum of streetlights flickering on and rush hour traffic filled the conversational void. After two blocks of mindless walking, Cora scratched the back of her head awkwardly. "I have a question."

Esme closed her eyes, bracing herself for yet another question. "Of course you do. What is it?"

Sounding tired, Cora asked, "Why can't we just go where we want to go right now? We can go from soul to veil and back in an instant, but we can't go to other places like a reaper bar? That's stupid."

Esme cocked her head to the side, almost in agreement. "It's not that we can't; it's more like not allowed." She stopped walking to explain further. "Up until maybe a year ago, we could zip in and out of any place we wanted. Apparently, our boss saw it as an abuse of power or something. I don't know if the other two feel that way, but he gets the final say."

Cora bit the corner of her bottom lip, lost in thought.

Esme took a step in front of her and placed her hands in her jacket pocket. A small smirk spread across her lips as she shook her head at Cora. "Out with it. What's the question?"

Cora narrowed her eyes. "You think I'm annoying, don't you?"

Without the need to think, Esme replied. "Pretty sure that's obvious. I know that isn't your question, so ask me what you're wondering before I count it as your question."

Unsure if she should feel insulted, Cora scratched at her jaw. "Who are the other two reapers you mentioned? No one speaks about them or any of the three of them."

Esme looked up at the darkened sky. "I personally know the big boss, since I work directly for and with him. The other two, I'm not exactly familiar with; our paths never crossed. I know them more by reputation. Thalia and Ansel. If it's a story you want, you'll find it with Camryn or Jensen."

Cora nodded and hurried her stride. Esme laughed and slowly walked a few steps behind Cora with a glimmer of mischief in her eyes. She focused on the city street's music and the feel of the icy air covering her. She lost herself in her thoughts until a hum and familiar glow of the pale blue neon light grabbed her attention. Conversation and laughter spilled into the alley as she looked in.

The Twisted Sickle

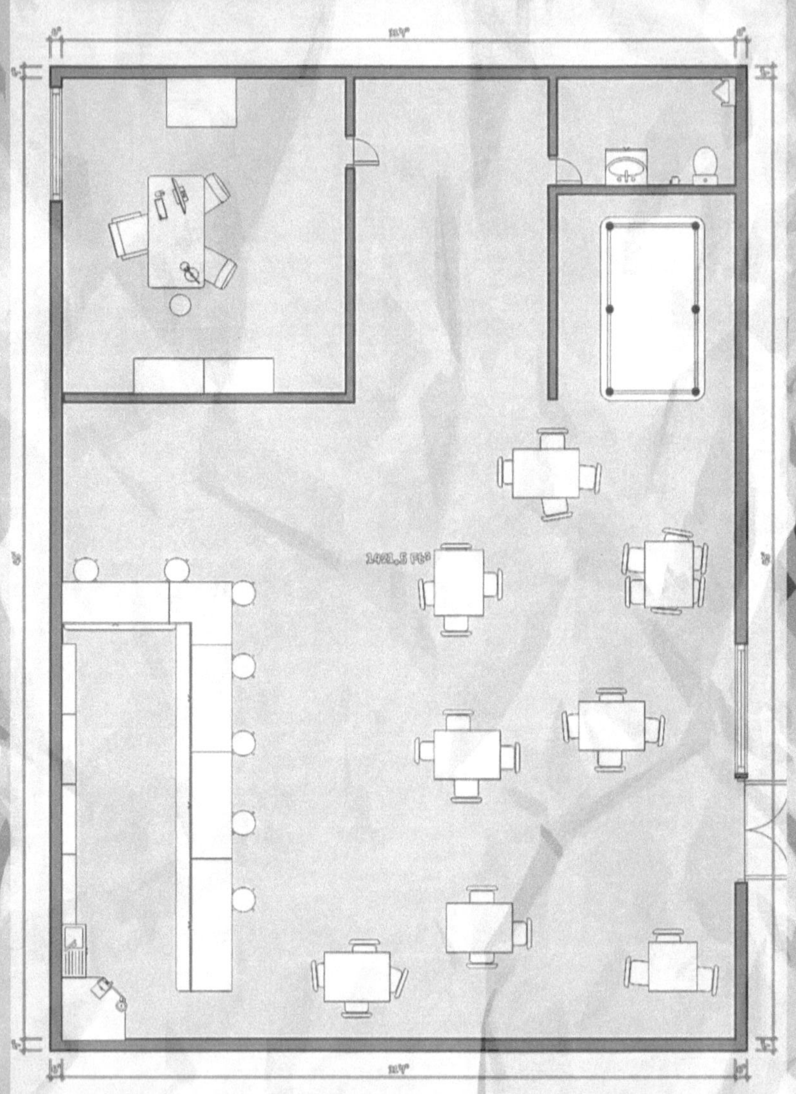

8

The Twisted Sickle was a hole-in-the-wall establishment down a dark alley. It was discreetly tucked away from mortal eyes. A single, pale, blue neon light in the shape of a twisted sickle called to the local reapers to relax and recharge with its soft buzz. Magic wards were woven into every brick of the local reaper bar. The wards in place made the bar forgetful to mortals who stumbled by it and difficult for others to enter without a reaper.

Inside the walls were a flint gray with dart boards hung throughout. Black cylinder pendant lights gave a warm, welcoming tawny glow. Distressed wood tables were scattered around the floor with matching chairs. Copper pipe shelves embellished the largest wall, holding every liquor imaginable. Around the sheet metal-wrapped bar with a dark wood grain top were swivel metal bar stools padded in tan leather.

Cora strolled in, searching for Camryn or Jensen. Her mind whirled wildly with the possible stories they could tell her about Thalia or Ansel. She stopped in the middle of the room, scanning for their faces. Esme casually strolled in behind her, spotting Camryn in his usual back corner, nursing his tried-and-true bourbon. He raised a glass in her direction. The bar's dim lighting shone through his glass, casting a soft amber glow on his face. She nodded in acknowledgment as her eyes moved to the ruby hall, where she could feel Jensen tucked away in his office. Their bond still tugging at her chest.

Cora had made her way over to the bar, looking lost more than ever. As she stood there, she began to chew the inside of her lip, studying the various bottles on the shelves.

Esme placed her elbows on the bar top, steepling her fingers on her lips. She never looked at Cora but offered a nod to the glass liquor bottles. "You know this isn't a test, right? Just grab a bottle, pour, then drink. Or don't. Choice is yours."

Cora raised a brow in question. "You mean there aren't any bartenders?"

Esme snorted an amused laugh. "When would we have time for that? It's not like we can pay a mortal to do so. Low profile, remember?"

Another voice chimed in. "I was shocked, too. I'm trying to convince everyone in this place to let me do it. Tough crowd, I tell you, tough crowd."

Both reapers whipped around. Esme slouched against the bar, studying the face in front of her. "You're the woman from the car accident this morning. Alicia, right? Why won't anyone let you pour them a drink?"

Alicia shrugged. "Ask the painfully handsome reaper busy brooding in the back office."

With different tones, Esme and Cora said, "Jensen."

Alicia let out a delighted laugh and giddily clasped her hands in front of her chest. "I can tell there are some juicy stories here, and I need to hear all of it. Since this morning, I have been stuck in this continuous happy hour, and I need more social interactions and attention. It's rude the way everyone ignores me here."

Cora had busied herself, opening a beer until she slammed the bottle down with a realization. "Wait! Why is a soul here? Why haven't you left the bar?"

Alicia twirled a purple lock of hair around her finger. "Apparently, I can't leave here without a reaper escort. Something about getting lost or stuck for all eternity."

Fascinated by Alicia's situation, Cora snatched her beer off the bar. "But I thought ghosts could go anywhere they wanted. At least within reason."

Esme pushed herself away from the bar top and walked behind the counter. She popped the cork off a bottle of red wine and poured it into a large glass. The wine swirled delicately in the glass as Esme moved her wrist in soft circles. "Ghosts can. She can't. She's still a soul, not a ghost. When a soul is taken into the veil, they become a ghost." Esme held the glass to her nose, inhaling the wine's aroma. "Dear Alicia here was never taken there. Hence why she's not a ghost."

Alicia raised her hands. "I've always been complicated. Why stop now, right?"

Both reapers could sense the turmoil of emotion brewing in Alicia's voice.

Esme quickly changed the subject. "As fun as this little girl's night out has been, I need to speak with Jensen. We have some business to sort out."

A devilish smile spread across Alicia's lips. "Is that what reapers call it?"

Cora choked on her beer, earning her an arched brow from both Esme and Alicia. Esme walked out from behind the bar. "Why are you looking flustered?"

Alicia bounced and gasped happily. "You have a crush on him, don't you?"

Cora stumbled on her words, never breaking her eyes away from the floor. "I do not. He's my mentor."

Alicia slid closer to Cora. "This just got even better. Crushing on the professor is one of my favorite things to read. I need to know everything. Spare no details."

A tinge of discomfort jabbed at Esme, but she hid it by taking a large swig of the wine. "You are entirely too comfortable and friendly around strangers. I'm done socializing now. I have work to get done. Cora, Camryn is in the back corner if you still want a story." She grabbed the rest of the bottle and made her way to the hall.

Alicia shouted behind her. "Working with a whole bottle of red, huh?"

Esme held her middle finger high in the air and kept walking.

Alicia couldn't contain her laughter, amused by Esme. She turned to Cora. "I like her. I heard your name is Cora. Who is she?"

Cora drummed her fingers on the neck of her beer bottle. "Oh, that was Esme. Pretty much everyone's boss. She's a little intense for me."

Alicia leaned forward on the old wooden bar top. "She's a little firecracker. I like it. She's not like the rest of you here. I completely support the limited-edition vibe." The young women stared at each other. "Why are you talking to me? Everyone else pretends I don't exist here."

Cora blinked repeatedly, at a loss for words. After several seconds of silence and unbreaking staring, Cora sidled away from Alicia, making her way toward Camryn's corner. "I could ask you the same. Everyone finds me annoying." As she walked, she could sense Alicia right behind her.

"I don't mind you talking. It's nice to have someone to talk to." Intrigue laced Alicia's tone. "You look like you're on a mission."

Cora glared back over her shoulder to see a smiling Alicia. "I am about to ask Camryn, a man who I seriously pissed off this morning, to tell me a story."

Alicia hurried her steps and whispered, "Who is Camryn, and what is the story about? In case you haven't figured it out, I'm totally tagging along."

Camryn sat in a dark corner, contently decompressing, when his buzzing phone caught his attention. A small smirk crossed his lips, seeing a message notification from Esme.

Tag. You're it.

Camryn wrinkled his brows in confusion, murmuring to himself. "What the hell is she talking about?" Two figures shadowed his corner further. He looked up to see Cora and Alicia standing in front of him. They had plastered grins on their faces. An obnoxious cackle came from the other end of the bar. Leaning to look past the two women in front of him, he caught sight of Esme laughing and waving in the hallway.

Camryn narrowed his eyes and pointed his glass in Cora's direction. "Whatever it is, hard pass. This is my time away from new reapers, souls, everyone. This is my me time."

Ignoring his protests, she pulled the chair he had rested his feet on and sat. "Why are you, Jensen, and Esme so jaded and cynical all the time?"

Camryn poured more bourbon into his glass, groaning his disdain for the intrusion. "Over seven billion. That's the world's population. Every year, one hundred forty million babies are born globally. Then there are fifty-six million deaths globally every year. Of course, these are averages. Do you know what that breaks down to?" He sipped from his glass. "One hundred six deaths every minute or one and a half every second. There aren't enough of our kind to keep up with the human population." Slouching farther into the chair, he slid his glass around in front of him. "Try and ask me again when you've been reaping for as long as we have." He took a sip and set his glass on the table, slung his arm on the back of his chair, and rubbed his eyes with his free hand. "So, are you going to tell me why Esme sent you over here to torture me tonight?" He kicked another chair out and motioned for Alicia to take a seat.

Alicia winked at Camryn as she sat. "Oh, you're Camryn with the stories. I'm Alicia. Aren't you going to offer me a drink?" A flirtatious smile grew on her face.

As he lifted the glass to his lips, his eyes darkened toward Alicia. "I would, but you can't."

Cora cleared her throat. "This is gross and awkward."

Camryn let out a husky chuckle as he sipped his drink. "What stories are you inquiring about?"

Cora sat up a little straighter while Alicia stretched her arms forward across the small table. Cora paused for a second, then clapped both hands before resting them on the table. "We—I-I wanted to know more about Thalia and Ansel."

Any hint of relaxation left Camryn's face as he set his glass on the table. "Why would you want to know about those two? This is only your first day; you don't have a specialty yet."

Cora gave him a saccharine smile. "Esme told me you told stories the best. She also mentioned you might know more about them, since she doesn't personally know them."

Camryn circled the glass around the table, contemplating whether to tell that story. Cora tapped her feet and let out a heavy sigh. "Well, are you going to tell us or not? If you're not going to, then I'll find Jensen and ask him."

He stretched his arms and shook his head wryly. He looked at the empty hallway. "Probably not the best idea right now. Safe to assume it's one intense conversation between those two right now." There was an underlying tension as he spoke.

Alicia perked up and spoke to cut the tension. "Let's put a pin in that story because I'm definitely coming back to it. Camryn, can you please tell us the other story we came for?" She batted her eyelashes at him.

Camryn cocked his head to the side and smirked. "Well, I can't say no to a face like that."

Cora frowned, looking between the two of them. "Guys, you can get a room later." Camryn and Alicia laughed at her expression.

Camryn poured himself another drink. Alicia eyeballed the half-empty bottle. "You're not too drunk to tell the riveting tale, are you?"

Camryn tipped his glass toward her. "Reapers, unfortunately, can't get drunk. This is just for fun. It helps to pass the time, just like eating. Even walking around helps, too." He sipped his wine. "All right, gather round, ladies. Story time is about to begin."

Anticipation fueled the air between Cora, Alicia, and Camryn. They pulled their seats in closer as Camryn lowered his voice. "Well, as you learned earlier, the Grim Reaper made his presence known around the 14th century."

Unable to help herself, Cora injected a question. "Does the Grim Reaper have a name?" It wasn't clear if the question was a personal thought spoken out loud or directed to Camryn. "What would I even call him?"

Camryn massaged the back of his neck. "Seriously? I'm one sentence into this story, and you're already interrupting me."

Cora held her hands up apologetically. He waved her off. "If he does have a name, he doesn't share it. If you should find yourself meeting with him, which is highly unlikely, you can just call him 'Sir.'"

Alicia rested her chin on her fist. "Great side note. How about we let Camryn continue?"

Camryn winked at Alicia as a smirk tugged the corner of his lips. "You're growing on me." He adjusted his seat and continued his story. "Thalia was the next reaper to show. I think it was around the fifteenth century. My understanding is she rather enjoyed Italy and Portugal. Can't blame her. Those were some lively and busy times." He took another sip of bourbon as he considered the story he was telling. "Thalia, and our boss always had a hard time getting along. He's headstrong, adjusting and adapting along the way, and she likes everything in order and by the book. Not to mention the distinctive styles they created when reaping souls."

Alicia slid her fist from her chin to her cheek and pursed her lips, thinking. "So, you're telling me they have a sibling rivalry?" She finished her thought with an amused laugh.

Camryn nodded. "Now that you mention it—yes, kind of like a sibling rivalry. He's more refined in his style of reaping. Rumor has it, he likes to operate in the gray of a black-and-white world. You didn't hear that from me." He pressed a finger to his lips before continuing. "Thalia is more of a blunt instrument. She doesn't waste time. Whatever needs to be done gets done, and she keeps it moving. In her eyes, the world is only black and white with no room for a shade of gray."

Cora craned her neck to look back at the hall behind her, thinking of Esme and Jensen. She squinted her eyes and tilted her head toward Camryn.

He couldn't help let out a laugh. "They certainly share some similar reaper traits." Camryn paused for several seconds, fixing his eyes on the two heavy energies swirling in the back office. He cleared his throat, trying to focus on the story he started. "Ahem, right. The first I heard of Ansel was at the tail end of the renaissance. Ansel is honestly the gentlest-natured of the three of them. He's eager to do the right thing, but his opinions often get overshadowed by the other two." Camryn stretched his leg out from under the table. "Ansel always played peacekeeper."

Cora sat back in her chair, drumming her fingers on her thighs. "What do you mean 'played?'"

Camryn lifted his eyes, resting his sight on the overhanging lights above the table. "I don't know if I should be telling you any of this. There's only a handful of us reapers who know this, including the big three." He brought his gaze back down to around the bar, dropping his voice to almost a whisper.

"Screw it." He sucked in a sharp breath and exhaled out of his nose. "I think you can speculate the three of them don't play well together. They work together only when necessary, usually in times of catastrophic events. Even then, they lead their own divisions, barely looking at each other. Something happened during the 1600s, causing a huge rift between the three of them."

Alicia perked up, eyes widening. "Do you know what happened during that time? It must have been one hell of an event to cause a rift to last centuries."

He knitted his brows in an unreadable expression. "That's just it. Not a single reaper out of the three knows exactly what happened. What I do know is, after that, the big guy spent time crossing continents, never staying in one place for long. His constant moving created a need for more reapers. With all the new reapers, someone had to be responsible to teach them. That's how our system was created."

Cora was gripping onto the edge of the table. "Okay, what were Thalia and Ansel doing while our boss was busy playing globe-trotter?"

He leaned in even closer. "That's just what gets curiouser and curiouser. Whatever happened between them, it ended up being Thalia and Ansel on one side, and the Grim Reaper on the other. However, wherever he went, the other two never seemed far behind."

Alicia gasped and covered her mouth. "I watched a lot of investigation shows in my life, and that sounds like they were totally stalking him! This is giving me goosebumps."

Camryn bit his lower lip. "Yeah, well, a lot has happened since then. Our specialties emerged; new rules were put in place. A lot of us have shuffled around to different countries and cities. Now, not many reapers get to see the big three."

Before she could even think a clear thought, Cora gaped out, "Esme said she work directly for the Grim Reaper."

Camryn shrugged carelessly. "Not strange. When you get a specialty, you fall under that original reaper. Esme works for the Grim Reaper, Jensen works for Thalia, and I work for Ansel. Esme is the Strategos. She goes where and does what he tells her to. Other Administrators in her department go through her if they need anything. Death is a busy being."

Alicia placed her hands on her lap and shifted in her seat. "So, what you're saying is, you work directly for them, as Esme does? Do you meet up with them? Can you ask them about me?"

Camryn poured the rest of his bourbon into his glass. "It's not that simple. As cut and dry as our reaper business appears, we have a lot of rules, and honestly, I think Jensen's got it handled. He has a friendly, personal, and more hands-on relationship with Thalia than I have with Ansel."

Alicia lurched herself across the tabletop, wide-eyed as her jaw dropped. "Hold on. You did not just say what I think you said."

Camryn quirked an eyebrow. "I didn't say anything."

Cora placed her fingertips on her temples. "What is my existence right now?" She sucked in a sharp breath through her nose. "You mean to tell me Mr. By The Book is sleeping with his boss?"

Camryn playfully shrugged. "I just said they were on friendly terms. Now, if you don't mind, I'd like to try and enjoy the rest of my night."

Cora crossed her arms and huffed in protest. "Oh, come on. I still have more questions."

Camryn scratched his head and stood, casting a large shadow over Cora and Alicia. "I'm sure you do, but I've already said more than I should have. Now, go annoy someone else. I have to talk with the grown-ups in the office."

Without saying anything else, he winked at Alicia and walked toward Jensen's office.

A knock at the door drew Jensen's attention away from the papers he was sorting through. The corners of his eyes softened at the sight of Esme leaning against the door with a bottle of wine and a glass in the other hand. "Please, come in." He stood and walked around his desk to meet her halfway. Gently, he plucked the bottle and glass from her delicate hands. "Only one glass?"

She shrugged off her jacket, draping it on the back of a chair. "You don't like wine swee—Jensen. You like whiskey. Neat." Sitting in the chair opposite his, she watched as he pulled an aerator from an intricately carved wooden box, then poured her a perfectly measured glass. "You keep an aerator in here?"

He put the bottle down and rubbed his chest. It always amazed him how he was always able to feel what she gave him hours or even days later. His touch never had lasted long for her. "I keep your aerator in here. It's that fancy one you said makes it taste better."

"Oh. Well, thank you. I didn't know you still had it." The thought of meeting in person being a mistake sprang in her mind. She reached for the glass, and their fingers brushed. Warmth crept up her hand, and her eyes darted, meeting Jensen's. The sadness and longing in his eyes splintered her heart. Pulling her hand away and setting the glass down, she straightened her posture. "We have souls to discuss."

"Straight to business, then." His posture deflated, he turned back to the shelf that held his favorite whiskey. It was kept in a special crystal decanter Esme had found for him. "What did you want to talk about, Es?"

The longer she spent around him alone, the more the eternal paramour bond called to her. Reapers experienced every human emotion, including love. It made them more adept to completing their job, given all the different circumstances death happens in. Having another to love for a reaper was not often found. Mortals had soul mates and twin flames. Celestials and Infernals have fated mates. Even witches and warlocks had their Solus Amor. But for a reaper to find an eternal paramour is rare. They are spread so far apart and constantly working that finding love is never a priority for them. Most either settle for casual connections or a chosen forever companion. When they find their eternal paramour, an invisible tether forms between them. They constantly long for each other. Their energies mix around each other, creating a harmonious buzz in the air.

"Please don't call me Es. That's a Camryn and me thing." Her voice faltered. She blinked away the gloss forming in her eyes. She cleared her throat and gave a tight smile. "Alicia isn't the only problem we have."

Instead of sitting in his chair behind the desk, he sat in the one next to her. "There's another soul who departed ahead of schedule?"

Esme reached for the glass and chuckled. "The opposite, actually." She took a few sips to clear her fogged head. "He didn't depart at all. It was the red collection I went on with Cora." She softly set the glass back on the desk. "Also, as the tonight's observer, she needs work. She was easily flustered. Please work on that with her. Curious thing, isn't she? So many rapid-fire questions." She rubbed her eye, causing a lash to float lightly onto her cheek.

Without hesitating, Jensen tracked the lash and brushed his thumb over her cheek. A small glow emanated from his caress and mixed with the natural blush on her cheek. He stilled, admiring how alluring she was with a glow more captivating than the setting sun. Esme inhaled sharply and turned her head. "Sorry, there was an eyelash," Jensen said.

The room was closing in; the floor moved under her feet, like waves in an ocean. Running her hands up her face and into her hair, she quickly tied her curled tresses into a messy bun. She stood and leaned her palms on the desk. This all seemed like a bad idea now.

Jensen stood and reached for Esme as the door opened without warning.

"What did I miss? I got the message you sent." Camryn shut the door behind him and made himself comfortable in the seat previously occupied by Jensen. "Was I supposed to bring my bourbon into this meeting?" He glanced at the open wine and whiskey.

Jensen dropped his head and sucked his cheeks in. "Don't even think about touching my whiskey, Camryn."

"Oh, please, everyone knows bourbon is better," Camryn said.

Esme rolled her eyes and drank the rest of her drink in a single gulp. "You're both idiots. Wine is the best. End of discussion. The only thing you missed was me telling Jensen that the soul Cora was set to collect tonight never departed, even though he should have."

Jensen made his way back around the desk before sitting in his chair. He and Esme both locked eyes. She stood straight and leaned her hip against the desk, focusing on both men. "So, we have one who wasn't supposed to die die, and one who was meant to not."

Camryn scratched his jaw, puzzled. In all his years, he had never come across a situation like this. "This isn't something I'm familiar with. Are either of you? Also, dick move, Es. I can't believe you sent those two to me."

Jensen's eye twitched at the mention of Camryn using the name Es. Jealously brewed in the pit of stomach. Even more when he saw the smirk grace her lips and how fondly they looked at each other. When was the last time he made her smile or laugh?

"I only sent one. I am not responsible for the other tagging along," she said, amusement clear in her voice. "The only thing I've ever heard of being close to this was back in the mid-1800s. It was a necromancer making deals. But that can't be the case here. There were no magic remnants to be found in either area."

The men leaned back in their chairs, neither having the amount of experience as the woman before them.

Esme's hand itched and burned, a high pitch ringing in her ears. She closed her eyes and shook her head. As she stood, her legs wobbled. She caught herself on the edge of the table, knocking her empty glass, crashing it to the ground. "Shit."

The men stood abruptly, both coming closer to help her. "I'm fine. It's just a broken glass. Do either of you have an idea on how you would like to address this? Or should I figure this out on my own?"

Camryn scratched his earlobe, trying to think of a solution.

"What if I reached out"—Jensen lowered his voice—"what if I reached out to my boss?"

Esme slowly rose from the ground, slamming the glass shards on the desk. The emotions she had worked hard to let go of rooted and festered. Her energy washed over every corner of the room, causing Camryn to sit and Jensen to stagger backward. "No."

One word: it was all she needed to say. One word to convey every emotion thrashing in her.

"Esme, she might be able to offer some kind of help. All three of us are out of our element here."

A sardonic laugh flew from her lips. "Oh, yeah. I'm sure she can be real helpful to you." Her energy filled the room like water on a sinking ship. Camryn and Jensen both fidgeted in their seats from the domineering energy.

"Es, try and take a deep breath and relax." Camryn gently grabbed her hand, rubbing his thumb over her knuckles.

She snatched her hand out of his. "Fuck off, Cam. Never tell a woman to relax. It does the opposite."

"Whoa, harsh and uncalled for. Still, message received." Camryn held his hands up in surrender.

Jensen sat in silence, realizing the mistake he had made, but it was the only solution he could come up with.

Esme whipped her head to Jensen. "If that is your solution, I'll do it myself. I'll call right to the top. If any of the three know, it'll be him. He's a busy man. It might be a few days. But do not"—she yanked her jacket off the chair—"do not call anyone else, do not ask anyone else. This does not leave the room. The last thing needed is for gossip to spread and panic to ensue." Her energy ebbed and flowed, chaotic and unstable.

"Where are you going Es?" Camryn could only think about how off she seemed this morning and even more so now.

"I have work to do and a list to complete." She jerked her jacket on and stomped toward the door.

Camryn stood and looked over his shoulder to Jensen. "You're an idiot."

"Esme, please. It was a stupid suggestion." Jensen jogged behind her as she slammed the door open. "I'm sorry. Esme, please come back in here."

Cora turned to Alicia, both staring at each other in silence for a few seconds until Alicia blurted her thoughts. "You better believe, since I'm stuck here, and Jensen works back there, I'm getting him to spill all those dirty little secrets. There's too much juicy gossip to not bring it up."

Cora slumped in her chair once again. "Okay, besides being 'friendly' with his boss, doesn't it seem like there's a whole lot more to this story?"

Alicia stood and stretched. "How would I know? Does it seem suspicious? Probably. But I can't be the judge. I'm not a part of this." She motioned her hands around the room and to the reapers around the bar. Could she consider herself to be a part of the reaping world? Where would a soul fit into that scenario?

Cora stood and made her way in front of Alicia. "You're basically stuck here for the foreseeable future; I'd say you are a part of this." Her tone was friendly as she rubbed Alicia's shoulder. She willed the ardor fragment to surface. It flickered mostly, but the feeling was present.

"What is that? Jensen did that to me earlier. Yours felt different, but I still feel all warm and fuzzy inside." She rubbed her shoulder where the tingling buzzed.

Cora offered a small smile. "Sorry, I should have asked if it was okay first. It's an energy sharing we do. It helps to relax and comfort souls. I'm not exactly good at it."

"I don't mind. I think you're doing just fine." Alicia beamed at Cora. "Are we becoming best friends? I feel like we're becoming best friends n—"

The office door flew open with a heavy thud. Esme stormed out of the office, followed by Jensen, then Camryn. Tense energy encircled the trio.

Esme blinked, pinching the bridge of her nose. She took a few unbalanced steps forward and held on to the wall.

Alicia leaned in toward Cora. "Is she wine-drunk right now?"

Cora whispered back. "Reapers can't get drunk, remember?"

Alicia cocked her head to the side. "Someone should remind her." She patted Cora's arm, then walked across the bar to another group of reapers, who were busy playing a game of pool.

Cora casually walked toward the hallway but lingered in the entryway. She could hear the tail end of the conversation.

"Guys, this is not the place to do this. Jensen, just back off and give her some space." Camryn's husky voice was slightly above a whisper, but the commanding tone lingered on every word.

Esme let out a frustrated groan. "Honestly, I'm fine. I just thought you should know what happened today. Give me a few days to dig some answers up myself. Right now, I have a soul to collect. Once that's done, I'm going home, then I'll try to get ahold of him in the morning."

Jensen's voice was barely audible. "Do you want me to go with you? I'm all done here for the night. I wouldn't mind keeping you company."

Esme snapped with a sharpness Cora hadn't heard before. "Absolutely not." She rounded the corner from the hallway and locked eyes with Cora before heading out.

Jensen ran after her as Camryn leaned into the frame of the hallway, giving Cora a side-eye glance. "Enjoying the show?" Before she could respond, he went back into Jensen's office.

Outside, Jensen caught up to Esme and grabbed her by the arm. "Will you wait a damn minute?" His eyes searched hers for answers. "Can we have a conversation that doesn't end up with one of us exploding on the other?"

"I don't know, Jensen. Are we even capable of having a conversation at all?" Esme pushed his hand off her arm. "We agreed to keep things professional. I'm holding up my end. Can you say the same?"

Jensen stepped closer to Esme. He gently reached for her hands, but she backed away from him. "Esme, this is killing me right now." His voice held the sound of defeat. It would be a lie to say his tone didn't have any impact on her.

Esme softened the angry lines on her forehead and took her time to gather her thoughts. "Jensen, I honestly don't care how you feel right now. You broke me first." She turned around and strode up the street. She stopped and yelled back. "I'm going to work. I'll let you know if I find anything out. Good night."

Before Jensen could say anything else, Esme disappeared into the night.

I O

The sun had just begun to rise, and the city streets were beginning to wake when Camryn sauntered into the bar as some other reapers were leaving. Cora, Jensen, and Alicia were all standing around the bar top.

"Oh, good, you're still here." He pointed to Jensen. "Was Es here? I didn't see her walk out."

Jensen flicked his eyes over to Camryn. "You weren't here at the meeting, either."

Camryn casually leaned an elbow on the wall. "Yeah, well, you know I don't go to these things. They don't apply to me, do they? Plus, you can't make me."

Jensen shook his head. "So, you haven't heard from Esme, either, then?"

Crossing his arms, Camryn took a closer look at Jensen's appearance. "Wow, you look like crap. But to answer your question, no, I haven't heard or seen her since that night."

Four months had come and gone since the three of them had their last encounter. The worry and stress of the passing days were beginning to etch themselves on Jensen's face. "Esme was going to find out some more information about—" He motioned his hands over Cora and Alicia.

Jensen placed his elbows on the bar top while resting his forehead in his palms. "Unclaimed souls and mortals dodging death are happening more and more in the city, and I'm trying to do damage control."

Camryn leaned in toward Jensen, dropping his voice to a whisper. "Should we be talking about this with them here? Isn't this a management-only issue?"

Jensen swiped a few items off his tablet before speaking. "Seeing as one of them is the issue, and the other witnessed the issue, I think we're past that already."

Cora rested her elbows on the counter as a dark expression crossed her face. "Esme already told me to stay quiet about all of it, and I plan on doing just that. Don't tell her, but . . . she kind of scares me."

Jensen snorted. "Yeah, she tends to have that effect on almost everyone." He continued to work on his tablet, unable to hide the worry and stress.

Alicia raised her hand as her eyes darted between Camryn and Jensen. "Quick question. Have either of you thought about checking Esme's apartment since you can't get a hold of her?"

Both men shared a mutual look. The thought never occurred to them, but it was swiftly abandoned. Camryn turned his full attention to Alicia. "How do you know about our apartments?"

Cora's furious head shook and hand motions for Alicia to be quiet went unnoticed by the bubbly soul.

Alicia gleefully said, "Cora's been taking me back to her apartment, so I won't be bored out of my mind here. A girl can only pour so many drinks until it feels like a purgatory punishment."

Cora sighed, wincing and dropping her head.

Jensen and Camryn swiveled their heads over toward Cora, who was trying to shuffle closer to the door, feeling the intensity of both reapers' gaze on her. She knew her attempt to sneak out of the bar was over. Cora took a deep breath and placed her hands on her hips, raising her voice. "What? It's rude to leave her here all by herself for days on end. It's not that big of a deal."

Camryn stepped back, shook his head, and clapped Jensen's shoulder. "Your apprentice, your problem."

Jensen gripped the edge of the counter and pushed back on his heels, attempting to collect his thoughts calmly. "Cora, the apartments are a reaper-only building. No other entity should be in there. It's against the rules. You could ruin the wards and sigils that keep us hidden."

When the hub in Philadelphia had been created, a coven of witches were paid handsomely to create wards on the apartments, headquarters, and bar. It was how they stay cloaked in a city crawling with mortals. Anything with the custom wards blended into the background.

Cora retorted, "You mean like this bar?" The defiant challenge in her tone hung in the air. She lifted her chin and dared Jensen with her eyes. "What's the matter? Out of rules and regulations to throw in my face?"

Jensen slammed his fist on the counter. His usual calm voice burned away with frustration and anger. "Don't speak to me in that tone again. I am not your friend. I am your Administrator and mentor who is trying to make you into a good reaper. All month you've barely made it to the veil on time. You even lost a soul for three days! Now I find out you've been escorting an unclaimed soul to our apartment building?"

Camryn covered his emerging smirk with a large hand, but his shuddering shoulders gave away his laugh.

Jensen focused his attention and rage on him next. "You. Why did you even come here? Something is happening in this city. Esme is missing, and you don't even care!"

Camryn all but lunged in front of Jensen. "Don't you dare try to assume anything about me."

A loud clap and whistle cut the tension in the room. The three reapers turned their heads to the noise.

Alicia had climbed on top of a table. "First, both of you are jerks for leaving me stranded here. So, neither of you gets to play the role of a righteous reaper. Second, neither of you have even answered the question of 'did you check Esme's apartment?' Third"—she shook her finger at the three faces in front of her—"I've got nothing else for a third, but I reserve my third notion to be used at a later time." She hopped off the table as Jensen and Camryn took a few steps away from each other. Cora walked back toward the group. Alicia confidently walked behind the bar. "Now, I may not be able to drink them, but I can pour them. Who needs a drink?"

All three reapers raised their hands, and Alicia met them with a smile and slid one whiskey neat, one bourbon on the rocks, and one pale ale down the counter.

Once they each had a drink and took a few minutes to let the air settle around them, Jensen spoke. "Like I said, before that night, in my office was the last time I saw Esme. I'm worried about her. She hasn't been acting like herself lately."

Camryn raised his eyebrow. "I'll agree she hasn't been acting like herself." He drew out a long sip from his glass. "But how did you think she was going to react when you told her your idea? That's probably the reason she's not talking to you."

Jensen gripped his glass tighter. "It's no different than who she was going to talk to. Besides, how does that explain why she isn't talking to you?"

Camryn shrugged. "We're low-maintenance friends." Cora and Alicia shared a knowing look. They dared each other to ask with glances at each other. He caught sight of their faces. "What's wrong with you two?"

"Well, I've already gotten in trouble today. I might as well keep the ball rolling." Cora gathered her courage and looked Jensen square in the eyes. "I'm guessing Esme stormed out of your office that night because you told her that you were going to talk to Director Thalia. Your boss. The one you've been sleeping with. Pretty different from her talking to the head honcho, who she hasn't slept with."

Jensen choked on his drink while Camryn trained his eyes on the bottle-lined shelves. "Who the hell said I was sleeping with her?" The outrage was undeniable.

As Cora stammered on her words, Alicia blurted, "Camryn."

Camryn ripped his eyes away from the bottles and glared at the women. "You take that back. I said no such thing! I said they were friendly!"

Jensen clenched and unclenched his fists as he opened his mouth, but Camryn interjected. "I've been contacting my own network. I also spoke with Tyler, seeing as they have the same specialty, he might have tabs on where Es has been reaping."

Jensen was still glaring at all of them. "That wasn't a terrible idea. Did he have any suggestions?"

Camryn shook his head, and as he was about to speak, the door to the bar opened. The backdrop of the sun in the city cast a silhouette around a woman. She was tall, with cascading dirty blonde hair. Her perfectly tailored white suit and emerald-green silk shirt accentuated her toned physique. The sunlight bounced off her high cheekbones and reflected into her gold eyes. She made her way slowly to the counter, carefully examining the outdated décor and dim lighting. She locked eyes with Jensen and gave a wicked grin.

Jensen pushed the sleeves of his shirt up his forearms. "Director Thalia, what brings you into the city and this bar?"

Cora leaned closer to Alicia and whispered, "Holy crap, that's Thalia?"

Alicia whispered back, "That's who he's screwing? I want to be mad—female solidarity and all that—but damn. I'd absolutely smash."

Before she could finish her sentence, Camryn shot a warning look and placed a finger over his lips. They both nodded their heads in understanding.

Thalia laughed at Jensen's question, but there was little humor in the sound. "You called me, remember? You sounded more stressed than usual and were throwing a lot of hypothetical questions my way." Her Mediterranean accent held a soft hint of seduction. Her eyes settled and narrowed on Alicia. Thalia's voice dropped and grew flat. "I see you have one of those hypotheticals behind the bar."

Alicia's nostrils flared. "Excuse me, I am a person, and I'm standing right here."

A sickly sweet smile spread across Thalia's face. "You're not a person, you're a soul who doesn't belong here. Now, if you don't mind, the reapers are speaking." She patted Alicia's cheek before turning her attention back to Jensen.

Jensen was still taking in the scene before him as Thalia grabbed his hand and stroked her fingers up and down his arm. He rolled his neck and stood, releasing his arm from her hand gently. "Why don't we talk in my office?" He held his hand out to lead her in the hall's direction.

Thalia's eyes darkened as she placed her hand into Jensen's. "Marvelous idea. I'm sure we have a lot of things to discuss." He pulled his hand out of hers. She looked back and saw him wiping his arm and his hand on his pants, a disgusted and pained look on his face.

Cora was the first to break the silence. "Does anyone not like her because I know I can't be alone?"

Alicia, who looked angrier than either of them have ever seen her, replied. "Besides being unfairly gorgeous, what is Jensen doing with her? Esme is way cooler than her. I take my smash back. I'd smash Esme in a heartbeat. Thalia can go sit on a cactus."

"I can't disagree with you. I told you Thalia was a blunt instrument." Camryn stood and stretched, letting out a heavy sigh. "As much as you don't like her, she might be able to help you."

Cora's phone beeped a reminder. "Oh, Alicia, it's time to go. The first collection of the day."

Camryn raised his hand, pushing it out. "This isn't my circus or my monkeys, but why is she going with you? You have to see how bad that is."

Cora looked away sheepishly. "It's innocent, and I'm not particularly good with kids. Alicia is amazing with them. She's my buffer. But don't worry, she doesn't come to the veil. That would be terrible. Tyler or some other reaper usually hangs out with her while I'm gone."

Camryn closed his eyes and bit his bottom lip. "There are so many things wrong with what you just told me. You're going to do this alone. You can't rely on another reaper, much less another soul, to do your job for you. Alicia is staying here for now. Helpful hint, talk soft, squat down to their level. Superpowers is usually a good topic to discuss with them."

As she tried to protest, Camryn furrowed his brows as he growled out a warning. "There is one of the big three in this bar right now who knows about Alicia. Now is not the time for you to break any more rules than you already have these past months. You are responsible for your job."

The bar door swung open, and a petite figure stumbled in. Camryn, Cora, and Alicia all stared, taking in the form before them. They all spoke at the same time. "Esme?"

I I

E sme tugged her jacket and attempted a smirk. "Don't tell me you guys missed me." As she walked toward the group of familiar faces, she grabbed her waist, wincing. "What?" She placed her phone on the counter and took a seat.

Camryn ran his eyes over her. "I've been trying to call you for months now, Es, months! Are you okay? You look a little rough there." He reached out, tucking a stray curl behind her ear. "Holy shit, that's one hell of a bruise. What—actually, no, how did that happen?"

Esme let out a dry laugh. "It's nothing, part of the job." Camryn went to open his mouth again. "Leave it be, Cam."

Sensing she was hiding something more, Camryn sat back and nodded. "Fine, don't tell me yet. I'm just glad you're here."

Cora nudged Camryn with her elbow and darted her eyes toward the office. He bit the inside of his cheek as his eyes were drawn to the hallway.

Thalia was sitting across the desk from Jensen while an uncomfortable silence fell between them. She sat quietly, studying him. "I guess I'll start talking. Jensen, I'm worried about you. Those questions you were asking me, what is that all about?"

Jensen slumped in his leather chair. "There are more unclaimed souls and more mortals who aren't departing when they are scheduled to depart. I have no idea how to fix this or why this is even happening. I've been trying to figure this out and keep hitting dead-end after dead-end. I called other Administrators in other countries to see if anything has been weird or off there. Fortunately, for them, and unfortunately, for us here, all is well elsewhere."

Thalia stood, hips swaying with each step around the desk, and crouched in front of Jensen before taking his hands in hers. "You don't have to handle this alone anymore. I'm here to help. Let me help you."

Jensen slipped his hands out of hers and pushed himself back to allow more space between them. "I'm not alone, as you saw. Also, the last time you helped me, things became—"

Thalia stood slowly, flicking her eyes to Jensen. She didn't even hesitate to say her thought. "Fun."

Jensen walked to the other side of his office, leaning against the wall, shoving his hands deep into his pockets. "I was going to say ruined."

A storm washed over Thalia's face as she made herself comfortable in Jensen's chair and spun around to face him. She meticulously folded her hands in her lap, regaining a regal composure, but her voice betrayed her face. "Jensen, please tell me you don't mean that ragtag group out there day drinking. You're better than that, darling."

Jensen set his jaw as every muscle in his body tensed. He pushed away from the wall, hands still in his pockets, and walked over to his desk. Thalia tilted her head up slightly as a smirk spread across her lips as Jensen stood over her. "I'm not your darling, Director. You're also sitting in my chair." A low growl overtook his voice.

As Thalia stood and flattened the wrinkles on her clothes, she trailed a finger down Jensen's chest. "Did I say something to upset you?"

"Don't touch me. I'm not yours to touch." Sidestepping around Thalia to reclaim his chair, Jensen stretched his arms in front of himself. "Thalia, please keep things professional. Do you have any answers for me or not? I do have work to get done. Also—" His and Thalia's eyes skimmed the heavy office door. Jensen's eyes widened. "She's back." He quickly rose to his feet, knocking pens off the table and rattling the computer monitor.

Noticing the wash of relief on his face, Thalia sucked her teeth. "Who's back?" Her eyes carefully studied Jensen and the energy he was walking toward. The energy rolled down the hall was familiar but strange at the same time. She rubbed her fingertips together, feeling for the energy attempting to place it. In a whispered gasp, Thalia muttered to herself, "It can't be." She lengthened her stride to catch Jensen's shoulder before he reached the door. "Jensen, who is back?"

His hand dropped as he reached for the door. Instead, he turned around to find Thalia swallowing a panicked breath. "Oh, it's Esme. Esme is the 'she' that's back. You can lump her in with the ragtag group who is figuring all this out. Just don't tell her." Jensen paused, noticing Thalia's hand still resting on his shoulder. "Do you mind keeping your hands to yourself, Director? What happened between us was a mistake, one I don't intend on repeating. Now, if you'll excuse me, I have some reapers I need to speak with." He paused, looking deep into the wrath-filled hazel eyes searing into him. "Unless you have any useful information to give me?"

A menacing gleam shimmered in her eyes. "You know, it's amazing how in all these years Death has kept her so busy. I've never officially met her. Perhaps I should go introduce myself. As for a useful piece of information, I might have something, but I'll save it for after I meet Esme." She snaked an arm around Jensen, pulling the door open.

All the stress and worry Jensen had been dealing with for months had just increased and boiled over. "Thalia!"

Giving a smile over her shoulder, she started walking down the hall.

Esme was on her second glass of wine as she caught up with Camryn and the mayhem ensuing in the city. "Cora, you must be out of your damn mind. Taking a soul to collect souls, bringing her to the apartments, and you still have trouble making it to the veil on time? Either Jensen is losing his ability to mentor, and you need a new one, or you just suck at being a reaper." Esme chuckled as she lifted the glass to her lips. "I will give you points for originality, though."

Cora pulled a newly frayed string on the hem of her shirt and shrugged. "It's not for a lack of trying. I'm just not good with anything other than expected deaths. The violent soul collections are way too intense for me, which makes sense why it suits you perfectly."

Esme furrowed her brows, adjusting herself in the barstool, attempting to her hide her wince. "What does that mean? Suits me perfectly?"

Alicia laughed as she cleared the other glasses off the counter. "Cora finds you intimidating."

Esme held a finger up, cutting the chatter. She slowly turned her head in the direction of Jensen's office. "Is that who I think it is back there?"

Cora coughed and twiddled her fingers, wrapping the frayed string around. "This has been a great reunion, but I have a soul to collect. Camryn, Alicia, thanks for the drink. Esme, glad you're back."

Alicia shot her an anxious glimpse just as Cora vanished. She looked back to Esme. "Maybe I should top off that drink for you."

Esme slowly turned toward Camryn. "Spill it. Is that who I think it is?" Her gray eyes grew dark as thunderstorms conjured inside her. She noticed the hesitation on his face. Her nostrils flared and breathing quickened. "He didn't call her, did he? Did he, Camryn? I told him to wait until I talked with our boss."

"You full-named me. You never call me Camryn. It's always Cam." He watched as her eyes darkened further. Camryn held his hands up, hoping it would be enough to shield himself from her fury. "I'm not saying I agree with him. I want to make that clear. You went missing for months. We both tried calling you and couldn't get a hold of you. The soul situation is getting out of hand here, and Jensen did the next logical thing. He called his boss." Once he finished his defense pitch, he swallowed hard, waiting to hear what Esme would say.

As Camryn finished his statement of defense, Jensen's voice broke out from the office. "Thalia!"

A deep scowl emerged from Esme. "This just keeps getting better and better." She finished her drink in one large swig. She slid off the barstool and took a deep breath before walking to the middle of the bar. Even though Thalia was walking confidently toward her, she locked eyes with Jensen as his steps quickened. He brushed right past Thalia and stopped short as his eyes drank in Esme. His expression fell as he noted the bruises on her face, the scrapes and cuts up and down her hands and arms.

Jensen went to reach for Esme's face, but he dropped his hand when she jerked her head back. His eyes disquietingly slid down her frame. "Esme, what happened? What or who did this to you?" Jensen felt a pang of guilt, seeing her this way. Anger boiled in the pit of his being. Anger at the fact that she would put herself in a position where something could happen to her but more at the fact that this happened to her, and he wasn't there to do anything about it.

She looked behind him, seeing Thalia callously standing behind Jensen. "It's not important right now." Esme plastered on a smile that didn't quite reach her eyes. There was more she wanted to say, more she had to say but opted to keep it a secret.

Jensen crossed his arms as worry lines deepened across his forehead. "I beg to differ. That looks pretty damn important to me, Esme."

Back at the bar top, Alicia cautiously walked around to take a seat next to Camryn as he surveyed the situation that was unraveling in front of them. Alicia leaned in close to Camryn. "Is this bad? This feels like something bad is about to happen."

Camryn leaned forward as he rested his forearms on his thighs, lacing his fingers together. "Oh, yeah, this is bad. This is bad on a lot of different levels. The history between those three is bad, but it's more than that. We're reapers. Being a reaper means we don't bleed, and if we don't bleed, we can't bruise."

She inhaled, a question forming on the tip of her tongue. "Then why does she look like that?"

Camryn turned to look at her. "Why indeed. There's little that can cause any harm to a reaper. But I've never seen anything like this."

"What exactly harms reapers? I thought you were indestructible creatures," Alicia said.

"Nothing is ever truly indestructible, Alicia. Celestial blades can cause damage, anything Infernal can hurt us. In the past, and I mean way back in history, covens would trap reapers. But none of that happens anymore. Some agreement above my paygrade prevents all that now."

Alicia cringed. "Oh, that sucks. The being able to get hurt thing, not the agreement."

Thalia stepped forward, lightly pushing Jensen to the side and held a delicate hand out toward Esme. Her eyes traveled up and down Esme's petite frame. "You must be Esme. Oh my, what is happening here?" Even though her voice sounded shocked, her eyes glinted with amusement.

Esme shook Thalia's hand in a surprisingly forceful grip that made Thalia lightly gasp. "Director." Even though Esme had to crane her neck, she never dropped her challenging gaze. The air grew frigid and stifled, with both reapers challenging each other in the other's grasp. Low, humming lights flickered. A flash of worry darted across Thalia as she ripped her hand out of Esme's strong grip.

Jensen noticed the change in the surrounding atmosphere. His eyes danced across the flickering lights, and oppressive cold air tickled his nape. A change in energy seeped from Esme. It didn't match her usual strong, warm, and measured pulse. It was cold, erratic, and stronger, as if ocean waves were crashing onto a rocky shore. An unrelenting, uncontrollable force. Trepidation brewed inside of him. Just what happened to Esme while she was gone?

Never looking away from Thalia, Esme spoke up. "As much fun as this has been, I'm going to head back to my apartment. I've had a long day and need some sleep before work tonight. I'll catch up with you all later." She looked at Jensen. "When you're not too busy, of course." She gave a half-hearted wave to Camryn and Alicia. "Thalia, it's been a displeasure. I'm sure we'll be seeing each other again." Without sparing a backward glance, she opened the door, allowing the sun to warm the cold air that settled into the walls. Once Esme was out of the bar, Thalia pivoted on her heels to face Jensen. He looked over to where Camryn and Alicia sat quietly.

Jensen stood there, replaying the sight of Esme in his mind. Carding his fingers through his hair, every muscle in his body tensed. His mind whirling with questions faster than he could put into coherent words. He brushed past Thalia, who was still standing in the empty bar, running through her thoughts. Jensen slumped against a pillar next to Alicia and Camryn. "So—he paused, his eyes trained into the distance—"that was unexpected."

Thalia's heels clicking against the wooden floor grabbed the reapers' and Alicia's attention. As she walked toward the group, she fidgeted at her thighs with her fingers, grasping for the remnants of energy Esme left behind. It was familiar, powerful but impossible. Ignoring the others, she set her sights on Jensen. "It's no wonder Death hid the infamous Strategos Esme." She delicately rested her hand on his arm. "There is something she's hiding. You saw her. She is not normal. You felt that energy she gave off. Normal reapers don't have those levels of energy."

Camryn cut her off with a protective tone. "You're right, even your energy isn't that strong." He stood from his seat, stretched his neck, and took a step closer to Thalia. His brawny frame overshadowed hers. His fist balled at his sides. "I get you're one of the big three, but you have no right to come in here and start talking about Esme. You don't even know her."

Thalia took a step away from Jensen, who was still mulling over what he had witnessed. She turned her full attention to Camryn. "If you know who I am, then you should learn your place before you get in over your head." A snarl crept across her lips. Her regal demeanor was fading, and she knew it. She cleared her throat, eerily put on a calm smile, and turned back to Jensen. "All I'm saying is, you should be careful around her. I know you have some strong feelings toward her, darling, but I would advise you not to put any more trust into her."

Jensen shook his head in disbelief and stood tall, squaring his shoulders. "I've known Esme for a while now. I know her, I trust her. We just need to talk. Also, I'm still not your darling." He pushed past both Camryn and Thalia as he reached for his phone that was left on the counter.

Alicia sat there, twirling a thick purple lock around her finger. Her head was down as she busied herself, watching her feet kick gently beneath her. Being an unclaimed soul in a bar of reapers was more than she had bargained for. The presence of Thalia made her skin crawl, and the intensity of everyone made her queasy.

As Jensen walked past, she tapped his leg with her foot, stopping him in his tracks. She lifted her face slightly so she could see him through lowered eyelids. He turned his face to see her.

Alicia took a shaky breath and whispered, "I can see you want to talk to Esme, but I would probably wait for a more private moment." She tilted her head to where Thalia's watchful leer fell upon them. Jensen nodded and put the phone in his pocket.

Thalia clasped her hands in front of her hips and arched her perfectly groomed eyebrow. "Well, then, this has been an eventful morning, and I can see emotions are running high. Why don't we all take a little break, hmm? I'm sure we all have a full list of souls to collect today."

Camryn dragged a frustrated hand down his face, sighing with displeasure. "I agree. I need to head out my collection list starts in a few minutes, and I have some things I need to check on before I get started." He narrowed his eyes at Alicia before speaking again. "Also, no more field trips, Alicia."

Feigning a shocked expression, Alicia rested a hand on her chest. "Camryn, whatever do you mean? I've been nothing but a model soul citizen." A playful smirk lifted the corner of her mouth.

Camryn rolled his eyes and glanced at the time on his phone. "You know exactly what I mean, and I'm being serious. You stay here."

Alicia crossed her arms and gave a slight pout. "You're no fun."

The bar door opened again, the sunlight creating a moment of blindness.

Tyler strolled in, clueless to what had taken place mere moments from then. "Alicia!" There was an extra pep in his step as he walked over to her. "You're looking particularly beautiful today. Did you do something different with your hair? Oh, wait, no. It's a new outfit, isn't it?"

Alicia dropped her arms and dissolved into a small fit of giggles. "See, Camryn, he's fun."

Camryn glared between them. "I'm responsible. Tyler, I already told her this, but I'm telling you, too. She stays here."

Tyler widened his eyes and slipped an arm around her waist. "What makes you think I was going to take her anywhere? Cora texted me and said our lovely friend here could use some company." He shot a sly wink to Alicia.

Thalia scoffed at the sight before her. "This is all utterly ridiculous. Perhaps while I'm here, I should also retrain all of you on reaper soul interactions."

Tyler leaned over to Alicia with a conspiratorial tone. "When did she get here? And why is she so mean?"

Alicia patted his arm and sighed. "I'll catch you up later."

Camryn straightened his jacket and darted his eyes between Alicia and Tyler, then over to Jensen and Thalia. He mumbled under his breath about the city and bar going to shit and walked out of the bar. Thalia made her way to the back office before stopping at the entrance of the hallway. Jensen was making his way to his office as well but stopped when he saw she was headed in the same direction.

Thalia smiled over her shoulder at him. "I hope you don't mind. I'll be using your office. I'm sure you'll be busy today, after all."

Jensen set his jaw before speaking. "I'll be at the hospital for most of the day. Try not to get too comfortable in there." He turned around and gave Tyler and Alicia a stiff nod as he walked out.

Tyler let out a slow whistle as he turned to Alicia. They were the only two left in the room. The tension lingered in the air. With a glimmer of mischief in his eye, he grabbed Alicia's hands and pulled her toward the door. "How about you tell me what I missed while we take a walk around the park?"

Alicia bounced in excitement, nodding her head. "I thought you'd never ask. Let's just try not to get caught. I'm on thin ice with Camryn and Jensen."

Tyler tucked Alicia's hand in the crook of his arm and smiled at her. "Don't worry about them. I'll have you back before they even notice you're gone." Alicia laughed and happily let Tyler escort her out of The Twisted Sickle.

As the pair made their way out the door, Thalia stepped out of the office and looked around the bar. Making sure no one was left around her, she pulled out her phone to scroll for a number. The other end quickly picked up. "I believe I found what we have been looking for." She paused, surveying her surroundings. "No, I still have to regain his trust. Yes, I know we are on a timeline now. Meet me at the Philadelphia headquarters. We need to get into that office and find it before anyone else does." Thalia ended the call and gave one last glance around before disappearing.

Escape couldn't come fast enough for Esme. Seeing Thalia was the last thing that was expected, wanted, or needed. Stepping out of the bar, she rolled her shoulders, breathing in the warm, light air once again. She walked to the corner but stopped when a pang of guilt hit her. The faces of her fellow reapers filled her mind. The worry and relief etched on their faces weighed on her. It was all because of her, and she was aware of it.

She owed them an explanation. They had a right to know where she had disappeared to and why she ended up looking the way she did. One large obstacle kept her from telling them everything. That obstacle was currently in The Twisted Sickle and had more authority than her. Esme knew if Thalia was around, she had to guard her secret.

Throbbing filled her head as she brought her fingers up to her temples, trying to stave off a migraine, letting out a shaky breath as her vision blurred. The amount of energy that unleashed itself during the confrontation with Thalia was beginning to take its toll. She looked back, sensing all the energies, swirling around and shook her head. Esme glanced around, making sure no one was around or following her. What she was going to do was not what the average reaper did. Her hand had a small tremor as she held it out in front of herself. Pinching her eyes closed, attempting to block out any pain coursing through her, Esme muttered a word under her breath. "Aperio." As soon as the words were spoken, a soft glow appeared before her that grew large enough to engulf her frame. The light snuffed itself out and Esme was no longer on the corner.

Esme stumbled out of the vibrant light pulsing in her apartment. She placed a firm hand on the navy-blue wall to steady herself. With a flick of her wrist, Esme whispered, "Claudere," extinguishing the bright light. "I need to get better at using that portal." A heavy breath escaped her. Pressing away from the wall, she stretched, and a long, satisfying crack traveled down her spine. With a groan, she rubbed the back of her neck.

The sun illuminated the living room's dark corners, but a cold, darkening still filled the space. The walls felt constricting. Her breathing grew frantic, and her chest tightened as she fought to breathe. Eyes widening, she slid down the wall that had just held her up. Esme's hands shook. "Not again." Cautiously, she pulled her phone out of her back pocket. Barely managing to steady her fingers, she scrolled to Jensen's name.

Her finger hovered over the green dial icon. She slid the phone across the floor instead, then placed both palms on her forehead. "Get a hold of yourself." Dragging her hands down her face, then resting them on her chest, she took one deep breath with a tap of each finger until she made it to ten. Blinking with a grunt, Esme pushed herself up off the floor and dusted herself off, then made her way to the bathroom. With each step, she stripped away layers of her clothing. As a new layer was shed, it was scattered across the floor carelessly.

She turned on the shower, letting the steam blanket the room. As the steam grew thick, she leaned over the sink, white-knuckling its edges. She wiped her hand down the foggy mirror and took a tentative step back, faintly recognizing the reflection staring back at her. Turning, she slowly stepped into the shower and pressed her palms against the tiles. As the hot water raced down her body, she hoped it would wash away all emotions threatening to surface.

Long, lazy minutes had passed, and the water ran cold. Finally, she felt calm and centered again. Once done, she wrapped a towel around her body, finding herself in front of her closet. Sifting through her limited wardrobe repeatedly, she settled on a pair of black jeans that were slightly ripped along the thighs, a fitted black shirt, and Doc Martens. Esme haphazardly gathered her tight curls into a high ponytail, but a few unruly strands skimmed the nape of her neck and ears. Her heels tapped as she walked out to her living room, searching for where her phone had slid earlier. Picking it up, she gave it a quick once over, making sure nothing was damaged and disregarded the horrifying number of unread messages. Esme checked the time and noticed she still had two more hours before her only reaping that night.

Looking around her, wondering how to pass the time, she decided to make a cup of tea and grabbed a book off her shelf. As she nestled into the mustard yellow couch with her book, she placed the tea on the coffee table to cool. Barely making it three pages into her book, her eyes felt heavy. She blinked rapidly until she could no longer keep them open, and her eyes fluttered closed.

Esme let out a guttural scream as she opened her eyes. Sweat was beading on her forehead and trickled down her back. Rogue tears tracked down her cheeks. One hand rested on her stomach as she placed the other over her eyes, trying to still her breathing. The nightmares wouldn't stop coming, they only intensified. Flustered, she sat up and threw a pillow across the room. The sun had faded, leaving her apartment dimly lit by moonlight filtering in, and her tea had grown cold.

She frantically searched and reached for her phone to check the time. "Crap, I'm going to be late." She hastily pushed herself away from the couch, making her way to the front door. Before reaching for the doorknob, she grabbed a black leather jacket off a wall hook and tugged it on. Feeling her pockets for her phone and keys, she ventured out into the night.

Stepping outside, Esme let the crisp cool air fill her lungs. There was something about the night's coldness that calmed her. Lights from the lamp posts twirled around with each passing car, casting shadows on the walls and sidewalks. Turning a few blocks away from her apartment building, she heard a deep growl from an alley. Esme turned her head and smirked in its direction.

Slowly rotating on her heels, she strolled toward the ominous sound. The darkened alleyway gave the illusion of stretching further than reality allowed. With slightly parted lips, Esme blew out a high-pitched whistle. The sound reverberated off the building walls and hollow dumpsters.

From out of the deep shadows, two menacingly glowing yellow eyes stared back at her. She planted her feet and squared her shoulders, challenging those eyes with a steely gaze of her own.

A louder growl emerged again from deep within the shadows. The growl was strong enough to quake within Esme's chest. She kept her gaze locked and stepped closer, flexing her hands at her sides, gathering fragments of her own energy, readying herself if need be. The light the moon offered was dimmer than a dying flashlight. As she braved another step forward, a large silhouette blocked her path. Before her prowled a massive hellhound, its wiry and coarse fur darker than the midnight sky. Its head aligned with her shoulder height. Thick opaque sprigs of slobber were flung through the air as it gnashed its teeth.

With hackles raised, he shook his fur. Embers flitted off the tips of the wiry fur. Every step the beast made imprinted into the chilled air as steam rose from the ground in his wake. The hound bowed to a low stance, ready to attack at a moment's notice.

Esme cocked her head to the side, studying and challenging the beast. They circled each other, leaning forward ever so slightly, their noses only a hair length away from each other. Its hot, rancid breath seeped into her pores. With its jowls still in a snarl, Esme let out a chuckle and reached out. The Infernal beast pressed its head into her palm. She pressed her gathered energy into the beast, and he pressed further into her palm.

Her hand was firm and steady as she ran her fingers up the bridge of his nose. She continued to trace her fingers over the large head, down the jowls and scratched his chin.

She smirked, and her eyes penetrated deep into the yellow pair before her.

"There you are. Ready to collect your bounty tonight?" A deep bark and snap of a jaw replied.

Esme straightened out her posture and walked toward the far back of the alley. She held out her hand. "Aperio." A familiar warm, glowing white light pulsed before her. Looking over her shoulder, she whistled to the hellhound. "Come." With a brisk shake of its neck, the vast beast lurked over, slinking into the portal. Taking in a deep relaxing breath, Esme looked into the glowing portal. "Okay, Samuel Carter, ready or not, here I come."

Taking a shaky step out of the portal, Esme took a minute to compose herself and establish her bearings. Waving a hand behind herself, she whispered, "Claudere," sealing the portal. With the hound close by, she scrutinized their surroundings. Fluorescent lights hummed from above while the sounds of machines whirred lazily in the background. Her focus switched between the sound of her heels and the scratching claws across the concrete floor. Scanning the room, she locked on to the energy she came to collect. Stopping mid-stride, she leaned in close to the hellhound's ear. In a voice barely above a whisper, she gave the command to begin his stalking of prey. "Hunt." Melting into the shadows, the hound stealthily began his stalking game.

Following Samuel Carter's energy, Esme quietly walked toward the stairs leading up to the offices. A chill ran down her spine as she drew closer to the energy source. It was dark, cold, twisted. Just being near the energy caused goosebumps to surface on her arms. She could only imagine what the sight of him must be. The scent of rusted metal filled her nose while the sound of grinding metal rang deep in her ears.

Eyebrows and eyelids pinched tightly together, Esme refocused on the energy that was pulling at her core and steeled herself. From out of the corner of her eye, she caught a sight of two familiar eyes gleaming from a dark corner. The air was stale and musky. She could feel the energy of what was about to take place. She could feel and taste death all around her. It pressed into her chest, oppressing every emotion in her. Rippling through the air came a blood-curdling scream. It filled the factory's every crevice.

A male's frantic voice followed soon after the scream. "Shut up, just shut up! Why did you have to do that? You shouldn't have done—"

A heavy clunk followed a bone-cracking smack. A few seconds later, a clang crashed on the floor above. Esme stood still, listening to the horror unfolding around her. Bile burned her throat, but she swallowed it as the anger growing in her chest was greater than her disgust. She cocked an eyebrow and set her jaw. Looking around the corner to a row of offices where light poured out from under the door, she sneered her next words. "Found you, Samuel."

Peering back to where the glowing eyes lurked, waiting for a single command. She pointed to the hellhound, then to the softly lit door and spoke the words to begin Samuel's end. "Claim your bounty." The hellhound bounded into the office's shadows, ready for its prey.

Esme opened the office door. Her eyes widened in horror, then disgust. Strewn across the room were ropes, zip ties, knives, and polished tools. Bloody rags were haphazardly tossed on the floor, along with torn clothing. Hurried footsteps caught her attention. Heavy pacing came from an adjacent room. Esme walked cautiously toward the adjoining door, listening to a muffled, gravelly voice. "No, no, no, this wasn't supposed to happen." Heavy wet coughs followed.

Sharpening her shoulders, she pushed open the door. The new room was smaller in comparison to the room next door. A lonely desk lamp poorly lit the room, but the shadows it allowed to waltz on the walls told a dark story of their own. In the far corner, Esme spotted a woman curled on the floor, gasping for breath. Blood glossed over her hair as it stuck to her forehead and dribbled down her face. A shadow flickered across the wall, grabbing Esme's attention. She spun around as a scrawny figure skulked near her. The woman gasped a plea and prayer behind her and said, "Help me."

Focusing her gaze full of fury on the figure in front of her, she addressed the helpless woman who clutched on dearly for life. "Sorry, hun, I'm not here for you, but another will be soon." She took a step closer to the figure, and a cold smirk tugged at the corner of her lips. "Hello, Samuel."

A deep, menacing growl rumbled the void in the room. The energy shifted around her, growing tenser and fear-filled by the second. A small wave of frightened energy from the woman tickled the hairs on Esme's neck. Just for a moment, she softened her tone. "You don't have to be afraid, sweetheart; the beast won't hurt you." The woman's energy was fading. Esme knew she only had minutes until this woman's reaper showed up.

Samuel's voice cut Esme's comfort off. "I'm not a beast." His voice was curt and shaky. As he stood in front of Esme, his body matched the shakiness of his voice. There stood Samuel Carter, a man who had killed five other women, the sixth currently being added to his list.

Esme eyed him, trying to make sense of how such a scrawny man and frail-looking creature could accomplish what he had. Mud-brown hair soaked with sweat clung to his forehead, pricking his beady eyes. His clothing and face were splattered with blood. One trembling hand held a wrench, slick with evidence of what he had done to that woman. The other hand clutched at his abdomen, where blood seeped into his shirt. He held the wrench up to Esme, trying to appear threatening.

Esme let out a wry laugh and crossed her arms. "You're not the beast I was talking about. You're hardly a man. I guess I expected more." She shrugged. "Samuel, Samuel, Samuel. Your time is up. I'm sure you can tell for yourself, though. You reek of stale piss, fear, and death." Her tongue swiped her bottom lips. The bitter and tart taste of death hung in the air.

Samuel gave Esme a wicked smile that crinkled the corner of his eyes. "I don't know who you are, but I'll kill you, too." Blood spurted out of his mouth as he coughed a laughed.

Esme circled him, eyeing him curiously. She pulled out her phone to check the time, then tucked it safely back into her pocket. "No, I don't think you'll get a chance to try." Her voice was taunting. "Ten, nine . . ."

He lunged at her with a raged-filled yell. Before Samuel could reach her, the hellhound leaped out of the shadows. The scruff on the hound stood on end while it snarled. Hunger surfaced in his eyes. Samuel dropped the wrench with a resounding clang on the ground. He stumbled backward as terror consumed his every fiber. "Get away from me!" Samuel shrieked as pure fear surged through him.

Esme's voice crept next to him. "Three, two, one."

Samuel's body lay motionless on the cold floor. All traces of terror forever frozen into Samuels's eyes. "What the hell is happening?" He stood there over his own body with his palms pressed to his head.

Esme slowly walked over with the hound. She reached up and grabbed his face. For the first time, she noticed the sunken dark circles under his eyes. Glancing over at the woman who was quickly fading on the floor, resentment flooded Esme's chest. Her fingers dug even harder into the hollows of Samuel's cheeks. "Even in death, you're still weak and pathetic." She let her grasp drop, letting her gaze rove over him.

Seizing the opportunity, Samuel tried to run out of the room, only to find his route of escape was blocked by a looming hellhound. Esme stood there calmly, assessing the situation. He clumsily took hurried steps backward as the nightmarish beast stalked toward him. Samuel held one shaky pleading hand out toward Esme. "Please, help me. Have mercy on me."

Tilting her head to the woman who desperately clutched to the last remaining threads of life. "Is that what those women prayed for? For help? For you to show them mercy?" Her tone matched her steely gaze. "Mercy and salvation are the last things you deserve, Samuel." She paused and crossed her arms. "Also, not in my job description."

Still fueled by fear, Samuel's eyes widened. "What does that mean? What is your job? Who are you? What is that thing?"

Letting out an exasperated sigh, Esme pinched the bridge of her nose. Her vision was beginning to haze again, but she knew she had to finish this job. "You're dead, Samuel. I'm your reaper, not your reckoning. But that beast is a hellhound. He's your damnation."

Samuel found he could no longer cower in the corner. A large, exposed pipe dug into his back. An unyielding dead-end captured him. His eyes grew larger as his worst nightmare crept toward him with bared teeth glossed in thick saliva. Samuel gulped hard, at a loss for words.

Esme turned away from Samuel and inhaled as she studied the photos on a nearby desk. With her exhale, she commanded the hellhound. "Eat."

The room filled with deep, petrified screams as the beast consumed Samuel piece by piece. Esme never turned around, training her eyes on the door. She rubbed her fingers together, feeling the new swirling energy forming on the other side of the door. Her eyes widened with a realization. "Oh, no." Anxiety bubbled in her.

Willing herself to look over her shoulder, she realized the screaming had stopped, and Samuel was gone, leaving deafening silence and a hellhound who stood there, licking his jowls.

A familiar voice made her stomach drop. The energy was one she knew and knew well. The stern voice drew all her attention to the door.

"Seriously, Cora? You've been doing this for how long now, and you still can't locate and pull a soul properly?" Jensen's voice was stern, mixed with exhaustion and frustration.

Esme could hear Cora's frustration match Jensen's. "I swear this isn't my fault! I had it and then some strange energy distracted me."

Esme wrinkled her face, knowing the strange energy that threw Cora off was the mixing energy of the hellhound with her own. The bickering ensued and Esme quickly captured the opportunity for her favor. She quickly whirled around, coming eye to eye with the hound. "Back to the shadows." With her whispered command, the hellhound retreated into the shadows and disappeared into the night.

She opened her hand and spoke the word to open the portal. "Aperio." A bright light filled the room. Not wasting any time, Esme ran through. As the portal closed, the office door opened, allowing Jensen and Cora to walk in to meet a frightened woman crouching in the corner.

13

Jensen wandered the hospital halls, listening to the rhythmic beeping of heart monitors and idle chatter. He had already completed two reaping's since leaving the bar that morning and was waiting for his third. Thoughts of Esme and Thalia played tug-of-war with his thoughts. Every fiber of his being wanted to call Esme and demand answers, but Thalia's warning pricked the back of his mind. Aimlessly, he wandered the halls, finding himself in a special spot.

It was a secret spot he and Esme would share when days were hard, and the nights were long. They would stand in front of the windowpane, talking for hours and creating stories. There, the air was alive with new bouncing energy while being oddly peaceful at the same time. This is the room not only held the beginning of life but the start of the end. Jensen rested his forehead on the cold glass, taking in all the new wrinkly faces, coos, and cries. He let out an emotional huff that fogged up the glass. Forcing himself away from the memories and pushing out any thoughts of the women who currently resided in his mind, he checked the time on his watch.

Double-checking the name on the list, he closed his eyes found the energy he was sent for. As his eyes opened, the setting was yet another sterile hospital room. Despite the room's coldness, the warm sunlight peeked through, slanting across the striped beige and pink wallpaper. In the middle of the room was a lonely bed and a disconnected machine. A woman dressed in a soft blue hospital gown with white trim sat on the edge of the bed. Her eyes were glued to the shell of her former self.

Jensen softly spoke. "Meredith, it's time to go."

Meredith stood and turned with vacant eyes. "Who are you, and where am I going?" Her Bostonian accent wobbled at the end of the question.

Jensen offered her his hand, palm up to usher her out. "I'm Jensen, your reaper. I'm taking you to the next stop."

Meredith stood rooted to the scuffed tile floor. She opened and closed her mouth several times. The words sat on the tip of her tongue but refused to leave her lips.

Jensen tried his best to put on a reassuring smile while walking over to the confused woman. "I know this is a lot to take in, but the veil waits for no mortal."

Confusion marred her face as she took a shaky breath. "This is it. I don't even recognize myself." Brushing her fingers over her lifeless hand. She was still reluctant to move. "I know I should be ready, but for some reason, I don't want to go."

Jensen closed the gap between them in two long strides and rested his hand on her shoulder. "This is weird, confusing, and new. New can be scary, but I promise it is painless." He gave her a gentle squeeze. "Now, we do need to be going."

Meredith looked up at the tall reaper standing next to her. His face was impassive while her eyes stung with unshed tears. Before she could utter another word, he transported them to the veil.

They both stood in silence as she processed her new surroundings. Those unshed tears flowed. "I don't understand. Why does this look like my parent's tailor shop?"

Jensen dropped his hand and took a step behind her. "The veil is designed to match the most significant place in a human's life. So, this place must be special to you."

Meredith nodded slowly, rubbing her fingers on the side of her neck. "I used to come here every day after school as a young girl. We spent a lot of family dinners in the back sewing room."

As Jensen stood there, listening to Meredith, one question kept nagging at him. "What did you expect this to look like?" In all his years of reaping, he never spared a thought as to what the people he brought to the veil were expecting. Every encounter he had ever had, he treated as nothing more than a transaction. But for some reason, curiosity got the best of him.

Twiddling her thumbs in front of her hips, Meredith laughed softly. "I don't know. I guess I was expecting a bright white light or a tall figure in a black cloak." She looked back at Jensen, who looked at her as if her assumption were a puzzle he couldn't figure out. She turned back to the tailor shop's double glass doors. "Cliché, right? The whole 'don't go into the light' concept."

Jensen rubbed his jaw as a small smile tugged the corners of his mouth. "Can't say I've ever witnessed a bright light in my line of work. Although, I have heard rumors of it." As he tugged his jacket sleeve up to check the time, his demeanor was stoic again. "It's time to go through that door now, Meredith."

Standing in front of those doors in a setting that was familiar but alien at the same time, Meredith felt dread choking her. "What happens if I don't? If I don't go in those doors? If I don't want to?"

Shoving one hand in his pocket while holding the other out in front of himself, Jensen spoke methodically. "Well, the truth is, you don't have to go. I can't force you to take that step." He darted his eyes past Meredith to the door behind her. "But if you choose not to go through that door, I can't bring you back to the mortal realm. My job is only to bring you to the veil. You'll be stuck here by yourself forever. Once I leave, all these cozy elements leave with me."

Meredith began to chew on her nails, contemplating her choices. Her hand hovered over the pull bar. She turned around to speak to Jensen, only to find Jensen was already walking away. She called out, "Why does it still feel scary?"

Stopping in his tracks and looking over his shoulder, he said, "If it makes you feel any better, there's some decent energy there." This was a small lie. The energy pulsing from the door was unsettling, something she didn't know. Being in the veil already made her skittish.

Mustering all the courage she could scrounge up; Meredith nodded to Jensen and pulled the door open. Once she was through, Jensen closed his eyes and left the veil. As his eyes opened, he found himself at the entrance of the reaper headquarters.

The sound of his dress shoes echoed throughout the lobby until he stopped in front of the elevator. As he reached for the up button, the doors slowly opened, revealing a broad shoulder man standing in the back corner. He was leaning against the railing with his arms crossed over his chest, his face devoid of thought. His copper tinted hazel eyes flicked up and registered the open door.

As the man walked out, he gave Jensen a friendly smile. There was something different about this reaper. The way the energy pushed off him wasn't like the regular reapers in the city. This energy matched Thalia, and maybe, just maybe, rivaled the energy he felt off of Esme earlier. For such a large man, his steps were barcly audible and extremely graceful. The elevator doors closed before Jensen stepped in. The new reaper turned to look at him.

Jensen turned on his heel, eyeing the reaper up and down. His brows wrinkled with curiosity. For the second time that day, curiosity got the better of him. The question slipped from his lips before he could process the words. "Have we met before?"

The other reaper pulled himself to his full height with an all too friendly grin plastered on his face. "Sorry, I don't believe so. I just transferred here." The lilting Welsh inflection poured off each word.

There was something about this reaper that didn't sit well with Jensen. He dared his curiosity further. "I didn't hear about any transfers coming in today. What did you say your name was?"

The other reaper turned toward the door. His baritone voice carried through the empty lobby. "I didn't say what my name was. Clearly, I'm not in your department if you don't know." He raised two fingers to his forehead and gave a small salute. "Have a good one." Even though his tone was cavalier, stress coiled in his shoulders.

Jensen watched the man walk away as an uneasy feeling settled in his mind. He jabbed at the elevator button. The dinging of his phone claimed his attention again. Looking down at the name on the screen caused him to let out an annoyed growl. He swiped to answer the call.

Cora's voice crackled to life. "So, I have another red reap tonight."

He didn't even try to hide the groan in his throat. "Hello to you, too, Cora. Yes, I know you do. I made your list." He pressed the button to his intended floor.

Cora let out her own protested grumble. "It's red. I'm not good at those."

Hard as he tried, he couldn't help but match her frustration with his own. "You're not good at any of this." He pulled the phone away from his ear and winced as a high-pitched shriek crackled through the other end.

"Excuse me? Correct me if I'm wrong, oh great and wise Administrator Jensen," Cora sucked in a sharp breath, getting ready for her tirade, "but isn't it your job and responsibility as my mentor to make sure I'm good at all of this?"

When the elevator doors opened, an unwelcomed sight met him. The onslaught from Cora became background noise in his ear. He averted his gaze and stepped out of the elevator. Casually leaning against a desk, thumbing across a tablet, was Thalia. Seeing him enter, she pushed herself away from the desk, smoothing her clothes while flashing a megawatt smile.

"My, my, isn't this a pleasant surprise." Her eyes roved over him hungrily.

Slowly lowering the phone from his ear, Jensen asked, "What are you doing here? I thought you were commandeering my office." His tone was flat and tired.

Thalia's long legs gingerly strolled over to Jensen. She ran a hand over his jacket and let out an airy laugh. She waved a delicate hand dismissively. "I had some business to attend to, nothing to concern yourself with." She reached up and smoothed a few strands of hair on Jensen's head as if she had done it dozens of times before. "Why are you here, hmm?"

Before he could respond, Cora's voice broke out over the phone. "Jensen. Jensen! Are you still listening to me?"

He lifted one finger in front of Thalia and raised the phone back to his ear. "Cora? Be quiet. Just come to the office building before that reaping, and I'll go with you, okay? Great. Bye."

Thalia inspected her cuticles as she leaned casually against a wall. A playful smirk stretching her mouth. She looked at Jensen through heavy-lidded eyes. Her tongue darted across her lips as she drifted her eyes across his frame.

Annoyance flashed across Jensen's face, but he put that emotion in check, and once again, put on his stoic mask. "My eyes are up here, Director." The words curtly slipped off his tongue. "Now, if you'll excuse me, I have work to get done. You know since my boss decided to storm in and take over my office." He huffed a hot breath, taking a large step away from her. The hungry look in her eyes caused him to shift uncomfortably. How he once fell victim to her seduction remained an enigma to him. Every second he spent near her was draining and intolerable. What he believed to be thrilling, passionate, and lustrous was uncomfortable, forced, and dull. Jensen knew everything about her, and their façade of a relationship was a massive regrettable mistake. One that cost him what he would define as his everything.

Eager to increase the distance between himself and her, Jensen walked briskly to an empty office. He could hear her snicker behind him, followed by her long, elegant, stilettoed strides. A few reapers bustled around the cubicles updating paperwork on the souls they collected or making plans to meet up after their respective shifts were over. A thick stack of green folders were sitting on the edge of the cubicle desk. Snatching the pile and rounding a corner, he found the vacant office, that was once his, and hurried into it. Jensen walked around the small desk and shrugged off his jacket. He tossed it on a corner chair and rolled his sleeves up, trying his best to ignore the stalker he now had. Taking a steady breath, he placed his palms on the cool desk and set a cold gaze on Thalia as she hovered by the doorway, studying him like he was in a petri dish.

"Jensen, darling. Why are you looking at me like that? We're not strangers in any sense. Plus, you called me. So, here I am. Let me be here for you. With whatever you need." Thalia purred out her words as she placed a stray hair back in its proper spot.

His yearning of space from her amplified with every word she uttered. His gaze never left her, and his voice dropped. "Don't call me your darling. Address me by name only. What we have is a professional relationship at best. I called you with a question you have yet to provide any answers to. Unless you have answers for me about what is happening in this city, go back to your own office in a different city, on a different continent. Please."

His words might as well have been a physical slap across her face. Thalia stood there, stunned in silence. The gears in her mind whirred rapidly, attempting to calculate how much hold and persuasion she still had over him. The flirtatious and regal demeanor vanished and a cold, calculating reaper stood in her place. "All right, then, Jensen." Her mouth formed a thin line. "You want answers? The answer has been in front of you the entire time. I already warned you about her. Your precious Esme is hiding something. There is something off about her, and you know it. Also, as for the mortals who have died ahead of schedule," She paused, trying to regain what little composure she had left. "Life and death are a balance. For the souls who didn't die one has to go in its place. Like that little soul, you keep stashed away."

Jensen stood there, tapping his foot on the worn gray carpet. As he placed one hand on the desk before him, the other dragged down his tired face. Between Esme disappearing and reappearing looking worse for wear without explanation and Thalia coming in like a whirlwind, he could feel the strain of stress wearing on him. Her tone softened once more, sensing Jensen's crumbling resolve and took small, graceful steps toward him. "I know this is a lot. There is a lot of chaos in this city. Let me be there for you. Let me help you." She reached out her hand and gently laid her long fingers on his forearm.

The tension between them was heavier than a wet wool blanket. As he clenched and unclenched his jaw, his eyes were drawn down to Thalia's fingers still laying on his forearm. His eyes traced the line of her arm, up past her shoulder, clavicle, neck, and landed on her eyes. A humorless snort escaped his lips as he plucked her fingers away. "Be there for me? Really, Thalia? You need to be here for those souls, not me. I have no reason to distrust Esme. Why would she be involved in this?"

Regaining his composure, Jensen stepped away, pulling out the desk chair and sat heavily. He rocked back in the chair as he rubbed the stubble on his jaw. Thalia was still speaking, but it became nothing more than white noise as his thoughts focused on Esme and Alicia. Could Esme have something to do with all this? How could he fix Alicia's situation? The onslaught of questions drained the last of his energy, and he closed his eyes in defeat of the day. After staring at a wall, he was drawn back to reality as Thalia tapped her nails on the door frame. He had missed the entirety of whatever she was droning on about except for the last few words as she walked out. "When you do, I'll be here waiting." Clicking heels faded down the hall.

Taking in a deep breath, Jensen willed himself to focus on the paperwork that needed to be filled out, signed, and filed. A knock on the door caught his attention. He blinked a few times, taking in the darkened space around him.

Cora leaned against the door, fiddling with a piece of loose string from her shirt. Her eyes darted around the room. "What are you doing here in the dark? I just spent the last fifteen minutes walking around trying to find you."

Rising from his chair, Jensen stretched his arms overhead, releasing the strain from his stiff muscles. "Why didn't you just call me instead of walking around aimlessly?"

If Cora had rolled her eyes any harder, she would have seen the inside of her skull. "I did, multiple times, in fact. I was about to call Esme to chaperone me on this. But then I remembered the fact that she scares me. Anyway, you told me to meet you here. Here I am."

Jensen scanned his phone and scratched the back of his neck. "I guess I left it on silent." After placing the phone in his pocket, he grabbed the discarded jacket and brushed past Cora. Tugging the jacket on, he noticed the now empty cubicles. A single thought ran through his head at this moment. He hated working in the main building. The Twisted Sickle was his domain. The thought of Thalia residing there disgusted him. To him, her presence tainted the establishment and its memories. He looked up at the ceiling, taking a calming breath to collect himself, then turned to Cora, who was still toying with that same piece of string. "Are you ready to try this again?"

Leveling her glare, Cora walked over to Jensen and slapped her hand on his back. "Am I ready for you to criticize me and tell me how horrible I am at my job? Nope. But seeing as you're my mentor, you need to help me. So, we're in this together." She pulled her phone out to find the name and location of the next soul. "Okay, Suzanna Baxter, let's do this."

Jensen rubbed his forehead and sighed. "You sound too excited about this."

Cora rolled her shoulders, aiming her eyes straight to avoid Jensen. "Let me do my thing. I hate red-coded reaps. This is how I get ready for them."

The last thing that was heard in the office before vanishing was Jensen replying with a sarcastic "uh-huh."

The factory was badly lit by broken streetlights, and the moon offered no more light than a nightlight. The energy surrounding the building was burdensome and dark. The entire block was quiet and lifeless.

Cora looked up and down the street, scratching her earlobe. Risking a glance over to Jensen, she could see the annoyance on his face. Still, something was off. Everything was eerily quiet, and the energy rolling out was wrong. For the first time, Cora experienced an emotion that made her clutch to Jensen's arm like a child. Fear took hold of her, and her nails dug into his jacket.

Feeling the darkness spreading and the pressure from the small hand clawing its way into his arm, Jensen turned his full attention to Cora. "Did you pull the soul like I taught you? Focused on her energy only?"

The only response was a muted nod from Cora. The cold air whipped around them, carrying muffled noise from inside the factory. He tapped her hand and nodded. "You know how you say Esme scares you? This emotional energy being pulled is raw fear. You need to push past it. It won't help you or Suzanna Baxter. Focus on her, pull her to you, and you'll end up next to her."

She inhaled a deep breath, letting that cold air numb her nerves, and nodded. She closed her eyes and focused again. Sensing that familiar pull, she quickly grabbed hold of Jensen's hand, and they disappeared yet again. This time, they didn't make it much farther, just to the inside the of building.

Trying to be optimistic, Cora said, "This is progress."

The blank stare Jensen gave her told her more than his words could. In reply to his wordless disappointment, she gave him a shy shrug.

Both reapers stood there, taking in the whirring machines, creating metal pieces. The concrete floor was cracked and stained beneath their feet. Jensen stood there stoically, while Cora worried her bottom lip. Silence stretched for a few minutes until a grating scream was released throughout the factory, overtaking the sound of machines. They shared a meaningful look, but neither moved toward the sound.

Finally, Jensen broke the silence, exasperated. "Cora, try again."

She swallowed a snarky reply. Reaching out for the soul she needed to claim, a darker energy caught her off guard. Instead of seeing a woman before them, all they saw was a door.

Frustration grabbed hold of them both, and it was clear Jensen couldn't take it anymore. "Seriously, Cora? You've been doing this for how long now, and you still can't locate and pull a soul correctly?"

Cora's frustrated tone matched Jensen's. "I swear this isn't my fault! I had it and then some strange energy distracted me."

Just before they could continue their bickering, a bright light flashed from under the door. Cora looked to Jensen for guidance, but his face was impassive. The energy from the other side stirred an overwhelming feeling in his gut.

Was it familiarity? Disbelief? Or could it be something else entirely?

Before Cora could ask what was wrong, he threw open the door. Peeking from behind his shoulder, she could spot a slumped figure on the floor and the matching soul crouching next to it. Jensen stepped aside to give Cora room, but she made little to no effort to move. Sweeping his arm toward the soul, signaling Cora that this was her show to get started, he walked over to the other body in the room.

Cora tiptoed toward the woman. "Suzanna? Suzanna Baxter?"

Wild eyes bore into Cora's. Pure, unadulterated fear was cemented on this woman. Cora gave her a small, kind smile and extended her hand. "Let's get you out of here. How does that sound?"

If fear was locked into Suzanna's eyes, it was etched into her voice. "No. Nope. Not happening. Not if you have one of those things with you, too."

Cora cocked her head to the side, trying to understand the mutterings coming out of the soul in front of her. "What things? I'm only your reaper, Suzanna. I'm not going to hurt you." She followed Suzanna's gaze to Jensen, who was silently studying the scene that had occurred moments earlier. "Don't mind the handsome, grumpy man. He's another reaper, my boss. Not a man of many words." Cora giggled, trying to lighten the mood. She was met with silence from Suzanna and a scoff from Jensen. Again, Cora offered her hand, and Suzanna hesitantly slipped hers in return.

A dim glow flickered between their hands, and Suzanna let out a small exhale. "All right, Jensen, are you walking back or coming with?" Secretly, she was hoping he would walk back somewhere, but a frown found its way to her face as he walked over to them.

His voice was contemplative. "I'm coming with you. I have questions."

Suzanna nodded while Cora arched her brow, questioning his motives but gave no further objections. While holding Suzanna's trembling hand, Cora closed her eyes as Jensen laid his hand on her shoulder. Within seconds, they were transported to the veil. Instead of the normal houses Cora grew accustomed to seeing, they found themselves standing outside a quaint bakery. The brick was accented by purple awnings and charming white lettering. Just the sight alone caused Suzanna to weep.

The woman crying made Cora uncomfortable, who blurted out the first thing that came to her mind. "Please stop crying. I don't do well when souls start crying."

Suzanna nodded her head, muffling a sniffle with her palm. "This is my bakery. It hasn't even been opened a full year yet."

Jensen's curt tone cut through the conversation. "Yes, it's a beautiful establishment. I need to know, what were you talking about back at the factory? What 'thing' were you talking about?" His honey eyes implored Suzanna for an answer. The intensity growing in his eyes emphasized the importance of her answer. Whatever answer she could give was the answer to a puzzle only he was trying to solve.

Suzanna looked over to Cora, who gave her a small encouraging nod. She took a shaky breath while beginning to pick at her cuticles. "It all happened fast and slow at the same time. I remember bits and pieces. I was blacking out when she walked in." Dropping her eyes to the ground, she continued. "The woman that came in before you two, she said she wasn't there for me. I remember her eyes—they were a cold color, but the strange thing was there was a spark of warmth in them."

Jensen stood there, waiting for her story to continue, his face never betraying any thought or emotion. Cora, on the other hand, found that string again and played with it as she listened intently.

Jensen spoke calmly, addressing Suzanna. "Do you remember anything else about this woman? What did she sound like? What did she look like? Was she alone?"

Running a trembling hand through her hair, a quiver broke out across her thin, chapped lips.

Cora quickly walked next to her and placed a comforting hand on Suzanna's cheek. "I know that was scary. You don't have to tell us if it's too hard to talk about. Just go to that door and leave all this behind."

Jensen's harsh tone altered Cora to the mistake of her words. "Yes, she does. We need to know what happened; this is important." He narrowed his eyes at Cora with a flat expression on his face. Cora squinted back at him in a poor attempt to figure out why this was important to him.

While the two reapers stared each other down, Suzanna made her way to her bakery door but stopped when a heavy hand grabbed her wrist. A small yelp escaped her lungs. Jensen had a firm hold on her. She shook her head in defeat. "If I tell you, will you let me go?"

Dropping her wrist, Jensen dipped his head and took a tentative step backward. As he waited for Suzanna to recount her last memory, he shoved his hands in his pockets.

She barreled through her final mortal memory, trying to remember every muddled detail. "The woman I saw, she was petite, cold eyes, dressed in all black, and I want to say she had dark hair, but I can't say for sure."

Sharing a confused glance with Jensen, Cora asked another question. "What thing did she have with her that was scary?"

A visible shudder cascaded over Suzanna. "It was a monster. I swear to God it was something out of a damn nightmare. Yellow eyes, large, something like a bear or a wolf. Holy crap, it was terrifying." Wringing her hands, she darted her gaze between both reapers. Their looks differed greatly. Cora looked as if she were trying to solve the world's greatest riddle, and Jensen looked as though he forgot how to breathe.

Silence loomed over the three of them.

In a meek voice, Suzanna broke the silence. "I'm sorry, that's all I remember."

Cora licked her lips, then fixed a smile on her face. "You did great, Suzanna. Thank you. But now, I believe it's time for you to open that bakery." She rubbed the soul's back, sparks of the ardor fragments flew where she rubbed.

The weight of the world notably lifted off Suzanna's shoulders. Grinning, she pulled open the bakery door, a charming bell sound rang out into the veil, and she was gone.

Jensen stood paralyzed in the same spot as Cora approached him.

She opened and closed her mouth, trying to urge the right question to come out.

Slowly, his eyes found hers. He shook his head in disbelief.

Finally, the words formed on her tongue. "What in the hell was she talking about back there?"

Jensen's voice was thick with hesitation. "Exactly that. It sounds like Infernals. But that energy didn't match any Infernal I know of. It felt more like . . ." The words died on his lips as if refusing to believe the evidence being presented.

Picking up his trailed thought, Cora quietly spoke. "You know who that description sounded like?"

Jensen held a singular finger up to Cora, stopping her thought. He knew exactly what or who she was going to mention, but he couldn't hear it said out loud. "Don't, Cora. Just don't. Let's get out of here. I have a certain reaper I need to speak with."

Thalia's words echoed in his mind. Esme is hiding something. It couldn't be right. It had to be wrong. Without another word, Cora grabbed hold of Jensen's arm, and together, they left the veil.

14

The bright portal closed as Esme stepped through into her apartment. Her clammy hand pressed into her forehead. An invisible vise tightened her skull, causing stars to burst behind her eyes. With her free hand, she clutched her stomach, feeling acid roll through her. Esme dared her feet to move, finding her knees quickly betraying her. "Oh, shit." She winced in anticipation of hitting the ground hard.

Before she could crash to the ground, a strong, muscled arm caught her. Startled would be an understatement for the look on Esme's face. Her eyes widened as she traced the lines of muscled arms up to a baffled, familiar face. "Holy crap. Hey, Cam, how did you get in here?"

Confusion sprawled across his face as he rapidly blinked at her. "You gave me a spare key a while back. I've been worried about you, so I came over to check on you. Alicia's idea." Camryn helped her stand straight but held onto her waist just in case. His hazel eyes narrowed, and his voice dropped a full octave. "Your turn. How do you explain how you got in here?"

A nervous laugh escaped Esme. "That, well. Hmm. That depends on what you saw."

Silent seconds passed between the two reapers. Camryn's hand was still on her waist while their eyes were locked in a battle of wills. His fingers gripping her lower back a little tighter. He finally answered her with one word, and what a damning word it turned out to be. "Everything."

The one word broke the last of Esme's will. Her eyes dropped, and a heavy sigh left her. The weight of all her secrets had finally taken its toll. The reserve well of energy now depleted. She nodded her head meekly. "We're going to need alcohol for this conversation." Esme let out a huff as she patted Camryn's hand.

Eyeing her cautiously, Camryn released her waist and asked, "Got any bourbon?"

Amusement flickered in Esme's eyes. "Sorry. You're in my place, remember? My place means wine."

Camryn scoffed as he followed her into the kitchen. A comfortable silence settled around them. She crouched low to reach into the wine fridge while he pulled down two glasses from a higher cabinet. This is how things had always been between them: comfortable, easy, no judgment. Even though there was a circus of elephants in the room, Camryn didn't push or rush Esme to speak. He only spared a few inquisitive glances toward her as they danced around each other in the small kitchen, pouring wine and gathering snacks. He motioned to the two stools at the kitchen island. She shook her head and waved him over to the living room.

Wordlessly, they sunk back into her couch and sipped wine. He looked around the apartment, looking at all the trinkets placed on her shelves. A large television mounted the wall, tucked in between two tall bookcases. He smiled at the books; it had become somewhat of a challenging game for him. He would try to memorize the titles on her shelves to see if she had added any new ones. One time, he had challenged her to not get any new books for two months. She lasted two weeks.

By the window was an overgrown calico kitten plant. Plants took over her office, living room, and bedroom. He understood why she had so many plants. She saw life ending in the worst ways possible daily. She had for centuries. Surrounding herself in plants like succulents gave her a chance to be around something alive that was hard to kill. After she had split from Jensen, she would find the most pathetic-looking plants around the city and bring them back to her apartment. She nurtured them until she could plant them in a community garden around the city.

The same went for her love of books. Once the story ended, she could always revisit those characters and worlds. It was something he admired about her, the softness in her that few witnessed. She was the one who taught him how important hobbies were. At first, he hated the idea of reading and still wasn't fond of it. But the museum was a place they visited quite often. She made it a point to go to one each month with him. Especially with so many in the city. He would pick a museum and ask Esme question to see if she had witnessed anything from that point in history, or he would share his experiences with her.

It wasn't until their sixth visit that he had asked why she decided to visit these places with him.

Her response was simple but impacted him to that day. "It shows us that, while tragic things happen, so do beautiful things. You can't appreciate the beautiful without the ugly." For years, he had known her, their friendship slowly blossoming overtime. But as she spoke her words while in awe of the art mortals had created, it dawned on him. She was the true masterpiece, and he was in awe of her.

Camryn set his glass down before casually pulling a single curl that had escaped Esme's ponytail. As he watched the curl spring back into place, he broke the silence. "So?"

A grumble formed in the back of her throat as her shoulders rolled forward in defeat. "Where do I even start?" She scrubbed a hand down her face, then nodded. Angling her body, she looked Camryn right in the eyes. "The Grim Reaper taught me to use portals about two years ago. It was more of a crash course. I never needed to use it until recently, when I started to lose my apparition ability. Not having used it, I'm extremely rusty." Camryn's eye never left hers as he wore a blank expression. Sensing he wasn't going to speak, Esme pressed on. "I work with a hellhound for all of my reapings."

The pregnant silence swelled as Camryn never blinked or moved a single muscle. "I think we need more wine for this." He emptied the bottle between them, pouring generously in his own. As he lifted the glass to his lips, his eyes found Esme over the rim. After a few gulps, he set the glass back down. "Please, tell me more. When did you start working with a hellhound?"

Simply nodding, Esme took a fortifying breath to calm her nerves before meeting Camryn's eyes once again, a faraway look creeping into her eyes. "I didn't always work with my hound. That started when I decided to stay in this city and learned how to use a portal. It was one of two conditions given to me by the Grim Reaper." As she paused to gather thoughts, she rolled the nearly empty wine glass between her palms. "The second condition was using portals, but it's not exactly an easy thing to master. No other reaper besides him has ever used them. They're finicky and energy suckers. I have to speak to open them, and sometimes, I don't even get the location right."

Camryn sat there dutifully, simply listening and nodding along as Esme spoke. When there was a break in her story, his brows pinched in concentration. He carefully mulled over how he wanted to phrase his question, knowing it had taken this long for Esme to start revealing truths. "Explain the bruises to me." He knew the phrasing had to be a demand and not a question. The thought of some other being hurting her fueled a heat in his chest. Reapers were not fighters; they did a job to keep both sides happy.

In the past, Celestials and Infernals had taken advantage of them, using them as pawns. That's why the Grim Reaper had banned them from socializing with anyone outside of their race. They stayed in their clustered groups and formed connections that way. It was because of Esme coming through different areas and redistributing them on occasion new reapers were introduced to new areas.

The serious tone with an undercurrent of worry in Camryn's voice made her wince. Esme had grown accustomed to the gentler, laid-back Camryn. The Camryn that never pushed her limits and accepted her and her decisions without question or judgment.

Guilt shot through her heart. She knew he worried about her, yet she kept these secrets preciously guarded to herself.

She knew he deserved the truth, but was tonight the night for this heavy heart to heart? The little energy she had left in her was leaving her body while her muscles ached, and the incessant throbbing in her head was increasing. Esme's outfit grew constrictive and irritating.

Squeezing her eyes shut, she let out a breathy "dammit." She shifted on the mustard-yellow couch and rubbed her hands down her thighs. "I'll tell you everything, I promise. Let me get changed. It's been a hell of a long week, and this is an even longer story." Esme didn't wait for Camryn to respond as she hastily stood to stretch and made her way into the bedroom. The clothing she had stripped off from earlier still littered across her floor. Esme looked down at them, contemplating picking them as she passed them; she decided stepping over the clothing was the better option.

Once she was in the comfort and privacy of her bedroom, she shut the door with a gentle click. The pressure of carrying the weight of the world released with a heavy sigh. A debate waged war in her mind. What was the best way to tell her best friend she wasn't what he believed her and known her to be all these years? Could she or should she even tell him the truth? Is there a correct way to say she wasn't just a run-of-the-mill reaper? With each passing thought, a new article of clothing was discarded.

Her black clothing laid in a pile by her feet. Pacing her room, she debated all thoughts entering and fleeing her mind. She stood in the middle of the room in her underwear, inhaling a bolstering breath, knowing what she had to do. Camryn deserved to know the truth. Lying to him was something that she couldn't bring herself to do anymore. He had been there for her through thick and thin. Esme made up her mind: she was going to tell him everything. That was the last thought she had before the world around her turned black as her bruised body buckled, meeting the hard ground.

The loud thump caused Camryn to jump from his seat, spilling wine all down his shirt. "Es?" No reply. "You good in there?" The panic in his voice was undeniable. Silence was the only reply to his calls. Knowing the state he found her in when she entered the apartment, he didn't hesitate to charge down the hall. He slid on scattered clothing in the hall before he slammed the bedroom door open. The door's impact against the wall caused a few hanging plants to fall from the wall, spilling dirt on the tidy, dark brown dresser.

His worried eyes landed on her crumpled petite frame on the floor instantly. She laid there on the dark floral area rug. Her face turned and reflecting in the trifold golden dressing mirror. Panic surged in his chest, followed by guilt. He knew something was wrong with her. He should have seen this coming somehow. She should have never left his sight. The strong energy that swirled around her just that morning was faint and flickering. He scooped her up gently into his arms, noticing how cold her body felt. Pulling her tighter to his chest, he gently called to her. "Es, can you hear me?" Her limp body held no reply for him. "Come on, open your eyes for me." Still no answer. "Please, I need to know you're okay," he whispered.

His eyes dragged down her body, noticing for the first time that she was only in her underwear. Camryn held her closer as he carefully stood and made his way to her bed. He tenderly brushed stray curls from her eyes. Cradling her with one arm, he turned down the silk sheets on her bed with the other, then proceeded to lay her on the mattress and tuck the covers tightly around her. He squatted down on the floor next to the bed. "You've always been there for me, and I've always been here for you. So, don't worry, Es. I'll stay right here. I'll watch over you until you wake up."

A pained moan left Esme's throat as she curled further into herself. "I just want help."

His lips brushed her icy forehead, a glimmer of warmth between them. She gently sighed as her face relaxed. Camryn stood from his position and clicked the side table lamp on. He walked to the door and found the light switch to the overhead before clicking it off.

True to his word of watching over her, he perched on the corner of her bed, looking down on her. "Dammit, Es, what is happening to you?" Hours passed with Esme asleep on her bed and Camryn watching over her. He thanked the powers that be he had completed his list earlier that evening. Leaving her felt wrong.

Camryn stood and looked around the room. The walls were onyx, and her black platform queen-sized bed sat in between the two windows of the bedroom. There were end tables on either side of the bed. Journals and a tablet lay on one, and the other was tidy, with only the lamp that cast a warm dusk light in the room. He shook his head when he perused the bookcase in her room. New titles were hidden in between well-loved books. "All right, let's see what these are about." Camryn picked a purple book off the shelf that only had the embossing of a black rose on the cover and an author name. As he skimmed the pages, his eyes widened. "Wow, kinky, okay. I feel like I'm seeing an entirely new side of you, Es." His eyes darted over to still form. He placed the book back and grabbed another, then made his way back to the spot on the corner of the bed.

Camryn admitted defeat to the war of keeping his eyes open when his phone rang, causing him to spring them open. The name scrolling across the screen caused him to still. Why would Ansel be calling him? While it's true, he worked directly for Ansel. He had never received a call from Ansel before unless it was urgent. Ansel was a hands-off reaper compared to the other two. He handed the curated departmental lists, and that was it. He put his faith in his Administrators to do their jobs accordingly.

The phone continued ringing as Camryn stood and quietly made his way out of the bedroom and into the bathroom across the hall. He wanted to be near in case Esme woke up but didn't want to wake her with his conversation. As Camryn stepped into the bathroom, realizing the wine stain was still on his shirt, he stripped it off while he answered his phone.

Two other reapers and an unlikely companion made their way through the reaper's apartment building. The elevator doors opened on to the top floor, and the unlikely trio stepped out.

"I can't believe you convinced me to bring her with us." Irritation rang evident in Jensen's voice as he spoke to Cora.

"What do you want me to do? Tyler was busy, and she's going stir-crazy in the bar. It's the right thing to do, and you know it," Cora smugly retorted.

Alicia, who was walking behind the pair, darted her eyes back and forth, watching, letting out an overly dramatic sigh, gaining the attention of both bickering reapers. "You don't have to fight over me. There's plenty of me to go around."

Jensen and Cora stopped walking and turned a dumbfounded expression to Alicia, who simply had a humorous grin on her face. "Oh, goody, you've both shut up now." She chuckled as she stepped in front of them and continued their walk down the hall. "This is it, right?" She pointed to a door at the end of the hall.

Jensen walked up to the door but froze as his eyes glazed over. He felt two different energies, one he knew for sure was Camryn, but the other was wrong. It couldn't have been Esme's. It wasn't warm, steady, or strong. This energy was barely noticeable, cold, flickering, but eerily powerful. Without a second thought, he dug out his keys that still had Esme's key attached to it.

"You have a key to her apartment? Aren't you going to knock first?" Cora asked in a high-pitched tone. "She doesn't even know we're all coming!"

The only response she received from Jensen was a half-hearted eye roll. "She never asked for the key back."

The trio walked into Esme's apartment and quickly noted the dim lighting, empty wine bottle, and glasses. The next thing to hold their attention was the scattering of clothing over the floor leading down toward the bedroom and the running of water in the bathroom. Jensen's jaw tightened as his knuckles turned white.

Alicia hesitantly placed a hand on Jensen and Cora. "You know what, this probably isn't the best time to ambush her with twenty-one questions. We should come back in, like, in an hour or three."

The flowing water stopped, and the bathroom door opened. Camryn felt the new energy in the apartment growing. He turned the corner, walking into the living room. The sight of a pissed-off-looking Jensen, a shocked Alicia, and an extremely uncomfortable Cora greeted him. "Hey. What are you doing here?" Camryn stood there, scratching his earlobe. Clearly not registering the situation.

A tired moan grabbed everyone's attention. They all turned to see a nearly naked Esme rubbing her eyes sleepily walking down the hall.

Something in Jensen snapped, causing him to see red. He found himself lunging toward Camryn.

Esme's Apartment

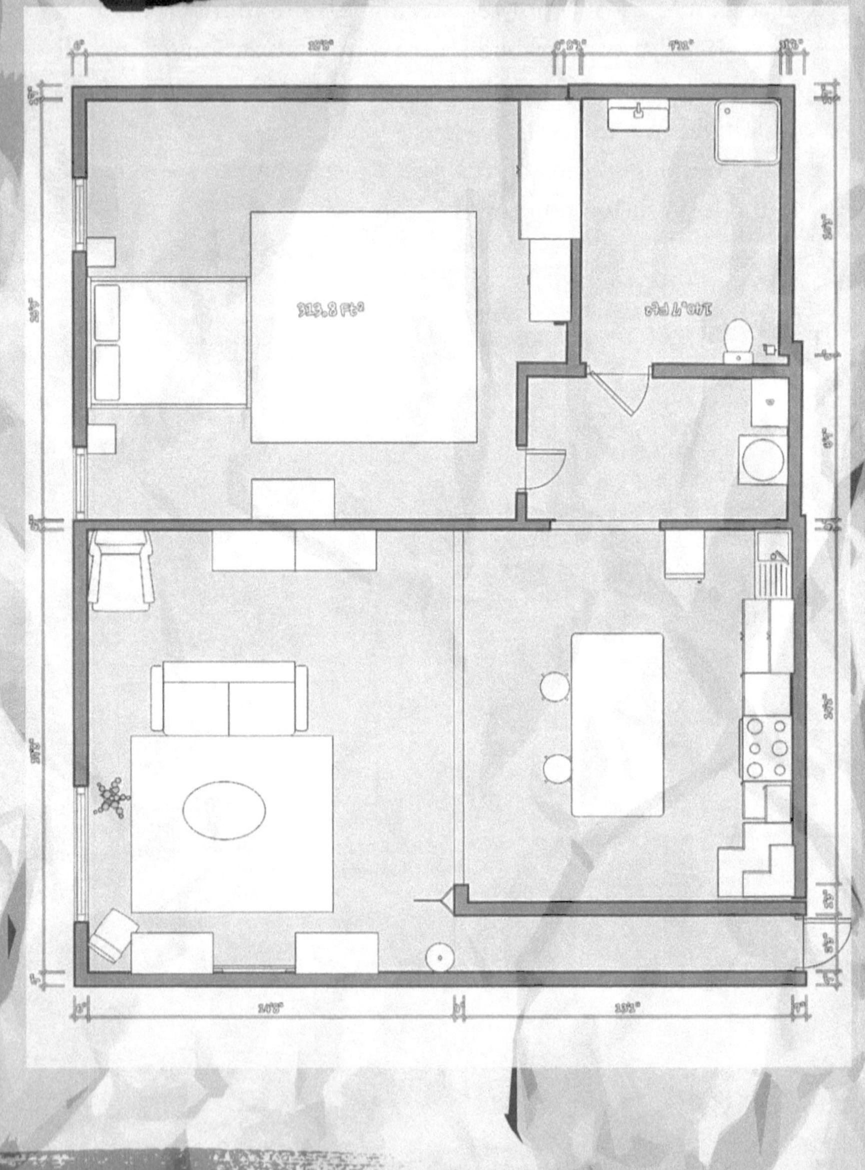

A solid punch landed square on Camryn's jaw. Alicia and Cora stood there with their mouths agape, watching a brawl play out in front of them.

"Dude, what the hell!" Camryn's rhetorical question was emphasized by a perfect jab to Jensen's eye.

As both reapers managed to land blow for blow and shoved each other into the living room, Esme threw her hands up and huffed in annoyance, mumbling about how these men were idiots. She stormed into her room and threw on an oversized gray sweater that grazed her mid-thigh and snatched an extra shirt for Camryn.

Bangs, thuds, and shatters filled the apartment. Shouting emerged from Cora and Alicia as they attempted to separate both men.

"I knew it! I knew I could never trust you. You were always looking for a way to weasel yourself into her pants." The words dripped like pure venom from Jensen's mouth.

"What the hell are you talking about? The only weasel here is you." Camryn shoved Jensen with all his might into the bookshelf, causing an avalanche of leather-bound novels and odd trinkets to fall. "Whatever you arrogantly assumed happened here didn't." He paused to collect his words and compose himself, but the straining tendons in Camryn's neck portrayed something else entirely. He pointed in Jensen's direction, who was now slowly standing. "Even if it did, it's none of your business. She's not your girl or concern anymore. You sealed that fate yourself."

Jensen could feel the anger festering. "No, you made sure of it. Always meddling and coming in to play the hero. Just admit it already: you never got over her, either. I see the way you look at her. It's clear as day."

A flash of resentment and displeasure flicked across Esme's face. She stood silently at the edge of the room. Her brows lowered, her lips drawn in a tight line. She watched as these two men turned her sanctuary into pure chaos. Energy stirred in her, making her muscles ache and her head pound again.

"Enough!" A formidable voice ricocheted in every corner of the apartment. Cold, dark, powerful energy rippled over every surface. The three reapers and Alicia froze for a second before slowly pivoting until they pinpointed the foreign voice.

Esme stood there, panting heavily as the energy rolled off her in droves. The voice that emanated from her was alien, even to her own ears. She took a few steps forward and stumbled as her vision blurred. Jensen rushed to Esme before her head could connect to the ground. That cold energy rolling off her flickered the lights, causing the bulbs to shatter. Glass confetti littered the floor.

Cora and Alicia yelped and scurried closer to Camryn, who pulled them closer to his chest. Jensen embraced Esme closer to him until he noticed the spastic movements in her body. He pulled away from her slightly to find her eyes had rolled back to show only their whites as she convulsed in his arms. Jensen froze, horror-stricken by what was unfolding in his arms.

When her body had finally stopped, the lights had been blown out. The once warm apartment was now only illuminated by the cold slivers of moonlight unfolding across the walls and floor. The silence was deafening.

Until Alicia spoke. "You're all reapers, right?"

Camryn hummed in response, since Jensen was still frozen holding Esme.

With a shaking finger pointing at Esme, Alicia posed what might be the most important question of that night. "Then, why is she bleeding?"

It was only then the others snapped out of shock to notice the trickles of blood leading out of Esme's nose, eyes, and ears. Jensen used the palm of his hand to gently wipe away the blood from her face. Cora sunk into the couch, massaging her forehead. Alicia scurried off to the kitchen to rummage a few dish towels to help Jensen with Esme. Camryn stood there, tapping his foot in thought.

Once Alicia was done wiping the trails of blood from Esme's face, Jensen lifted her carefully and strode into her room. She grabbed the extra shirt that had fallen to the floor and handed it off to Camryn.

Jensen sat on the queen-size bed, still cradling her as if she were made of glass. His eyes traced the lines and curves of her face when the sound of a small knock brought him out of his trance. He looked up to see Alicia in the doorway.

"Camryn wants to speak with all of us." Alicia's voice was barely above a whisper as she looked at Jensen with soft eyes.

Jensen nodded, afraid that his voice would crack. Never in all his existence had he experienced the panic and fear that blossomed in him over Esme. So many things had gone so right for them and so wrong at the same time. As he tucked her back into bed, Alicia stepped next to him.

"You're in love with her, aren't you." Alicia stated it as more of a fact rather than a question.

Jensen still nodded his head in agreement. "I never stopped being in love with her. How could I? She's the reason the world stills."

With a gentle tone and tapping of her toes, she asked, "What's it like, loving her?"

A large smile that could outshine the sun stretched on his face. "It's like catching smoke in your hands. The thrill and joy of catching it just sweeps you up. Then, when you do have it, you're almost too afraid to open your hand to see if it was there at all." His smile faltered. "But when you open it, you witness the most magnificent whirlwind of colors. You cherish it and admire the feel of it twirling in your fingers."

Rubbing his back, she sighed. "Maybe, one day, you can catch that smoke again."

He let out a deep sigh and a tired smile and walked into the living room.

Cora was placing books back onto the bookshelf while Camryn swept up pieces of broken glass from the trinkets that fell onto the floor. Jensen winced a little, looking at the broken trinkets. He knew Esme had collected those during her years of travel and were irreplaceable. Alicia skirted by him and picked up the wine bottle and glasses to place them in the kitchen.

Looking around, he decided he would pick up the clothes laying on the floor. As Jensen gathered Esme's clothes in his arms, he thought back to when they lived together. He would be sitting down, reading, and Esme would come home after finishing her list. She would give him a deep kiss and strip her clothes off as she walked into the shower. He would always follow the trail as an invitation, and they would get lost in each other for the night.

Jensen placed the bundle of clothing into the washer and shook his head, attempting to rid his mind of those memories for the time being. He walked back into the living room, where everyone else was sitting on the couch or perched in reading chairs. His eyes were drawn to an elegant red velvet chair pushed off into a darkened corner of the living room. It sat alone, the walls around it bare compared to the rest of the space with no light source anywhere near it. Letting out a sigh, he picked up his old chair, the one he had to convince Esme to let him move into her apartment and settled near the rest of the group.

"All right, Camryn, we're all here, sans Esme. What do you know?" Jensen was eager to find the underlying cause of this mystery.

Rolling his shoulders and giving a firm nod, Camryn decided to tell them everything he learned about Esme. He started with how she came into her apartment, the hellhound, and the deal she had to make. "I know there was more she was going to tell me but then she collapsed. I stayed with her for a while when I got a call from Ansel. After that call, you all came in, and you know the rest."

"I'm sorry. I think I heard you wrong. Did you say she works with hellhounds?" The incredulous tone matched Jensen's face.

Cora sat in a round, gray reading chair trying to process all the new information, knowing everything in this situation was well beyond her. "Here I am, struggling to collect souls the traditional way, and Esme is over here portal jumping with hellhounds." The statement was simply a thought left unfiltered and meant for no one in particular. Alicia couldn't help but laugh at Cora's train of thought. Her laughter was soon followed by the chuckles of Camryn, then Jensen.

"I know this is like super serious and whatnot"—Alicia started with a glint of admiration in her eyes—"but Esme seems even more badass now."

"The point is not to be badass, Alicia." Jensen scrubbed his hands down his face, then turned toward Cora. "Cora, pop quiz."

Cora groaned and rolled her eyes. "Please, no."

"Cora. Why is it a bad idea for Esme to be working with hellhounds?" Jensen leveled his gaze over to Cora, waiting for her answer.

While Cora tucked her knees into her chest, trying to find some comfort in the little armchair, she fidgeted with her fingers. "Well, um. Ah. I . . . I guess it has to do with us reapers being impartial and not working directly for any side?"

Camryn smirked. "I see you're good with theory, just not the practical application."

She knew his assessment was right. She shrugged, defeated. Feeling someone staring at her, she turned her head and caught Esme leaning against the wall, silently observing everyone. "Holy crap, Esme! You're up. I didn't even sense you come in."

All eyes turned to Esme as she stood there. Something was quite different about her. Her energy was different from before; her body now looked fragile. Her once warm eyes reflected on everyone coldly. "Thank you, Alicia. It can be badass working with hellhounds. Also, it's a hellhound. Singular. I only work with one, mine. One is more than enough." She smiled at Jensen, but it didn't quite reach her eyes.

The tension in the air was making the other reapers and Alicia squirm in their chairs. Alicia raised a shy hand in the air. "Question. Actually, a few questions for Esme." She sat up a little taller. "First question, what did Jensen mean when he said Camryn never got over you, either? Second question, why did you have to make a deal to stay here? There's another question somewhere in my mind, and I'll think of it."

At the second question, Esme's eyes darted over to Jensen and softened before hardening them again. It was so quick no one else noticed it, except for the man it was directed toward. He couldn't help but feel curious about the answer, too.

Before answering the questions, Esme's eyes searched for a place to sit in her living room. She was never one to have large gatherings, since all the reapers would just gather at the bar, so her seating was limited. Seeing Jensen sitting on that red velvet chair brought back so many memories and emotions for her. She was transported back to when it was just the two of them. Tucking herself into his chest as he wrapped his arms around her while he read. As if the same memory was playing in his mind, Jensen adjusted himself on the chair and gave her a knowing and inviting smile. To say she wasn't tempted would have been a lie. A large part of her craved to be near him, to feel his caresses and kisses again. But the larger part of her reminded her of everything else, all she did for him, and all he did to her.

Esme's eyes narrowed, and her tumultuous energy picked up again. The air became oppressive, any fragments of warmth in the apartment quickly dissipating. Everything turned cold, the air, energy, looks, her. The tension grew palpable, and Cora quickly got up from her selected seat and offered it to Esme while squeezing herself in between Alicia and Camryn.

Esme leaned into the back of the chair, sitting with one foot underneath her. She let out a breath, and the energy rolling off her became gentle ripples. "Well, to answer your first question, Camryn and I had a fling back in the 1940s in Europe. He was new to the area, and I had been there for quite some time. I showed him all the local reaper haunts. We had fun for a while, but that's all it ever was. We both knew it was never meant to go any further than that." Her answer was simple, honest, and straightforward. "It was years, and I mean decades, before I had even met Jensen. Both Camryn and I moved on from that. Apparently, Jensen holds grudges over things predating him."

A heated look intensified between Esme and Jensen as he grumbled incoherent words under his breath. Camryn simply nodded while placing his cheek on his fist, reliving a memory. Alicia couldn't help but get consumed with the drama as she scooted closer to the edge of her seat. For the first time in the night, Esme grew uncomfortable as she bounced her knee repeatedly. "Now, I guess I should tell you why I had to make an agreement." She gave a small smile to no one in particular as her gaze was set on the wall opposite her. The smile never reached her eyes. "I was never meant to stay in this city. Hell, I was never meant to stay in this country. Before I came here, I was known as the 'roaming reaper.' I traveled everywhere with Death. It's not common to have our kind globe-trotting anymore because of the headquarters placed in every major city. So, seeing a reaper traveling with the Grim Reaper constantly, and looking the way I do, caught the attention of others. Then I got my nickname 'roaming reaper' at a dive bar in Berlin."

Esme paused her story to stand and stretch her sore muscles and pushed open the curtains in the living room, allowing more moonlight to sweep in. "I came here because this is where Death sent me. The city was having issues, and I needed to resolve them. I never questioned—just followed—and completed the tasks he gave me. I bumped into Camryn at the office, and we decided to catch up at The Twisted Sickle once his list was done for the day. That's where I met Jensen."

Jensen stretched his arms over his head. "I remember that night. I remember seeing you and thinking an angel walked in. There was an overwhelming need to be near you.

So, I invited myself over to that table you had covered in papers. Then we felt the tether of the eternal paramour." He chuckled, lost in memory, before scrunching his face. "What does how our relationship started have to do with you working with a hellhound, Es?"

Esme bit her lip and shook her head. This was something she never told him. She never intended for him to find out, especially like that. "You don't get to call me Es. I've already told you that. Also, it has everything to do with you. I did it all for you."

"What?" All three reapers and Alicia asked in unison, but Esme could only focus on the pained questioning voice that belonged to Jensen.

"Three years into our relationship, I was still roaming around. You asked me if I could stay here. I told you I would ask, but what you didn't know was it came with a cost. I asked Death if I could stay here, at least on a trial basis. He asked me why I wanted to stay. I gave a half truth. My reason was that this city needed new Administrators. The green department never had anyone, and it was bogging down the system. Drew was transferred from this city's red Administrator position to fill a vacancy in another country after her mishap, leaving the red Administrator position vacant here. I offered to be the red interim Administrator, giving myself more work while I found someone else. I never intended to find anyone because, if I did, I would have to leave. A stipulation of being Strategos is always moving. I'm not allowed to settle down. No one is allowed to follow me, but I figured, if my other half was of equal standing, he would see the benefit of having two of us roaming. Sharing the title and work."

Jensen stood, shoved his hands in his pockets, and started pacing. "You hid the truth about us? What do you mean, equal standing?"

All eyes were on Esme. She let out a small breath of defeat. "I didn't want you to find out, not like this. I convinced him to promote you to Administrator. Not just because I wanted to be with you, but you worked hard and deserved it. Thalia never promotes any reaper in her division. She's too much of a control freak. He always had to promote for her and always took my input into account." She wrung her hands. "There's more. I'm also the fourth reaper to be created alone. I have no memories of ever appearing at the falls like everyone else. I was just here. After me, the rest followed in groups."

Guilt riddled Esme's face, while Jensen was emotionless and trying to pinpoint the emotion that permeated in his essence. "How does the hound come into play here?" Jensen's voice was thick.

"For me to stay here, I had to agree to work with a hellhound. Making my own department and specialty while the hound helped to mask my whereabouts. He told me it wasn't safe for me to stay in one place. In the past, other beings have tried to abduct me or do unspeakable things to me. Wouldn't a one-of-a-kind reaper fetch a pretty price? This was the solution. The hound acts like a bodyguard.

"He's never too far from me." Her eyes were downcast, but her words were straightforward.

Camryn interjected. "Es, why didn't you tell anyone? Why do look so banged up?"

That was it, the moment where all cards needed to be laid on the table. Esme just didn't know if they were ready for the truth. She stood there, contemplating omitting certain aspects; it wasn't exactly a lie, since she still didn't know if it was safe to say anything at all. While she struggled to form words, her bottom lip worried between her teeth. It was a nervous habit she hadn't done in months. Jensen fixated on her lips, longing to rub his thumb on her bitten lip to tug it free. But everything that was just confessed nagged at him.

He had the status because of Esme. The reason she began working on the side of Infernals was for him. The reason Thalia took notice of him was because of Esme pushing for his promotion, even though he knew deep down he never actually earned it. During that time, he was more laid back doing the bare minimum. His head kept spinning; did she say she was the fourth created? As in singular? She had her own department? "Dammit, Esme! Start talking. None of this makes any sense."

She released her swollen lip from her teeth and snapped a cold stare at Jensen. "I couldn't tell anyone. I took an oath to keep my hound and job a secret. The answer to why I look like I went nine rounds in a cage fight is something I figured out on my own when I went missing. I'm not a normal reaper like the rest of you. I'm half mortal."

The collective silence spoke volumes. Every movement in the apartment became idle, even the twinkling stars in the night sky stilled. What Esme had confessed was not possible. Reapers were not mortal in any way, shape, or form.

In all the unfolding truths, Cora found her voice to break the pregnant silence. "How? How is that possible, and how do you know?"

Jensen's pacing stopped abruptly, and he recalled what Thalia had told him earlier. Not to trust Esme that she was hiding something. She was hiding quite a bit. The truth was, he wanted to know the answers to Cora's questions as well because none of this was okay or made any sense to him.

"Remember how I went missing for months? Well, after Cam, Jensen and I had met up to discuss Alicia's situation, I left to collect my soul. I wasn't feeling like myself, but this soul had a contract that was about to expire, and I had to collect on it. Unwisely, I pushed through the throbbing pain that grew in my head and portal-jumped to meet my hound and fetch the soul." Esme turned her attention toward the books on her shelves, silently admiring the leather-bound tomes. It helped to distract her from the intrusive and accusing looks were aimed at her. "Working with a hellhound is different than how we normally collect a soul. I show up before the soul departs the human body because the hound hunts the soul down. I make sure that the hound does indeed hunt successfully and devours the soul. I'll admit that the hunting aspect is a bit thrilling, but I'm not one to enjoy the devouring part." She turned around and was met with horrified looks on her fellow reapers' faces.

Alicia was completely engrossed as if she was hearing a ghost story at summer camp. "That particular soul ran, thinking he could outrun death." Her laugh was dark and sent chills crawling across the bodies in the room. "It wasn't the first time a soul tried, but I couldn't pull him to me like others because he was for the hound to devour, not for me to escort. I didn't have a tie to him, so I had to chase him. What I hadn't counted on was for my body to appear solid as I ran across traffic to catch up with the hound. One minute, I was running, the next, I was hit by an SUV."

Alicia winced, remembering her moment of demise. "That's not fun. I would know."

Esme tapped the tip of her nose, then pointed at Alicia. "I woke up in a hospital as a Jane Doe hooked up to machines. I was too weak to go anywhere. I had no choice but to remain in the hospital and pretend I had amnesia. I had my phone on me, but I couldn't call any of you because of my oath. I called Death instead."

Camryn sat there with his hand covering his mouth, wrapping his mind around everything. Cora looked out of her depth. She was only there to confirm what she and Jensen heard in the veil. Jensen had his hands shoved so far down his pockets they were beginning to strain at the seams. With the lack of interruption, Esme continued her story. "When I had enough energy, I opened a portal and left the hospital. I've called him repeatedly; there's no answer. I haven't been able to get ahold of him for I don't know how long now. He's missing. I've called my contacts everywhere. No one has seen or heard from him."

Jensen slotted his fingers in his hair. "Mortal? You're part human? That's why you're bruised, and you bleed. But how are you human? That isn't possible."

Esme spread her arms out wide. She had hoped that finally telling them the truth would lift a weight off her shoulders, but it complicated things more. More questions sprung than she had answers for. "I wish I knew the answer, but I don't. That night, you called me to evaluate Cora. I was in the office, going through his personal library, trying to find an answer."

"Did you find anything?" Camryn chimed in.

"I didn't," Esme replied. "I didn't get a chance to finish researching. I had to go meet up with Cora. You've never seen the amount of books in there. I would need to spend days in there or have a team to properly research everything."

Jensen arched a brow and pointed at Esme. "How did you get into his office? You need a special key to access that floor." Suspicion laced his tone.

Esme looked flabbergasted; of all the questions he could have, that's what he wanted to know.

She rubbed her temples. "I work with him, Jensen; I have my entire existence. He gave me the key when that office was built. I have access to every office he has around the world. I always have. Strategos, remember?"

Jensen shook his head. This is all too much, too wrong. "Esme, this is all wrong. Both you and the Grim Reaper knowingly sided with Infernals. Also, how are you sure you're part human?"

"Since I woke up in that hospital room. Heart monitor beeping kind of gave it away. Try and keep up." She fixed her eyes on Jensen. The emotions playing across his face were enough to make her feel guilty about all the secrets. She didn't want to admit any more truths, but what would be the point of holding any more secrets? "I guess I'll admit I'm the reason why we aren't allowed to apparat all over the place. It was another security measure to keep me hidden."

Cora shot up from her seat. "You lied to me! You told me that other reapers were abusing that ability, so it was put to a stop."

Esme leaned against the shelves and picked some lint off her sweater. "I partially lied. During my inspection of the city years ago, there was a small group partaking in voyeurism."

Jensen laughed incredulously. "You're pretty good at this lying thing, Esme."

Camryn stood, casting a menacing glare at Jensen. "That's not fair, and you know it. What the hell do you expect her to do? It's amazing that she was able to hold it all in for this long."

Jensen crossed the living room with quick and precise strides. His mind was unable to form any logic to any of this.

Thalia was right all along; Esme couldn't be trusted. "Can't you see how insane this all is?"

Her truth bared for this group had Esme feeling vulnerable. This was a new feeling for her, and Jensen's reaction fueled the inferno of emotions that had been kept as embers. "Oh, fuck off. I'm so sorry my existence doesn't fit into your perfect color-coded world. I don't know what more you want from me. I'm in all this because of you. I literally gave you everything you have, everything you claimed you wanted. I gave you everything I could give, all of me, and more!"

Her words hit like a smack to the face. "I didn't know you did all that, Esme."

She walked back to the armchair and slumped down. Her energy was flickering, and she was trying her best to rein it in to avoid another blackout moment. "It shouldn't matter if you knew or not. You asked me repeatedly to stay, and I found a way to make it work. Not you, me. You never proposed any solutions. I found one, and I paid the price. For fuck's sake, I'm still paying it. Do you know why? Because all that mattered to me was you and being with you, being enough for you. You are—were my other half. I would have done anything for you because love makes you stupid and do stupid things. I love—loved you more than I loved myself."

"Dammit, you were enough. You are enough. You've always been more than enough. We could have found another way to make it all work." Jensen moved closer to her, but Camryn blocked Esme's body.

Esme stood, sidestepping Camryn, and stalked closer to Jensen, not caring at all that she had to crane her neck to meet his eyes. "That's real rich coming from you. I clearly wasn't enough. If I were, you wouldn't have pounced on the chance to be with Thalia. On several different occasions, might I add. When Camryn called me to say where you were with her, I went to Depravity and confirmed what I had been denying to myself, and it broke me. I gave everything I had and sacrificed everything, and it still wasn't enough. Don't give me that crap line of finding another way to make it work. You clearly lost interest when you didn't have to chase me anymore and strung me along until the next big opportunity came sauntering your way."

The small apartment shrunk with the energy flaring from the three standing reapers. Jensen turned his attention to Camryn. "You were the one that told her?"

"You're damn right. I saw you and Thalia all over each other in the Infernal infested club, knowing that you were supposedly in love with Esme. I called her because she deserves better than you." No regret laced Camryn's voice. "Thalia had somehow found out that I was the one who told Esme, which caused her to lose her shiny new toy. That's why I got put on training duty. Because I told my friend what she deserved to know."

Cora scooted closer to Alicia as they both watched the scene playing in front of them. The other three had completely forgotten they were even there. Cora leaned in. "Are you following what they're arguing about?"

Alicia sat back farther into the couch, pulling her knees into her chest before whispering, "Kinda, but I'm pretty sure we missed a few seasons." Their conversation was cut short by raised voices.

"I never knew she did that or why she would do that Camryn." He rubbed his clavicle. "But, Esme, I told you— begged you to let me fix this, fix us. It all sounds like total bullshit, but I can't recall the moment I decided I wanted her or ever thought I would want her. I could never want anyone other than you. You're my reason for everything. You are my eternal paramour. Just you, and no one else." Jensen's voice broke. So much he didn't know what involved and revolved around him, and it was eating away at his conscience.

A bitter laugh escaped Esme. "I've already told you: there is no fixing this or us. You broke me. You left me broken and shattered in pieces and dumped in a grave. Now I'm stuck in this mess, and I can't find a way out."

"I could have fixed it if you let me. I wanted those pieces, Esme. I wanted all those broken pieces of you because they're mine. Hell, I still want them. Those are my beautiful, perfect pieces because you're mine, broken, shattered, or whole. You've always been mine, and I've always been yours. I loved you, dammit, and I'm still in love with you! I never stopped. I honestly don't know how to explain what happened with Thalia. I truly don't. There is no reason or excuse for it. But it is the biggest regret I will ever have. What I do know is that a handful of moments with her will never equate to a single second spent with you." Jensen's chest heaved. He had never gotten a chance to pour out his words.

Esme stood there, emotional turmoil playing on her face. She refused to let his words take up residence in her mind. She convinced herself that she was better off without him. She was over him; she didn't need any more lies from him or her own. In her mind, what he did was unforgivable, she made have hidden truths, but he was disloyal. She forced her eyes to the ground, refusing the words being spoken enter her essence. Esme's now cold and raging energy mingled with Jensen's warmth and steadiness. Both energies spiraled around them, creating a hauntingly perfect harmonious buzz.

"Let me help you out of this mess, Esme. You're in this because you did so much for me. I can get you out. I'll find a way out of all of this." For the first time that night, Jensen's voice was soft. He dared to drift closer in her personal space. He knew with his cards on the table there was nothing left for him to lose. He dared to go a little further, reaching out to tentatively tuck a stray curl behind Esme's ear while her eyes were still locked on the floor.

Feeling the tingles of his energy on her skin caused her eyes to dart up to meet Jensen's. Her face glowed where his touch lingered. The torture in his eyes held her captive, and soon, she was drowning in honey pools. The world stopped around them. Esme's secrets, the missing Grim Reaper, the hellhound, Thalia's warning, and the distant grumbled protests of Camryn faded. In this frozen moment, his only concern were those large steel-gray eyes peering up at him. Everything else be damned. It was always her, just her, secrets, faults, and all. Before he or she could come back to their senses and the magic moment dissipated, his lips crashed down on hers. He dug his fingers into her hair, pulling her face closer to his, while his other hand traveled to her hip. Her magnolia and amber scent enticed him even further.

Feeling emboldened since she hadn't protested, he tugged her hips until they were slotted perfectly with his. He could feel her body dissolve into his. His tongue swiped the seam of her lips, seeking entry, but she wouldn't give him that. Esme was regaining her senses and snapping out of the moment, but Jensen wasn't ready to crash back down into reality just yet. He needed to pour his emotions into her because words always failed him. Biting her bottom lip, he found the perfect opportunity to brush his tongue over hers when she gasped. Jensen's tongue explored her mouth, tasting every piece and corner of her. It's what he had been missing for months, and he could sense she missed it, too, by the way she leaned into him. She tasted like home.

Being wrapped up and lost in this perfect kiss was home for her. Her fingers roamed freely up his arms and chest and brushed softly over his nape. She wanted to live in this kiss forever. It was warm and familiar, like a favorite sweater. Only she didn't want to be in her favorite sweater. It had been worn and snagged too many times. A fear deep within her told her that if she wore that sweater again, it would succumb to tatters completely. Gathering what little resolve she had left, she pushed Jensen away from her. His warmth vanished as he stepped back. She kept her eyes closed, secretly basking in the warmth that had infiltrated her mind and quickly spreading down to her toes. As she opened her eyes, cold washed over her body, her eyes glassy from unshed tears. It was all overwhelming. She felt too much.

Jensen simply stood there, watching her with hopeful eyes. Hoping she could understand what she still meant to him, hoping that she would give him a chance to fix everything and redeem himself. He ignored Alicia's giddiness, the unease of Cora, and the daggers that were being shot by Camryn. They stood there, glowing from their kiss and touch. Each a nightlight in the dark for the other.

He decided on driving his point home, seeing Esme's resolve hanging on by a single thread. "Please, Esme, I love you."

Those unshed tears that she had been fighting back descended her cheeks. "I know you do." Her voice quivered. "I'm sorry." She choked out and waved her hand over Jensen's feet and whispered. "Aperio." A bright light filled the room as Jensen fell through the portal that opened under his feet. "Claudere." With that one command, the portal closed. She turned around with a finality, walking away from the source of her pain.

"Holy crap, that was intense." Alicia spoke louder than she intended.

"Oh my God! Esme, what did you do?" Cora had finally snapped back to her senses and panicked. She had just witnessed Esme using portals and using said portal to transport Jensen to who knows where. "Where did you send him?"

The only response was a shrug, as if Esme couldn't care less where she had sent Jensen. Truth was, she didn't send him anywhere. He was just stuck in a never-ending light tunnel, since she wasn't there to give him an exit. It may have seen rash or cruel to those around her, but in that moment, Esme could only care about herself, her thoughts, her feelings. Everything was too much. She felt everything closing in around her. What she did gave her a reprieve from the overwhelming moment Jensen had thrust upon her. This was the moment where she had to put herself first for once.

Opening and closing his mouth several times, Camryn finally managed to string together enough words to voice his thoughts. "Listen, Es, I like Jensen about as much as you do right now on a daily basis." He couldn't help the chuckle in his voice or the fact that he did find this to be amusing. "You can't just leave him wherever it is. I can't believe I'm saying this, but you need to bring him back. I don't condone what he just did but bringing him back is the right thing to do."

Esme peered over her shoulder to Camryn to observe the concerned expression taking over his face. Then she looked over to Cora, who had an indecipherable expression. Then to

Alicia, the calmest of the bunch, sported a smirk but nodded in agreement. Esme let out a defeated sigh and whispered while flicking her wrist. The bright light once again filled the room. Three sets of eyes glanced in her direction. She dramatically flourished her hand in front of her. "Go on, go get him. I can't hold this open forever. It's a bit draining." Cora blatantly nodded to Camryn in the portal's direction. He, in turn, placed his hands on his hips and dropped his head. He took a step toward the portal before stepping in. He looked back at Esme, narrowing his eyes. "Oh, come on, Cam, I promise I won't lock you in the portal, too. I have no grudges against you."

He took in a deep breath as if he were about to plunge into the ocean and walked into the light. As he walked in, he had to squint while his eyes adjusted to the blinding white light. That's all there was, just light and nothingness. "Jensen!" You would think that a never-ending tunnel would have a possible echo, but the surrounding nothingness swallowed any sound. "Jensen, where are you? Come on, man, let's go back. Es can't hold this open forever." He wasn't sure if it was only seconds or minutes that passed, but Jensen jogged up to him, appearing out of nowhere, looking bewildered. "Oh, there you are. Where did you come from?"

Jensen squinted and scratched his head. "I think from that direction? I honestly don't know, but I'm ready to get out." They walked in silence, hoping it was the right direction. As they continued to walk, a familiar sight of the apartment began to form in a haze in front of them. "Is it weird that I'm not bothered by the fact that she sent me through this?"

Camryn chuckled and shook his head. "You deserved it."

Jensen walked into the apartment first, quickly followed by Camryn, to find an uneasy feeling floating about the living room. Cora played with the hem of her shirt as her eyes narrowed on Esme. Alicia looked worried as Esme braced herself against the bookshelf. Camryn realized what Esme meant when she had said she couldn't hold the portal open forever. The longer the portal stayed opened, the more it drained her energy. She heaved herself away from the shelves. "Oh, good, you're both back." Then she flicked her wrist once more. "Claudere." She closed the portal. Esme studied Jensen as he studied her back, then she turned and walked back down the hall. The sound of her door closing filled the void, ending all conversations.

Jensen's mind caught up to what she had said before she sent him on an impromptu portal trip. He saw a small ray of hope. Far too much passion passed between them for her to be completely out of love with him. She never said he couldn't try to make her fall in love with him again. It was now his mission to win her over again, even if he had to harvest the stars, because she deserved the universe. He never knew she gave up everything for him. He realized he never gave his everything to her and that Camryn was right. She deserved someone better than him, and he was going to be better to be deserving of her. He was going to be better than his past self.

16

The sun rose, dotting the apartment in warm orange light. The reapers and Alicia hadn't realized how quickly the night came and went. Every being present mirrored the way they felt unequivocally depleted. Before anyone could leave or truly process events prior, Camryn said, "What Esme said about the Grim Reaper checks out. That phone call I mentioned from Ansel—he told me that he and Thalia had a scheduled meeting. The Grim Reaper never showed. Instead, they found his office in disarray. Books were tossed everywhere, papers on the desk scattered on the floor. The worst thing they found is that the scythe is missing."

Jensen scrubbed his jaw. Nothing about this new information sat well with him. "How do they know that it's missing? What if he just took it with him? It is the Grim Reaper's scythe."

Camryn nodded. Jensen had valid questions, but the answer to them was damning. "The case it's housed in when he isn't using it was smashed. They both picked up traces of residual energy around it. The real question is, who would have taken it and why? Only the Grim Reaper can use it."

The silence lingered between them. The noise of shuffling reapers in the hallway leaked in. Another day had begun. Another day filled with more problems and questions rather than solutions and answers. Even with this ever-growing mountain of issues being in this space, thoughts of being with Esme flooded Jensen. She was the only thing that mattered to him. Her body was breaking as a perfect depiction of what he did to her emotions. He had to fix it. Jensen knew he had a new list to complete, but knowing what happened to her, seeing it firsthand, he had to check on her. He needed to know she was okay, and maybe he could start making her fall in love with him again. He made his way to the bedroom, but Camryn short-stopped him.

"Move, Camryn. I need to check on her." He stood there in the hallway, staring Camryn down.

"Not right now, man. She went through a hell of a lot last night." Unmoving, Camryn crossed his arms over his chest, blocking Jensen from getting to Esme. Jensen opened his mouth. "Just stop. Can't you sense it? Focus on her energy. It's not what it used to be. It's rocky and flickering now. She needs space to calm down and recharge." It bothered him to not be near her, but Camryn was right: the only logical option for him was to nod and turn away.

Pinging sounded throughout the apartment, reminding the reapers once again that there were souls that needed to be collected. Each reaper let out a sigh while checking the new list on their phones. Alicia sat silently, chewing away at her nails before she spoke up. "So, obviously, you all have to get to work. I can stay here until Esme wakes up." Just by her gaze alone, everyone could tell this idea was meant to help Jensen be more at ease with the current situation.

"Are we not going to talk about the ticking time bomb in the other room?" Cora stated in disbelief. "I'm pretty sure we all saw the same unhinged Esme, right?"

Alicia rolled her eyes. "She isn't unhinged, babes. She's just going through a season. It's obvious she's processing a lot."

Cora stood there in disbelief. How could anyone say this is a "season?" Even though she was new to the reaping business, judging by the two older reapers in the room, what had just transpired was not normal. Letting out a short sarcastic laugh, she said, "This isn't a season! This isn't just something that happens to reapers everywhere." She paused, absorbing the faces. That wasn't the first time being around this group, where everyone looked at her as if she had "stupid" engraved on her forehead. Even with all the stares, her thoughts rolled off her tongue. "You can't seriously think this is just a coincidence, right? The Grim Reaper is missing, then, suddenly, Esme is acting all kinds of suspicious. Everything about her is different. Even I can tell, and I've only had a few close encounters with her."

"Cora, that's enough." The city sounds were trickling in as Camryn shoved his phone into his pocket. "Cora, you don't know Esme like we do." He pointed to himself and Jensen. "We don't have the whole story. Whatever you're implying or story that your brain is concocting, let it go."

She couldn't decide if everyone had gone blind to what had occurred around them or if she had entered a parallel universe. How was it possible these other reapers who are senior to her, who have years of experience and have seen more than her, could see no issue with what was happening? Cora couldn't help debate whether this matter concerned her, but seeing as she was sucked into this whirlpool, she would stay with it. "You're both so biased and blinded by her that you didn't even realize she was working with Infernals!"

If anyone should have an issue with Esme, it would be Jensen. He was the one who she had sucked into the portal. Obviously, he didn't agree with Esme working with Infernals, but her reasoning had been given. He knew that was a discussion that was still left unresolved. What he was more concerned with was the fact that she was part mortal and had apparent changes in her energy. He had determined that if he could win Esme's heart back, he could sway her to not work with Infernals and work out all the other problems together. But the most pressing matter was the fact that the Grim Reaper was missing. "Cora, drop it already! You don't know what you're talking about. Focus on getting your list done correctly, then maybe you can have a say in all of this." After the night he had experienced, Jensen was ready to snap.

Cora spoke through gritted teeth. "Oh, that's right because I'm too stupid to do anything right. Maybe if you would step up as a mentor and get your nose out of Esme's ass, I'd be capable in your eyes." Her eyes darted over to Alicia, who was unusually quiet during this heated discussion. The only reaction she received was Alicia's eyes glued to the floor. "Really, Alicia? Do you have nothing to say? Do you agree with them?"

Alicia's eyes snapped up. What was she supposed to say? She was a lost soul in a world of reapers. "I mean, I don't really have a place in this conversation. What I do know is that your phones keep buzzing, and you three have souls to escort. So, I'll stay here. I could use a change in scenery." She shooed the three reapers out, as if she were a mother sending her children off to school.

The three reapers shuffled out of the apartment. Just as Alicia was about to close the door, Jensen turned around, worry pinching his brow. "What if something happens while we're out? You can't leave here without one of us. I should stay and redistribute my list to someone else." Behind him, Cora looked at him as if he were a lost puppy, while Camryn smirked with amusement.

"Well, lucky for you, she has a phone, and I know how to use technology. We'll be fine." Alicia rolled her eyes and gave a mock salute as she quickly shut the door. She leaned her head back on the door, closed her eyes, and drank in the silence. Time trickled slower than sand in an hourglass. She wandered around the apartment, opening and closing every drawer, closet, and cabinet. Curiosity got the better of her when she found herself in the bathroom. More specifically, looking in the medicine cabinet. "Oh, let's see what fun treasures you have hidden here."

"Find anything interesting?" Esme's voice caused Alicia to let out a small yelp and knock a lit candle over. "Good thing I'm a reaper, and you're already dead. You could have burned down the apartment, and we would have suffered death by fire." Esme rolled her eyes at her own statement. "Trust me, it's not a pretty sight."

Alicia shivered. "I'll take your word for it. Also, to answer your question, no, I didn't find anything. Unless you find expired lip balm interesting. Oh, and that floral-scented candle."

Esme stood there as memory surfaced. A smile tugging the corners of her lips, and she finally gave in. The laugh that came out was one that she hadn't felt in quite some time. "Sorry to disappoint. Besides, that candle is an old gift." Esme muttered almost to herself, "I give him an antique watch, and he gets me a candle." Then she shook her head and laughed.

Alicia smirked and shrugged before hoisting herself on the bathroom counter. "So, how are you feeling? Because, to be honest, you look like crap."

Esme rolled her eyes and placed her hand on her chest. "You say the sweetest things." She turned on her heel and padded her way into the kitchen to brew a pot of coffee. As the coffee dripped, she searched the apartment for her phone and tablet. Even though her world was in disarray, reaping didn't stop. Scrolling through her obscenely overfilled inbox containing reports and contracts, the aroma of coffee flooded her senses as the couch dipped next to her.

"So, what are we working on?" Alicia had an eager look that made Esme chuckle.

"What do you mean 'we?' I'm working on reports, contracts, as well as reviewing my list for today. You, I don't know why you're here."

Alicia took a moment and narrowed her eyes as she chewed on the inside of her cheek, thinking. She didn't want to say that Jensen refused to leave, and she volunteered to ease his troubles. Her eyes scanned the apartment until they landed on the finished coffee pot. "I'm your personal assistant for the day." She then stood from the couch and made her way over to the kitchen. She began to pour a large cup of coffee. "How do you like it?"

Esme rolled her eyes, knowing Alicia was either unceremoniously left behind or left there to play babysitter. She continued to reply to emails and restructure the lists that needed to be sorted for the upcoming weeks, when she replied to Alicia. "However, I can get it." The clattering of a spoon followed by a full belly laugh snapped Esme from her work. She looked up to find Alicia doubled over in laughter when she realized how her reply had been interpreted.

"You're such a child." She shook her head, refocusing on her work.

Alicia giddily replied. "That's my secret to never getting old."

The unfiltered thought slipped past Esme's lips. "I thought your secret was dying."

Alicia pressed a hand to her chest and cocked her head back. "Wow, Esme. Now I'm going to assume you take your coffee black. It'll match that hole where your heart should be. Or your soul if you had one"—she set the drink down—"your beverage, ma'am."

Letting the rich bitter taste of the dark hot liquid explode over her tastebuds, she hummed in satisfaction. "Dark and bitter. Just like me." Esme set the mug down and stood. Just then, a soft knock tapped on the door. Alicia looked at Esme, and Esme raised an inquisitive brow toward Alicia. "Well, as my assistant, you should go see who that is."

Alicia skipped over toward the door. "I swear if Jensen came back because he wants to helicopter, I'm going to smack him. I don't care if he's a reaper or not." Esme chuckled as she tidied the books and blankets around her living room.

"Oh, hey, Tyler. Do you have an appointment today?" The high-pitched professional voice from Alicia was such a contrast to her normal voice it was slightly comical. Seeing

Tyler's eyebrows pinch in confusion, she leaned in to whisper, "I'm Esme's assistant for the day."

The hallway had quieted with reapers either resting or out completing their lists. He stood there for a minute as what Alicia just told him registered.

He let out a deep laugh. "In that case, no, I did not have an appointment with her highness." Tyler paused for a minute and scratched the back of his head. "I thought I was collecting a soul, but I ended up here instead. Kind of strange, but oh well. So, I decided to see what's up. I haven't seen Esme in a while."

"Wow, that is strange, but unfortunately, now is not the best time for a meeting with the boss. So, I'll have her people call your people, and we'll set up a meeting." Alicia rocked on her heels and darted her eyes around. "Have fun with your reaping, may your harvest be bountiful."

He stood there, expressionless, then threw his head back, bursting of roaring laughter. He bent over with laughter, clutching his side.

"Oh, shut up." Alicia rolled her eyes and closed the door.

Esme was sitting on the kitchen counter, trying to contain her laughter and failing miserably. She held her hands up in surrender as Alicia huffed. "May your harvest be bountiful. That just made my day." As she stretched, she looked over to Alicia and realized she was going to be there until someone came to get her or to be dropped off at The Twisted Sickle. A large part of her was okay with the idea of having some new company. "Well, I'm going to shower, then I have a list to get started on."

Alicia's eyes widened. She didn't know the first thing about reaping, especially the way Esme went about it, but she could tell the fatigue was taking a toll on the reaper before her. Esme's complexion looked paler, her cheeks were hollowed out, and the dark circles under her eyes could be seen from miles away. A shiver ran down her spine as the thought entered her mind: Esme looked like walking death. "Shouldn't you, I don't know, maybe take the day off? Rest could do you some good."

Esme began her journey to the bathroom, stating, "Death waits for no one."

"Well, do you at least know what's wrong with you? You know, the fainting and bleeding from different orifices and stuff? Maybe we could get you some medicine or something."

Esme snorted with amusement. "You'd think after being around for a few centuries I'd have an idea, but sadly, I have no clue."

"Can I use your tablet?" Alicia asked.

The question caught Esme off guard. "Why do you need it?" There were names, places, contracts, and other things that not just any being was privy to seeing other than Esme and a select few involved in those contracts.

Alicia locked her hands behind her back, rocked on her heels, and lifted her chin. "I'm going to search your symptoms to the all-knowing internet."

Esme gave a contemplative stare before walking to the table where the tablet rested and typed a few things in. She handed the tablet over. "Have at it, kid." A smirk played on her lips as she watched this unclaimed soul skip over to her couch and nestle in with that tablet. She scrubbed her hands up and down her face. A warm, sticky substance on her hand caught her attention, followed by the stinging in her eyes.

Esme wiped her eyes with the back of her hands. Sure enough, she was bleeding again.

Why her, why now? These questions played on a continuous loop as she made her way to wash away the new and encrusted blood from the previous night.

17

The sounds of the city street whirled and buzzed while the sun warmed the crisp, cool morning air. All three reapers stood in front of the apartment building, allowing the energy to swirl around them. Cora's stance was stiff as she paced in a tight line with her arms akimbo. Her mind was a continuous racetrack with no checkered flag in sight. Sparing a side-eye to Jensen and Camryn, she made up her mind. Those two idiots were blinded by a pretty little half-reaper to see the situation clearly. Her thoughts were broken when Jensen's voice carried over to her. "No, I'm not going to the bar right now. She still has my office hostage, and right now, Thalia is the last being I want to see."

Something curious burned in the back of her mind. There's an entire headquarters building in the middle of the city just for them. Why would Jensen get his own space? The question nagged at her brain and grew louder in her mind, and she just couldn't help it. "Why do you hold meetings and have an office at the bar when there is an entire building of offices?"

Jensen pinched his face in concentration. Why did he still work out of there? "Well, when Esme and I started dating, I didn't have an office. I wasn't an Administrator yet." His eyes glazed over, his mind finding and getting lost in memories.

Camryn looked up to the sky, watching the clouds before nudging Jensen slightly, waking him from his thoughts. "Anyway, all the reapers would use the bar as our central hub. With working different lists and shifts, Esme and I didn't always see each other. She surprised me by making an office in the back of the bar for us." Jensen's eyes cast down toward the sidewalk, where he scuffed the bottom of his shoe on the pavement. He couldn't help but chuckle as a thought infiltrated his mind. Esme did do everything for him, for them.

Silence ensued for a few heavy seconds until Camryn chimed in. "That's why lover boy here is hell-bent on staying there. It's sacred to him."

Jensen shoved his hands in his pockets and huffed out, "Shut up, Camryn."

Camryn gave a knowing smirk before walking into the city's crows. Jensen grumbled incoherent words as he marched into the flow of people, catching up to Camryn. Cora chewed on her lip as her mind formulated new questions and ideas. Noticing she was left behind, she scurried into step with the other two reapers. "Is Thalia still there?"

Jensen continued his pace without sparing a glance in Cora's direction. "Unfortunately, yes, she is."

Cora stopped abruptly, her eyes wide, her fingers fidgeting against her thighs. "Oh, shoot, I have some souls to collect. Don't want to be late. So, yeah, great. Bye." Camryn and Jensen stood there in the middle of a busy sidewalk, blinking as people walked distractedly around them. They both appeared to be puzzled by Cora's behavior, and neither of them knew what to make of it.

"What do you—"

"No idea, man. She's not my apprentice." Camryn then proceeded to pull out his phone to check the time. "Well, I've got a few stops to make, so I'm going to get going." With that, Jensen was left alone with his thoughts as he continued to the headquarters office.

Camryn continued walking until he reached the city park. There was something about being in this park that calmed him as he readied himself for the day. Perhaps it was the contrasting sounds of nature to that of the chaotic city. Maybe it was the sight of happy families laughing and playing with their children that gave him a different view of what his job did. He found himself standing on the bridge that arched over the steady stream. Off in the distance, old men were gathered around small tables playing chess, while adults jogged with dogs down the winding trail. Closing his eyes, the surrounding sounds created a melody in his mind while the crisp, cool air brushed against his face.

The sterile scent and crackling intercom forced Camryn's eyes open. He found himself in both his favorite and most hated place in the world, the children's hospital. The way his department operated was vastly different from the other two. Reapers who worked with the innocents got to spend time with smaller children to gain their trust and make the transition easier. To the humans around them, the reapers were nothing more than imaginary friends that children created as coping mechanisms. Since the reapers never knew which child would be on their list, they interacted with as many as they could. There were times when the list included those souls who were not in this hospital, but that place is where they spent much of their time.

"Camryn!"

The high-pitched squeal caused him to turn around. There he was, the first one on his list today, Alexander Kelly. He was always a lively boy with wild, unkempt red hair, deep green eyes, and freckled skin. He giggled, running over to where Camryn stood and greeted him with a smile. Camryn towered over him but crouched down to eye level. This was it, the hardest part of what he did. He put his hand out, and they performed an elaborate handshake just as the sounds of hysterical crying filtered into the polka-dotted hallway. "Camryn, I think my mommy is sad."

He took a breath, giving Alexander a small smile. "Yeah, kiddo. I think she is sad."

Alexander looked up with big innocent doe eyes. "Is this what we talked about last week? Do I get to go to the new place now where I won't be sick anymore?" He nodded in response. "Will mommy and daddy be there?"

The explanations were always the hardest, but for Camryn, he kept his explanations in the simplest forms. "Well, they'll be there eventually but not for a while." He tilted his head to the side when he saw uncertainty and fear setting in. "Hey, would you like a piggyback ride while we walk?" The little boy eagerly nodded, earning a deep chuckle from Camryn as he turned around, allowing him to climb onto his back.

"Whoa, everything looks different from up here." Delight was now clear in the little voice. "Hey, Camryn?" He paused as they walked down the hallway. Other reapers walked in and out of rooms, smiling at them as they played and chatted with other children. "Will there be kittens and puppies there? Or other kids?"

Camryn was walking in a zig-zag pattern as he thought about how to answer the question. "Would you like there to be kittens and puppies and other kids there?"

Small bubbly giggles filled the air as Camryn walked in his silly pattern. "I really would. It would be nice and super cool. I could always use more friends. Plus, I always wanted a pet that wasn't a goldfish. I mean, what am I supposed to do with a goldfish, Camryn? I can't even pet it!"

A deep laugh left Camryn, and Alexander began his rant on why goldfishes were the worst pets anyone could ever give to a kid. For a six-year-old, he was opinionated. Camryn couldn't help but wonder what this little boy's life would have been like if he got to experience a full human life. The boy quieted when he saw a memorable sight before him. Somehow, during his rant, he ended up at his grandmother's house.

It had been such a long time since he or his family had been there. All the amazing memories flooded in and any worry or fear he may have felt left. His wiggling around gave Camryn the cue to squat down so that he could hop off his back. The delicious scent of snickerdoodles wafted from the open window. He bounced on the balls of his feet but was still hesitant to go. "Are you going to come inside with me, Camryn? I'm sure grandma made plenty of cookies. She always does."

Camryn bent down, giving a gentle hug, along with a soft smile. "Not this time. I have to go visit some more friends today."

Nodding, he heard barking coming from inside the house.

"It sounds like your grandma has a puppy in there. Why don't you go on inside and see for yourself?" Alexander giggled as he ran off with his arms stretched like airplane wings toward the house.

Stopping midway, he turned, then ran back toward Camryn and threw his tiny arms around Camryn's waist. "Thanks for being my friend. I'll save you a few cookies for when you come back to visit me." He gave him a big smile that had a few teeth missing and ran into the house. He watched the boy fade into the house before letting out a breath he didn't realize he was holding. This was just the start of a long day for him and another name on an ever-growing list.

On the other side of town, Cora found herself in front of a pale blue neon light. Her mind was made up, and she knew exactly what she was about to do. She just hoped it was the right decision. Nodding to herself, she opened the door and walked in. A few reapers lingered about, but it was mostly empty. Two strong energy sources pulsed from the back office. Shaking out her nerves, Cora faked her confidence in what she was about to do. As she strolled in through the bar, the sound of smashing and a shrill scream. This would be the moment to turn around and leave. To rethink her decision and go on about her day. This was the last chance, but it was a missed chance. With hesitant determination, Cora lifted her fist and knocked on the wooden door.

Seconds passed as hours; the rapping of her knuckles echoed against the ruby walls. The bar was silent. More life and sound could be found in a graveyard. All the fake confidence Cora had mustered quickly deflated when the door swung open. A large man towered over her in the doorway. She tilted her head back, allowing her eyes to meet his gaze. His copper eyes held her hostage. Crunching and cracking glass broke Cora from her daze. "Ansel, who is that?" A sharp female voice ended the silence. Ansel? Bells rang in Cora's head, and her eyes widened. She staggered back, taking in the reaper before. His broad shoulders and height filled the door frame. His face was sculpted, from his angular jaw, sharp cheekbones, and straight nose. Everything framed his copper eyes perfectly. "Ansel!" The voice then registered with both Ansel and Cora.

Ansel rolled his eyes and staged whispered to Cora. "She's always been a touch on the dramatic side." He sighed. "I'm not sure, Thalia, I didn't get to ask over your screeching." Thalia's heels clicked angrily against the floor, followed by the door violently widening farther. Turbulent eyes analyzed Cora from head to toe, assessing every twitch. "Are you done staring down this young reaper? Please say yes because you look a tad constipated, and it honestly isn't flattering." Boredom and mockery glazed Ansel's words.

If looks could kill a reaper, Ansel would no longer exist with the searing look Thalia was giving him. She hollowed her cheeks and gave an inquisitive look to Cora. "I know your face, but not your name. Who are you, and what do you need?"

Cora's chest heaved. "I'm Cora. Jensen is my mentor. Or at least he's supposed to be. His mind is preoccupied with someone else." Her tongue darted out to lick her lips nervously. Changing her mind was no longer an option, but her nerves were increasing and becoming harder to control. The amount of energy exuding off the two reapers before her was enough to bring a being down to their knees. She lost herself in one curious thought. Two of the three original reapers had the same amount of overpowering energy combined that Esme had held on her own.

Rapid light taps on the door brought her out of her thoughts, and she noticed piercing gold eyes on her. "As for what I want." Cora gave a sheepish smile before continuing. "I want to be better at what I do and help you find what you are looking for."

With a flip of her hair and an unamused scoff, Thalia turned on her heels and proceeded to walk into the disarray. However, Ansel stood there with glee twinkling in his eyes as he crossed his arms, causing the fabric to strain around his biceps and chest. A sensation grew within Cora she couldn't quite describe. Whatever the feeling was showed on her face. Ansel winked and smirked, then flourished his hand, signaling Cora to walk into the office. The floor was littered with pieces of glass and tidbits from items that were on display. "You do know that this isn't your office, right? I mean, it's kind of rude to trash someone else's things." Intense energy vibrated through the room. It was obvious that it came from an agitated Thalia. Cora raised her hands slowly. "Just saying."

Ansel grinned at the interaction, or lack thereof, between the two women in front of him. Something about Cora intrigued him. For someone to actively seek out a deal with an original reaper was rare. What could she be after? It couldn't possibly be to be better at soul collection. No reaper was that bad. He studied the way she carried herself closely. All his centuries spent around different beings and observing their behaviors told him her stance was false confidence. "Thalia, maybe we should hear her out for just a moment. We have exhausted all other options and leads."

He tilted his head, rolling his bottom lip between his teeth. "Besides, I have a good feeling about her."

"Oh, for heaven's sake, Ansel, think with the head on your shoulders, not the one in your pants. She is of no value to me. I've read about her from Jensen's reports. The girl can barely manage to take a soul to the veil on time and is constantly breaking rules." Thalia spewed her words in a trickle of poison.

Cora inhaled, fighting off the tremble of her lips. Did everyone see her as useless and incompetent? Sure, she wasn't great with the innocent crowd, but she always had Alicia tag along for moral support, and that made it easier. The violent deaths caused her stomach to roll, and she never knew how to interact with a distraught human. As for the so-called normal collections that didn't exactly go her way, that could be entirely Jensen's fault. He was hardly a mentor and viewed her as nothing more than an inconvenience.

She didn't fit into any category, but that didn't mean she couldn't learn to be better while providing and gaining valuable information. "First, if you want to cast judgment on me about my skill of soul collecting or lack of skill, you can start with blaming your boy toy. Second, it shows how flawed your stupid training system is. Third, judging by the state of this mess, you're desperate to find whatever it is you're looking for."

Dragging the chair out from behind the desk, Thalia sat and propped up her stiletto-clad feet. "What makes you believe that you, a brand-new reaper, has anything to offer to me?"

"She means us," Ansel quickly chimed in. "What do you have to offer us?"

Picking at the hem of her shirt, Cora gave a quick nod toward Ansel. "Whatever it is that you're looking for is obviously connected to the big bad Grim Reaper, right?" She paused, observing both reapers before her, but their faces were emotionless masks. All Cora could do now was hope that she was on the right track, and all this was not in vain. "Right, well if that is the case, you need someone close enough to someone who knows him better than you do. And, um, yeah, that's where I come in."

Thalia and Ansel shared a glance, communicating purely with their eyes. Cora squirmed in her spot from the silent conversation around her. A deep exhale broke the silence as Thalia reclined further into the chair. "I still don't see how you are valuable to me, Cora. You say that you can get close to someone who is close to the Grim Reaper, yet I already have someone who is close to that person. So, again"—she paused and scratched her nose—"what do you have to offer me?"

Maybe an argument could be made for a temporary moment of bravery or an argument could be made for a brighter moment of stupidity. Cora may not be the best at soul collecting, but she excelled at one thing: annoying others. That was exactly what she decided to accomplish in that office. "Are you talking about Jensen? I think you are, but I find that funny because he hates you. Just last night, he confessed his undying love for Esme. You remember her, right? The one who looked like she had been through hell and back? Yeah, that Esme. Oh, that's the same Jensen who bluntly said—" Smashing and trickling thuds boomed over Cora's monologue. She stilled, assessing everything around her. A ceramic jar that connected with a framed photo was the culprit of the smash while the pens it contained rolled across the floor. Her eyes continued to roam until they landed upon a reaper blazing with fury.

Ansel leisurely strode toward Cora and turned to fully her. A giant grin graced his sculpted face. "If you can cause her to mentally destruct like this, I think I'll keep you." He winked at her and kicked a few pens away. "You do seem rather observant; I'll give you that." Deciding that taking over the impromptu meeting was for the best, Ansel took matters into his own hands. "Who do you have that can offer us information of what we're looking for, and why would you put yourself in this situation?"

Something close to warmth radiated through Cora's chest. Was there finally someone who saw her? Was this someone who saw actual value in her? She had only spent a handful of shared minutes with Ansel, but something about him put her at ease, made her feel safe, heard, and not a burden. "Esme. She said herself that she works directly for the Grim Reaper, always traveling with him." Thalia and Ansel shared a knowing look. "The reason for why is simple. That group doesn't want to help me. I'm a burden who asks too many questions and talks too much. I just want to be better. Maybe even the best one day."

An unsettling smile spread across Thalia's face. Maybe there was use for Cora after all. But what had her giddy was that the answers to all her questions were under her nose. "How close are you to Esme? I do not need someone who occasionally chitchats with her. I need someone who knows her, who is close to her." The hint of excitement and unbridled curiosity was evident in Thalia's tone.

Offering up information without anything in return was not on the agenda for Cora. She knew she needed a guarantee and had to decide how much information she was willing to give. "What are you going to give me in return?" Her voice trembled. Maybe, just maybe, she should have thought this through more and given her emotions a chance to settle. Everyone else was bounded by some unspoken devotion that they would rather drink acid than speak the ugly truth about their precious Esme. She was the outsider looking in, witnessed a power that was madness and needed to be stopped. She was the only one who felt and experienced the daily criticisms. This is the exact reason why Cora had to do this. It was all for the greater good, right?

Ansel sat on the edge of the desk, legs stretched and crossed in front of him while he clasped his hands together by his thighs. "You want to be accepted somewhere. You want someone who will see your potential and value you. It's nothing to be ashamed of, Cora. Every being is motivated by something. I can guarantee you that you have a place here. Next to me and somewhere in the same vicinity as Thalia. Nothing personal—she just doesn't like anyone."

Thalia stood from her chair and walked around the desk until she was next to Ansel. She examined her nails. "He's not wrong. I don't like many beings. I mostly tolerate them. You want to be accepted; you have Ansel. Do you want to be better than the rest of the reapers in this city, or even this country? I'll teach you how to be the best. In no time, you'll be better than Jensen and even rival Esme." The air was thick and charged with energy as an elegant hand reached forward. "Do we have a deal, Cora?"

Casting her eyes down as she contemplated one last time, toying with the hem of her gray sweater. She nodded, bracing herself as she met the two faces before her and shook the outstretched hand. "Good girl." Ansel clasped his large hand over the two others. "Now, tell us what you know about Esme."

Cora pulled her hand back and rolled her shoulders. "I know that her energy is unstable. It's like her essence is leaking out of her. I witnessed it last night when a pulse of energy shot out of her, and all the lights in her apartment exploded. Also, she works with a hellhound." She could tell them she knew Esme was part mortal, that she's bleeding from every place imaginable. She could tell them that Esme uses portals to transport instead of apparating from place to place. But there was no need to mention all that for the time being. It isn't breaking the agreement if she omits part of what she knows. They still have to live up to their end before the continuing her trickle of insider knowledge.

"Hellhound?" Ansel and Thalia questioned. Whether it was rhetorical was unclear, so Cora just hummed in reassurance. Thalia looked over to Ansel. "This may complicate things a little." He nodded in agreement.

"Uh, um, excuse me. Question here"— Cora paused to card her fingers through her long hair—"why would a hellhound complicate anything? Also, what is there to complicate?" It was at this moment that Cora realized that she should have been brave enough to ask more questions as she usually did. Why would a hellhound concern these two powerful reapers? Why do they seem to salivate at the thought of being able to get information on Esme? She finally realized she never asked what it was they were looking for. So many mistakes were made, and whether they could be undone or fixed seemed like wishful thinking. "Piggybacking off those questions." A nervous giggle left her lips without realizing she had let it slip. "I guess I should have asked before I made a deal, but what is it you're looking for?"

"Oh, my dear Cora, take a deep breath and try to relax. You have nothing to fear from us." Ansel flashed her an easy smile. He strolled behind her and rubbed his hands soothingly up and down her arms. "We will answer all your questions. That's the only way you can effectively help us, anyway. What we have now is mutual, understanding, respectful honesty. This way, we all get what we want."

While his touch was nice and warm, it did little to relax her. "What is it you actually want?"

Thalia rolled her eyes as she picked up an old leather journal and skimmed the pages. "You do ask a lot of questions." She glanced at Cora, then refocused on the old journal. "Since Ansel promised you our honesty, we're looking for the scythe."

How Cora tilted her head to the side in confusion was comical to Ansel, her eagerness to prove herself, but the innocence of it all was something he couldn't help but find endearing. Still confused, she said, "Wouldn't the scythe be with its owner, you know big daddy death?"

Ansel let out a deep chuckle. "Big daddy? That's a new one. But yes, you are correct, it would be with him if he were still around to own it."

Her eyes widened, and it became all too hard to swallow the lump forming in her throat. "What does that mean, exactly?"

The journal snapping shut caused Cora to jump. Thalia made note of how skittish Cora naturally was. "Mind your place, Cora."

Ansel glared at Thalia and wrapped Cora in a warm hug while running his hands through her hair. "What Thalia means is that is something you simply don't have to concern yourself with right now. He's simply missing, that's all. You focus on learning to collect those souls better. Let us worry about the other things." He gently removed his arms from around Cora and ushered her toward the door with his hand on her lower back. "Now, your training starts today. Find your list and wait for us out there. Perhaps have a drink. This was an exciting morning."

Cora shook her head. "It's not even noon, Ansel, and I haven't even collected a single soul yet, and here you are encouraging me to have a drink."

She truly was amusing to him, and he laughed once more. "It's merely a tool to occupy your idle time. You don't have to; the choice is always yours." She gave him a tight smile and walked out of the office. He shut the door softly after she walked out and turned swiftly back to Thalia. "Well, now, talk about unexpected, pleasant surprises. Now you don't have to waste any more time on that lover boy. It was counterproductive, anyway. He never told you anything of real value. According to our new little friend, he despises you." Ansel reveled in the delight of the revelation and made no attempt to mask it in his voice. Without warning, Thalia chucked a stapler toward his head, which he managed to duck and miss at the last second. "Honestly, woman, and you call me childish."

It was Thalia's turn to be amused, but she hid it behind her stone faced demeanor. "You are childish, Ansel. I was right, though. I told you it was Esme that we were looking for. Jensen was leading me toward her, but this is quicker. Do you think she has the scythe or knows where it went?"

His Italian leather dress shoes crunched on the debris scattered on the ground. He clasped his hands behind his back. "It's possible. It would explain the hellhound. Only Celestial or Infernal energy is strong enough to mask his energy and that of the scythe. I highly doubt a coven would be willing to hide it, anyway. But the real question is why her? Why would Esme be the one to receive it and how?"

Thalia walked to a corner chair and picked up her Vicuña wool jacket. "Those answers will reveal themselves in time. Right now, we need to simply find the scythe. The balance of life and death is off-kilter. There is no one to hold meetings with fate, or the other counsel members. They will not recognize me without that damn scythe."

Ansel bit the inside of his cheek and inhaled sharply. "Yes, of course. So"—he helped Thalia put on her jacket—"off you go to help Cora. I will stay here and oversee how things play out." He turned back to the desk, clicking through files. "I'll distribute what I can from what remains of the lists we have."

Thalia found Cora tucked away in a corner, scanning her phone. As she made her way over, Jensen walked in, looking exhausted and irritated. Cora noticed them both and turtled herself into her sweater.

Thalia was the first to speak. "Stand up Cora. Lesson one, stand straight, shoulders back, and head up. You'll never effectively do anything in your existence if you're not confident in yourself."

Cora diligently nodded and did as she was told. Jensen chose this time to approach both women.

Jensen addressed Cora but eyed Thalia. "Cora, what are you doing here? You have a list to complete." Something about her was starting to unsettle him. His eyes flickered over to Cora, waiting for her response.

Thalia stepped closer to Jensen, staring down her nose at him. "Don't look at her, look at me. Cora is no longer your concern. Seeing as how you have been more than lacking in your mentorship of her, I am taking over her training immediately. You will be under review to see if you are still effective in your current position." She brushed past him, making her way out of the bar. "Come along now, Cora, time to bring out that reaper in you." Cora gave a quick regretful glance and scurried behind Thalia.

Jensen was left there, astounded. How did Thalia go from throwing herself at him to threatening his position so quickly? What did Cora do or say to have his boss believe that he is ineffective? His mind was racing, everything was going wrong, and he just needed a moment and a space to collect his thoughts. His office had been his sanctuary before Thalia took residence there. Knowing that she had left, he hoped to reclaim the place where everything was in order and made sense.

He turned the door handle, but his body stilled at the sight before him. "Who are you and what the hell happened to my office?" The strained tendons in his neck could easily be seen from across the room. That's when the familiarity of the face occupying his seat struck him. "You, I've seen your face before, but I don't know who you are."

"How rude of me. I'm Ansel. Pleasure to finally meet you." Ansel clapped his hands, laughing. "You sound like Thalia when she met Cora. You remind me of her."

Jenson scoffed and walked into the office, observing the damage that was done. "I remind you of Thalia?"

Ansel settled further into the chair. "Don't sound offended, but yes."

Jensen bent down, picking up random papers that he spent time meticulously sorting and color coding, but paused. Just like Thalia? He shuddered at the idea. "I'm not sure that's something to not be offended by." He stood, papers in hand, and gave the reaper his full attention.

Narrowing his eyes, Ansel quirked the side of his lips. "That's an interesting response for someone you have a relationship with. A taboo one, but one nonetheless."

As Jensen approached the desk, he placed the stack of papers on the keyboard. He shoved his hands in his pockets, looking as though he was trying to solve the world's hardest mystery. "I'm not in a relationship with her. I don't think whatever it was that we had could be classified as that. To be completely honest, I don't even know how that happened. I love my Esme. Always have and always will."

"A witch's tonic and spell. I swear she keeps witches on retainer." The mumble from Ansel was too deep for Jensen to completely believe he heard correctly. But still, he had to be sure.

"Are you telling me that bitch cast a spell, which is forbidden for reapers to do, by the way, and cost me everything? Why? What kind of vile creature does that?"

Ansel thrummed his fingers on his chin and responded. "I believe that kind of vile creature is called a Thalia. I believe you've met one. I hear they'll stop at nothing to get what they desire. A Thalia will even go as far as to hunt, stalk, and kill their prey. Obviously, something about you caught her attention. I vaguely recall her mentioning it. She would pour it into your drinks when she was supposedly training you. It was really to make sure she still had your attention. But your

Esme, as you put it, was in the way. That bond you had was something. It kept pulling you out of the tonics effects."

Jensen didn't know what to make of this response and quickly circled back to his original questioning. "You still haven't answered my question. What happened to my office?"

Ansel stood, rounded the desk, and held his hand out. "Oh, yes. Thalia is what happened to your office. She was rather frustrated and needed an outlet for those brewing emotions, I suppose. Quiet the mess to straighten out, isn't it?" He waved his hand around nonchalantly. "It was interesting meeting you, Jensen." He smirked. "I must be on my way now. Souls to collect. I'm sure you understand." In a blink, Ansel vanished from the office, leaving Jensen to pick up the wreckage.

"Esme! Esme! Help me!" Esme was midway through, buttoning up her silk shirt when Alicia's scream sliced into the calm stillness in the apartment. Forgetting all about the shirt, she ran down the hall into the living room. She found Alicia cowering behind the red velvet chair with fear imprinted on her face. "It was right there. Something was here. It was watching me. I swear." Sobs racked through her.

A putrid burning stench wafted in on a gust of deathly freezing air. Random sadness, anxiety, and fear were palpable. Esme's eyes darted around the corners of her home, analyzing every shadow. She moved cautiously closer to Alicia until she could crouch to meet her in her corner of safety. "Are you okay? Are you hurt?" Esme cupped Alicia's face in her hands, scanning her as a mother would a child. Hiccups were all that Alicia could manage. Esme's grip tightened; her eyes hardened. She could tell her energy was going haywire again.

Alicia gasped and ran a shaky hand across Esme's face. "Your eyes. Esme, your eyes are changing." Before Esme could say anything, a deafening hum surrounded them, and vanilla and fresh-cut grass masked the rotting singed odor. The energy in the room spread like wildfire, causing a burning and tingling sensation to flow through every atom of Esme's body. She shielded Alicia the best she could with her own body. There it was again, that metallic taste, the same taste that had been haunting her. Searing pain ripped through her chest, causing her to fall backward. A clank echoed across the room. Esme balanced herself on all fours as her wet hair from the shower earlier clung to her cheeks. It was all a blur, a painful, redundant blur. Blood bubbled from her lips with each cough until nothing but silence remained.

Sitting on her haunches, Esme hoarsely questioned, "You okay?"

"Me? I'm fine. Are you okay? You coughed up a good amount of blood again, and your eyes . . . Esme, your eyes were turning black. Not to mention your hands felt ice cold." Alicia whispered the last part of her questioning.

They both walked to the middle of the apartment, from where the clanking resonated. It was there in all its silver and juniper glory.

"Well, this can't be good," Esme said.

"Is that?" Alicia cocked her head in fascination.

"Yep."

"Like?"

"Yes, that one."

"How?"

"No idea."

Annoyance fueled Esme. Lately, questions were in ample supply while the answers were in a shortage.

Alicia leaned closer to it, but Esme yanked her arm and pulled her back behind her. "Don't get too close and don't even think about touching it unless you have some kind of desire to be tethered to that forever."

"Forever?"

"Well, until the Grim Reaper releases or delivers you." Something was wrong. Why would his scythe show up here? Especially in the way it did. With the tip of her toe, Esme nudged the handle, causing the blade to scrape against the floor. Skidding, screeching metal caused Esme to close her eyes and wince. She bent down, slowly reaching for the long, aged juniper handle. It was odd seeing it out of its case or out of the hand that would hold it. As her delicate fingers grazed the handle, a crack whipped through the air, and Esme flew backward into the window, causing the pane to spiderweb. "Ow." She stood, stretching her back, rubbing the back of her head. Her hand was wet and sticky. As she focused her eyes further, glistening ruby-red blood dripped down each finger. "Son of a bitch, I just showered, too." She snatched a blanket from the corner chair. It was unceremoniously tossed over the scythe.

Alicia was still frozen, unsure what to think or do. Even more fearful of touching the scythe and being eternally bound to an object. "So, what do we do now?"

Circling the now covered scythe, Esme released a frustrated groan. "Well, you certainly can't touch it, and I don't feel like getting body slammed by it again"—she tentatively sidestepped around Death's instrument—"we're going to have to call Jensen. Or Camryn." Her eyes met

Alicia expectantly. "You're my assistant. You can make that call."

Crossing her arms, Alicia snarkily replied. "You just don't want to talk to Jensen."

"I don't know what you mean. It's not like I'm avoiding him or anything." Esme huffed, examining her red-stained fingers.

She sucked in her cheeks and walked over to where Esme's phone was charging, then disconnected it and wiggled it in her face. "Is it because he gave you a kiss worthy of a romance novel?"

"Just—call him, please. I need to clean up again." The resolve in her voice cracked. Hearing the cracking of her voice, Alicia looked up to notice unshed tears caged in long lashes.

"Hey, Esme. I know it's not my place, and I don't know both sides of what happened." Alicia chewed on the next words carefully. "It's okay to want to try again. I know I would give anything for another chance for someone to look at me the way he does you."

"I don't know if I can." Esme smiled, down turning her brows. That told more than her words ever could.

Raising the phone to her ear as she mumbled, "maybe the reaper in you wants to see things end and be final, but maybe the mortal side wants to try again." She wasn't aware whether her words were heard, but they were. They were loud enough to cause a falter in Esme. "Hey, Jensen, it's your favorite friendly neighborhood soul."

The apartment door swung open. "Where is she? Is she okay?" Jensen's deep, velvet voice floated down the hallway. His frantic footsteps racing toward Esme drowned out whatever Alicia was saying. She was sitting at the edge of her bed pulling on her spiked heeled boots, whipping her head up at the door being opened. Taking large strides, he closed in on her, pulling her up and wrapping her in a crushing embrace. "Oh, thank God you're okay. I came as soon as I could."

"Yeah, I'm fine. Are you?" Her voice was muffled from her face being pushed into his hard chest.

Another deep voice filtered through the doorway. "Careful with her, Jensen, Esme is a fragile little thing now."

She pushed her face away from Jensen's chest, still working on getting the rest of her body free from his arms. Camryn stood there, a sad glint in his eye, observing the pair. "Fragile? Did you just call me fragile? I may bleed or pass out occasionally, but do not call me fragile, or we'll find out which of us is truly the fragile one." She tilted her head up to look closely at Jensen, who still had her wrapped up tightly. "Can I have the rest of me back now?"

"Oh, right. Sorry." He gently let her go, taking a small step back. "Alicia called me. She said there was an emergency, you were hurt and bleeding. I should get here quickly."

Camryn folded his arms and huffed. "She told me a little development came up and to get here when I could. Why did she give you the dramatic version?"

Esme narrowed her eyes at Alicia, who was slightly hidden and sheepishly waving behind Camryn. "Was I hurt? Yes. Was I bleeding? A little. An emergency? Not exactly." She tucked her hair behind her ears. "Let me show you what was classified as an emergency." Leading everyone out to the living room, she pointed to the covered object on the floor.

Jensen and Camryn both felt the pressing energy radiating from under the blanket. They simultaneously asked, "Is that—"

Esme nodded and hummed in response. "It goes without saying, but Alicia can't touch it and probably shouldn't be near it. Also, I can't touch it. I already tried, and the energy from it threw me back into that window." She pointed behind herself with her thumb to the splintered window. "I need one of you to move it."

Camryn swallowed roughly while Jensen tapped his fingertips against his thighs and asked, "Why is it here?"

Esme was chewing on her bottom lip and wringing her hands together. "I'm not sure, but it can't be good. Grim Reaper is missing as if he vanished from the face of this earth and now the scythe shows up in a peculiar manner. I don't know why it's here, how it got here, or why I have it. Whatever the reason, I can only assume it's for safekeeping. So, if you don't mind, can one of you please pick it up and move it into my bedroom?" She looked over to spot Alicia standing the furthest away, nudging Jensen forward and whispering something behind him.

He snapped out of his daze and squared his shoulders. "Of course. I'll take it and put it in the closet. It'll be safe and sound."

Camryn rolled his eyes and muttered, "you're overdoing it now."

Hiding the fact that he was scared to touch the scythe that had tossed Esme like nothing more than a rag doll, Jensen reached out his hand and gently grabbed the worn handle. The weight of it was shocking to him. It felt heavy and unbalanced, but still, he picked it up and held it upright. Squinting, he noted small cracks not only in the handle but also chips on the edge of the blade. "It feels weird to hold this. It's like I'm doing something wrong. I never would have guessed how worn down it is."

Esme drew closer, taking in every little detail with intense scrutiny. "Because it was never this worn down. I've seen this a million times. It never had these markings. Look at where the blade meets the wood." She hovered her index finger, careful not to make contact again. "Those are burn marks, and the energy is wrong."

"Wrong how?" Camryn asked while tugging Alicia to his side.

Her eyes were fixed on the scorch marks around the juniper. "Slow, steady, measured—that's what it should feel like. This is sad and chaotic. The energy is off balance." She cleared her throat. Her mind went to the impossible, but in her current situation, what did impossible mean? "I'll clear some space in the closet." Jensen followed behind her, careful not to get too close.

They both went into her room and awkwardly shuffled around each other. Holding the object, even for a short amount of time, was starting to wear on him. Uncomfortable tingles ran up his arm while the scythe was starting to feel heavier with each passing second. She shuffled and shoved some dresses out of the way, then backed up, allowing Jensen to place it into the far corner of the closet. While nestling it away, his eye roamed past the dresses and landed on a couple of sweatshirts that belonged to him. He shook his head and smiled to himself.

He couldn't help but wonder if she wore them at night or while she watched a movie, tucking her feet into the hem of it. The memory of her in his sweatshirt, messy hair, and lounging around only increased his longing for her. When he turned around, he noticed Esme putting on a long black lapel cashmere coat. That's when Jensen noticed how she was dressed. The Esme he was accustomed to seeing wore T-shirts, faded jeans, and waist-length jackets. Seeing her in silk, leather, and cashmere was out of character to him, but she wore it like a second skin.

She turned around, pulling her hair out from the collar. "Sorry to disrupt your day. I know you're probably busy with Cora. You're not being too hard on her still, are you? I know she's annoyingly curious, but that's not always a bad thing." She noted the way he shuffled his feet. "Jensen. What did you do?"

His mouth formed a tight line as he recalled the earlier encounter. "Honestly, I don't know. What I do know is that I am no longer Cora's mentor. That role now belongs to Thalia."

Her eyes widened and a feeling of unease set in the pit of her stomach. "How the hell did that happen?" A shrill scream cut off their civil conversation. "What now?"

Esme and Jensen shared a tired look before making their way to the commotion. Once in the kitchen, the sight of Camryn boxing Alicia into the corner of the counter with his back against her chest just outright confused Esme. Who screamed? Why did they both look terrified? As she pondered the situation, her world literally turned upside down when Jensen tossed her over his shoulder. "Jensen! What are you doing? Put me down now."

"Like Hell I will. Is that what I think it is?" Jensen was making his way back to her bedroom, causing Esme to have to lift her chest and strain her neck to determine what the 'it' was in this situation. Then she caught sight of the thing that had everyone in the room terrified.

The beast redirected his attention to Jensen, stalking closer. "Seriously, Jensen, put me down. That's my hellhound. He won't hurt me or any of us."

"Yeah, okay. Sure thing. It's a hellhound, Esme! You can't trust that thing any further than you can throw it." The only thing Jensen did was tighten his grip around her waist.

"If you keep walking away with me like a caveman, he might attack you. You're going to make him think that you're a threat to me. I promise all of us will be safe." He hesitated but let her down slowly. She slid down his body, delicately landing on her feet. Their eyes never leaving each other. Her breath hitched as his fingers dug into her hips.

Shaking out her hands, she turned and faced the beast that was pacing like a caged animal. Esme stood tall, placing her hand out, and gave one command. "Come." The hound stopped its growling and walked over to stand in front of Esme. She circled him, wondering how he made it into a building designed just for reapers. Then realized that she still had a soul to collect. "It's fine, guys. He's not going to hurt you. We have a soul to hunt. So, if you don't mind."

"Does he have a name?" Alicia, while looking scared, also appeared wildly excited as she started to edge closer to the hound. Camryn snatched her and shoved her behind him again. "She said it wouldn't hurt us. I want to pet him."

Esme looked between them and said, "Which one of you screamed?"

Without hesitation, Alicia replied, "That was Camryn."

"I am not ashamed" was his only response.

Her shoulders shook as a cackle escaped her. "I'm sorry. I've just never heard you scream like that before. I thought it was Alicia. It's not like it's your first close encounter with a hellhound, Cam. No, he doesn't have a name. I never gave him one"—she lifted one finger—"and you absolutely cannot pet him."

"Yeah, it wasn't a great encounter, then, either," Camryn mumbled.

"How do you not name him? You call him yours, and he's protective over you. He deserves a name, Esme." Everyone stared at Alicia. This was a massive hellhound, not a puppy from the animal shelter.

"Naming a hellhound was never on my priority list, Alicia." She ran her hand over the muzzle.

"Hank! You should name him Hank. Oh, wait, Paul, wait, no Keith. I had an ex named Keith who was a bastard."

The hellhound growled at Alicia. "Down, boy," Camryn said sternly, reining in a determined Alicia.

"Esme, you actually think it's a good idea to go collect now?" Jensen did his best not to make direct eye contact with the beast in the room. While he trusted Esme, he did not trust this Infernal monster.

She tilted her head while her hand rested on the black fur. "I have a job to do, and I will do it. This is not up for debate or questioning, Jensen."

A delighted gasp broke the serious conversation. "Cuddles!" The hound barked and gnashed its teeth. "Okay, not cuddles. How about Scott-Lauren?" While the beast snarled, dripping thick saliva on the ground, the three reapers all dotted different forms of disbelief on their faces.

"Scott-Lauren? Where did that even come from?" Jensen couldn't help but get himself involved in this conversation.

"What? It sounded majestic. But I don't think he likes it." Alicia pouted and slumped to the ground.

Esme pointed a stern finger. "You're not naming my hellhound Alicia; he obviously is taking offense to every name you have thrown out there. Jensen, I'm going to collect this soul that is on contractual time. Camryn, you need to relax. He's not going to eat you."

Alicia stretched her legs out and huffed. "He should still have a name."

The hound lifted his head, casting his yellow gaze to Esme. His eyes pleaded with her. Was it to escape the craziness that was ensuing, or was it because he wanted a name? A twitch started forming in her eye. "Dominic. Okay? We'll call him Dominic. Happy? Are we all happy now?"

Dominic licked his jowls, flexing his long claws, and stretched his back.

Alicia clapped in delight. "Can I call him Domi for short?"

"I don't care. Knock yourself out." Esme rolled her shoulders, trying to ease the tension out of them.

"As much as I hate to admit this, Jensen has a point, Es. Is it a good idea for you to be doing this?" Camryn questioned, observing Dominic.

The room spun as she pinched her brows, taking deep breaths. "Good idea or not, it's happening."

Jensen shook his head, then scratched the corner of his eye. "You are the most stubborn being I have ever known."

She bit back a smile, letting the corners of her full lips quirk slightly. "You always liked me stubborn." It was clear how her heart called for him, but her mind pushed away from the thought of him. Her eyes traveled over to Alicia, who was still on the floor looking at the interaction occurring with longing in her eyes. Thinking back to what Alicia had mentioned earlier, Esme did one thing she never thought she would ever do. "You could tag along with me. If it makes you feel better."

Jensen's eyes lit up. Perhaps this was the opportunity he needed to show her that she didn't have to do this. That working with the beast was wrong. It was the opportunity to reconnect with her. "Okay, that's a good idea."

She rolled her eyes at his poor attempt at schooling his emotions. She nodded at Camryn. "Keep an eye on my assistant, will you?" Then smirked at Alicia. "Aperio." She snapped her fingers, and the bright portal opened. "Dominic, go." The hound entered the portal, and Jensen groaned. "Are you coming or not?" She tossed an expectant glance to Jensen before walking in herself.

"You better hustle." Camryn wore a stern expression. Jensen gave a glare in return. "Hey, Jensen. Don't fuck it up this time. If you do, I swear I really will castrate you this time."

Jensen nodded. "Deal." The light vanished as soon as it engulfed him. Camryn sighed and slid down to the floor next to Alicia.

"You love her, too, don't you?" For someone who was new to this world, Alicia was connected with those around her.

He gave a deep, half-hearted chuckle. "I always have, always will. But I'm not the one she wants, and I'm okay with that. I'll be there for her when she needs me, however she needs. That's enough for me."

Alicia rested her head on his shoulder and patted his thigh. "You're a good man Camryn. I wish I would have met someone like you when I was alive."

He rested his chin on her head. "I'm glad you didn't. You might think they're better than me." They sat in comfortable silence, enjoying each other's presence.

The light flashed as the portal closed behind Jensen. He looked around, observing the luxury around him. "Where are we?"

"Penthouse of Teague Niles." She walked to the wall of windows, basking in the light that warmed the space. The city life hustled below, cars racing, traffic lights and string lights turning on corner cafés. He walked next to her, admiring how the light glowed on her face. "It's a shame"— she pulled her jacket off her shoulders and tossed it on the leather sofa—"selling something precious for something that you can't even take with you at the end."

"Selling? I thought you were here to collect a soul." A questioning unease lingered between them. Jensen eyed her as she walked to the kitchen, disappearing behind the island. "What are you doing? Where is the soul?"

Esme's voice floated from behind the black marble counter. "I'm not purchasing what he's selling, Jensen. He already sold that to a crossroads demon years ago. I'm here to collect on payment now." She chuckled deep and curt as she stood, brandishing a bottle of wine. "Mr. Niles is preoccupied at the moment, given that he still has time on his contract. I get to the locations early, just in case." Her eyes darted to a dark corner of the room and smirked as she popped the cork on the bottle.

"What are you doing? You're enjoying this a little too much." He didn't conceal his growing worry at her nonchalant behavior.

"I'm having some of this rare vintage wine because it would be a crime for it to go to waste. Enjoyment is subjective. This is just another Tuesday for me. That's how long I've been doing this, Jensen. Need I remind you why?" The bitterness of her words was unintentional but exposed her true feelings. Why was moving forward difficult? Did she want to give him another chance? "Sorry." To keep from saying anything else, she swirled the vintage cabernet.

"I'm sorry. I don't want to fight anymore. I understand why you do this. How long though, Esme? How long do you have to work with that hellhound? We're reapers. That's not what we're meant to do." As he approached her, she found herself trapped between the counter and his chest.

Biting her lip, she hopped onto the counter to be eye level with Jensen. "I'm not exactly a normal reaper now, am I? So, maybe those rules don't apply to me. It's more of a gray area." She took a small sip, savoring the floral notes. "Besides, I've grown pretty attached to Dominic." She laughed before downing the rest of her wine.

Moans filtered down the hallway into the open space, followed by the sound of smacking flesh. Esme snorted at the flat gaze Jensen wore. "They're not actually, you know? Are we waiting for him to finish?" The most uncomfortable sentences came tumbling off his tongue. Never had he had a reaping like this. "Is it always this way?"

She couldn't help but beam a smile while swinging her legs off the edge of the counter. "Yes, Jensen, they are, in fact, having sex back there. Wanna go watch?" He sputtered, causing Esme to turn her head away but burst into laughter. "I'm sorry, it was too easy. I had to. But I'm not saying I haven't done that before. It can be fun and erotic." She took several breaths to recompose herself. "This makes me wish you were there with me when I apparated into the middle of an orgy. The 18th century in Britain was wild." She flashed a nostalgic smile and shook her head. "You can always find a succubus or an incubus in that crowd."

Trying his best to ignore the sounds that were growing louder, he focused on the giggling reaper sitting in front of him. When was the last time he saw her smile like that? The sound of her laugh was a beautiful melodious tinkling that made others laugh with it. "Why did you bring me with you? I thought it violated the set of rules you agreed to."

She poured herself a second glass, biting her bottom lip. The debate started in her mind about whether to tell him that she wanted to see if they could get along. Should she admit that she was deciding if she wanted him back? Maybe it was cowardly, but she went for the option that brewed easiest in her mind. "Well, it is, or at least was. Considering I already told you and everyone else everything, I'm pretty sure it doesn't matter anymore. Our entire world is going to shit, souls left uncollected, people departing when they aren't meant to, and Grim is missing. I think bringing you with me is the least of our worries." She ran her finger around the crystal glass's rim. "Plus, it made you feel better to not leave me alone." She gave a careless shrug, trying her best to playoff any emotions she felt.

"I never wanted to leave you." The murmur was quiet from him, but Esme pretended to not hear it as she chugged her second glass of wine. "Are you okay to drink that? Being half mortal and all?"

She raised a brow. "Good question. Well, my lips do feel a little weird." She swiped her tongue across her bottom lip. "I feel a little hot." She unbuttoned the top button on her shirt. "Let's find out, shall we?" Her concentrated gaze landed on Jensen's honey eyes and traveled down to his bobbing Adam's apple as he roughly swallowed. Their faces grew closer, a whisper of a space left between their lips. His breath fanned over her parted lips. Esme's eyes fluttered closed as his fingers caressed the edge of her jaw.

A deep growl emanated from the corner. It signaled the time was near for Dominic to begin his hunt. Esme's demeanor changed instantaneously. The fading glow on her cheek and his fingers was the only evidence of what could have been. A door opened and shut, followed by the sound of heavy feet. A man came out with a towel slung low on his hips. "Who the fuck are you?" The man's raspy voice echoed in the empty space. "I didn't order any other girls or guys tonight."

Esme hopped off the counter and sauntered into the living room. She made herself comfortable on the leather couch. The setting sun cast a fiery glow around her. "Teague Niles?" Noting the man's hesitation, she continued. "No need to lie.

I've already reviewed your contract that has your picture and scent."

"So what? You did a quick internet search, not enough for me to be impressed or scared. Now, who are you and pretty boy in the corner?"

Teague had alarms blaring in his mind, trying to remember if he had met this woman before. Perhaps she worked for someone who he had gotten into debt with, but the answer wouldn't come to him.

"I'm not a pretty boy." Jensen pouted over in the corner, observing Esme and the power she was suppressing while tracking the shadow that was creeping along the floor.

"Not now, love." She cleared her throat and readjusted her shirt, realizing the name she called Jensen. Jensen was beaming in the corner. It may have been a simple term of endearment or even just a slip of the tongue, but it rolled off her tongue effortlessly. "Mr. Niles, fifteen years ago, you signed a contract with a crossroads demon. All this luxury and a career as a noted photographer in exchange for something that you wouldn't miss too much. I believe it was your soul. The demon upheld her end of the bargain. Now it's time for you to do the same. My name is Esme. I'm a reaper who is here to collect that payment."

"Fuck you. I don't owe a thing. I told that bitch that I was done. I was out. Plus, I'm not dead. Aren't you supposed to wear a raggedy black cloak and have a spear or some shit?" Teague was backing away slowly, attempting to make his way back to the bedroom.

"You signed a contract in blood and sex. She was a succubus, remember? You can't just say you're out and be out. Maybe you should have read the fine print more closely. Either way, it's not my concern. You can take it up with her when you meet her in the underworld. Second, you are correct, you are not dead, yet. Your contract expires in two minutes as agreed upon on the terms of said contract. I can produce it if you want to reread it, but you wouldn't have enough time to scan each page. Third, don't stereotype me. Oh, and it's a scythe, not a spear or some shit." She rose from the seat, the leather creaking as it expanded again. "This is happening whether you want it to or not. I suggest that with the last minute you have left, you tell whoever is back there they should leave. And don't bother running, it just gets Dominic more excited."

Teague glanced over to Jensen, who shook his head. "Not me. She's talking about the hellhound that's behind you." It was only then that a hot huff that caused the hairs on the back of his neck to stand. He pivoted to run but tripped over his own feet.

A somber expression took over Esme's face. "Was it worth it?"

Teague scurried across the floor, slamming a door behind him. Muffled yelling and shuffling were heard coming from the bedroom.

"Jensen, make sure they can't see you." Just as he nodded, two women emerged from the bedroom, jackets and shoes in hand, storming toward the door. As the women left, Esme looked at Jensen, who cocked his head in question.

Her posture was rigid. This part, while she was accustomed to it, was new for Jensen, and she wasn't sure if him being here was a good idea anymore. "This bit is uncomfortable. Don't look over there, okay? It's better if you keep your eyes closed." His eyes narrowed, but he nodded and kept his eyes trained on Esme's face. He was taken aback by the power that radiated off her that was hidden this entire time.

"Dominic, eat." A rumble traveled across the floor boards, followed by scratching. All emotion wiped from her face when they heard it.

Jensen's eyes were shut tight, but he darted his arms out to encase Esme. Once she was in his arms, he spun around, so his back was to Dominic, who was tearing Teague apart. He clutched her head tighter to his chest, muffling the sounds with his hand over her exposed ear. As Dominic devoured the man, flesh and soul, Esme peeked from under Jensen's arm. Even though the sight and sound of gargled screams, blood misting the air, and bones crunching were grotesque, she couldn't help but smile to herself at the way Jensen held her out of protection for her or comfort for himself. In his arms, she didn't feel tired, worn, or lost. It felt right.

She pulled out of Jensen's arms. "Dominic, back to the shadows." He let out a deep growl of disapproval and stalked closer to her and Jensen. She traded places with Jensen, unleashing all her energy. It stifled the hellhound's and Jensen's energy. Her voice deepened and grew lethal. "Go back to the shadows and deliver which you devour!" Dominic growled, darting his eyes to Jensen before dragging his claws across the floor and disappearing below. "Sorry about that. He gets a little overzealous when he gets to have flesh and soul." She turned to face Jensen, who gave her a look she couldn't decipher. "Why are you looking at me like that?"

He lifted his head to look down the hall where a man was just delivered to the underworld in the most gruesome act he had ever witnessed. "This is what you do? This is what you agreed to do to stay here with me?" Blood had been sprayed on the walls and misted on the doors.

"With you." Her lips set in a straight line. She calmly walked back to the couch and reached for her coat.

"Esme, I . . ." He was taken aback by everything. It's one thing to hear about it, it's another thing entirely to witness it firsthand.

She flicked her fingers in front of herself, whispering "aperio" and walked through the portal, leaving Jensen to decide what he wanted to do for himself. As she walked through, his fingers entwined with hers before the portal closed. When they stepped out, Jensen found himself surrounded by the onyx walls he knew well. They were in Esme's room. "I'm sure you can find your way out from here. I have some paperwork to file and more research to do over at headquarters." Something between them was changing again, but she wasn't sure if she was ready for yet another change.

"Please don't shut down and push me away. You can send me into another blinding and empty portal again if it makes you happy. I'll find my way out and come right back here again. I'll do it over and over again if it makes you happy because I want to make you happy again."

Esme found her tongue unwilling to release any words as her lips parted. Her brows pulled in as she looked down.

This was the moment he needed to seize. He went for it once more. Laying his heart open and bare for her to see. His heart had always been hers to do with as she pleased. "I know what you're going to say. I know I broke you in the worst way possible, and there aren't and will never be enough apologies in our existence to ever make it better. By breaking you, I broke myself, too. Every day is pointless, meaningless. It's pure endless torture. I broke us, Esme, I take full responsibility for it." He closed his eyes, taking a calming breath as he noticed his words begin to quicken.

"Please let me take those broken pieces, big or small. Let me take both of our pieces. Creating what we had before is almost impossible and isn't what I want, but"—he carded his fingers through his hair—"maybe with these pieces, we can make a beautiful mosaic. Like the ones from Barcelona you love and always talked about."

Jensen shoved his right hand into his pocket, flourishing the other. "Being without you is something I don't want to keep doing. I love you, Esme. Only you. It's you I want and have ever wanted. If you say no right now, I'll respect it and leave you be. I will walk out of here, and you'll never have to see me or hear from me again unless you want to. Please, Esme. One more chance."

The pain in his eyes and the tremor in his voice were the last she could take. Her walls crumbled like ancient ruins. Taking a small step toward him, she spoke one simple sentence. "Please don't break my heart again."

"Never." One word, one promise, was all he could utter. The awe and relief on Jensen's face was enough for her to fist his shirt, pulling him into a fervent kiss.

Sparks erupted where their lips met, igniting a dormant passion. "I love you, too, Jensen. I never stopped."

This was the moment he had been yearning for, and it was far better than anything his mind had conjured in her absence. He skimmed her brow with a delicate brush of his fingers, pushing the curls away from her eyes. Unable to resist the sparks and tingles, she leaned her head into his palm, placing a kiss on his wrist. His hand slipped into her hair as his fingers wove into every curl, clutching them greedily, bringing her in closer for a bruising kiss.

The way she hooked her arms around his neck caused a deep hum of satisfaction to escape him, making Esme giggle against his lips. Jensen broke the kiss for only a moment to gaze into her eyes. "I love you. I missed you." He whispered as his hands stealthily traveled down her waist to the back of her thighs.

In one swift motion, he hoisted her up, and she matched his eagerness by anchoring her legs around his waist. She leaned in, their foreheads touching, tips of their noses brushing, and said, "Show me how much."

His restraint dissipated as he pressed her back against the wall, and she responded by pushing her chest into his. Her nails harshly scratched across his shoulders, up his neck, and into his hair. Jensen's nose traced a line from her lips, down her chin, and to her neck. Her scent and taste were intoxicating. It was better than the richest flower fields and finest wine this world had to offer. He wanted and needed more of her. He made sure more is what he had as his tongue massaged the soft flesh of her neck and gently bit down, teasing her sweet spot.

"Jensen," she panted, her need for him building deep within her increased with every passing second.

Hearing his name roll off her tongue added fuel to their fiery passion.

Before Esme could register that she was being carried off, her body was laid on the soft plush mattress. He stroked her face as he stood to his full height. Maintaining eye contact as he kicked off his shoes, he pulled his shirt off and slid his pants down, discarding the constrictive clothing carelessly. With her eyes following every ripple of muscle, she shamelessly admired the perfect man in front of her. "See something you like?" He smirked and bit his lip.

She nodded, unable to hide a growing smile. He leaned over her, placing his forearms on either side of her head.

Looking directly into her eyes, he asked, "Are you sure this is what you want?" While he was all in and more than ready, he had to make sure this is what she wanted, too. The last thing he wanted was for her to be filled with regret in the morning and go back to hating him.

There was lust evident in Jensen's eyes, but the love that was lurking in them outshone everything else. Had he always looked at her like this? Being engulfed by him, breathing him in, sinking into those warm pools of honey that bore into her very essence, she had never felt more sure of anything. This is where she belonged. This was her home, her heaven, her sanctuary.

A delicate hand lifted to brush the hair from his eyes. "I'm sure."

Their lips clashed against each other, and their tongues battled for dominance until he won. He brushed her sides with his fingertips and down to her hips, eliciting a shiver. He held her close, pulling her up to strip each layer off of her. She fell back onto the bed once the final layer had been removed. Her curls splayed about the silk sheets in a dark halo. His eyes roved over every inch of her, drinking her in as if he were a man dying of thirst. The more his eyes lingered on her, a knot grew heavy and tighter in the pit of her stomach. She clenched and rubbed her thighs, craving any kind of friction to ease the ever-growing knot.

"Beautiful" was the only word he could utter. Jensen wanted to call her enchanting, stunning, divine, breathtaking, but his mind had forgotten every word he had ever learned except for beautiful. He peppered kisses over her face, down her neck as his hands wandered freely. The hitch in her breath encouraged his further exploration. Her lips found his shoulders and biceps while her hands wandered down his chest. As she neared his cock, he tilted his hips away from her searching fingers, earning a pout from her. "This first round is all about you. Be a good girl for me and just relax. I'm going to take care of you." She bit her lip and moaned with anticipation and excitement at his words. His lips found her pebbled nipple, and he took it in his mouth, brushing it with his tongue while his other hand rolled and pinched the other. Gently, he bit it, causing her hips to eagerly seek his. He pulled her breast with his mouth, lifting it from her chest before releasing it. "Well? Are you going to be a good girl for me?"

Esme's mouth had gone dry, and her core dripped. She could feel how slick her thighs had become as she squirmed under his intense gaze. "I'll be a good girl for you."

He gave her a devilish smirk that made that knot in her stomach tighten further. With his deft fingers, he traced down the valley between her breasts, the flattened plane of her stomach, over the peaks of her hips and up her toned thighs. Her eyes fluttered closed when his fingers reached the pool forming at her center. "So wet and ready for me already?" His teasing tone matched the rhythm of the circles he conducted across her sensitive bud. "Let's see how ready you are." He dipped one finger into her, languidly moving in and out.

A frustrated groan fled from Esme's lips. "Please, Jensen." Her mind was a haze of love, lust, and need for this man.

"Please what? I'll give you anything you want and need, love. Use your words and ask." He continued his slow, tortuous movements. Alternating between circles and a whisper of a thrust.

"More. I need more, Jensen. I want more of you." Esme was ready to beg him for her release. The way he touched and caressed her was perfect. It was better than what her memories had replayed for her. He played her body like his own personal instrument, getting every sound he wanted, as he wanted, when he wanted.

His lips brushed her earlobe, his breath tickled her neck. "Don't worry, beautiful, I'll give you more." He added a second finger to his teasing rhythm, scissoring them inside of her. As his fingers curled, her nails drew beautiful red lines down his arms. Jensen's lips were not far behind his nimble fingers. Having memorized the map of her body into his mind, his lips trailed over every dip, curve, and line they could find.

His lips covered her core as his tongue traced her delicate folds before plunging in to savor and drink every drop he could. She choked back a moan as her hips bucked up toward the ceiling.

He responded by wrapping his arms firmly around her thighs, splaying them farther apart.

Lifting his head, he said in a husky voice, "If you want to swallow something, I'll give that to you later. But don't you dare swallow those moans. I've earned those."

"Fuck, Jensen." The way she breathlessly chanted his name was both prayer and plea. Her sounds were a siren's song that he would gladly fall victim to over and over.

He could feel her ready to reach her crescendo, but he wouldn't allow her that ending just yet. "I almost forgot how good you tasted." She reached for him, bringing his face up to hers. His lips and chin glistened with the evidence of her arousal. His fingertips rubbed gentle circles over her sensitive nub, keeping on the edge he danced her to. Bringing him closer, she kissed him eagerly, tasting herself on his lips.

"Now you're ready for me." Her eyes rolled back, and her back arched beautifully, like a newly formed crescent moon, as he slowly slid himself into her. With every delicious thrust, he brought her closer to the edge of bliss before bringing her back again. His hands squeezed and caressed her breasts and thighs freely, committing her form to memory and turning her into a moaning mess. "Open your eyes, beautiful." His voice was soft and assertive. When her gaze fell upon his, he noticed how blown out her pupils were. Leaning in close, he said, "You're mine." He pulled out of her before slamming back in. "Who do you belong to, Esme?" His movements slowed, waiting for her response.

Esme's voice was raspy from her moans and cries of pleasure. "You. I belong to you, Jensen."

"Good girl. You belong to me, and I belong to you." Slamming roughly into her, he sat back on his knees and allowed his fingers to anchor into her hips. Continuing his thrusts, he placed her ankles over his shoulders and slid his arm under her lower back. Her walls tightened around him, and he sped up the rate of his hips. Stunning goosebumps covered her skin. When she reached her climax, her neck stretched. He leaned in, sucking the skin on her neck as the muscles in his back coiled as he found his release.

His head rested on her shoulder, and her arms encased him. Her legs slid down his shoulders, cocooning Jensen's chest in the warmth of her thighs. As Esme's fingers ran gently through his hair, they both relished in the feel of one another. Before the night was through, he would make sure she knew and believed they belonged to each other. They spent the night entangled in each other, bouncing their moans, grunts, and cries of pleasure off the onyx walls.

It was dawn by the time they were both spent, and she had fallen asleep, bare in Jensen's arms. As she slept, he caressed her wild, dark, frizzy locks, stretching the twists and turns of each strand between his fingers. His eyes traced the lines of her leg that slung across his hips, and the arm that rested on his chest. The sun trickled in, painting the room with the warmth of the new day. With the rising sun, the warm light kissed Esme's exposed rich tawny skin, and for one irrational moment, Jensen found himself jealous of the sun because it was the first to kiss her today. He stifled his laughter the best he could at his own absurdity.

He laid there, admiring the afterglow that radiated off her. During the night, he had made sure every inch of her body was kissed and caressed. Skating his fingers across her collar bone, he traced the outline of the etching that the eternal paramour bond had left on her. It was a mirror of his. The image of an intricate abstract swirl that reminded him of feathered angel wings shimmered with each pass of his digit.

The etching was a marking that bonded reapers once they had found and accepted their eternal paramour. An identical image formed on each pair but was different from any other pair. It was the easiest way to show your devotion to each other and share in the ardor fragment. During their separation, the etching had slightly faded to appear as nothing more than a faded tattoo. But then, it was back to the warm gold contrasting effortlessly with her own natural glow.

Esme began to stir, and he mentally kicked himself. The last thing he wanted was to wake her. She needed to rest. He knew she had been through so much already and how her body was fighting itself. Her body shivered against him as she let out a small whimper. His brows pinched as he pulled her closer to him and pulled the sheets higher over her shoulders. He held her tighter, tucking her head under his chin as the shivers continued to trek through her body. "Jensen. Jensen." Hearing her whimper, his name broke him.

A loud pitch rang through her ears. She grabbed at her ears to muffle the sound, but it was useless. The pitch had penetrated her brain, and her eyes began to burn. Then she felt it. With no warning, the cold metal blade ripped through her chest. Two figures stood before her as another came running toward her, screaming for her. A black blur swept in front of her vision, followed by screams. Smoke and sparks surrounded her.

Esme thrashed around the sheets, unable to feel Jensen's attempts to wake her from the ongoing nightmare. "Esme, Esme wake up, love." He cradled her close as he sat up, leaning against the black velvet headboard, rocking their bodies. She awoke with a pained scream and tears rolling down her cheeks. "It's okay, love. It's okay, I'm here. I got you. You're safe." Jensen kept whispering reassurances while kissing the top of her head. He was at a loss of what else he should do. Normal reapers don't dream, let alone experience nightmares. "Do you want to talk about it?"

She wiped tears from her eyes. "There's not much to talk about. It's the same dream I've been having for months now. It was just slightly different this time." Esme cleared her throat, adjusting herself against his chest. "It's always me in an open, empty space of some kind and there's a noise that makes my ears hurt. Then I get stabbed. Except, this time, there were other people there. I couldn't make out who they were." She looked up from beneath her lashes. His face contorted in concentration.

He continued to play with her hair and spoke. "I'll never let anything happen to you, as long as I can prevent it."

Esme chewed on her bottom lip and gave voice to her biggest fear. "Jensen, what if I die?"

Jensen slid down the bed, allowing himself to be at eye level with her. He took in her glassy eyes and trembling chin. "What do you mean by that?"

She turned to face him, resting her head in the crook of her arm. "I'm half mortal. I don't know if that means I can die. I don't want to die. But look at what my body is doing. Do I have a soul? Would I go anywhere if I did die?"

Jensen rested on his elbow and reached over to push a rogue curl out of Esme's eyes. His face hardened, voice resolute. "I just got you back. I will pitch a damn fit if I were to lose you. The only place you're going is home, with me, every day." He leaned down, placing a gentle kiss on her forehead. "Even if there is a small chance that you could die, we'll cheat death. Who better to find a way to escape death than reapers?"

Just as she reached up to cup Jensen's jaw for another lingering kiss, the door creaked open, showcasing Alicia in the doorway. "I heard screaming, and not the fun kind from last night. But in case it was, I decided to give you a little extra time. I didn't know if you two like to get extra kinky or not."

Esme laughed as she hid her face in Jensen's bicep. Jensen was stunned into silence. "I thought I told Camryn to take care of you before we left?" Esme spoke, unable to make direct eye contact.

"Oh, yeah, he totally kept me company for a while, but he had a list thing or something to do. So, I stayed here just in case you needed someone to talk to when you got back." Alicia twirled a purple lock around her finger and hollowed her cheeks. "But it wasn't needed. Those sounds will forever live rent free in my mind. I'll go make some coffee." She turned to close the door behind her and shouted before it clicked closed. "You guys look super cute together!"

"Thank you, Alicia!" Esme chuckled.

"Sure thing, boss lady." Before scurrying back down the hall, she cracked the door open a few inches. "Good job catching that smoke, Jensen!"

Esme pursed her lips. "Smoke?"

He rolled himself on top of her, adoring the curiosity in her eyes. "No idea what she's talking about." He pressed a long kiss to her lips as he grazed her skin with his fingers until he found his mark. Her eyes fluttered closed, and a sigh floated from her lips. "Good morning, beautiful."

"Good morning, handsome." She moaned as his fingers delved into her core.

20

Five months had come and gone since the scythe had found its way to Esme, and the reaping world was in a continuous downward spiral. Lists had become few and far between and growing into extinction. Souls were wandering around cities across the globe without any reaper to escort them. Mortals were dying ahead of schedule or not at all. The worst part was, the Grim Reaper was still missing. No one had seen or heard from him for several months. All reapers looked to upper management, who looked to Ansel and Thalia for instructions.

Esme, Jensen, Camryn, and Alicia were making their way to the Grim Reaper's office. As they walked the streets, Esme grew increasingly agitated. The normally crowded sidewalks, with mortals racing to go nowhere, were now full of lost, unclaimed souls who could not go to the veil. "This is ridiculous. How does the Grim Reaper just vanish off the face of the Earth? It's stifling here, and the human world is becoming depressing." Esme sneered. She rolled her neck as energy pulsed around her, creating a bubble, allowing space for them to walk untouched.

Camryn and Jensen could have easily apparated with Alicia to headquarters. It was because of Esme they found themselves walking. Apparating with anyone left her tired, and her portals had become unstable. She had begged them to go ahead without her so she could meet them there. Esme had felt like she was becoming a burden, even though the others voiced differently. They went out of their way to make sure she was comfortable and had everything she needed. Jensen, true to his word, never left her side. He loved her and cared for her as if she is what made his world go round.

They had spent their nights curled up together on that red chair as he wrapped her in a green waffled blanket and read to her. Every night, she had fallen asleep in his arms and awoken the same. Even though her energy and abilities waned, the love between them only increased. Jensen lifted her hand as their fingers were still entwined and placed a small kiss on her palm. "Try and relax, love. I know it's a lot, but hopefully, we'll find some answers in the office." He brought her in a little closer to place a gentle kiss on her temple. She gave a sigh of content as his lips touched her skin.

"If it makes you feel any better, the human world has always been depressing. It just had small glimmers of happiness with cute cat videos and laughing babies." Alicia chimed in as she wrapped Camryn's arm around her shoulders. He simply glanced at her, amused at her happiness, and pulled her in closer.

The buildings closed in around Esme. The air grew stale and heavy. The feeling of being watched caused the hair on the back of her neck to stand on end. Even though her mind was racing, and her eyes ping-ponged to every corner, she remained still. Whoever or whatever was currently watching her made her feel like a caged animal waiting to be poked and prodded. Jensen squeezed her hand, gaining her attention, giving her a concerned look. She shook her head and gave a tight-lipped smile, trying to brush the feeling off, and continued to the office.

Snow fell around them, and the air nipped at any exposed skin it could. In the passing months, Esme had shown more signs of being mortal. Her fainting spells were more common. When vast amounts of energy were exerted, she would end up in a seizure and hemorrhage. Recently, the cold sliced right through her, carving itself into her bones. She was the only reaper who still had a list to work. All were contract collections, but she never went alone anymore. Jensen was always there with her in case he needed to apparat her out.

"Are you sure she's not holed up in there again?" Esme scowled.

Camryn spoke from behind her. "I have it on good authority that she isn't there today." Since the scarcity of collection lists, they had been attempting to get into the Grim Reaper's office, but Thalia claimed that office her own, and when she was not in it, Ansel was. Cora was never far from either of them, much like a loyal pet.

"Do you think Cora is here?" Alicia hadn't seen or spoken to her first afterlife friend since the portal incident. Even when Thalia and Ansel were in town, Cora never sought out her original group, and they never tried to seek her out, either. "Side note, it's weird being in the cold and not feeling the cold."

Jensen looked over his shoulder, watching Alicia play with Camryn's fingers and try to catch snowflakes on her tongue, as he asked, "Whose authority is it?"

As Camryn was about to answer, Tyler came out of the mirrored building, shaking his head. "Hey, there reapers, and soul. I haven't seen you in a while." There was a slight tilt in his head that was easy to miss, but the way his eyes scanned Esme had her noticing immediately. "You okay there, boss lady? Esme?"

Her eyes were busy capturing every living and nonliving person around them. Her mind was in overdrive. Everything felt overwhelming: the sounds, sights, smells, and energy coming from every direction were all too much. It was a corset cinched too tight, limiting her breaths. She looked down at her left hand. If someone were to tell her that there was a fire burning under her hand, she would believe them from the intense burn she was feeling.

Colorful spots flashed behind her eyes. "I'm fine." She gave a tight grin, mimicking the tension in her fingers that squeezed Jensen's. Two squeezes are what he gave her in return, letting her know he had her. A silent conversation, much like all the others they have shared, knowing looks, quiet arguments, and I love yous with only their eyes. These squeezes told him that she needed to get out of there—and fast.

"Who are they, and what are they doing?" Alicia nodded over at two creatures circling a group of souls.

"Fucking low-level demons." An unexpected burst of energy spurted from Esme. The buildings whirled around her as a vignette skirted her vision. Jensen cupped her face and kissed each eyelid.

Camryn tucked Alicia closer to him. "Those are soul snatchers."

"Soul snatchers?" The title alone caused her to burrow deeper into Camryn's warmth and safety.

"Those Infernals are becoming bold. They normally have to work harder to get a soul before a reaper does. Without the big guy around telling reapers who to escort it's a buffet for them. Nothing we can we do, either. That's why it's important for Death to be around. One thing is certain, the underworld is going to be in disarray, with all these snatchers vying for power." Her eyes lit up with understanding, and Tyler shot her a wink as he felt proud of his explanation.

Esme and Jensen seized the opportunity of Alicia's question to make their way into the building unnoticed, except by Camryn, who nodded. The last thing they needed was another reaper asking questions about Esme that they didn't have answers for. Their world was already in disarray. Rumors about a fellow reaper would help no one and only incite panic. That's why they were there that day, to scour through every book they could find in the Grim Reaper's office. With two walls stacked with more books than anyone could count, there had to be an answer hidden somewhere.

The lobby's energy was a restless buzz that caused Esme to grit her teeth. Reapers were never meant to be stagnant; they had a single purpose only resting to recharge their energy. Stagnancy is a cancer to any world; it leads to restlessness, which turns into recklessness that becomes chaos, and ultimately, forms into anarchy. Signs of that slippery slope had already begun. Reapers would spend all day at The Twisted Sickle, arguing among each other, creating conspiracy theories as to why the Grim Reaper left. Others made themselves noticeable to the mortals and interacted with them as a source of entertainment.

They both stood in front of the elevator, waiting for the doors to open as Camryn and Alicia kept Tyler entertained. As the door opened, they quickly entered, and Jensen jabbed at the Close Door button before any other reapers could enter. When the doors finally closed, Esme slotted the special key into the hole of the button panel. The hole was easy to miss unless you knew it was there. The Grim Reaper valued his privacy, and only he and Esme had keys to his offices.

That is what stumped Esme the most. She couldn't figure out how Thalia and Ansel entered his office without a key. As far as she was aware, they all hated each other. Her stomach churned, uncertain if it was from the elevator or the nefarious thoughts in her mind. She was certain of the feeling something truly terrible had happened.

Stepping into the private office, shock took over Esme's body, freezing her in her tracks.

Jensen analyzed the walls, flooring, and shelves. It was clear by the look on his face that this is not what he was expecting. Gone were the moss green walls and intricate chair railing. The wooden desk and brown high back leather chair were nowhere to be seen. In their place were blinding white walls, a white L-shaped marble desk with a seven-point white chair behind it. White tile had even replaced the flooring. Any trace or memory that this office had once belonged to the Grim Reaper had been scrubbed clean.

"What in the sanitary space station?" Tyler's voice floated through the air, causing Esme to spin a little too quickly, crashing into Jensen's chest. He grabbed hold of her hips to steady her from falling as she regained her bearings. Their silent conversation began.

"I'm waiting for the smell of bleach to invade my nostrils." Alicia piped up behind Tyler as she freely perused the office. Camryn was hot on their heels, looking more frustrated than anything. He gave a quick glance, trying to convey an apology. Alicia snorted as Tyler sniffed the air for traces of the potent scent.

In a stage whisper, Tyler leaned into Alicia and Camryn. "Why are they staring at each other like that?"

Wordlessly, Camryn made his way to the shelves to scan book titles, leaving Alicia to answer. "Oh, mom and dad are probably arguing again."

He snickered and clapped his hands. "What are we doing here or looking for? I need something to do. Put my idle to work hands before the devil makes use of them."

They all shared a look, then waited for Esme's lead. "Just looking for anything that could tell us where the boss man is. Or if there is a way to bring those lost souls to the veil."

Tyler's naturally playful demeanor shifted slightly as he focused solely on Esme. "Wouldn't Thalia or Ansel be looking into that?"

Not appreciating the way Tyler was staring at Esme, Jensen angled his body to slightly cover her. "I don't know, would they? It's been months, and they've been silent. There's no harm in us doing some research of our own. Also, as management, I think it's okay."

"Right, but how did you get in here?" His eyes still never leaving Esme. Tyler studied her and with every passing second, he saw deeper into her essence.

"Do you want to help or not?" Camryn questioned and threw a book at Tyler, who caught it with a slight fumble.

He sat on the floor since there was no other option and opened the book. "Oh, come on, man, you gave me one that doesn't have any pictures. It's also in German."

Alicia plopped a notebook and pen down next to him. "Do you speak German?"

"Oui." Mischief twinkled in his eyes as he wore a winsome smile.

Hours had passed, and the group was no closer to finding any answers. Plenty of books and scrolls chronicled the Grim Reaper and reapers in general. They found passages of witches, covens, and spells, which had led to talk about getting help from witches to do a summoning spell. The biggest problem with that was that witches had all but gone underground. Any witch or warlock worth their salt was a rarity to find, and magic never came cheap. The wards master that had performed the wards for all the reaper buildings in Philadelphia and friend to Death, had passed away twenty years prior and left no information for his coven or wards apprentice.

Esme grew increasingly tired and frustrated, and it was becoming apparent. Huffing and rolling her shoulders, energy rippled off of her, causing a shock wave to spread across the room. Lights flickered and a few books flew off the shelf. She cleared her throat and said, "Sorry," only there wasn't any remorse in her voice.

Voices leaking from the other side of the door caused the room to still. Cora and Ansel entered together, cutting their own conversation short. "Well, hello." Ansel strolled into the office and made his way behind the desk. He sat, looking at the desk and his surroundings with clear disdain. "I just want to unleash a horde of toddlers armed to the teeth with markers in here." He rested his Italian leather shoes on the desk. "What brings you lot in here?"

"Storytime." Tyler waved a book in the air.

Cora glanced around until she made eye contact with Esme. The way she carried herself was different. She no longer appeared unsure or meek. Her chin was lifted as she walked with purpose. Esme couldn't help but let a slight sneer flicker on her face. Cora was resembling too much of Thalia, even in the imitation of clothing.

Just like all other reapers, Cora was taller than Esme and made it a point to accentuate it, too. She looked down her nose at Esme. "It's been a while since I've seen you. I'm honestly surprised to see you walking around with everyone. Since, you know, the last time we saw each other, you sent Jensen into a portal and looked like you were on a death bed. You still look like you're on a death bed."

Esme looked uninterested in the reaper before her. "Oh, Cora, that is you. I would have never guessed, seeing as though you resemble Thalia now."

For being physically small, her presence alone took up more space than a mountain. Without inching closer, hardening her eyes, and speaking sternly, Esme asserted herself. "Don't try and stand before me as if you're a chess master when you just grasped the concept of tic-tac-toe."

After months of working with Thalia to be better and the best, Esme saw her, the real Cora, the same reaper from the start of training, and reduced her down to nothing yet again. All the confidence she learned to carry dissipated faster than fog on a sunny morning. Seeing her shrink in size, Esme felt a sense of twisted pride. She didn't want to make Cora feel small, but she needed to remind her not only of her place in this world but also who she is. She needed Cora to know that pretending to be someone doesn't make you that person. "Now, seeing as you came to me, what is it you need?"

"I'm pretty sure I've learned all that I can from Thalia. I was wondering if I could shadow you when you work with that hellhound." Her voice was small and uncertain.

"No." Esme replied.

"No? Why?" Cora asked.

"Maybe you've been on vacation and haven't heard the news. I'll catch you up. There are next to no lists. Without lists there is nothing to do." This wasn't a lie, just a slight omission of the truth.

"Oh, you mean Domi? He's sweet once you get used to him." Alicia chimed in from her spot on the floor, still surrounded by books.

"The thing has a name. You named an Infernal like an adopted pet?" The way she still twiddled with her fingers and pulled at the hem of a shirt gave away the discomfort Cora was feeling.

Esme turned her back, no longer caring for the conversation. "What brings you here, Ansel? Last I checked, this was the office for the Grim Reaper."

He lifted his chin, resting his thumb under it, and his index finger on his lips. "Yes, well, seeing as though he is." He coughed and cleared his throat. "Thalia is now attempting to take full control of the reaping world one office at a time, I suppose."

He tossed a worn black leather journal on the desk. The thud echoed in the tensely quiet room as all eyes locked on it. The journal appeared as nothing more than an inkblot on an empty white canvas. "To answer your question, my dear, I was simply seeing if the scythe had found its way here. I've checked every other possible location and have returned empty-handed." He held his arms out to the side, almost childlike, to show how futile his searching had gone. "It's extremely important that we find it. Not only is it necessary to carry out a mass collection of these poor lost souls"—he shook his head as he placed his folded hands on top of his lap—"anyone possessing such an instrument of death could technically call themselves the Grim Reaper, since the Grim Reaper has . . . vanished."

Camryn and Jensen darted their eyes to Esme, both looking worried and confused. Alicia squirmed uncomfortably on the floor. Esme's brows lowered as she paced the cold tile floor. The soles of her shoes caused a faint squeak to linger around them as she paced. "Please explain this mass collection and how someone can call themselves the Grim Reaper. The scythe was made for him and him alone. No one else can use it."

"It's simple. The veil is partly powered by the energy of the Grim Reaper. The scythe was intended for mass collections, considering it was created before there were, well, you. The Grim Reaper would go around, town to town, city to city, and find the center of it. Once he was in the right location, he would slash the air around him with the blade, then quickly pound the Earth with the bottom of the scythe. Then, after a few minutes, all souls would be drawn to the energy and light, it would omit. Once a soul was touched by the scythe, it would be tethered to it until reaching its final destination, the veil." He stood, smoothing the wrinkles on his pants. "While, yes, it is meant for him to use, I would assume any original reaper could wield it with some practice, taking into account that we are only slightly weaker than him in terms of energy."

Cora observed everyone's interactions. She couldn't help but find it interesting how tense everyone had become at the mention of the scythe. Thalia would certainly want to hear about this. Her eyes found Ansel, and she signaled she was heading out.

Ansel walked over to the group in front of him, rubbing his fingers against his chin, and glanced at the door. "Listen, I know you don't know me. I don't know what happened between all of you and Cora, but I'm worried about her. When she came to see us, she made a deal with Thalia. She was so lost, like a child trying to find their place in the big, scary world. But now"—his eyes searched their faces and landed on Jensen—"she's become just like Thalia, and we know that Thalia will never stop to get what she wants." He gently placed his large hands on Esme's small shoulders and bent his knees to lock eyes with her. "Whatever you do, if you find the scythe or know where it is, do not tell Cora or Thalia. She's been obsessed with becoming Grim Reaper. She hated him and everything he did. The scythe is the only thing Thalia needs now. If you happen across it, Camryn has my number."

Her bottom lip rolled in between her teeth before pursing them together. "I don't care much for Cora at the moment. What do you mean, 'The only thing she needs now?'"

Ansel curled his fingers into Esme's shoulder, tightening his grip. His eyes were hard, and his voice was barely above a whisper. "The Grim Reaper is gone. He no longer exists. Thalia killed Death with his own scythe." A whoosh of air left Esme's lips. "She's now fixated on you."

21

Once Cora was out of the office, she apparated to a loft in a nearby building. The creaking floors showed their age with veined cracks and a dull luster. Exposed brick on three walls and floor-to-ceiling windows on another, metal beams on the ceilings, and exposed metal piping did nothing to fill the cavernous area. A crushed blue velvet couch and matching armchair had been positioned to face one another by the window.

In the armchair, Thalia sat, waiting. She watched Cora like a hawk. "So, what did you learn?"

Cora plopped down on the couch, kicking her pointed stiletto heels off with a sigh. "Well, I think you're right,"

"I didn't ask if you thought I was right, Cora. I inquired about what you learned." A scowl had found its way on Thalia's face. Her long nails thrummed against the armchair's padding.

Cora sat up a little straighter, tucking her hair behind her ears. "Right, well, they're just fine. Alicia is still hanging around them as if she were a reaper. Camryn was Camryn, silent as always." She held her right elbow with her left hand and shrugged. "Those rumors are true. Esme and Jensen are together again. He hovered over her, never leaving her side. She, on the other hand, looks haggard. Like death personified. Oh, and they certainly know something about the scythe, too."

This piqued Thalia's interest. Leaning forward in her chair, motioning for Cora to continue. Her eyes sparkling with excitement and anticipation.

"When Ansel mentioned the scythe, they got quiet and kinda tense"—she scrunched her face—"now that I think about it, they all looked at Esme. For what, I don't know, but all eyes were on her."

"Perfect"—a sinister smile spread across her lips—"the little witch is finally being drained."

"Witch?" Cora snorted. "More like bitch."

"If they look to her, she's obviously the one in control. She must know where the scythe is. One word should never make someone uneasy if there is nothing to hide." Continuing her monologue and completely disregarding Cora, she chewed on her nails, thinking of how to proceed. "Was Ansel still with them when you left?"

She nodded in response. "There was something odd about him, too. The way he was acting."

"He's none of your concern. Ansel knows his role to play in getting me the scythe, just like you know yours." Thalia's voice sent chills down Cora's spine. "Once I'm the Grim Reaper, you'll be one of us. Just like in our agreement. How would anyone dare look down on you when you're the one in the position to tell them what to do?" There was no room for doubt now. She had a plan, and it was coming together perfectly. She wouldn't let anything—or anyone—stand in her way now, especially a young reaper who could so easily be swayed.

"You're right. Esme still has the hellhound but claims that she no longer works, just like the rest." Cora swung her legs on the couch to stretch out a little more.

Ansel walked into the loft with a content look on his face. He picked up Cora's legs and placed them on his lap as he sat. "Hello, ladies." His fingers skimmed the back of Cora's calves, continuing a trek up her inner thighs where he drew lazy circles. "All went according to plan." He winked at the now blushing young reaper.

"If you two are done with your school yard flirting," Thalia ridiculed, "I have an inkling of where we should look next." She gracefully stood and sauntered to the large windows. Clasping her fingers behind her back, she said, "Our dear Cora has done remarkably well. Telling us all the dirty little secrets she knows. That is why you will go with me on this scavenger hunt. You've been there before."

The world opened up under Esme's feet. Dead? Killed? The dread she was feeling, the nagging in the back of her mind, her worse fear came true. This couldn't be right, could it? All for power? Could Thalia be that power-hungry, that she would kill the Grim Reaper with his own scythe? There had to be more to this.

"What are we missing? We must be missing something here, right? What drove her to want to become the Grim Reaper?" Camryn was pacing along the bookshelves, racking his brain for a plausible reason.

Alicia stood twirling and untwirling her hair, deep in thought. "Wait!" She jumped up and down. "Camryn, remember when you told Cora and me the story about the three of them? You said something happened back in the 1600s, right? Then he was constantly on the move. What if that rift is what had him on the move for centuries?"

Stopping mid-stride, Camryn turned and faced everyone else. He snapped his fingers, then pointed at Alicia. "She might be on to something. The timing seems correct. What if Thalia had tried to kill him before? So, he took off to maintain balance. Think about it, she kills him, and the balance of life and death becomes unbalanced. He knew it would happen and tried to avoid it."

Jensen was leaning his hip against the desk with his hand in his pocket. "But why not just kill her first, then? If she could use the scythe on him, it would be child's play for him to use it on her. What do you think, love?" He turned his head to look at Esme, who was slouched in the desk chair.

Her unfocused eyes were glassy. She continuously rolled her bottom lip between her teeth. Every book that lined the shelves was sent flying through the air and skidding across the floor. "Did you know that he would always try and talk people out of Infernal contracts? He always said every life was worth living and saving no matter how big or small because they were all part of the balance." She let out a humorless chuckle.

Jensen cocked a brow. "He was there for the contracts you collect on now?"

She hummed in response. "If the contract was big enough, yes. Look at where we are now. If one mortal is meant to die and escapes death, another must take its place. That upsets the balance of life and death. The Grim Reaper has to reset the balance. To answer your question, he would rather not kill anyone, even Thalia, because she had a purpose as well."

She flicked her eyes to Jensen. "Why did Ansel focus on you when he mentioned Thalia not stopping at anything to get what she wants?"

He stretched his neck, clearing his throat. This was not something he wanted to mention to Esme, especially without proof. "Well, when Cora defected, Ansel was in my office and had mentioned that Thalia used a witch's potion on me. It was a potion to have me be with her, only her." Roughly swallowing, he darted his eyes to Esme.

"She used a binding tonic on you? That's why you"—she licked her lips and dug her fingers into her thighs—"you knew this before we got back together and didn't tell me?" He nodded and cast his eyes down. She wasn't angry with Jensen; she was furious with the situation and how Thalia was responsible for every horrible thing that has happened so far. As her thoughts lingered on Thalia, her hands clenched into fists. She slammed her fist down on the marble desk, causing it to crack in half and Jensen to stumble. The floor vibrated, and chasms formed along the veins of the marbling in the tile. "I'm going to kill her."

Tyler, who was leaning against the wall, watching and listening to everything, spoke up. "You can't kill her, Esme. It's not you. You're too good to do that."

"The fuck I can't. If she could kill the Grim Reaper, I can return the favor. I spent my entire existence with him. He made me who I am today, and she took him from me. She is the reason for the pain and suffering Jensen and I went through. I don't know who you think I am, or what I am or am not capable of, but I will do this. It is who I am." The chair flew into the wall behind her as she stood. "I am a reaper, who is half mortal, who works with a damn hellhound! Nothing is impossible for me to do."

"You're part mortal?" Tyler shook his head. He was taken aback by her declaration and revelation. It made Esme's current appearance and her shift in energy understandable. "I guess that explains why you're different from the rest."

She sighed and rubbed at her temples, willing the oncoming migraine to disappear. It was foolish of her to admit it to another reaper. No one else should have known about her. She slowly crept closer to Tyler. "I swear to the powers that be, both Celestial and Infernal, that if you so much as hint anything about me to any being"—her lips formed a snarl, her voice low and menacing—"I will end you, too." The lights flickered overhead.

He lifted his hands in surrender. "I promise, you have nothing to worry about from me, boss. You are a very scary lady, and I very much like my existence."

She eyed him up and down. She didn't know if he could be completely trusted. While they got along well and had a friendly relationship with each other, they still didn't know one another well. His record was hazy and incomplete. Tyler didn't always work in Philadelphia. His transfer papers from France were misplaced during the last Administrator changes. Not knowing information on anyone never sat well with Esme, but Tyler still had no reason to be disloyal. "Since you're wrapped up in everything now, how would you like to make yourself a little more useful?"

Tyler gave a big smile. "Idle hands, remember? I am at your disposal to work as you will it."

She gave him a quick smile and a pat on his shoulder. "Go see if you can find Cora, Ansel, or Thalia. If you do, follow them for a bit and see if they meet up with anyone and where." No fiber in her body trusted that group. Especially not Thalia and Cora. He saluted and vanished in a blink of an eye.

"What do you want to do, Es? Obviously, you can't give the scythe to Thalia. So, why not give it to Ansel?" Camryn couldn't help but think that was their best option. He is one of the originals and warned them about Cora and Thalia. Ansel revealed the truth about the Grim Reaper.

Jensen was standing near Camryn. There were plenty of thoughts in his mind and chewed on the words before speaking. "Camryn has a point, honey. What if Ansel is the key to fixing everything. The reaping world and the mortal world could go back into order, the way it was meant to be."

Camryn, Jensen, and Alicia all stood on one side of the room, while Esme stood in the center of the book-riddled floor. "Absolutely not. I know nothing of him, except for the fact that he is always by Thalia's side. How do we know that he isn't just going to give it to her? What do you truly know about him? Other than he's an original reaper and the head of a department. If that's the requirement, I can say the same for myself." Her voice grew loud and impatient.

All of it didn't make sense. "If that is your logic, then ask yourself, why did the scythe end up in my apartment? Why not end up in his hands or Thalia's hands? I will not give up the scythe, not yet."

The energy in the room was stifling the more Esme paced and kicked the various books out of her way.

"What about all those souls out there, Esme? Don't they deserve a chance to move on? I think the guys are right. Ansel might be the best choice." Alicia's voice was small and unsure. She could only speak from a soul's perspective. The thought of moving to her afterlife had crossed her mind on more than one occasion. Maybe this would be her chance to move on, too.

Lights and spots began to prance in the corner of Esme's vision, and the floor wobbled beneath her feet. Her breathing became short and fast. As she lifted a shaking finger toward the desk, she muttered, "Black spot."

The impact of her head made a sickening crack that echoed off the walls. A flash of bright white light filled the room for a fraction of a second. Once the light disappeared, Esme did. A pool of shining thick crimson blood was left behind, the books surrounding it soaking it in and filling their pages with the new ink.

"Holy shit! Where did she go? Is she dead? Wait, can she die? What black spot was she talking about?" Alicia's mouth moved faster than a lightning strike.

"I have no idea where she is. We don't know if she can die, but she better fucking not be dead. I just got her back. She's not allowed to die in any way, shape, or form."

Jensen closed his eyes as he spoke, trying to find the chaos that is Esme's energy.

While Jensen concentrated and Alicia was speaking her unfiltered thoughts, Camryn surveyed the room. What could Esme have meant by the black spot? He thought the answer could be something as simple as she saw black spots before vanishing like a magician. Then again, nothing was or is ever simple with Esme. He paced the office space, avoiding the red pool on the ground, then he paused. Standing where she stood, he bent his knees slightly to be able to see what she saw from her perspective. His eyes traced the line to where she pointed, and he smiled in victory to himself.

In a room of white, the black journal that Ansel discarded on the desk would look like a black spot to anyone. It now laid on the floor, hidden under the crumbles of marble. As he wiped the white dust, the detailing caught his eye. The spine had cracks and creases, the cover's edges had long since faded from black to tan. The flat leather twine had frayed from constant use. Finger marks were permanently embedded from where a large hand had held it repeatedly. Oxidation had taken its toll on the pages, turning the exposed edges and corners yellow.

As Camryn opened the journal, the leather's quiet groan filled the room. The handwriting in it was elegant, beautiful, skillful. It was clear that whoever wrote this did so with clear thoughts and purpose. The writing was only on one side of each page, probably because the author of this book did not want the ink to seep through the fibers, ruining their most precious thoughts.

The world faded around him as he read the pages. His hands trembled with every turning of the page. Why did Ansel have this artifact? Did he leave this as a token and sign of good faith? Or was it done by accident? More questions grew in his mind as he skimmed pages and reread others. "Oh, fuck."

Alicia and Jensen stopped what they were doing to see what had caught Camryn's attention. He held the open journal to Jensen, no other words leaving his lips. Jensen grasped it gently. His eyes to skim across the yellowed pages. Every flourish of black ink engrossed him further into the journal entry. Alicia leaned in close to allow herself to read.

Her hand covered her gasp, and Jensen just stared at the pages, almost waiting for the words to change. "We have the Grim Reaper's journal." Jensen's voice matched the disbelief on his face. "How do we tell Esme about what this says?"

Camryn placed his hands on his hips and shook his head. "We don't tell her." He looked at the two beings in front of him. What they discovered changed everything they had ever known. Everything they have ever been taught would—and will—change. Esme had already been through hell and back, and she kept coming out on top. Granted, she never came out unscathed, but she always came out better. The worry that took up residency in him clawed at his chest like a feral cat. This could be the tipping point that finally broke Esme forever. "She needs to read it for herself."

Jensen and Alicia nodded, the same feral scratching growing in them as well. However, Esme not only deserved to know, but she needed to know. "Her energy is ping-ponging everywhere. Most traces of her energy are all over the city, but the strongest pull is back at her apartment. It might be old but, I say we start there." Jensen tightened his grip on the journal while Camryn grabbed hold of Alicia and quickly apparated to Esme.

22

Energy radiated out of the apartment, seeping through walls, filling every void. They all called for Esme; the only response was the pulsing hum calling from the dark corner of the closet. As they searched every possible spot for her, Jensen scratched his head, puzzled her energy was here, but she was not. They searched in closets, even in cabinets. Alicia went to search the bedroom one more time. Slamming doors from the bedroom caught Jensen's and Camryn's attention, followed by a piercing cry.

The bedroom door flew open, cracking the wall behind it as they collided. Esme's clothes were tossed from the closet and now littered the floor, trailing to Cora and Thalia. The scythe was held in one hand by Thalia while she dug her nails into Alicia's arm. Cora couldn't meet the men's eyes. Guilt crept in her as she kept her eyes glued to the floor beneath her pointed stiletto heels.

"Please, let me go." Alicia's plea swelled Cora's guilt. Taking Alicia was not part of the plan, at least not part of what she was told.

Camryn's jaw tightened. "What the hell, Cora? You don't need to do this. Whatever it is, we can come up with a solution." His eyes softened toward Alicia. "It's okay, Alicia. Everything is going to be okay."

Rolling her eyes, Thalia scoffed, "no point in lying to the poor soul. You are in no position to reassure her of anything." The scythe's handle was placed across Alicia's chest, pushing itself and her into Thalia's chest. "She belongs to me now, as does the scythe."

Jensen's focus locked onto Thalia and the scythe. "Thalia, that doesn't belong to you. You and I both know that. Just let it go and walk away. There is no need for all this senselessness."

Maniacal laughter filled the space. "Jensen, darling, I always believed you were smarter than you look. Perhaps I was wrong. If I want something, it will belong to me. Now, be a good boy and give me Esme."

Deep grumbles left both Jensen and Camryn. "She isn't here. I have no idea where she is." Jensen spat his words as he clenched his fists. "Even if I did know, she would be nowhere near you."

"Well, aren't you the fierce protector? If you want Alicia here to not be lost like all the others out there. Or have her sold off to a soul snatcher." The back of her knuckles stroked down Alicia's cheek before landing a sharp back-handed smack. "Then, you'll find Esme and bring her to me." She shoved Alicia into Cora and apparated away with the scythe. As soon as Thalia left, Alicia disappeared before getting the chance to say anything.

"I'm sorry." That saddened apology was all Cora could muster as she, too, apparated.

Camryn and Jensen stood there, unsure of what to do next. Jensen shuffled his way to the bed, tidying the room as he made his way. So many things were out of his control, and just when things were beginning to settle, another hurdle caused him to trip. He slumped down on the bed, pushing his hair out of his eyes.

"So"—Camryn leaned against the doorframe, picking at his nails—"when we find Esme, are you going to tell her about the journal first or that Thalia has Alicia and the scythe?"

Whipping his head toward the door, Jensen narrowed his eyes. "Why do I have to tell her all of it?"

Camryn chuckled. "You're her boyfriend."

"You're her best friend. You can tell her, too." A smile was forced onto Jensen's face. "I'll tell her about the journal. You tell her the rest."

Camryn rolled his neck, reluctantly agreeing to share the new load of messy news that has become their reality. "First, we need to find where in the world Esme is."

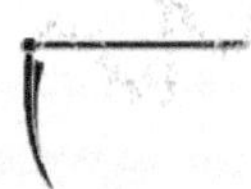

It was dark, cold, and wet where Esme awoke. The blood that ran down the back of her head had congealed into her curls, causing a red cast to form around them. The floor was hard and uneven. As she turned to lay on her back, something dug into her spine. She flinched at the intrusion. Her eyes struggled to acclimate to the darkness, but she forced herself, using what little energy she could gather to see better and stand. Gaining her bearings, Esme noticed the stalagmites that jutted from the floor, and the stalactites overhead. Some joined, forming columns throughout the cave she found herself in.

Waving her hand, Esme attempted to open a portal back to her apartment. Time ticked with every droplet that fell from the rocky ceiling, and still, the portal would not open. She shouted in frustration as the walls shouted their frustration back at her. The continuous echoing of her shout caused her ears to ring and her head to pound. It built pressure within her, causing her to fall to her knees and cry out in pain. Crimson tears ran down her cheeks as she clamped her hands over her ears in a desperate attempt to dull the sounds. She pulled the skin on her lips with her teeth, causing cracks and tears to form as she bit back and choked on the sounds that still tried to escape her.

Exhausted and wary of any noise she could make, she let out a small sigh. The pain and sounds had dulled, and she felt blood crust on her cheeks as it dried. Knowing that she was fully depleted of any energy, she sat on a ledge that had formed out of the rocks. It was only then she noticed the cave's entirety. Sigils were painted on various walls, stalagmites, and stalactites. Years of candles were melted everywhere. Plants and herbs were hung throughout. Clay pots held chalk and powders of different colors.

Esme cocked her head back, feeling the dark energy that weaved itself everywhere. It had been years since she had felt energy like this. It wasn't the same as reapers, Celestials, or Infernals. This energy was magic-based, but not just any magic; it was old dark magic. Debris had settled around the objects, making it clear that it had been untouched for some time. As her eyes scanned the walls, studying every sigil that either warded against or trapped different entities or beings, Esme found an odd object wedged in between two rocks.

Hoisting herself off the ledge, she slowly made her way to the mystery item. The energy pulsed rhythmically, calling and calming her like a mother singing a lullaby. Normally, she would check for traps or things that looked out of place, but seeing as she was already trapped in the cave for the foreseeable future, Esme did not hesitate to pull the book from the cave's hold.

The book was ancient, with hand stitching holding patch-worked leather as a cover. It was heavy and thick, the pages damaged from the humidity and battered by the passing of too many hands. As she opened the book, pages slid out, drifting to the rocks beneath her feet. She picked the fallen pages up and sat to read the ancient texts before her. The book was filled with dark magic, talks of sacrifices as offerings, necromancy, binding spells, and rituals, conjuring Infernals and so much more. What caught her attention was who the book belonged to.

The Unhallowed Shadow Coven was a coven of dark witches about whom Esme had only heard stories of during her travels. The coven had supposedly fallen, and members had dispersed when the coven's maiden, who was newly married to a distant necromancer, mysteriously vanished. The maiden was set to take leadership of the coven as the new mother. Opening the book, she found an inscription scrawled on the last page:

> *May the powers that be find our lost sister, the maiden to be mother, and return her to her rightful place. We call on the shadows to find her darkness and bind together, allow her to rule evermore.*

Mother Sybil Blackwell

Crone Mathilda Blackwell

Time was irrelevant to her now. Her energy was not increasing, but it wasn't draining. She found herself lost in the old tome's pages when a growl ricocheted around her. A smile that could light the darkest night formed on her lips at the familiar growl. As she stood, wiping the dirt from her pants, she came face to face with yellow eyes. "Dominic, how did you find me? I hope you can get us both out of here." She ran her hand over his snout when dark azure and ebony sparks erupted between them. Energy filled her faster than white water rapids. She snapped her fingers, and a purring portal opened.

It wasn't her normal portal of blinding white light. This portal had black mist surrounding the light. She wasn't straining to keep the portal open; it was as if it was simply an extension of her. Figures could be seen pacing the other side. The closer she walked to it, the clearer it became. His voice was the first she heard.

"What is that?"

She smiled and breathed a sigh of relief at Jensen's voice.

"Good boy, Dominic, let's go home." The excitement in her could not be contained as she clutched the grimoire tighter and stepped through the new portal.

Her face was crushed into a solid wall of muscle as soon as her feet met the apartment floor. "Oh, God, Esme. Where were you? Are you okay? Why does the portal look like that?" Before she had a chance to speak, Jensen tilted her head up, placing her face between his palms. He kissed her as if she were life itself, and he was a dying man.

"I could be wrong, but maybe if you take your tongue out of her throat and let her breathe, she could answer your question." Camryn's statement floated from behind them. Dominic growled in his direction. "Easy boy, I'm just making an observation."

She lifted her hands to hold Jensen's and brought them to her lips. She kissed his knuckles. "I missed you too, honey. I was only gone for what, a few hours, maybe a day?"

"Try eleven days," Camryn said as he walked around the portal that was still open, metrically pulsing.

"I was in that cave for eleven days? It didn't feel that long." She looked behind her and snapped her fingers again, closing the portal in front of Camryn's nose. He jerked his head back, shooting a glare at her as she shrugged as it were nothing. "I don't know why I ended up there. I was trying to come here." She began to tell them about all the things she had found, showing the grimoire, and how Dominic showed up and creating the new portal. She squinted and looked around the apartment. "Where's Alicia?" She rubbed her chest, feeling slightly winded.

Camryn and Jensen openly stared at each other. Jensen pulled Esme to the couch to sit close so that their thighs touched. He pointed looked at Camryn, who winced and rubbed the back of his neck. He dragged the red velvet chair closer and plopped down. "Thalia and Cora broke in, stole the scythe, and are holding Alicia hostage." Whether he did it on purpose, his words came out rushed and in a single breath. Jensen smacked his own forehead and ran his hand down his face.

Esme sat there, blinking. "Try that again with a few more inhales added in along the way."

Clearing his throat and sitting up straighter, he recounted what happened the day she went missing. As he finished, her icy gray eyes turned black, and Camryn as well as the chair he sat on flew backward before slamming into a wall. The mirror that hung on the wall crashed to the floor. Shards of glass covered the floor like glitter. "Sorry, I didn't mean to direct that to you. It just came out."

Camryn stood from the floor, shaking the shards of the mirror out from his hair and picking up the chair. "It's okay, I know you can't help it, Es. No hard feelings. I promise."

Jensen laughed nervously. "Maybe I should have gone first."

She pivoted her head with a hardened glare. "Why should you have gone first? What else happened?"

He stood and walked to the kitchen counter and set the black journal down on the coffee table. "This is the Grim Reaper's journal."

Her eyebrows pinched as she looked at the journal before her. "I know what it is. I saw him with these all the time. Why do you have it?"

"Ansel left it, and Camryn found it after you disappeared. Have you ever read them? This one in particular." She knew that Jensen was dancing around the topic but still entertained his question.

"No, Jensen. These are his personal thoughts and feelings. I respect that." Her eyes peered deeper into him.

"Well, we read it." He squirmed as her energy pushed against the walls in a flare. "There is something you need to read. It was meant for you to read." He opened the journal to the perfectly written page.

My dearest Esme,

Words can never do justice to the pride I have for you. You have grown into such a beautiful and talented reaper despite you never belonging in this world. It saddens me that you are reading this now because if you are that means Thalia has finally succeeded in her conquest for power. She most likely ended my existence because I refused to give you up. How could I? That would be breaking the last promise I ever made to your mother. I loved her dearly and love you just the same. I could never hand over my own child to that maddened creature. You are my daughter, my darling Esme. You are a part of me and a part of your mother. You are a child of death and life. Something that should never be possible, but here you stand. I am afraid that I have failed you. I know that I had many chances to reveal myself to you, but you were flourishing so impossibly perfect that I never found the need.

There is so much I want and need to tell you my dear child, but I know that all will reveal itself to you. For now, I must implore you that to keep the scythe safe when it finds its way to you. Never let it fall to her hands, she will use it not for the balance of life and death but to her own advantage. Perhaps one day we will see each other again. Until that day, continue growing, learning, and loving. There is nothing impossible for you to accomplish since you are proof that the impossible is possible.

Forever yours,

Father

She sat there, hands shaking, lips quivering while the world was in free fall. How? That was the only question replaying in her mind. How could death have a child? How could she be that child? How could he have kept this from her for centuries? How is she supposed to keep the scythe safe when she can't even touch it? How? The more the thoughts played in her mind like a carousel, the tighter her chest grew.

Her breathing became labored, and the apartment was a blur. She could hear voices but couldn't make out the garbled words. The pain in her chest faded and came back with vengeance as if it were playing a cruel prank. She slid off the couch, spewing a puddle of blood. Crimson rivers flowed freely from her eyes, joining the glittering pool on the ground. In a shuddered exhale, her eyes rolled back, and her body limply collided with the floor.

Jensen screamed her name as his knees thudded on the ground, turning her over. Camryn rushed behind him, his hand covering his mouth. Jensen bellowed repeatedly as he rocked Esme's lifeless body, pleading for her to come back to him. Tears blinded him, and his body shook with each unabashed sob that left him. "Esme, love, wake up. You have to wake up. You're not allowed to leave me! We were going to find a way around this, remember? Wake up, love. Please wake up." One sharp tug in his chest is all he could feel. He couldn't feel her; their tether had snapped. The very crux of her vanished. "Esme!"

Her name was ripped from his heart and out of his throat. Jensen screamed her name repeatedly. It wasn't supposed to happen like this. They had just found their way back to each other. Over and over, he screamed. No matter how much he yelled and cried, her body remained limp in his arms. What was the point of existing? She was the center of his universe. He couldn't breathe. The emptiness in his chest began to devour him whole. Camryn pulled Jensen to him, hugging him and Esme. He didn't know what else he could do.

Dominic stalked forward from the shadowed corner he lingered in. He sniffed her body and pawed at the ground. The ground grew warm with each scratch. He rubbed his snout against her hand, spreading the warmth that came from the depths. Dominic let out a pained howl and trudged into the shadows. A distressed cry exploded from Jensen's lungs as her body vanished, leaving a vacant hole in his arms that matched the one growing in his heart.

Nothingness, that's what surrounded Esme when her eyes opened. From the energy that wrapped around her, she knew she was in the veil. It was perplexing how there was nothing there. No home, no door, just nothing. "Hello, Esme." She turned at the sound of the voice.

Her eyes widened. "Tyler?"

23

E sme stared at Tyler in disbelief, releasing a small laugh. "So, I died, and you're my reaper?" Spinning around slowly observing the nothingness, her questions continued in her mind.

"Well, this is going to be awkward, but, yes, you did die, or at least a part of you did. Sorry about the way I had to bring you here. Time is of the essence now." He watched as she cocked her head to the side. "Also, no. I am not your reaper. In fact, I'm not a reaper at all. My name isn't Tyler, either." His body swayed left and right as he watched her face.

Esme closed her eyes, breathing in deeply. She pointed a finger at the man she knew as Tyler. "If you're not a reaper, or Tyler, then who and what are you?"

He happily trotted over to stand in front of a skeptical Esme. "Let's start over, shall we?" Flashing a smile and holding his hand out, he said, "Hello, Esmerelda. I'm Atticus, also known as Fate."

A statue held more movement than she did at this moment. Atticus simply chuckled. Her eyes squinted as an avalanche of thoughts and questions thrashed in her mind. One question slipped out first. "Why did you call me Esmerelda?"

"Because that's who you are. Esmerelda is the mortal you. The you that was born into the world in 1674." Atticus stretched his back and proceeded to lay on the ground. "You might want to get comfortable. It's an exciting story." Esme remained standing, silently watching with caution. "Fine, suit yourself. Not like you can get tired now, anyway." Atticus folded his hands behind his head as he began. "As you found out, your father is, or rather was, the Grim Reaper. He was fascinated with humans, especially since it was only him for such a long time. But one human caught his eye in a way that it should never have." Turning his head slightly, he asked, "Did you get a chance to find out who your mother is?"

Esme remained silent but shook her head.

"Your mother was one of the most powerful witches to have ever lived. Sybil Anne Blackwell." He arched his brow. "I believe you found the family grimoire." Her eyes widened further. "I'll explain that in a minute." Atticus rolled onto his side, propping his head up with his hand. "You were created by pure dark magic, love, and a little extra ingredient of an unknown flavor. You should have never existed. Life coming from death is a bit ironic." He chewed his cheek. "The closest creatures that you compared to are Nephilim's."

"Half angels and half human. They aren't a myth?" At this point, if she were told the tooth fairy was real, she would believe it.

Atticus shook his head. "No, not a myth but extinct. They held too much power for a mortal body, and it made other beings feel insecure. Every last one was hunted down. Much like how Thalia was doing to you." He sat up, resting his arms on his knees. "But you, Esmerelda, you are so much more powerful than they could have ever been." Wonder twinkled in his eyes as he looked at the woman before him. "Your mother named you Esmerelda. Your father molded you into Esme when he was forced to hide you." Esme sat unceremoniously in front of Atticus. "You lived 20 years as Esmerelda before becoming Esme."

"How can I be Esmerelda Blackwell? That would mean I'm the lost maiden of the Unhallowed Shadow Coven. I don't remember any of that. I only know myself as—"

With a dismissive wave, he said, "Yes, yes, Esme, the roaming reaper and Strategos. In the beginning, you had a soul, kind of. But yes, you were the maiden of the Unhallowed Shadow Coven. I had a plan for you. It was tricky, I'll admit. I never had to plan or account for something like you. But it was fun and exciting! Finally, I had a challenge, something to really flex and show my talents.

You had finally married a man from another coven. Let me tell you, finding someone to balance you that you actually liked was not easy. You rejected just about any person I sent your way. It was thrilling to see you about to become the new mother, the leader of your coven. Then Thalia had to come along and try to play judge, jury, and executioner."

Atticus threw his hands up, exasperated by the mere mention of Thalia. "She was jealous of Sybil and a spiteful bitch. What Thalia wanted, she couldn't have. To have what she wanted, she needed all obstacles removed. The only issue for her was whether you were the child of death or just an insanely powerful witch. Either way, you were too close to the Grim Reaper, as was Sybil. She needed you both gone."

Esme cast her eyes down, processing this new information. "Why would she be jealous of Sybil and need us both gone?"

"You really don't know? Oh, this is a gripping tale now. Thalia and Death were eternal paramours. He tried to make it work with her for years but couldn't stand being around her. Not that I blame him. They clashed in every way possible. Since he never fully accepted the bond, it was a painless rejection. At least for him, it was. Your father disappeared for some time once he fell in love with Sybil. He still did his job but would always come home to his family. Thalia, with revenge in her heart, saw him as unfit to lead her and Ansel. When she finally did find him, he was with Sybil, and you were an adult. The amount of magic you had could have easily cloaked your parents. In Thalia's mind, you were nothing more than a powerful bodyguard in witch form. Especially how you almost trapped her for coming too close to your family and coven. You would have had her, too, if it weren't for Celestial or Infernal intervention. The details on who she brought with her as an army is a little fuzzy. I wasn't there. Whoever or whatever it was, almost killed you."

"This sounds like a well-thought-out fairytale, but why don't I remember, and why did we have to run from her?" Buzzing was forming around her, filling the soundless, empty space.

Atticus rubbed his hands. "Now we're getting somewhere." His wide smiled made her uncomfortable. "As you were dying, Sybil cast a spell to make your soul dormant, allowing only the reaper energy that flowed through your veins to be in complete control of your body. Think of it as a supernatural embalmment. When the soul is separated, or in your case, dormant, it is no longer that being. When your reaper abilities surfaced, you were named Esme and kept under the close watch of your father. Thalia was still hell-bent on revenge. She wanted to take everything from Death. If she found out, you really were the child of Death—" He let the statement hang in the air as he picked imaginary lint off his shoulder. What would happen didn't need to be said out loud because it already happened.

He stood and paced, clasping his hands behind his back. "When Thalia killed your father, the world was thrown into pure turmoil. She thought she could simply kill him and control the scythe. She never accounted for you. The scythe is tied to the Grim Reaper's energy. You share the energy of your father." Atticus stopped pacing to fully face Esme. "The scythe recognized you as the Grim Reaper."

Esme furrowed her brows and shook her head. "That doesn't make any sense. The scythe was in his office when he disappeared. It freakishly showed up in my home and catapulted me across the room when I went to touch it. Why are you lying to me?"

His hands rested on his hips as he rocked on his heels. "I promise I'm not lying to you. I may have omitted a few things about myself, but never lied. The scythe was in his office because you were there. Wherever the Grim Reaper is, so is the scythe. You became the default Grim Reaper when he died, and you had your first touch of death."

Esme shot up from the ground and gasped. "Alicia."

Atticus nodded. "She was not meant to die, but it just happened that you touched her at the exact moment your father was killed. You restarted the balance unknowingly and in the wrong way. To restart the balance properly, you would have had to escort the soul yourself. The longer she stayed out of the veil, the more life and death was thrown off. Now it's all in shambles and wouldn't matter if Alicia went or not. The rebalancing needs to be rebalanced yet again. As for not being able to touch the scythe, it's straightforward." He held out his hand as he spoke. "Your soul was dormant, not gone. Technically, you were still mortal, and mortals can never touch an instrument of death."

"Okay, say I buy into all this. Why was I having nightmares? Why would I bleed and faint. How did I end up in that cave? I thought of my home and ended up in a cave. Explain that, Fate." She crossed her arms, calculating her slow steps as she neared Atticus.

"Nightmares? Well, that was probably because Esmerelda was a powerful witch and seer. Those were most likely visions. It's safe to bet that your soul was waking at the threat of danger. Your body was at war with itself, having been separated for centuries. It was a battle of Esmerelda the witch, versus Esme the reaper. The winner took control of your body. The more Esme won out, the more it killed Esmerelda. Essentially, the reaper was possessing the witch."

Esme dropped her arms and laughed sarcastically. "Well, given the fact that my entire being is here, I would say that both sides of me lost."

He scuffed his shoe on the ground and continued. "When you thought of home, you weren't specific. Esmerelda was vying for control, and she won that battle and went to what she considered home. The grimoire called and pulled. Only your witching abilities would work in that cave." Atticus thrummed his fingers together giddily. "This is where it gets fun. You have a choice to make. You can either stay here and find your way into the afterlife, if there is one for you, or—"

She leaned in closer, intrigued by the option. "Or?"

He placed his arm around her shoulders. "Or you can leave here and become the Grim Reaper."

Esme raised her brow in thought. "So, I would go back without a soul. Esmerelda would be gone forever. Basically, a part of me dies. Then, what does that make me? Just Esme?"

"Oh, my dear, you have never been 'just' anything. But I might be able to manage a thing or two if you like. I am Fate, after all, that means I get to play with lives."

A surge of anger speared her chest. Why didn't he stop all this before it became insanity in the mortal world? "All those times, I felt like I was being watched. That was you, wasn't it? Why not just tell us the truth from the beginning and stop all this madness?"

He solemnly nodded his head. "That is the downside to being me. Yes, I was following you. Only because I was making good on a promise I made to your father when you refused to leave Philadelphia. I promised him I would look in on you from time to time. If anything, I am a man of my word. Being Fate, I can never directly interfere, with Celestials, Infernals, or Reapers. Their choices are all their own. Call it a limitation of my abilities. Hence, Tyler."

"Would this not count as interfering?" She pushed his arm off her and circled him.

Atticus threw his head back, laughing. "This is more of a loophole. Theoretically, I'm speaking to Esmerelda, not Esme. There is nothing in cosmic law that says I can't speak with souls; I'm just not allowed to directly interfere with the business of others like us. Seeing as you were dormant, you never had the opportunity to play out your many choices, so consider this your last choice." He flashed a smile, proud of himself for finding a gray area to play in. "I am not ashamed to admit I am hoping you pick to go back. Thalia would destroy not only the reaping world but the mortal world as well."

"What about Ansel?" Esme knew little about this reaper and didn't know whether to trust him. The only response she received was a single shoulder shrug. She huffed in annoyance. "The man I love is still there. That scythe is my legacy, and my friend is held hostage by that psychopath. You bet your ass I'm going back."

"Yes!" Atticus yelled in excitement.

"I want to keep the witch powers; the soul can stay here." Her face was emotionless, her voice hard.

"Wait, what?" The excitement drained from his voice. He knew this was a possibility, but he was hoping that she wouldn't ask this. Never had he done such a task. "Dark magic and Grim Reaper energy would make you god-like."

She stared at him blankly.

"I can't promise the soul bit, but I'll do my best." Atticus cleared his throat and shrugged his shoulders. "Okay, let's bring in a new era, shall we?"

Atticus paced around her, examining her hands, hair, eyes. He pulled, pinched, and tied at the air around her. It was difficult to tell how long this went on, since time was irrelevant in the veil. Once he was satisfied with his work, he took a step back, his eyes quickly flashing to all white. "I've done what I can, but it came at a cost. Now go, set forth, and conquer."

Atticus winked at her and disappeared, leaving her alone in the veil. "You didn't tell me there was a cost, jackass! What's the cost?" Her temper flared as familiar azure and ebony sparks erupted around her. She studied her hand as the sparks continued. She snapped her fingers, conjuring a flash of light and black mist to engulf her.

Once the mist dissipated, she found herself at the edge of the city. Everything felt new and strange. The energy from every living being and lost soul invaded every pore on her body. Her hands itched while feeling oddly empty. Then she felt it; they called to her. The scythe longed to be with its master while Infernal heat grew in the other. Thundering paws against the Earth sounded behind her, followed by deep growls.

A smirk graced her face as a snout pressed against the hand that grew hot. She looked down at the hound, who stood next to her. "You know, you don't need to be with me anymore. You're free of me now." Dominic snapped his jaws at her as he pressed his body into her side. "Well, in that case, how would you like to hunt a reaper with me?"

Dominic's hackles raised as he snarled. He salivated at the thought of a hunt with a reaper as a prize. "First, we need to see Jensen."

Dominic grumbled in protest, knowing the hunt was delayed.

24

aze covered the windows. The usual buzzing neon light that called to reapers to relax was off. Normally, the energy around The Twisted Sickle was light and vibrant, but this was hollow, murky, lethargic energy. A sound of discontent left Esme as she stood on the edge of the corner, looking down the alley that housed the bar. She looked down at Dominic, who stood at her right, his eyes in a constant state of dance. Swiping her tongue over her teeth, she snapped her fingers and found herself in the middle of the bar while Dominic curled himself into a dark corner that faced the entryway.

She made no effort to hide her disgust. Dust blanketed every visible surface, cobwebs strung on shelves. The air was thick and smelled of stale liquor and musk. The small chattering that floated around the air came to a halt. She felt a pinch of guilt and sadness for a moment, knowing that it was Alicia who had always kept up with bar duties ever since she arrived there. This place was missing the sunny disposition Alicia added to the atmosphere. Everyone had grown accustomed to the lively soul who knew every name and drink belonging to that name. Tilting her head, she examined all the reapers that lingered around the bar top and random tables. Her eyes locked on a table that sat directly in the center of the bar. Pendant lights swayed with every step she took. As she neared the table, her eyes narrowed at the reaper who sat with a being that did not belong in The Twisted Sickle. Esme's face hovered only a few inches away from this young reaper as she looked deep into his eyes. "Why is a mortal in here?"

"I don't have to tell you anything." As the young reaper finished what was meant to be a retort full of bravado, Esme let out a dark chuckle as her irises flashed to pitch black. He fell backward out of his seat, scurrying to stand.

"Fix it before I do." Her voice grew low and lethal as she pushed ripples of her power and energy into the nooks and crevices of the bar. Every reaper present gasped and murmured to each other. A saddened shout from the hallway shifted her focus.

Jensen sat at his desk, shaking out the last remnants of whiskey from his current bottle. Seeing yet another empty glass bottle only reminded him of the hollow feeling that still lived in his heart. With every gulp, he hoped and prayed that the lingering burn from the caramel liquid would consume him and destroy the images in his mind. It was a constant loop of Esme seizing on the floor until she disappeared in his arms. Leaving him to cradle nothing but air.

The memory haunted him as he allowed every ounce of grief and anger that was shoved deep down, festering, to unleash again. Pouring all his emotions into one single scream, he threw the bottle against the wall. Glass skittered down the wall in a race to shatter on the floor.

"That better not be the vintage crystal decanter. I can't get another one of those." That voice was impossible. His shoulders hunched forward as he turned his head to catch a glimpse of where that impossibility came from.

Jensen's eyes grew wide as his lips set to a tight, thin line. "Who are you?"

Esme stood there, leaning against the doorframe, ankles and arms crossed. She allowed her eyes to freely roam the man in front of her. His hair had grown past his shoulders, the usual scruff evolved into an unkempt beard. Bloodshot eyes told her that he had not rested enough or at all. He no longer wore his typical button-down shirt and casual work pants. Instead, he had worn-out jeans and a plain black tee shirt. "I could ask that same thing of you." She quirked an eyebrow at Jensen.

"Esme is dead, so who are you? What kind of sick joke is this?" Jensen inched forward, slowly balling his fists. The woman who stood before him had Esme's likeness but was slightly different. Her pure gray eyes had flecks of black. Her face was sharper instead of the soft curves he had memorized. Whoever this was, was more serious than his Esme. Then there was the energy that was all wrong. This energy was strong, bold, and cold, it was overpowering. Not even Ansel or Thalia could compare to this.

Pushing herself away from the door, she took long, measured strides until she stood before him. "Technically, Esmerelda is the one that died, not me. This isn't a joke. I'm here, love." Her hand ever so gently brushed down his cheek, neck, and arm and grabbed his hand. "I gave you this watch for our anniversary. You gave me a candle." She smirked as she watched his eyes dart between hers. The glowing trail of her touch on his face stretched her smirk. She never took the time until now to appreciate how excruciatingly handsome he looked when glowing.

Tightening her grip on his hand, she snapped her fingers. They were in the hospital, standing in front of the nursery window. "This is our special spot. We would play pretend here." With an airy laugh, she bit her lip. "We would pretend to be a mortal couple and pick one or two of these babies as if they were ours. For hours, we would make up a story about our pretend family, names, jobs, hobbies."

With shaky fingers, Jensen traced the angles of her face, the line of her nose, and her soft, full lips. "How?" He was too in awe of her to form any long coherent sentences, so one word would have to do.

A gentle smile graced her lips. "I have so much to tell you." Again, she snapped her fingers, and they were back in Twisted Sickle's office.

He cupped her face in both his hands, drinking in the sight he thought was lost to him forever. "You know I made you that candle." His breath was stolen as her smile grew wider, crinkling the corners of her eyes. Not giving her a second to respond further, he leaned his face down and captured her lips with his. As their lips glided against each other, he breathed out a sigh of relief. She was back by some miracle. Grabbing the back of her thighs, he hoisted her up and walked them over to the desk. Swiping everything off with one hand, he sat her down in their place.

His teeth grazed her neck as his fingers nimbly undid the button of her pants. Encouraged by her panting, and the blush that was rising from her chest, he stepped back to deftly discard his own shirt. She watched him with lustful eyes as she slid her own cardigan off her shoulders, followed by her shirt over her head. "I missed you so fucking much." He whispered against her lips. Cradling her back until she was on her elbows, she lifted her hips, allowing him to slide her remaining clothing down, followed by his own. For a moment, he was lost in her eyes as the irises flickered from speckled gray to all black.

Her hand reached around his neck, lowering his face to meet her own. "I missed you, too."

She gasped, and her eyes rolled back as two of his fingers toyed with her folds. A smirk of satisfaction spread across his face, finding her wet for him already. "More, please, Jensen. I need more of you."

"Don't worry, beautiful, we're just getting started. I'm going to take care of you." His voice held a husky timbre, and his pupils were blown out with lust. Working his fingers in her, he slipped one, two, then deftly added a third, slowly curling them deep within her. He watched as goose flesh broke out across her perfect form. Her etching pulsed hypnotically, mirroring his. He used his thumb to rub delicate circles on her engorged, sensitive bud. The moans of pleasure that leaked from her lips were more beautiful than a symphony. She slid further on her elbows, grabbing the edge of the desk with one hand. Her other hand crept forward, grabbing his girthy length as her thumb ran quick circles around its rosy head. "Fuck, Esme." He exhaled roughly against her chest as she began to pump her hand faster.

He leaned down as his long lithe fingers continued thrusting into her core with reckless abandon and took her supple breast into his mouth. His tongue swiped and rolled over her pebbled peak, and her hand fisted his hair tightly. Releasing her breast from his mouth, he trailed kisses up her chest. He stopped to kiss and bite her etching, dragging his tongue up her neck and slid his fingers out of her. "Such a good girl for me. With that needy tight cunt of yours." He proceeded to lick his fingers clean of her sweet essence.

He wrapped his arms around her waist, flipping her over in one fluid motion. "Ass up."

"Holy shit." Her mouth had run dry, and her brain was a haze of desire and exhilaration. She was eager to see what he would do to her body. Rising on her tiptoes, she allowed her back to arch and hips to tilt, fully exposing herself to him.

"God damn, baby. You are perfect." He placed his hand in between her shoulder blades and pushed her chest down onto the desk. Without warning, he burrowed into her ravenously. The ramming of his cock knocked the wind from her lungs. A strangled moan passed through her lips. As he continued his assault, she could feel her wetness drip down her thighs. "I love how wet you are for me." He kicked her legs further apart and lifted her hips higher. Her toes barely brushing against the cold floor, and the heat that was passing between them sent shivers down her spine. "You're going to take all of me. Do you understand?" His hands moved from her hips, grabbing her plump ass cheeks, and splayed them open. "I should punish you right in this tight ass for leaving me again." His fingers dug into her cheeks harder. "So divine and perfect." Bending over her, his nose drew a line over her shoulder, up her neck and to her ear. Pulling out of her, he whispered, "You're mine."

Esme propped herself on her elbows. Her hair was tousled from the friction of the desk, and her chest heaved with desire. She watched as he sat in the desk chair and stroked himself. Sliding off the desk, she made her way to stand in front of him. Leaning closer to him, so her breast swayed in his face, and her hands rested on the back of the chair, she whispered in his ear. "What is it you want? How can I make up for leaving again?"

He slid two fingers down her folds and teased the entrance into her before repeating the same motion. "I want you to show me just how much you missed me, too. Use those beautiful lips to show me how sorry you are."

She pulled his hand away and dropped to her knees. With the tip of her tongue, she traced the thick, throbbing vein on his cock. He threw his head back, groaning deep within his throat. She stretched her lips around the head and took him into her warm mouth. His hands gathered her wild tresses into his fist. His mouth dropped at the sight of what this woman was doing to him. She swallowed him, bobbing up and down. Tasting herself on him, she hummed in satisfaction. He bucked his hips in tandem with her bobbing. Her thighs were slick, and her core ached, feeling how hard he was for her. Instinctively, her hand slipped between her legs, trying to alleviate the ache that grew with each passing second.

Jensen tracked the motion of her hand and watched as it disappeared. "Oh, beautiful, no one touches what's mine. Not even you." He slipped out of her mouth and ran his thumb over her red and swollen lips. "If you need to be fucked, just ask nicely."

She continued playing with her sex. "Please, Jensen? Will you please fuck me? Hard."

He swatted her hand away. "Stand up." She did as she was told. Seeing him in control thrilled her to no end. "I'm not going to fuck you. You're going to use my cock to fuck yourself."

With a sly smirk, she offered her fingers to him to clean while straddling his hips. He sucked each one of her fingers clean as she slowly slid down his length. Cupping his face, she said, "Please, keep looking at me." Their eyes locked in a sex filled haze, and she bounced herself.

His fingers dug into her hips the closer he came to his end. This moment was far too perfect for an ending. He held on as he stood and lifted her while still in her before pushing her back against the wall. Every plunge he made caused her to scratch deeper down his back. He hissed in pleasure while her legs tightened around his waist and shook with pure ecstasy. "Just like that." She panted as she clawed at his back, resting her forehead on his. "Yes. Just like that."

Her walls gripped his cock tight. "That's right, love, take what's yours. Milk your cock dry." With every one of his thrusts and every single one of her small moans, he felt his heart piece itself together again. A radiant golden gleam swam over them. With one final plunge, he watched her in all her beauty as she fell over the edge, then allowed himself to do the same. They embraced each other, relishing in the feel of one another. Both their bodies basked in the afterglow and the warmth it offered. A sharp tug in their chests hinted at their bond being restored. Kissing his cheek, chin, lips, and nose, Esme looked deep into his eyes and whispered, "I love you, Jensen."

Moving around the room, picking up and putting on their discarded clothes, Esme spoke. "How long was I gone for this time?" She shrugged on her oversized cardigan and turned to Jensen, who was zipping up his pants.

"One year this time." He shook his head, blinking away tears. "It was a long, painful year. I watched you die in my arms." His voice quivered at the memory. "I'm so glad you're back, but how are you back?" Jensen ran his knuckles down her cheek, mesmerized by the woman in front of him.

A shift in energy that bounded down the hall caught Esme's attention. "News still travels fast around here." The door swung open as Camryn rushed in. He crushed Esme to his chest. As he hugged her tightly, he picked her up off the floor and shook her side to side as if she were a rag doll eliciting a small, giddy yelp from her. "It's good to see you too, Cam." Her muffled voice seeped from under his arm.

He set her down gently, placing his hands on her shoulders. "It really is you. It's so good to see you, Es." His eyes darted over her face, noting how she was the same but different. "You look good—different but a good different."

She playfully rolled her eyes. "Thank you, Cam, for noticing. That's because I am different."

He pulled his eyes away from his best friend, "Jensen." The greeting was short and dull, and Jensen acknowledged him in the same gruff manner. The two men had stopped speaking to each other two months following Esme's death. Camryn despised the fact that Jensen opted to drown himself in bottle after bottle while he still searched for ways to separate Thalia from the scythe. Camryn observed Esme's rumpled clothes and disheveled hair and took a deep breath. "It smells like whiskey and sex in here."

Esme punched his arm harder than she intended, causing him to wince and rub the spot on his arm. "Shut up." Turning around, she noted various objects littered on the floor. With a flicking motion of her fingers, the objects parted on either side of the room, clearing a path as she walked. "I guess I should go first. Then one of you or both of you can fill me in on what I missed." She sat at the desk and motioned for the other two to do the same. "You should get comfortable." With that, she began from the beginning, telling them about Tyler, who is Atticus and Fate. She told the whole story, leaving no details untold. Both men were on the edge of their seats, absorbing and processing every syllable in every word. "I'm the Grim Reaper."

Silence hung in the air. They looked at her as she looked at them. As minutes stretched, the staring became increasingly annoying. Esme drummed her short nails against the desk, feeling irritated by the lack of response. Closing her eyes, she took in a deep breath and sucked in her cheeks. When she opened her eyes, Camryn and Jensen still wore blank stares. "I'm pretty sure that, in the year I was dead, you didn't lose the ability to speak."

"This is, this is just a lot. Do you feel different?" Jensen looked at her, realizing why she seemed different. Sadness pricked at part of him, knowing there was part of her that was never coming back because he truly loved every bit of her.

Did she feel different? Truth is, she hadn't considered it. "I guess, in a way, I do feel different. I feel stable. I don't feel like I'm falling apart at the seams. It's like I can touch and taste the energy. I have the magic that Esmerelda had, but I'm not sure how to access or use it. It is there, though. I can feel it flowing and mixing with my energy."

Camryn and Jensen shared a look. They found it peculiar how she referenced the magic belonging to Esmerelda as if that was an entirely different person. Even though they both thought the same, neither dared to say anything. While, yes, she was still Esme, she was the Grim Reaper now, and that comes with a level of respect.

"We have to get you the scythe. Not only does it belong to you by birthright." Camryn tilted his head, processing the information. "But you are the rightful Grim Reaper, and Thalia has gone insane trying to wield it."

She leaned back in her seat, rolling her neck, preparing herself for what she had missed. "All right, boys, what have I missed?"

"Since your death," Camryn began, "Thalia felt there was no one who could challenge her as Grim Reaper. Except even with the scythe, the Infernals and Celestials would not recognize her. Fate was not present during her tried and failed claim to power."

"I guess we know why he wasn't there," Esme smirked.

"The scythe continued to vanish, and she would send Ansel and Cora on wild chases to find it and bring it back to her." He looked at Jensen.

Jensen brushed his fingertips over his thighs. "Things only went downhill for Thalia from there. In one city, she attempted a mass collection. The energy from the scythe rebounded and pushed the lost souls even further away. Now we don't know where they are. But it gets worse."

Esme sat up straighter and nodded for him to continue.

"At first the other reapers looked to her and Ansel, but when they noticed how little control she had, they began doing their own thing. Selling souls to soul snatchers, some completely went off grid and intermingled with mortals. A small faction attempted to claim the scythe and power for themselves. She attempted to put a stop to us socializing with other beings, keeping us contained to only the apartment or here. The office has been shut down." His eyes went from Esme to Camryn, who gave him a nudging look.

"What aren't you telling me, Jensen?" Her face was stone, her voice curt.

"Any reaper that doesn't do exactly as Thalia decrees, she eliminates. She's easily killed over half of our kind globally with the scythe. More every day." Jensen dropped his eyes to his fingers that fidgeted on his lap.

Black eyes looked back at the two reapers. The steady rise and fall of her breath concealed the rankled outrage in Esme's chest over Thalia. Slowly, she stood, flexing her fingers, then paced the room. Dark smokey tendrils rose from the pool of ink-black shadows, swaying their way up her body. They caressed her skin and twirled in her hair. Tendrils cascaded down her back, melting down into the floor once more.

More smokey tendrils joined the delicate dance, forming the appearance of a cloak on her back. Azure sparks rippled down her arms, weaving around her fingers in a constant loop. Where the shadows pooled on the ground, Dominic emerged with hackles raised, salivating more with every shake of his head. He released a deep, nightmarish growl while pressing his body into Esme. She scratched her fingers down his head repeatedly. Where her fingers scratched, blue smoke rose from the friction of the weaving sparks against the wiry fur.

Camryn and Jensen sat with tight shoulders, gulping down their breaths. It wasn't clear if fear or awe had paralyzed them, but neither dared to flinch. As the tendrils moved around Esme, Camryn broke his frozen state and poked Jensen's face. Jensen slapped his hand away but kept his eyes on Esme. "Esme, love. You okay?"

Camryn rolled his eyes to the side and pointed at the woman pacing the room. "Does that look okay to you?"

"I don't know. I never met her father to know if this is normal Grim Reaper shit or if this is her witchy side," Jensen harshly whispered back.

While they argued behind her, Esme focused her thoughts on scouring every energy signature, locking on to the one she desired the most. She looked over her shoulder, onyx eyes still piercing her surroundings. Her voice wasn't her normal tone; it was deep, churning with other voices. "This ends now." With a snap of her fingers, she, along with Dominic, and the tendrils vanished in a flash of hazy light and blue sparks.

They stood at the same time, knocking their chairs over. "Camryn, do you think—"

Camryn smoothed his hair back. "Just breathe, man. We need to stay calm. She's fine. She's going to be fine. Esme's the Grim Reaper with witch power, remember?"

"In case you forgot, that psycho bitch Thalia killed the last Grim Reaper, you know, Esme's father!" Jensen's voice grew louder and louder, and his body shook. "We have to go and find her. I can't let her do this on her own."

Camryn nodded. "Into the lion's den we go."

The building's energy ebbed and flowed as Esme entered. Ansel and Cora came rushing from around a corner and stopped mid-stride.

"Holy shit, I thought you were dead? Is that a hellhound?" Cora's voice held fear and confusion.

"Sorry to disappoint you." Esme leaned closer to Dominic and whispered in his ear. "Hunt." Dominic bounded into the air straight for Cora, missing her by mere centimeters, disappearing into the shadows. Cora screamed and latched herself to Ansel's arm.

"Thalia sent us out here to see what was emanating the Grim Reaper's energy. I must say, I'm not completely surprised to see that it's you. You are his daughter, after all. But I will admit that I am glad to see you." Ansel soothingly patted Cora's hand. She craned her neck forward at the news of death having a daughter. "Trust me, I'm on your side here. Thalia is mad with power and needs to be stopped. I cannot. I believe only you can."

"Then, stay out of my way. Both of you." Sensing the energy and the scythe calling to her from the top of the building, she snapped her fingers and vanished.

"His daughter? Ansel, is this going to work?" Cora was uncertain Esme could take control and do what was necessary with Thalia.

Ansel's eyes twinkled as he smiled. "Have faith, Cora. This is going to work out splendidly."

"I still can't believe you haven't given up this stupid idea of yours. Obviously, this just isn't the career path for you." Alicia spoke to Thalia as she sat cross-legged on the ground.

For one year, she had been kept away from everyone by Thalia. Locked away in a corner sitting on a sigil that trapped her. The only reason she wasn't taken and left to become lost forever or sold to the underworld was because of Cora. She had begged Ansel to speak to Thalia. Alicia was her first friend, and she couldn't fully turn her back on her.

"Does anything intelligent ever come out of your mouth?" Thalia's eyes were crazed. Her once perfectly manicured nails were broken and jagged as she chewed on the cuticles. She hugged the scythe to her chest, fearing it would leave her again. Her tempo quickened as she sensed the oppressive energy nearing. "This is impossible. The title is mine, and mine alone. I am Death. I am the Grim Reaper. They'll see. They'll all see I'm right."

Alicia rolled her eyes. "Does anything not crazy come out of your mouth?"

A flash of light and smoke filled the room. "I believe you have two things that are near and dear to me." Esme's voice bounced off the brick walls and metal beams.

"Esme! I am so happy to see you. I've been attention-deprived. I'm starving for social interactions. I miss my reapers! Not to mention, I hate being stuck in this corner like I'm in timeout." Alicia ranted as Esme slowly smirked.

"It's good to see you, too, Alicia. Just give me a minute, and we'll talk." She crept closer to Thalia, who paced around as if she were a captive animal in a cage.

"No, you died. You can't be here. This is mine, and I will not give it up." Screeching, she charged at Esme, catching her off guard, swinging the scythe wildly. Esme dove out of the way, crashing to the floor, barely missing the scythe. Thalia took this opportunity to rip a vial from her neck, then smash it on the floor. Green liquid traveled around the concrete ground, encircling Esme, siphoning and suppressing her energy. "Funny feeling, isn't it? I used the same potion on your father before I killed him."

She threw her head back, cackling, a sound ripped straight from a child's nightmares. "He never deserved to hold all that power and never use it. Instead, he wanted to be like them." She pointed a shaky finger in Alicia's direction. "He wanted to play house like a pathetic mortal. I would have let him. All he had to do was give up the title and power that came with the scythe and being himself. But ever the stubborn one, he just had to refuse. Then he somehow impregnated that whore he called his wife." The words spewed from Thalia's mouth like a venomous geyser.

Esme dragged her body away from the potion that was thrown at her, desperately summoning what energy hadn't been stolen by that potion. She had come too far for this to be the outcome. Thalia noticed Esme's movement and clumsily chopped at her with the scythe. Esme rolled away, managing to stand on shaking legs, fatigue grabbing hold of her. "Is that meant to offend me? If it was, I'm pleased to tell you that it doesn't. I honestly don't care about any of that since that is not who I am and never was." Her hands itched and burned. She knew Dominic was near, and the scythe was ready to leave Thalia's clutch.

The scythe was barely recognizable, the blade chipping and warped, the handle splintering. A toothpick looked stronger than this instrument of Death. That's when Esme realized that it looked like this because of Thalia's senseless destruction of their kind. "My father may have believed that letting you continue your existence was for the greater good, but I am not him. You are a cancer to the reaping world, and the mortal world. I have no issue with cutting that cancer out."

Jensen and Camryn apparated into the building in front of Ansel and Cora. "Where is she?" They spoke simultaneously to Ansel.

"Probably trying to convince Thalia to hand over the scythe. You shouldn't be here. There isn't anything for you to do." Ansel's eyes held worry, seeing how both reapers in front of him were determined to aid Esme. "Top floor," he sighed. "It's useless, you know. Only Esme has the power to end this once and for all. You'll only get in the way."

"Wonderful. Thank you for your unsolicited opinion. You're both coming with us." Jensen spoke quickly as he snatched Ansel and Camryn grabbed Cora.

Esme charged at Thalia, and Thalia ran full force into Esme as an energy blast exited both women, but Thalia's momentum was stronger. She pinned Esme against the rough brick. "If any of us is a cancer, it's you. You don't belong here; you should never have existed. I think I'll cut you out instead." She dragged the blade down the wall, sending sparks across Esme's face and hair. They landed in Esme's eyes, causing them to water and burn small freckles on her right cheek.

"Yet, here I stand. You were pathetic then, and you're pathetic now. You need a vial from witches to even stand a chance against my father or me." Esme laughed in the maddened reaper's face before she pulled Thalia down by the shoulders, kneeing her in the stomach and bashing her forehead straight into Thalia's face. A crack echoed in the charged air.

Thalia stumbled back but quickly regained her footing. Esme pushed herself away from the wall and reached out to rip the scythe out of the rogue reaper's hands. Turning quickly, she evaded Esme's hands. In the process, she rammed her elbow backward into Esme's nose, causing a crunch to vibrate through her ears. Jensen, Camryn, Ansel, and Cora entered the room while Thalia and Esme landed blow after blow on each other, each attempting to ensnare the scythe in their own hands. With an angry grunt, Esme jumped, reaching for Thalia. She grabbed a handful of the long strands, ripping them downward, dropping Thalia to the ground.

The scythe slid across the floor. Both women stilled for a hair splitting second before scurrying in its direction. Esme's fingers brushed the handle just as long fingers wrapped around her ankle, yanking her away. Thalia yanked her further from the scythe and crept herself closer to the instrument. Esme released a yell filled with rage as Thalia's hand encased the staff of the scythe. She launched herself on

Thalia's chest, entwining her fingers into the hair on the sides of her head. With every ounce of might she could muster, she lifted and smashed Thalia's head onto the ground. The ground buckled and cracked with every pound. She yanked her head forward, and as their noses touched, a snarl rippled across Esme's lips, and she crashed into her enemy's skull on the ground once more.

Still gripping the scythe, Thalia skimmed the blade across Esme's chest. Searing pain shot through Esme. She screamed, releasing the hold she had on Thalia as she clutched the open wound in her chest. Swirls of gold light and glittering black wisps seeped from the gash.

Jensen released his hold on Anscl and attempted to run to Esme. Ansel held him back. "Don't. This isn't your fight. Esme has to end this."

Thalia scooted away on her hands and rose from the ground. She jabbed Esme's mouth with her fist, making her head snap back.

Esme rolled her neck and laughed through the pain radiating from her chest. "You hit how you act. Like a little bitch." As she stood to her full height, one hand still covered the wound that attempted to weave itself together. She lifted her foot and kicked it directly into Thalia's knee. A sickening snap echoed as the knee bent back, creating a new arc in the long, slender leg.

Ignoring the pain in her knee, Thalia struggled to steady herself as she hacked away at the air with little precision. She swung as close as she could as Esme bobbed and weaved under the swipe.

As they continued their match, Esme grew tired and angry, tendrils forming around her, ascending her body.

"That's new," Ansel whispered. "No reaper has ever done that."

Jensen stood there, helpless, watching this clash of power. His fingers twitching at his thighs. "That's because she isn't just any reaper. She's the best of us."

Camryn stood by Jensen, watching his friend in this battle. Everything in him wanted to run over to where she was, but he knew he would only get in the way. What could an average reaper like him do compared to the god-like power he was witnessing?

The tendrils danced around Esme's hands and onto the scythe, helping her pull the object closer to her.

"No! I will not allow this to happen." Using what strength she had left, she ripped the scythe from Esme and the tendrils and used the handle to swipe her feet. Esme fell to the ground, the smokey tendrils dispersing around her. Jensen ran toward Esme as Dominic surged from the shadows that stretched along the ground. Esme stood on tired legs.

Thalia lifted the scythe above her head.

"Esme! No!" Jensen apparated in front of her, covering her frame with his own. The blade ripped through his back and protruded through his sternum. The cracking of wood filled the now quiet room. He fell to his knees as Thalia tore the scythe from his back. Pure gold light cascaded down his back and chest. His hands held on to Esme's forearms as her eyes followed him to the ground. Her body shook with wrath as her irises turned black. The overhead lights sparked, the metal beams creaked as they bent. Azure sparks and ebony smokey tendrils surrounded Thalia, covering her legs and pulling the scythe from her grip.

Esme's voice changed once more. Her eyes never leaving Jensen. "Dominic, eat."

Dominic barked and snarled as he circled Thalia. Standing on his hind legs, he shoved as the tendrils yanked her down. This was a prey worth savoring. His teeth dug into her bicep, tearing her arm out of its socket, while his claws dug into her chest, pinning her further to the ground.

The tendrils held her securely, tightening their iron grip as Dominic ravenously ripped shreds off her. He played with each new shred, purposefully prolonging her suffering. He mauled her face, tearing off chunks of nose and cheek with enthusiasm. Esme flicked her gaze to Dominic. There was a twisted, sadistic satisfaction that expanded in her as she watched this vile woman being torn to pieces.

Thalia's shrill shrieking rippled in all directions. He ripped her piece by piece, savoring every drop of energy that spilled from her mutilated body. The tendrils continued to help by holding the pieces Dominic tore off her in place. Saliva stretched from his mouth to the ground as he swallowed her reaper flesh. The other reapers stood in silent horror. Cora hid behind Ansel, no longer wanting to see the gruesome sight as he stood, quietly watching. Alicia sat in silent terror. Camryn stood motionless. He wanted to look away, but the sight was too ghastly. Esme refocused on the man who laid at her feet.

She assumed the pain would have consumed her, like how the mortal movies portrayed: instant tears and sadness. That's not how it felt. She was in a vacuum, with no sounds, no movement from the outside world. There was an internal snap that emanated from her chest. It burned. Something tightened in the pit of her gut as her lungs seized mid-breath. A guttural cry came from somewhere so deep it sounded animalistic.

The world moved again when the concrete came up to meet her knees. Cradling Jensen's head to her chest, she hugged him tightly. Blowtorches couldn't scorch hotter than the tears that blinded her. "No, no, no, no, no. You self-sacrificing idiot! Why would you do that?"

"Because love makes you stupid. I love you, Esme." Although Jensen's voice grew weaker with every syllable, a serene smile rested on his face. The tears that poured from her eyes fell onto his cheeks, dampening his face like a rainstorm. He continued to smile. Drinking in her tears because, even when she was crying and in pain, Esme was still the most beautiful creature his eyes had the privilege of seeing.

She tried to speak through painful hiccups. "You. You promised me, remember?" Her hand slid into his hair. "You promised me you wouldn't break my heart. I asked you to never break my heart, you said 'never.' You promised me, never." Her words induced a cascade of tears as she allowed herself to pour out all her emotions to him. "You're not allowed to leave me. Please, Jensen, don't break me again. I need you. Don't do this. Don't leave me. Please don't leave." She clutched him tighter as his energy flickered, his warm honey eyes dimming.

He brushed his knuckles up the wet tracks on her cheeks and whispered, "Kiss me."

Esme allowed a sad laugh to escape her lips. She knew her face was splotchy, and her eyes were glassy obsidian. Yet, he still wanted to kiss her. How could she refuse a request from her eternal paramour? Her lips met his just how they did countless times before, effortlessly gliding against each other. As she went to deepen their kiss, the softness against her lips was gone. Peeling her eyes open, her mind struggled to believe what her eyes were capturing. There was nothing there but an empty space in her arms. He was gone. Jensen was lost to her forever.

She wrapped her arms closer to herself. Her throat unable to release any sound. In her mind, she believed if she held herself as tight as she could, she could keep the pieces of herself from falling apart. Whimpers emerged from her as her lip and chin trembled, and she clung tighter to herself. Her left hand slipped off her right shoulder.

A scream erupted from her, cracking the silence open with the weight of a sledgehammer. Energy scorched the ground and air around her as she bellowed, sending all the reapers flying in every direction and Dominic running to the corner where Alicia sat frozen.

The ground cracked beneath her as she stood. Blue sparks rising from the newly formed crevices. The scythe had been forgotten and discarded, skidding along the floor, landing near Ansel. With every breath, Esme's back coiled tighter.

Cora was the first to stand, gaping like a fish out of water. This was never in the agreement. Thalia wasn't supposed to try and kill Esme. Jensen certainly wasn't meant to be annihilated. It was never meant to be this way. "Esme, I—" Her steps were small, much like her voice and stance. "I didn't mean for—"

"You didn't mean for what, Cora?" Sparks flew from Esme's hands as the tendrils formed up her back. "You didn't mean to play on the lunatic's team? You didn't mean to have a hand in this!" Her words were sharp, but her voice was piercing. Everything about Esme was cold, tactical, calculating. "I once told you to push aside your pride." She stood and walked toward Cora, moving like an apex predator. "Instead, you clung to it and nurtured it into betrayal."

"Betrayal? That's what you call what I chose to do? I did what was right, Esme. You were unstable working with a hellhound for fuck's sake. Look at you, you still are. This isn't right or natural. You were the one who was never loyal. If you were loyal and cared about our kind and the balance of life and death, you would have just given the scythe willingly."

Esme bitterly laughed. "Loyal? You want to stand here and speak to me about loyalties when you don't even appreciate what defines the word. Who taught you your concept of loyalty? Those two who betrayed the original Grim Reaper? Who betrayed my father?" With every question, her tongue lashed harsher than a whip. "Those two, who wanted to steal my legacy? Was it Thalia who taught you loyalty? The one who was driven to insanity over her lust for power? Or was it the one who stood by watching as she was devoured? Does that sound like loyalty to you, Cora? Does it?"

Cora watched as Ansel quietly stood eyeing the scythe. "Oh, please, what are you loyal to?"

Pushing her hands forward and up, Esme willed the tendrils forward, slamming Cora against a warped metal beam. "My loyalty is to the great equalizer. My loyalty is to death."

Cora clawed at the tendrils that crept up her throat. "So, your loyalty is to yourself?"

"Yes." As Esme went in for the kill, she sensed Ansel behind her. Spinning around, he held the battered scythe over his head. She sent the tendrils that held Cora flying to Ansel.

"For centuries, I endured the constant whining from Thalia and your father about each other. Thalia thirsting to be in control, not just because he chose to have fun with mortals and start a silly little family, leaving her sad and pathetic with a broken heart. It was because she thought herself to be better than everyone and everything. She couldn't stand the idea of your father being more powerful than her. Then we have your father in a forbidden love, creating a disgusting creature like yourself. Both of them were unfit."

Cora gasped for air as she scurried away from Esme. Esme tried her best to aim every spark and tendril at Ansel, but with so many emotions still flowing through her, it became hard to control. Ansel ran from beam to beam, escaping the sparks that exploded from the cracked floor and the tendrils that swarmed in the air. "I had it all planned out. I finally convinced her to kill him, and she did. I had the scythe and journal. Did you know he hid all his precious thoughts in that glass case? Hidden secretly under the scythe in a compartment. I grabbed the journal, and the scythe vanished. So, I kept it safe, waiting for the right moment. I plant his journal for you to find. You did. Then I let that fester in your mind, making you want to take control so you can kill her. Clearly, there were a few hiccups with you dying, and your lover was never meant to die, I assure you." He dodged a group of tendrils that swiped at his face. "In the end, I can't complain, since it all worked out. Now I just have to finish you once and for all."

Camryn had landed behind the blue couch as his head bounced off the brick wall. Ringing spread through his ears, but he could still make out Esme's voice. He peeked over the back of the couch, catching a glimpse of Ansel with the scythe. He sprinted from his hidden spot, taking the opportunity during Ansel's rant to rush at him. He yelled as he tackled Ansel to the ground from behind. The scythe clattered on the floor, breaking into pieces. Ansel pushed Camryn off him and ran to the largest piece of blade his eyes could find. Before he could reach it, Esme flung her arm in his direction, sending him crashing into Cora. She summoned the tendrils, ready to attack, when a scream filled her ears. Turning her head, she saw the tiny pieces of the scythe heading for Alicia. She knew that if those pieces entered Alicia, she would no longer exist. Esme couldn't afford to lose anyone else. The tendrils that were aimed at Ansel and Cora were sent to intercept the deadly metal shards.

Ansel took Cora in his arms and welcomed the distraction. He took the moment that allowed them both to escape.

"Fuck!" She displayed the anguish that fueled her. Standing in the aftermath, only thoughts flitted about her mind. The scythe lay shattered and useless. Jensen was gone, leaving her shattered once more. The ones responsible had escaped. What did she have left? What was this all for?

25

With her tear-stained face, Esme stood in the aftershock of death and destruction. Walls crumbled around her, lights hung and swayed by a few measly wires. Cracked and broken concrete crunched beneath her feet. Seeing the anarchy that was left provoked a deep wrath within her. Her energy pulsated, filling every newly formed crack and crevice. "Cam, take Alicia and leave." Her voice was shaky and strained from containing the boiling emotions.

Alicia noticed the sigil that housed her was cracked, so she poked a toe out of the circle to test. When nothing snapped her back like a rubber band, she hopped out as Camryn neared her. "Esme, we can stay. I don't want you to feel—"

"Get out now." Esme's voice rumbled and bounced off the debris.

"It's okay, Alicia. She needs space right now." Camryn glanced back at his friend. A woman who was always so strong, who was hit so many times and always stood back up. He saw her truly broken. This time, he feared there was no piecing her back together.

Alicia wrapped her hand around Camryn's arm. "Come on, Domi." Dominic darted his yellow eyes to his master and bowed his head before walking behind Alicia and Camryn.

Buzzing filled Esme's ears as a shape darted in the corner of her eye. "Bring him back, Atticus."

Kicking rubble as he walked closer, Atticus stopped where Jensen had been wiped from creation. "I can't do that. I don't create reapers. I'm not supposed to create at all making you is going to raise all kinds of hell with the counsel. I just play with the things that were created." He stroked his jaw and sighed. "I truly am sorry, Esme. A price had to be paid. It was either him or watch the mortal world burn."

"I would have gladly burned the world to ashes for him!" The tendons in her neck tensed. Azure sparks flew from her fingertips as the smokey ebony tendrils resurfaced from the ground. The walls quaked, and the floors began to buckle.

Atticus observed the mayhem that she was producing. He knew, when he let her remain with her witch abilities, she would be a force to be reckoned with. What he saw was a force that was barely controlled or contained. Esme was death and destruction in one small package. Left unbalanced, she could rip the mortal world in half. "You sound like Thalia, Esmerelda."

"I am not Esmerelda. My name is Esme. Don't you ever compare me to Thalia again. If you do, I promise it will be the last words you ever utter." The building shook as her words rippled through the air, the tendrils making their way to Atticus.

He pointed a stern finger at her face and tightened his lips. "Then act like Esme. You're the fucking Grim Reaper now. It's what you wanted when I offered."

Her lips curled into a snarl. "You never mentioned there being a price to pay until it was all over. You know I would have said no or thought of something else. Bring him back. Find a way and bring Jensen back now, dammit."

"He is gone, not coming back, and I am sorry. But you are Death. Death is your purpose so pull yourself together and balance the scales again. You have a job to do." His eyes flashed white, and he vanished.

All the energy left in her was used to summon all the sparks and tendrils. The tendrils stroked her limbs, wrapping her tightly until they engulfed her. Darkness surrounded her. She felt comforted by the tender caress of the dark. She kneeled on the ground, threw her arms up in the air, and crashed her hands to the floor. Esme screamed her anguish into the devastation around her as the building's windows exploded and every wall crumbled. If fate wanted her to balance the scales, then balance them, she would.

On the street below, people continued as they normally did, completely oblivious to the torment and shifting of powers happening in an everyday city building. At least, they continued until the glass was blown from that building, and the ground quaked. Camryn spun around, eyeing the building, his chest constricted in pain for Esme. Alicia hid her face in his chest, crying her own silent tears. Not only did she lose her life two years ago, but out of the four closest friends she had made in her afterlife, two were lost to her, and one changed forever. What could a lost soul like her do?

Sirens filled the air and lit the evening sky, adding their own somber song to the events that passed. Atticus appeared before Camryn and Alicia. "Before you threaten me, try anything or do anything"—he licked his lips and put his hands up in surrender—"just know that I tried my best to create the outcome with the least amount of pain for everyone."

Alicia's lips pouted as her brows pinched. "What are you talking about? Camryn, what is Tyler talking about?"

Camryn's voice trembled. "Your best? You broke her. She's been through enough, and you destroyed her, Atticus."

Atticus threw his arms up. "I had to break her fully so she could rebuild herself to be better than her father, and all others." Fists akimbo he turned, facing the building. "She needs help. Esme's witching power is stronger than I anticipated it to be. She needs help learning how to use and control it."

Camryn gnawed at the inside of his cheek as he thought about Esme. "What do you need me to do?"

As the emergency lights lit up the buildings and sidewalks and bustling conversations of first responders about gas leaks and exploding pipes, Atticus spoke to Camryn. There were few witches or warlocks left who had dealt in dark magic that was similar to what Esme possessed. But there were some who could do it. One came to mind. The one he thought of lived in a small, cloaked town inhabited by others in their coven, tucked away in the woods. It was the home of a husband and wife, but Camryn needed to get assistance from the husband since he was the one who held the power most similar to Esme. "Consider it done." There wasn't anything Camryn wouldn't do for Esme, especially after what had happened to Jensen.

"Okay, I get that Esme's dad was the Grim Reaper, and now, she has that job. But what about the scythe? How can Esme be the Grim Reaper without that?" Alicia pondered her question aloud.

A mischievous glint resided in Atticus's eyes. "Esme's an intelligent and capable woman who has access to the greatest grimoire ever created. I'm sure she can figure out how to get these souls to the veil with it while a replacement is being created." Giving an impish wave, his eyes flashed white, then once again vanished.

Finally realizing all the parts of the conversation, Alicia glanced at Camryn. "Why did you call Tyler Atticus?"

"Not now Alicia." He nodded his head in the direction of the building.

Esme walked out of the building, cloaking herself from the mortals that ran in and out. Any evidence of tears had been wiped away, methodical steps and hardened stares replacing grief. She tucked an object into her waistband, coming to a complete stop. "I have work to do. There has to be some way to gather all these lost souls without the scythe."

"You could check in the grimoire. Jensen, we left it at your apartment on your bed." Camryn swallowed the lump in his throat, not wanting to cause any more pain to Esme.

Vacant obsidian-flecked eyes stared back at him. "That's where I'll be, then. If there's a sigil like the one that contained Alicia, there must be more." She tapped her thigh, and Dominic stood by her side. She snapped her fingers and disappeared in a smokey white light.

Alicia looked up at Camryn as he looked down at her. "So, we have a warlock to find, right?" She gave a watery smile as Camryn held her hand and nodded. "You need to catch me up on what I missed."

Everything was pristine and orderly; she could tell Jensen was there and taking care of her apartment. Not a single speck of dust could be found. Her books had been rearranged by genre and alphabetical order. A fond smile passed her lips as she remembered how she would set books any which way to purposely irk him when she was mad at him. On her reading chair was the green waffle blanket that Jensen had gotten her before her death. He would make jokes about how she was becoming too mortal for the cold. A whine unwillingly slipped from her lips. She cleared her throat to rid the sob that threatened to overflow.

There was work that demanded her attention, but with her focus still on losing Jensen, work would have to wait.

Dominic stretched his back and yawned. He found a dark corner, curled himself tightly, and quickly fell asleep.

She made her way to the shower, hoping the scalding water would burn her sorrow away. As the hot water licked at her olive skin, turning it an angry red, she slid down onto the shower floor. The searing water charring her flesh was nothing compared to the flaming tears she let flow from her eyes as the cold tiles absorbed her sobs.

Steam tickled her skin as she wrapped the towel around her body. In her closet, she found the most comfortable and comforting thing. Pulling his old sweater over her head, she spotted the grimoire. It was where Camryn had said it would be, but it was different. Upon closer inspection, loose sheets of paper were sticking out from various sections.

Esme picked up the old book, careful not to disturb any of the note-filled papers, and slid into the sheets. The scent of cedar, leather, and oranges wafted into her nose. How many nights had Jensen spent lying in that bed for his scent to be so prominent? Tears threatened to spill, but she stuffed them down. It was not the time for tears again. He died saving her, and she was determined to make sure his sacrifice meant something. Hours ticked by with every turn of the page. She quickly discarded any spell that spoke of needing a sacrifice, enough had already been sacrificed in the past year.

Her eyes blurred from staring at the endless pages. She was ready to call it quits until his notes fell out. Esme rubbed her eyes and took a deep breath. "Holy shit, you did it, love." Words fell into the quiet night. Jensen had devised a way to patch work, a summoning ritual that would call the soul of a lost love. The only work she needed to do was find a way to tweak the ritual to call on all lost souls. The sigils would be easy but needed to be placed in different areas in a country. She had to figure out a way to get every reaper involved.

Scavenging her room, she found her phone and sent a message to Camryn.

> *Leaving the city for a bit. There's a ritual that could work, but I need ingredients. It should only take a few hours. Meet you at The Twisted Sickle when I get back.*

Not waiting for a reply, she hurriedly pulled on a pair of jeans and boots, shoved the phone into her pocket, and disappeared into the light.

"Are you sure this is the right place? I thought Tyler said it was in the woods. I was expecting a creepy witchy cottage. This is charming, in an off-grid sort of way." Alicia spoke swiftly as she scrutinized the small cabin before them.

"First, his name isn't Tyler, remember? It's Atticus. Apparently, he's Fate." Camryn rolled his eyes. "It's a long story, and I'll fill you in more later. Second, this is where he said to go, so here we are."

Cautiously, they walked up the worn pathway, passing an iron gated garden that held flowers, herbs, and plants that neither of them had ever seen before. Camryn pulled Alicia behind him as a precaution. He had never had an encounter with a witch or warlock before, especially one as powerful as the one he was sent to retrieve. Rapping his knuckles on the door, he squared his shoulders and let his energy surface more than usual.

The door opened and a tall man with a strong build filled the entire frame. Alicia peeked out from behind Camryn, and her eyes widened as her jaw dropped. "Holy Adonis and marble sculptures."

Her eyes scanned him from head to toe. His hair was pitch black except for a streak of gray that ran from his temple to the nape of his neck. It flowed in soft waves in a medium length windswept backward. Cobalt blue eyes stared through them as his lips curled upward. "His jaw was meant to cut thighs."

"Alicia!" Camryn scolded her as he pushed her behind him again.

"Camryn." Her tone was mocking. "I've been socially deprived. I can't help it."

The man tossed his head back, laughing, placing his large hand on his chest. "So, who and what are you? Also, why are you bringing me this cheeky soul?" His heavy British accent lingered in the air.

"Camryn." She staged whispered with glee from behind Camryn's back. "He has an accent, too."

"I'm Camryn, a Reaper. Are you Leo?" Camryn asked, completely ignoring the swooning that was happening behind him.

Folding his arms across his chest, sending a ripple of muscle through his shirt. "I am. But why is a reaper bringing me a simple man, might I add, a soul?"

"He can see me. How can you see me?" She poked her head out again.

"I see with more than just the eyes, darling. It's an innate ability." He gave his reply with a toothy grin.

Camryn dropped his eyebrows, unimpressed and unamused by this so-called powerful warlock. "You aren't a simple man, are you, Leo?"

Leo darted one finger into the air. "I've given up my dark magical ways, thank you very much."

Camryn pointed to the strange garden. "Really?"

"It's an innocent hobby, good for the soul," Leo retorted.

"The Grim Reaper needs your help. Fate led me to you. The choice to come along willingly is yours. Just so you know, I have zero issues dragging you with me." Camryn's chest puffed out, matching Leo's size.

"Grim Reaper you say? Well, that changes things a bit. I'm going to wager I should pack a few things, yeah?" Leo thrummed his fingers on his forehead, calming the racing thoughts flitting about in his mind. "Feel free to come in; I'll be a few minutes. Clothes, toiletries, amulets, charms, potions. You know, the essentials."

Alicia giggled. "Nothing simple about that, man."

As they walked into the cabin, Camryn felt his energy slightly drain, and he raised a brow at Leo. "Sorry about that, mate. It's a dampener. Makes the big, bad, scary things not so big bad and scary." He went down a short hallway and closed a door behind him.

Camryn and Alicia wandered around the small room, taking in the plants that crawled out of planters. Jars filled with liquids that glowed, sparkled or were entirely opaque. Books were stacked on the floor, and scrolls were tossed on a large desk that was lined with vials. If this man was married, as Atticus had said, there was no trace of another person.

Camryn was about to pick up a stone that pulsated with energy when Leo entered the room with a large duffle bag. "I wouldn't touch that if I were you. It strips any being of their power or abilities, making them human. Made it myself, but I haven't had the opportunity to use it yet, so not sure how long it would last."

Alicia slapped Camryn's hand away. "Why would you make something like that?"

Leo tensed as anger dashed in his eyes. "I have my reasons."

A phone beeping broke the tension. Camryn fished it from his pocket and read the message from Esme. "Looks like we're meeting back at the bar." He gave a quick smile to Alicia, who smiled back. He turned his attention back to Leo, who was patting down his pockets. "Do you have everything you need?"

Walking to the desk, Leo picked up a square piece of suede and covered the stone, placing it in his pocket. Then he picked up a pen and a blank sheet of paper. "Just leaving a quick note in case anyone from my coven comes looking for me." He dropped the pen, hovered his hand over the paper, muttering a few words. When he was done muttering, indigo-colored fire sparked over the paper, sending it in flames. "All right, now I'm ready." He brushed past his visitors and walked out the door. Camryn and Alicia shared a confused look and followed Leo out of the cabin.

Esme appeared in The Twisted Sickle's back office. Broken glass still crowded a corner, chairs still tipped over, all remnants and painful bitter reminders. In her arms were bags filled with jars of powders and plants. She gently set the bags on the desk and went to the corner with glass. She crouched down and began picking up the shards that were still dipped in whiskey.

Camryn held on to Alicia and Leo and apparated to the bar. When they appeared on the corner of the reaper hangout, Leo spun around, dropping his duffle bag and retched the contents in his stomach. "Can't say I've ever traveled that way before. A little warning would have been nice." He wiped the corners of his mouth with his sleeve and righted himself. "Oh, not the bloody city. I hate the city. It's far too populated for my liking."

Huffing out and scratching his head, Camryn replied, "I've never transported a mortal before. So, we're even." He couldn't tell if it was from traveling with a mortal or a warlock, but he felt his energy was close to being depleted.

Leo picked up his bag and straightened his jacket. "I'm not just a mortal. I'm a warlock. Technically, I'm not exactly mortal anymore, either."

Alicia's ears perked up. "How does that work?"

Leo chuckled and patted her arm. "Buy me a pint, and I'll tell you."

The three of them walked into the bar that was now buzzing with reapers gossiping about Thalia and Ansel. A few even made small conversations of the Grim Reaper. Camryn ushered Leo to the back office as Alicia walked silently behind them. The door was closed, but her energy pushed against it.

Turning to Leo and Alicia, he spoke. "Just wait out here for a minute. I forgot to mention that I was bringing you a long. Didn't exactly run it by the boss." Camryn knocked on the door before entering. He saw Esme placing shards of glass in a trash can. "Got your message Es. Also, I brought someone along who might be able to help. At least Atticus thinks so."

Esme stood and wiped her hands on her jeans. "To be quite frank, I'm over what Atticus thinks. Besides, I think I found everything I need for the ritual." She paused to blink back tears. "Jensen did all the leg work when he was trying to find me."

Camryn chewed the inside of his cheek as he hung his head. "I feel like a dick. I criticized him because I thought he was just downing bottles of whiskey. I thought he wasn't doing anything to find you. I was wrong. Now, I can't even tell him, so he can gloat about being right."

She let out a soft sigh, grabbing both of his hands. "It's okay Cam. He grieved how he had to, just like you did. Like

I am now." She gave him a watery smile as he nodded in agreement.

Leo stood in the hallway listening to the two voices converse. His hands grew clammy, and his heart thudded in his chest, threatening to fracture his ribs. "Impossible."

"What's impossible?" Alicia asked worriedly.

He ran into the office, his world stopped spinning. Breathing was an exercise his lungs forgot how to perform. "Esmerelda?" His voice cracked at the end of her name.

Esme turned her head, and her obsidian-flecked eyes locked onto the cobalt orbs gazing at her. "My name is Esme. Who are you?"

His heart shattered to millions of pieces. Was this some cruel joke? He wasn't the best or kindest man to ever walk the planet, but he believed he certainly didn't deserve this stunt from fate. "Angel, it's me, Leo. Your Leo. Leofstan Craven, your husband."

Esme paled as she felt the sensation of bile crawl its way up her throat. "My name is Esme. You are not my husband. I am not your wife and most certainly not your angel. You, Leofstan Craven, are mistaken." Her mind spun with thoughts until she remembered the story Atticus told her. Esmerelda was newly married to a necromancer. Could her past, the one she had no recollection of, be catching up to her now? Her eyes widened in horror. She refused to believe what was happening. She just lost Jensen, the man she loved and still loves. There was no room, need, or want for any other man.

"No, you are Esmerelda Blackwell. In fact, it's Esmerelda Craven. I think I would know my wife. The wife I have spent centuries scouring the globe for." Pain and anger rooted in his chest. How could she not recognize him? Sure, he had aged and looked slightly different. Centuries would do that to a being. Yet he knew her solely from the sound of her voice. The voice he dreamed about night after night. Her face was unmistakable. She was left untouched by the cruel hands of time. Her beauty still rivaling the Gods of old. He could see the struggle with denial in her eyes. Some part of her knew it to be true. No matter how small that part was, he knew this beautiful being recognized him as her husband.

Now was not the time for someone new to enter her existence. Then she realized how Fate had sent this man back into her path once more, but this was a game she was not willing to play with Atticus. As she pierced the depths of Leo's soul, her voice was strong and final. "My name is Esme. I am the Grim Reaper."

THE END

Dear Reader,

I truly hope you enjoyed A New Era. This book is my debut novel and the start of a series and the amount of fun I had creating this world was worth every minute. Thank you for reading this book and giving this new author a chance.

Find out what happens with Esme, Leo, Camryn, Alicia, Atticus, Ansel, and Cora in "Call of the Coven" The Reaper Tomes Book 2. Releases in 2023. Make sure to follow me on social media or be on the lookout for my newsletter with the most up-to-date information.

Follow this link or scan the QR code to visit my website for all the links.

While I finish crafting Call of the Coven, check out my free novella Fated Deals (The Reaper Tomes Novella 1). It takes place three years before A New Era and will introduce to new characters who will reappear in Call of the Coven. It's available for free download on my website.

Until then, Happy Reading

ACKNOWLEDGMENTS

The undertaking of this book would not have been possible without some truly special and important people to me. First and foremost, I have to thank my husband, Colton, even though this book is already dedicated to him. He is the rock that I cling to and my biggest supporter. Thank you for supporting my wildest dreams.

Even though they are not old enough to read this book and I wish they would sleep in a little more often, thank you to our sons. Because they get up before the sun does, so do I. You two give me more hours to work and to spend with you both.

I'll forever be amazed by the small crew that helped make this large dream come true. This crew includes my best friends Andrew, Kevin, Chris, Gloria, Katie. I can't forget about my friends and beta readers Hannah, Shaymus, JD, and KB for giving the blunt honesty that helped to shape this story. They always answered the hypothetical questions I conjured at odd hours and cheered me on when this entire series was just hopeful dreams. If it wasn't for my best friends and my amazing husband, I would have shelved this project and hid it from the world.

To my editor and formatter Samantha Pico at Miss Eloquent Edits, you're the best and thank you for elevating this story with your talent.

Lastly, I want to thank my past self for being brave enough to write this story even when it felt impossible. Thank you for being bold enough to share it with the world. So future me don't you dare give up because we just made little girl us, who was awkward and had trouble fitting in, extremely proud.

About the Author

Marilu Moser is a Latina fantasy and romance author, born and raised in the state known for its chocolate, crayons, and Independence Day history, Pennsylvania. She is a military wife and stay-at-home mother to two rambunctious little boys and holds a Bachelor of Arts in Psychology.

She is a self-proclaimed connoisseur of dad jokes and perpetual optimism with a weakness for root beer floats and pizza who possesses a snort-laugh that is uncontrollable. When she's not creating worlds full of memorable characters, she enjoys losing herself in between the pages of other books curled up next to the two family dogs, binge-watching crime shows, playing with Hot wheels, and winning every board game against her husband.

9 7 9 8 9 8 6 4 2 6 1 0 5